The

SHAMUS
WINNERS

America's Best Private Eye Stories

Volume I: 1982-1995

Collected and Introduced

by Robert J. Randisi

Founder, Private Eye Writers of America

Perfect Crime Books

"What You Don't Know Can Hurt You" by John Lutz, copyright © 1982 John Lutz, originally published in *Alfred Hitchcock's Mystery Magazine*. "Cat's-Paw" by Bill Pronzini, copyright © 1983 Bill Pronzini, originally published by Waves Press, Richmond, Virginia. "By the Dawn's Early Light" by Lawrence Block, copyright © 1984 Lawrence Block, originally published in *Playboy* magazine. "Eight Mile and Dequindre" by Loren D. Estleman, copyright © 1985 Loren D. Estleman, originally published in *Alfred Hitchcock's Mystery Magazine*. "Turn Away" by Ed Gorman, copyright © 1987 Ed Gorman, published in *Black Lizard Anthology of Crime Fiction*. "The Crooked Way" by Loren D. Estleman, copyright © 1988 Loren D. Estleman, originally published in the *New Black Mask*. "The Killing Man" by Mickey Spillane, copyright © 1989 Mickey Spillane, originally published in *Playboy* magazine. "Final Resting Place" by Marcia Muller, copyright © 1990 Marcia Muller, originally published in *Justice for Hire*. "Dust Devil" by Nancy Pickard, copyright © 1991 Nancy Pickard, originally published in *The Armchair Detective*. "Mary, Mary, Shut the Door" by Benjamin M. Schutz, copyright © 1992 Benjamin M. Schutz, originally published in *Deadly Allies*. "The Merciful Angel of Death" by Lawrence Block, copyright © 1993 by Lawrence Block, originally published in *The New Mystery*. "Necessary Brother" by Brendan DuBois, copyright © 1994, originally published in *Ellery Queen's Mystery Magazine*. "Lucky Penny" by Linda Barnes, copyright © 1986, originally published in *The New Black Mask #3*. "Dying in the Post-War World" by Max Allan Collins, copyright © 1991, originally published by Foul Play Books. "A Little Missionary Work" by Sue Grafton, copyright © 1992, originally published in *Deadly Allies*.

Library of Congress Cataloging-in-Publication Data
The Shamus Winners. America's Best Private Eye Stories. Volume I, 1982-1995/
Robert J. Randisi, editor
1.   Detective and mystery stories, American   I. Randisi, Robert J.

ISBN: 978-0-9825157-4-7

Contents

Introduction

by Robert J. Randisi

THERE WAS a collection of Shamus winners about fifteen years ago called *The Eyes Still Have It*. Since then the Eyes have continued to have it, we just haven't been able to put together another collection of these fine stories until now. Since there have been twenty-seven winners, we decided to split this collection in two.

Volume I covers from 1982 through 1995. Volume II will cover 1996 through 2008. We have added several bonus stories, which could easily have won in their years — witness their authors' continued popularity.

Volume I opens with John Lutz's "What You Don't Know Can Hurt You." (Read the title carefully.) This was the first short story to win a Shamus, as the Private Eye Writers of America, the organization that makes the award, did not have a short story category its first year. Since the publication of this story, John Lutz has gone on to write hundreds of short stories and many, many novels. Now he is writing a succession of best-selling serial killer novels set in New York City, the most of recent of which is *Urge to Kill* (Kensington, 2009). When the subject of this story comes up, he still advises people to read the title carefully.

"Cat's-Paw" was the next winner, written by Bill Pronzini and published by a small establishment called Waves Press. It features Bill's "Nameless" private detective, who has become one of the longest running PI series characters. Bill is a three-time Shamus winner, including the debut award for best novel (*Hoodwink*) while he was the organization's first president. He noted during his acceptance speech that "the fix was in," but it wasn't, I swear. The most recent "Nameless" novel is *Schemers* (TOR, 2009).

"By the Dawn's Early Light" is a significant story in Lawrence

Block's Matthew Scudder series. I had invited Larry to write a Scudder story for the first PWA anthology, *The Eyes Have It*, back in 1983. He replied that he had done all he could with the character—but then called me later and said he'd come up with a story he thought would work. The story appeared first in *Playboy*—Larry wanted his work to be close to those interviews. Not only did "Dawn's" win the Shamus, it also became the basis of *When the Sacred Ginmill Closes*, which a couple of years later was nominated for a Shamus for best novel. Larry has continued writing about Scudder, the most recent book being *All the Flowers Are Dying* (William Morrow, 2006).

Ed Gorman, who won the 1988 award for "Turn Away," is the current President of PWA and a prolific author of mystery, western and horror novels. We have been friends since 1986 and co-founded *Mystery Scene Magazine* together. There are some who say that Ed's short work is his best, and this story is a prime example. His novels are first rate, too, and a new one, *Ticket to Ride,* came out from Pegasus in 2009.

"Eight Mile and DeQuindre" and "The Crooked Way," two winning stories by Loren D. Estleman, are both in his Amos Walker series. Loren has also nabbed a Shamus for best novel and continues to produce Walker books. *The Left-Handed Dollar* will appear in 2010 from TOR Books.

"The Killing Man" was a popular winner in 1989, because it was written by private-eye icon and arguably the best-selling writer of mysteries ever, Mickey Spillane. And yes, it was a Mike Hammer story. Fittingly enough, it appeared in *Playboy*.

"Final Resting Place" by Marcia Muller was the winner the following year. The story featured her series sleuth Sharon McCone, who many feel is the mother of all female PIs. Well, Mother is still hard at work. *Locked In* (Grand Central Publishing, 2009) is the 26th book in the long-running McCone series.

Nancy Pickard, not a name normally connected with the private eye genre, was the winner the next year with "Dust Devil," a story that appeared in *The Armchair Detective*. Her Shamus award simply points out the versatility of this talented author, whose most recent novel was the stand-alone thriller *The Virgin of Small Plains* (Random House, 2007).

"Mary, Mary, Shut the Door" by Ben Schutz is perhaps one of the most anthologized short stories in the PI genre. Once you read it you'll know why. It features Ben's series detective, Leo Haggerty. Sadly, Ben was taken from us suddenly and much too soon in 2008, at 58.

The 1994 winning story, "The Merciful Angel of Death," is Larry

Block's second contribution to this volume featuring Matt Scudder. That same year, Larry won his second award for best private-eye novel with *The Devil Knows You're Dead*. Lawrence Block holds our record with four Shamus Awards.

"Necessary Brother" got the first of Brendan DuBois's two awards for Best Short Story; his other winner will appear in Volume II. Brendan holds a distinction of another sort: things get messed up with his Shamus awards. On the first, an extraneous letter worked its way into the story's title. On the second, the award never arrived. Brendan took these mishaps with grace; in fact, he didn't mention the missing award until years later.

Each of the bonus stories that made it into this volume could have been a winner. "Lucky Penny," by Linda Barnes, which introduced the character Carlotta Cortez, has been often anthologized. Linda's most recent Carlotta novel was *Lie Down With the Dead* (St. Martin's Press, 2009).

Max Allan Collins has won the Shamus for Best Novel twice with Nate Heller books, *True Detective* in 1984 and *Stolen Away* in 1992. Almost every Heller novel has been nominated. Indeed, Al holds the record for most nominations: no numbers here; he might have another by the time this comes out. His novella "Dying in the Post-War World" was nominated in 1992—one of the years when Max Collins graciously permitted other writers a moment in the sun, and the award went elsewhere. The first Nathan Heller novel in almost a decade, *Bye Bye, Baby*, dealing with Marilyn Monroe's death, will be appearing soon.

The final bonus story comes from Sue Grafton, who is the only three-time Shamus winner for Best Novel. She also has been nominated many times in the short story category, and "A Little Missionary Work," featuring her sleuth Kinsey Millhone, was a deserving candidate in 1993.

All these authors have been heaped with praise and awards over many years. Lutz, Pronzini, Block, Grafton and Gorman have been presidents of PWA. Lutz, Pronzini, Block, Spillane, Muller, Grafton and Collins have received the Lifetime Achievement Award.

You'll find the quality of these stories consistent from first to last. And there are more to come in Volume II.

Robert J. Randisi received the Private Eye Writers of America's Lifetime Achievement Award in 2009. He is the author of more than five hundred published novels.

What You Don't Know Can Hurt You

by John Lutz

"YOU ARE NUDGER?"

"I am Nudger."

The bulky woman who had leaned over Nudger and confirmed his identity had a halo of dark frizzy hair, a round face, round cheeks, round rimless spectacles, and a small round pursed mouth. She reminded Nudger of one of those dolls made with dried whole apples, whose faces eerily resemble those of aged humans. But the apple dolls' usually are benign; the face looming over Nudger came equipped with tiny dark eyes that danced with malice.

Behind the round-faced woman had stood two silent male companions. She and the two men hadn't spoken when they'd entered Nudger's office without having sounded the buzzer and in workman-like fashion had begun beating him up.

"Who? What? Why?" a frightened Nudger had asked, wrapping his arms around his head and trying to think of who other than his former wife would want to do this to him. He couldn't divine an answer. "I don't need this!" he'd implored. "Stop it, please!"

And they had stopped. Extent of damage: sore ribs, cut forehead, but no damaged pride. Nudger was still alive; that was the object of his game.

But there was more to it. He'd felt his shirtsleeve being unbuttoned, shoved roughly up his forearm. And the abrupt bite of a dull hypodermic needle as it was inserted just below his elbow.

Sodium Pentothal, he deduced, before floating away on a private, agreeable cloud. His mouth seemed to become completely disassociated from his brain. He was vaguely aware that he was answering questions posed by the round-faced woman, that he was rambling uncontrollably.

Yet he couldn't remember the questions or his answers a few seconds after they were uttered.

Then an emptiness, a breathtaking slippage of light and time.

Nudger opened his eyes and wondered where he'd been dropped. It didn't seem proper that he should be slowly revolving. Then the sensation of motion ceased, and with relief he realized he was lying on his back on his office floor. He felt remarkably heavy and comfortable.

Moving only his eyes, he gazed around and took in the open desk drawers and file cabinets, the papers and yellow file folders strewn about the floor. He remembered the hulking round-faced woman and her greedy pig's eyes and her two silent masculine helpers. He tried to recall the round-faced woman's questions but he couldn't.

Nudger struggled to a sitting position and a headache fell on him like a slab from the ceiling. When he'd become somewhat accustomed to the idea of enduring throbbing pain for the rest of his life, he stood, dizzily staggered to his desk, and sat down. The squeal of his swivel chair penetrated his brain like a hot stiletto.

What was it all about? What could he know that the round-faced woman wanted to know? All he was working on now was a divorce case, like dozens of other divorce cases he'd handled as a private investigator. The husband was sleeping with his secretary, the wife had a compensatory affair going with her hairdresser, the husband had hired Nudger to get the goods on the wife. That would be easy; she was flaunting the affair. All of these people were suburbanites who wouldn't know a round-faced woman who shot up people with sodium Pentothal; they were mostly concerned about who was going to come away with the TV and the blender.

Nudger made his way over to where the coffeepot sat on the floor by the plug in the corner. He tried to pour a cupful but found that the round-faced woman and friends had emptied the pot and spread the grounds around on the floor. Maybe it was diamonds they were looking for.

Sloshing through a shallow sea of papers and file folders, Nudger got his tan overcoat from its brass hook, wriggled into it, put on his crushproof hat, and went out, not locking the door behind him. He took the steep steps down the narrow stairwell to the door to the street, feeling the temperature drop as he descended. He shoved open the outer door and braced himself as the winter air stiffened the hairs in his nostrils. The sudden rush of cold made his headache go away. He almost smiled as he stepped out onto the treacherous pavement and walked quickly but gingerly in a neat loop through the door of Danny's Donuts, directly above which his office was located.

Nobody was in the place but Danny. That was the usual state of the business. Nudger breathed in deeply the sudden warmth and cloying sweetness of the doughnuts and unbuttoned his coat. He sat on a stool at the end of the stainless steel counter. Without being asked, Danny set a large plastic-coated paper cup of steaming black coffee before him. Danny was Danny Evers, a fortyish guy like Nudger, and, some might say, a loser like Nudger. Even Danny might say that, aware as he was that he made doughnuts like sash weights.

But what he said was, "You cut yourself shaving?" as he pointed at the cut on Nudger's forehead.

Nudger had forgotten about the injury. He raised tentative fingers, felt ridges of blood coagulated by the cold. "I had a visit from some friends," he said.

"Some friends!" Danny said, changing the emphasis. He put some iced cake doughnuts and a couple of glazed into a grease-spotted carryout box. He was a sad-featured man who seemed to do everything with apprehensive intensity, a concerned basset hound.

"Actually I never met them before this morning," Nudger said, sipping the coffee and burning his tongue. "So naturally we were curious about each other, but they asked all the questions."

"Yeah? What kinda questions?"

"That's the odd thing," Nudger said. "I can't remember."

Danny laughed, then cocked his head of thick graying hair and squinted again at the cut on Nudger's forehead. "You serious about not remembering?"

"It's not the knock on the head," Nudger assured him. "They shot me up with a drug that made me a regular mindless talking machine. It's called truth serum. It works even better than cheap scotch."

"Maybe you oughta see a doctor, Nudge."

"Find me one that doesn't charge twenty dollars a stitch."

"I mean about the memory."

"That kind of a doctor charges twenty dollars a question."

Both men were silent while a blond secretary from the office building across the street came in, paid for the carryout order, and left.

Nudger smiled at her but she ignored him. It took a while for the doughnut shop to warm up again.

"I could drive you," Danny offered. "Emil is coming in to take over here in about fifteen minutes." Emil was Danny's hired help, a sometime college student working odd jobs. He made better doughnuts than his boss's.

"I've got my car here," Nudger said.

"But maybe you shouldn't drive."

"I won't drive anywhere for a while," Nudger said. "What I'll do is go back upstairs and straighten up my office. If you'll give me another cup of coffee and a jelly doughnut, and put them on my tab."

"Straighten up why?" Danny asked, reaching into the display case.

"It's always a mess after friends drop by unexpectedly," Nudger told him.

"Some friends, those boys and girls," Danny reiterated, dropping the doughnut into a small white bag. It hit bottom with a solid smack.

As he trudged back up the unheated stairwell to his office, Nudger tried again, with each painful step, to surmise some reason for his interrogation. He could think of none. Business had been slow ever since summer, and he had been a good boy. Danny's horrendous coffee had started his stomach roiling. He'd take a few antacid tablets before drinking a second cup.

He stopped at his office door and stood holding the sack. It was a morning for surprises. In the chair by the desk sat a slender man wearing a camel hair topcoat with a fur collar. On his lap were expensive brown suede gloves. On his gloves rested pale, still, well-manicured hands. The man's bony face was as calm as his hands were.

"There's no need to introduce myself, Mr. Nudger," he said in a smoothly modulated voice. "On your desk is a sealed envelope. In the envelope is five thousand dollars. You've proved yourself a clever man, so you can't be bought cheap." A thin smile did nothing for him. "But, like all men, you can be bought. I know your present financial status, so five thousand should suffice."

The man stood up, unfolding in sections until he was at least four inches taller than Nudger's six feet. But he was thin, very thin, not a big man. He gazed down his narrow nose at Nudger with the remote interest of a scientist observing familiar bacteria.

"The problem is," Nudger told him, "I don't know who you are or what you're buying."

"I'll make myself clear, Mr. Nudger: stay away from Chaser Heights, or next time you'll be paid a visit of an altogether more unpleasant nature."

He turned and left the office with wolflike loping strides.

Nudger stood stupefied, listening to the man's descending footfalls on the wooden stairs to the street. He heard the street door open and close. The papers on the floor stirred.

Nudger went to the office door and shoved it closed. He walked to his desk, and sure enough there was an envelope, sealed. He opened it and counted out five thousand dollars in bills of various denominations. Earning this money would be a cinch, since he'd never been near any place or anyone named Chaser Heights. Then he reconsidered.

There was little doubt of a connection between the round-faced woman and the tall man. What bothered Nudger was that if these unsettling characters thought he'd been around Chaser Heights at least once when he hadn't, what was going to keep them from thinking he'd been there again? And acting forcefully on their misconception?

Now the five thousand didn't look so good to Nudger. This occupation of his had gotten him into trouble again. He put the money back into its envelope and tucked in the flap. He opened a desk drawer and got out a fresh roll of antacid tablets. He wished he knew how to paint a house.

After his stomach had calmed down, Nudger set about putting his office back together. Small as the place was, the task took the rest of the morning. Most of the time was spent matching the foot-printed papers on the floor with the correct file folders. When he was finished he looked around with satisfaction, straightened the shade on his desk lamp, then went out for some lunch.

At a place he knew on Grand Avenue, Nudger drank a glass of milk, picked at the Gardener's Delight lettuce omelette special, and studied the phone directory he'd borrowed from the proprietor. Within a few minutes he found what he was looking for: Chaser Heights Alcoholic Rehabilitation Center, with an Addington Road address way out in the county.

Nudger knew what he had to do, even if it cost him five thousand dollars.

He finished his milk but pushed his omelette away, jotted down the Chaser Heights address on a paper napkin, and put it into his pocket.

Outside, he slammed his Volkswagen's door on the tail of his topcoat, as he invariably did, reopened the door and tried again, and twisted the key in the ignition switch. When the tiny motor was clattering rhythmically, he pulled the dented VW out into traffic.

It had been a large and palatial country home in better days, with sentry-box cupolas, tall colonial pillars, and ivy-covered brick. Now it was called Chaser Heights, which Nudger gathered was a sort of clinic where alcoholics went to tilt the odds in their battle with booze. It was isolated, set well back from the narrow road on a gentle rise, and mostly surrounded by woods that in their present leafless state conveyed a depressing reminder of mortality.

Nudger parked halfway up the long gravel drive to study the house. He realized that the longer he sat there in the cozy warm car, the more difficult it would be to do what he intended. He put the VW in gear and listened to the tires crunch on the gravel as he drove the rest of the way to the house.

He entered a huge foyer with a gleaming tiled floor that smelled of pine disinfectant. There were brown vinyl easy chairs scattered about, and behind a high, horseshoe-shaped desk stood a tall elderly woman wearing a stiff white uniform. The starch seemed to have affected her face.

"May I help you?" she asked without real enthusiasm, as if she risked ripping her lips by parting them to speak.

"I'd like to see whoever's in charge," Nudger told her, removing his hat. He leaned with his elbow on the desk as if it were a bar and he was about to order a drink.

"Do you have an appointment with Dr. Wedgewick?" the woman asked.

"No, but I believe he'll want to see me. Tell Dr. Wedgewell that a Mr. Nudger is here and needs to talk with him."

"Dr. Wedgewick," his mannequin corrected him. She was so lifelike you expected her eyes to move. She picked up a beige telephone and conveyed Nudger's message, then without change of expression directed him down a hall and to the last door on his left.

He entered an anteroom and was told by an efficient-looking young brunette on her way out that he should go right in, Dr. Wedgewick was expecting him.

And Nudger was expecting Dr. Wedgewick to be exactly who he turned out to be: the tall, camel-coated unfriendly who had delivered the five thousand dollars. He was wearing a dark blue suit and maroon tie and was seated behind a slate-topped desk a bit smaller than a Ping-Pong table. There wasn't so much as a paper clip to break its smooth gray surface. Behind him was a floor-to-ceiling window that overlooked bare-limbed trees and brown grass sloping away toward the distant road. Probably in the summer it was an impressive view. He didn't get up.

"I am surprised to see you here," he said flatly.

"You'll be more surprised by why I came," Nudger told him.

Dr. Wedgewick arched an inquisitive eyebrow impossibly high. Obviously he'd practiced the expression, had it down pat, and knew there was no need for words to accompany it.

"I'm here to return this," Nudger said, and tossed the envelope with the five thousand dollars onto the desk. It looked as lonely as a center fielder there. "Its return should prove to you that you've made a mistake. I can't be who you think; I can't sell you whatever it is you want to buy, because I don't have it and don't know what it is."

"That is nonsense, Mr. Nudger. You've been followed from here several times by Dr. Olander, observed going to your office by the back entrance, observed emerging at times and coming here, snooping around here. Where you hid the pertinent information regarding your client, and how you managed to fool Dr. Olander when she administered her drugs, I can't say, nor do I care."

"I didn't fool her," Nudger said. "I have no client and I didn't know the answers to her questions. But I understand somewhat more of what's going on. Dr. Olander and her two silent helpers couldn't make any progress with me their way, so you came around and tried to buy me."

"We live in a mercantile society."

"The thing is, there was no reason for Dr. Olander to hassle me, and there was nothing I could tell her. I wish there were some way to get you to believe that."

"Oh, I'll bet you do."

"And I wish you'd tell me why a doctor would want to follow me to begin with, me without medical insurance."

Dr. Wedgewick smiled with large, stained, but even teeth. "Dr.

Olander is not a medical doctor. You might say hers is an honorary title. She is chief of security here at Chaser Heights."

"Then I needn't expect a bill." He felt in his pocket for his tablets.

"What you should expect, Mr. Nudger, is to suffer the consequences of being stubborn."

Nudger saw Dr. Wedgewick's gaze shift to something over his left shoulder. He turned and saw the round, malicious features of Dr. Olander. She had taken a few silent steps into the office. Now she stood very still, staring through her gleaming spectacles at the bulge of the hand concealed in Nudger's coat.

He realized that she thought he had a gun.

"What's this wimp doing here?" Dr. Olander asked. "I thought he'd been taken care of."

Nudger, still with his hand inside his coat, perspiring fingers wrapped tightly around his roll of antacid tablets, backed to the door, keeping as far as possible from her. His stomach was fluttering a few feet beyond him, beckoning him on.

Dr. Wedgewick said, "He brought back the five thousand dollars." He looked somewhat curiously at Nudger. "Someone must be paying you a great deal of money," he said. His slow, discolored smile wasn't a nice thing to see. "You'll find that it isn't enough to make it worth your while, Mr. Nudger. You can't put a price on your health."

But Nudger was out into the hall and half running to the lobby. There were a few patients in the vinyl armchairs now. One of them, a ruddy old man wearing a pale blue robe and pajamas, glanced up from where he sat reading *People* and smiled at Nudger. The waxwork behind the counter didn't.

Nudger shoved open the outside door and broke into a run. He piled into his car fast, started the engine, and heard the tires fling gravel against the insides of the fenders as he drove toward the twin stone pillars that marked the exit to the road and safety.

All the way down Addington Road to the alternative highway he kept checking his rearview mirror, expecting to be followed by troops from Chaser Heights. But as he turned onto the cloverleaf he realized they didn't have to follow; they knew where to find him.

When he got back to the office he parked in front, out on the busy street, instead of in his slot behind the building. As he climbed out of the car he noticed that the tail of his topcoat was crushed and grease-stained where he'd shut the door on it again. The coattail had flapped in the wind like a flag all the way back from Chaser Heights. For once Nudger didn't care. He went up to his office, locked the door behind him, and sat for a while chomping antacid tablets.

When his stomach had untied itself, he picked up the phone and dialed the number of the Third Precinct and asked for Lieutenant Jack Hammersmith.

Hammersmith had been Nudger's partner a decade ago in a two-man patrol car, before Nudger's jittery nerves had forced him to retire from the police force. Now Hammersmith had rank and authority, and he always had time for Nudger, but not much time.

"What sort of quicksand have you got yourself into this time, Nudger?" Hammersmith asked.

"The sort that might be bottomless. What do you know about a place called Chaser Heights, out on Addington Road?"

"That clinic where drunks dry out?"

Nudger said that was the one.

"It's a second-rate operation, maybe even a front, but it's out of my jurisdiction, Nudger. I got plenty to worry about here in the city limits."

"What about the director out there? Guy named Dr. Wedgewick?"

"He's new in the area. From the East Coast, I been told." Nudger heard the rhythmic wheezing of Hammersmith laboriously firing up one of his foul-smelling cigars and was glad this conversation was by phone. "Anything else, Nudger?" The words were slightly distorted by the cigar.

"How about Wedgewick's assistant and chief of security, a two-hundred-pound chunk of feminine wiles named Dr. Olander?"

"Hah! That would be Millicent Olaphant, and she's no doctor, she's a part-time bone crusher for some of the local loan sharks."

"Isn't that kind of unusual work for a woman?"

"Yes, I would say it is unusual," Hammersmith said dryly, "and I meet all sorts of people in my job. You be careful of that crew, Nudger. The law out there is the Mayfair County sheriff, Dale Caster."

"What kind of help could I expect from Caster if I did get in the soup?"

"He'd drop crackers on you. Let's just say it would be difficult for a place like Chaser Heights to stay in business if they didn't grease the proper palms."

"And they grease palms liberally," Nudger said. He expected Hammersmith to ask him to elaborate, but the very busy lieutenant repeated his suggestion that Nudger be careful and then hung up.

Nudger sat for a long time, leaning back in the swivel chair, gazing at the ceiling's network of cracks that looked like a rough map of Illinois including major highways. He thought. Not about Illinois.

He thought until the telephone rang, then he picked up the receiver and identified himself.

"This is Danny, downstairs, Nudge," came the answering voice. "Your ex, Eileen, was by here about an hour ago looking for you. She was frowning. You behind with your alimony payments?"

"No further than with the rent," Nudger said. "Thanks for the warning, Danny."

"No trouble, Nudge. She bought half a dozen cream horns." "Then she's doing better than I am."

When Nudger had replaced the receiver in its cradle he sat staring at it instead of Illinois, and he remembered something Danny had said this morning. "Some friends, those boys and girls," he had said. But Nudger hadn't mentioned Dr. Olander-Olaphant's gender.

Nudger put on his coat and tromped downstairs, gaining more understanding as he descended. He went outside, but instead of taking a few steps to the right and entering Danny's Donuts, he cut through the gangway and entered the building through the rear door, then opened another unlocked door and was in the aromatic back room of the doughnut shop. On a coat tree he saw Danny's topcoat, similar to the rumpled tan coat he, Nudger, was wearing and Danny's sold-by-the-thousands brown crushproof hat that was identical with Nudger's. Nudger and Danny were about the same height, and seen from a distance and wearing bulky coats they were of a similar build. Things were making sense at last.

Nudger walked into the greater warmth of the doughnut shop proper, nodded to the surprised Danny, and sat on a stool on the customers' side of the counter. He and Danny were alone in the shop; Emil got off work at two, after the almost nonexistent lunch trade.

"I shoulda said something to you earlier, Nudge," Danny said, no longer looking surprised, nervously wiping the already gleaming counter. "I seen them people from Chaser Heights go up to your place this morning, but I couldn't figure out why until you came down here and told me you'd been roughed up."

"You've been sniffing around there, haven't you?" Nudger said.

Danny nodded. He poured a large cup of his terrible coffee and placed it in front of Nudger like an odious peace offering.

"You were spotted at Chaser Heights," Nudger went on, "and they followed you to find out who you were. You're close to my size, you were wearing a coat and hat like mine, and you came and went the back way. They checked to see who occupied the building and naturally figured it was the private investigator on the second floor. Whoever did the following probably staked out the front of the building and verified the identification when I left my office."

"It was a mistake, Nudge, honest! I didn't mean for you to come to any harm. Absolutely. I wouldn't want that."

Nudger sipped at the coffee, wondering why, if what Danny had said was true, he would serve him a cup of this. "I believe you, Danny," he said, "but what were you doing reconnoitering at Chaser Heights?"

Danny wiped at his forehead with the towel he'd been using on the counter. "My uncle's in there," he said.

"Is he there for the cure?"

Danny looked disgusted. "He's an alcoholic, all right, Nudge. That's how he got conned into admitting himself into Chaser Heights. But what they really specialize in at that place is getting the patients drugged up and having them sign over damn near everything they own in payment for treatment, or as a 'donation' that actually goes into somebody's pocket."

Nudger tried another sip of his formidable coffee. It was easier to get down now that it was cooler. "Does your uncle have much to donate?"

"Plenty. Now don't think small of me, Nudger, but it's no secret he plans to leave most of it to me, his only living relative. And he's not a well man; on top of his alcoholism he's got a weak heart."

"And Chaser Heights is about to get your inheritance before you do. Have you tried talking to your uncle?"

"Sure. They always tell me he's in special care, under detoxification quarantine—whatever that is. So I went back there a few times in secret and hung around thinking I might get a glimpse of old Benj and get to talk to him, at least see what they're doing to him. But they've got him doped up in a locked room with wire mesh on the windows. Some quarantine. I'm worried about him."

"And his money."

"I don't deny it. But that ain't the only consideration."

John Lutz

Danny rinsed his towel, wrung it out, and started wiping the counter again. Nudger sat slowly sipping his coffee. Growl, went his stomach.

"You help me, Nudge, and I'll pay you a couple of thousand—when the inheritance comes."

Nudger eased the coffee cup off to the side. He looked at Danny. "I think it's time your Uncle Benj checked out of Chaser Heights," he said.

"You know a way to manage it?"

Nudger always figured there was a way. That was a two-edged attitude, though, because he always had to figure there was a way for the other guy, too. All of which didn't help Nudger's nervous stomach. Nor did the knowledge that he had to go back out to Chaser Heights that night and case the joint.

The next evening, Nudger and Danny parked Nudger's Volkswagen on a narrow dirt access road that ran through the woods behind Chaser Heights. Nudger was glad to see that Danny was only slightly nervous; the fool had complete faith in him. Both men put on the long black vinyl raincoats with matching hooded caps that Nudger had rented. They pinned badges on the coats and on the fronts of the caps. The sun was down and it was almost totally dark as they made their way through the trees and across the clearing to the rear of Chaser Heights.

They huddled against a brick back wall. Nudger checked the tops of the leafless trees, where the moon seemed to be nibbling at the thin upper branches, to verify which way the breeze was blowing. From a huge pocket of his raincoat he drew a plastic bag stuffed with oil-soaked rags. Danny drew a similar bag from his pocket. They laid the bags near the rear of the building, in tall dry grass that would catch well and produce a maximum amount of smoke. Danny was smiling confidently in the fearlessness born of incomprehension, a kid playing a game.

Nudger used a cigarette lighter to ignite the two bags and their contents. While Danny crept around to the side of the building to set fire to a third bag, Nudger forced open a basement window and lowered himself inside. He had noticed the sprinkler system in the halls on his first visit. Following the yellowish beam of a penlight, he made his way to the system's pressure controls in the basement and turned the lever that built the water pressure all the way to high, hearing an electric pump hum to life and the hiss of rushing water.

12

With a hatchet strapped inside his coat, Nudger broke the lever from the spigot with one sharp blow and then headed for the stairs to the upper floor. He opened the door to the back first-floor hall and then the rear door to admit Danny. Already he could hear movement, voices. And as Danny stepped inside and both men put on their respirator masks, Nudger saw that the burning bags and weeds were creating plenty of smoke, all of it drifting away from Chaser Heights.

Just then the pressure built up enough to activate the sprinkler system in the halls throughout the building, raining a cold spray on anyone caught outside a room. There were several startled shouts, a few curses.

Each carrying a hatchet, Nudger and Danny bustled down the halls in their badge-adorned black slickers and hoods, the respirators snug over their faces. They pulled the respirators away just enough to yell, "Fire department! Everyone remain calm! Everyone out of the building!" They began kicking doors open and ushering patients through the watery halls toward the exits. Nudger was beginning to enjoy this. Not for nothing did small boys want to be firemen when they grew up.

In the distance they could hear wails of sirens. The genuine fire department had been called and was on the way. A white-uniformed attendant, one of the thugs who had been in Nudger's office, jogged past them with only a worried glance.

"Where do you suppose Wedgewick and Olander are?" Danny asked.

"You can bet they were among the first out," Nudger said. "Go get Uncle Benj and head for the car."

Dr. Wedgewick's office was empty, as he'd thought it would be. Through the wide window behind the slate-topped desk, Nudger could see more than a dozen people gathered on the front grounds. Beyond them flashing red lights were approaching, casting wavering, distorted shadows; the sirens had built to a deafening warble. The Mayfair County fire engine even had a loud bell that jangled with a frantic kind of gaiety, as if fires were fun.

The door of a wall safe was hanging open. Nudger went to it and found that the safe was empty. After glancing again out the front window, he left the office.

Everyone in front of Chaser Heights seemed to be shouting. Volunteer firemen were paying out hose and advancing on the building like an invading army. Patients and staff were milling about, asking questions. Nudger joined them. At the edge of the crowd stood Dr. Wedgewick, holding a large brown briefcase,

"Are you in charge, sir?" Nudger inquired from beneath his respirator.

Dr. Wedgewick hesitated. "Yes, I'm Dr. Wedgewick, chief administrator here."

"Could you come with me, sir?" Nudger asked. "There's something you should see." He wheeled and began walking briskly toward the side of the building. All very official.

Dr. Wedgewick followed.

When they had turned the corner, Nudger removed his respirator. "The briefcase, please," he said, not meaning the please.

"Why, you can't! . . ." Then Dr. Wedgewick's eyes darted to the hatchet Nudger had raised, and remained fixed there. He handed the briefcase to Nudger. His hand was trembling.

"Millicent!" Dr. Wedgewick suddenly whirled and ran back the way they had come, all the time pointing to Nudger.

Nudger saw the unmistakably bulky figure of Millicent Olander-Olaphant. He took off for the woods behind the building. He didn't have to look back to know Millicent and the good doctor were following.

Running desperately through the woods, Nudger shed his cumbersome coat, hood, and respirator. He kept the axe and briefcase, using both to smash through the branches that whipped at his face and arms. Behind him someone was crashing through the dry winter leaves.

Nudger had the advantage. He knew where the car was parked. He put on as much speed as he could. The pounding of his heart was almost as loud as his rasping breath.

As he broke onto the road, Nudger saw a dark form in the VW's rear seat. Still wearing raincoat and hood, Danny stood leaning against the left front fender with his arms crossed.

"Quick, get in!" Nudger shouted as he yanked open the driver's side door. He tossed the briefcase and hatchet onto the backseat next to Uncle Benj. His chest ached; his heart was trying to escape from his body.

Danny was barely into the passenger's seat when the engine caught and began its anxious clatter. As Nudger hit first gear and pulled away, he saw the fleeting shadows of pursuing figures in the rearview mirror.

"Who was chasing you?" Danny asked, straining to peer behind them into the darkness.

"My quarrelsome friends from that morning in my office."

"You think they'll get the cops, Nudge?" Danny sounded apprehensive.

Nudger snorted. "1 think it's going to be the other way around." He jerked the VW into a two-wheeled turn, bounced over some ruts, and was back on the main road, picking up speed.

From behind him came a chuckle and Uncle Benj said, "Hey, young fella, where's the fire?"

Nudger thought it wise to stay in the presence of witnesses while he had the briefcase he'd taken from Dr. Wedgewick. He'd known that Dr. Wedgewick wouldn't have paid off the county sheriff, Caster, without keeping some sort of receipts. And when fire supposedly broke out at Chaser Heights and Dr. Wedgewick hurriedly cleaned out the safe, it figured that the doctor would number those receipts among his most valuable possessions.

In Danny's Donuts, Nudger examined the briefcase's contents. There was a great deal of money inside. Also some stock certificates. And among other various papers a notebook containing the dates, times, and amounts of the payoffs to Sheriff Caster. There also were several videocassettes, which the notebook referred to as documentation of the payoffs. Nudger had to admit that Dr. Wedgewick was thorough, but then wasn't the doctor the type?

Nudger went to the phone and called Jack Hammersmith at the Third Precinct. Hammersmith said he'd be around in ten minutes. "I don't understand how you manage to emerge from these misadventures relatively unscathed," he said. He was quite serious.

"Pureness of heart very probably is a factor," Nudger told him. Hammersmith broke the connection without saying good-bye.

"I forgot to give this to you earlier, Nudge," Danny said, holding out a small lavender envelope. "It's from Eileen. She said she could never find you and I was to deliver it."

Nudger grunted and crammed the envelope into his shirt pocket. "Ain't you gonna open it?" Uncle Benj asked, from where he sat near the end of the counter.

"I know what it is," Nudger told him. "It's from my former spouse and makes more than passing reference to neglected alimony payments."

Uncle Benj chortled. "Women can do that to you—drive you to drink if you let 'em." He sat up straighter and drew a deep breath. "You know, Danny boy," he said heartily, "despite the drugs and all the arm-twisting out at that place, I ain't had a drop of the sauce for weeks and I think my stay there did help me. I feel great, like I'll live to be a hundred!"

Danny bit his lower lip glumly, then he smiled and ducked behind the counter.

"Have a doughnut, Uncle Benj," he said.

Nudger thought about Danny's inheritance, about the rent due upstairs, about the envelope from Eileen.

"Don't forget to give him some of your coffee," he said to Danny with a meaningful nod.

If Uncle Benj was going to escape the bottle, maybe he'd fall prey to the cup.

Cat's-Paw

by Bill Pronzini

THERE ARE TWO PLACES that are ordinary enough during the daylight hours but that become downright eerie after dark, particularly if you go wandering around in them by yourself. One is a graveyard; the other is a public zoo. And that goes double for San Francisco's Fleishhacker Zoological Gardens on a blustery winter night when the fog comes swirling in and makes everything look like capering phantoms or two-dimensional cutouts.

Fleishhacker Zoo was where I was on this foggy winter night—alone, for the most part—and I wished I was somewhere else instead. Anywhere else, as long as it had a heater or a log fire and offered something hot to drink.

I was on my third tour of the grounds, headed past the sea lion tank to make another check of the aviary, when I paused to squint at the luminous dial of my watch. Eleven forty-five. Less than three hours down and better than six left to go. I was already half frozen, even though I was wearing long johns, two sweaters, two pairs of socks, heavy gloves, a woolen cap, and a long fur-lined overcoat. The ocean was only a thousand yards away, and the icy wind that blew in off of it sliced through you to the marrow. If I got through this job without contracting pneumonia, I would consider myself lucky.

Somewhere in the fog, one of the animals made a sudden roaring noise; I couldn't tell what kind of animal or where the noise came from. The first time that sort of thing had happened, two nights ago, I'd jumped a little. Now I was used to it, or as used to it as I would ever get. How guys like Dettlinger and Hammond could work here night after night, month after month, was beyond my comprehension.

I went ahead toward the aviary. The big wind-sculpted cypress trees that grew on my left made looming, swaying shadows, like giant black dancers with rustling headdresses wreathed in mist. Back beyond them, fuzzy yellow blobs of light marked the location of the zoo's cafe. More nightlights burned on the aviary, although the massive fenced-in wing on the near side was dark.

Most of the birds were asleep or nesting or whatever the hell it is birds do at night. But you could hear some of them stirring around, making noise. There were a couple of dozen different varieties in there, including such esoteric types as the crested screamer, the purple gallinule, and the black crake. One esoteric type that used to be in there but wasn't any longer was something called a bunting, a brilliantly colored migratory bird. Three of them had been swiped four days ago, the latest in a rash of thefts the zoological gardens had suffered.

The thief or thieves had also got two South American Harris hawks, a bird of prey similar to a falcon; three crab-eating macaques, whatever they were; and half a dozen rare Chiricahua rattlesnakes known as *Crotalus pricei*. He or they had picked the locks on buildings and cages, and got away clean each time. Sam Dettlinger, one of the two regular watchmen, had spotted somebody running the night the rattlers were stolen, and given chase, but he hadn't got close enough for much of a description, or even to tell for sure if it was a man or a woman.

The police had been notified, of course, but there was not much they could do. There wasn't much the Zoo Commission could do either, beyond beefing up security—and all that had amounted to was adding one extra night watchman, Al Kirby, on a temporary basis; he was all they could afford. The problem was, Fleishhacker Zoo covers some seventy acres. Long sections of its perimeter fencing are secluded; you couldn't stop somebody determined to climb the fence and sneak in at night if you surrounded the place with a hundred men. Nor could you effectively police the grounds with any less than a hundred men; much of those seventy acres is heavily wooded, and there are dozens of grottoes, brushy fields and slopes, rush-rimmed ponds, and other areas simulating natural habitats for some of the zoo's fourteen hundred animals and birds. Kids, and an occasional grown-up, have gotten lost in there in broad daylight. A thief who knew his way around could hide out on the grounds for weeks without being spotted.

I got involved in the case because I was acquainted with one of the commission members, a guy named Lawrence Factor. He was an attorney, and I had done some investigating for him in the past, and he thought I was the cat's nuts when it came to detective work. So he'd come to see me, not as an official emissary of the commission but on his own; the commission had no money left in its small budget for such as the hiring of a private detective. But Factor had made a million bucks or so in the practice of criminal law, and as a passionate animal lover, he was willing to foot the bill himself. What he wanted me to do was sign on as another night watchman, plus nose around among my contacts to find if there was any word on the street about the thefts.

It seemed like an odd sort of case, and I told him so. "Why would anybody steal hawks and small animals and rattlesnakes?" I asked. Doesn't make much sense to me."

"It would if you understood how valuable those creatures are to some people."

"What people?"

"Private collectors, for one," he said. "Unscrupulous individuals who run small independent zoos, for another. They've been known to pay exorbitantly high prices for rare specimens they can't obtain through normal channels—usually because of the state or federal laws protecting endangered species."

"You mean there's a thriving black market in animals?"

"You bet there is. Animals, reptiles, birds—you name it. Take the *pricei*, the southwestern rattler, for instance. Several years ago, the Arizona Game and Fish Department placed it on a special permit list; people who want the snake first have to obtain a permit from the Game and Fish authority before they can go out into the Chiricahua Mountains and hunt one. Legitimate researchers have no trouble getting a permit, hobbyists and private collectors are turned down. Before the permit list, you could get a *pricei* for twenty-five dollars; now, some snake collectors will pay two hundred and fifty dollars and up for one."

"The same high prices apply on the other stolen specimens?"

"Yes," Factor said. "Much higher, in the case of the Harris hawk."

"How much higher?"

"From three to five thousand dollars, after it has been trained for falconry."

I let out a soft whistle. "You have any idea who might be pulling the thefts?"

"Not specifically, no. It could be anybody with a working knowledge of zoology and the right—or wrong—contacts for disposal of specimens."

"Someone connected with Fleishhacker, maybe?"

"That's possible. But I damned well hope not."

"So your best guess is what?"

"A professional at this sort of thing," Factor said. "They don't usually rob large zoos like ours—there's too much risk and too much publicity; mostly they hit small zoos or private collectors, and do some poaching on the side. But it has been known to happen when they hook up with buyers who are willing to pay premium prices."

"What makes you think it's a pro in this case? Why not an amateur: Or even kids out on some kind of crazy lark?"

"Well, for one thing, the thief seemed to know exactly what he was after each time. Only expensive and endangered specimens were taken. For another thing, the locks on the building and cage doors were picked by an expert—and that's not my theory, it's the police's."

"You figure he'll try it again?"

"Well, he's four-for-four so far, with no hassle except for the minor scare Sam Dettlinger gave him; that has to make him feel pretty secure. And there are dozens more valuable, prohibited specimens in the gardens. I like the odds that he'll push his luck and go for five straight."

But so far the thief hadn't pushed his luck. This was the third night I'd been on the job and nothing had happened. Nothing had happened during my daylight investigation either; I had put out feelers all over the city, but nobody admitted to knowing anything about the zoo thefts. Nor had I been able to find out anything from any of the Fleishhacker employees I'd talked to. All the information I had on the case, in fact, had been furnished by Lawrence Factor in my office three days ago.

If the thief was going to make another hit, I wished he would do it pretty soon and get it over with. Prowling around here in the dark and the fog and that damned icy wind, waiting for something to happen, was starting to get on my nerves. Even if I was being well paid, there were better ways to spend long, cold winter nights. Like curled up in bed with a copy of *Black Mask* or *Detective Tales* or one of the other pulps in my collection. Like curled up in bed with Kerry. . . .

I moved ahead to the near doors of the aviary and tried them to make sure they were still locked. They were. But I shone my flash on them anyway, just to be certain that they hadn't been tampered with since the last time one of us had been by. No problem there, either.

There were four of us on the grounds—Dettlinger, Hammond, Kirby, and me—and the way we'd been working it was to spread out to four corners and then start moving counterclockwise in a set but irregular pattern; that way, we could cover the grounds thoroughly without all of us congregating in one area, and without more than fifteen minutes going by from one building check to another. We each had a walkie-talkie clipped to our belts so one could summon the others if anything went down. We also used the things to radio our positions periodically, so we'd be sure to stay spread out from each other.

I went around the other side of the aviary, to the entrance that faced the long, shallow pond where the bigger tropical birds had their sanctuary. The doors there were also secure. The wind gusted over the pond as I was checking the doors, like a williwaw off the frozen Arctic tundra; it made the cypress trees genuflect, shredded the fog for an instant so that I could see all the way across to the construction site of the new Primate Discovery Center, and cracked my teeth together with a sound like rattling bones. I flexed the cramped fingers of my left hand, the one that had suffered some slight nerve damage in a shooting scrape a few months back; extreme cold aggravated the chronic stiffness. I thought longingly of the hot coffee in my thermos. But the thermos was over at the zoo office behind the carousel, along with my brown-bag supper, and I was not due for a break until one o'clock.

The path that led to Monkey Island was on my left; I took it, hunching forward against the wind. Ahead, I could make out the high dark mass of man-made rocks that comprised the island home of sixty or seventy spider monkeys. But the mist was closing in again, like wind-driven skeins of shiny gray cloth being woven together magically; the building that housed the elephants and pachyderms, only a short distance away, was invisible.

One of the male peacocks that roam the grounds let loose with its weird cry somewhere behind me. The damned things were always doing that, showing off even in the middle of the night. I had never cared for peacocks much, and I liked them even less now. I wondered how one of them would taste roasted with garlic and anchovies. The thought warmed me a little as I moved along the path between the hippo pen and the brown bear grottoes, turned onto the wide concourse that led past the front of the Lion House.

In the middle of the concourse was an extended oblong pond, with a little center island overgrown with yucca trees and pampas grass. The vegetation had an eerie look in the fog, like fantastic creatures waving their appendages in a low-budget science fiction film. I veered away from them, over toward the glass-and-wire cages that had been built onto the Lion House's stucco facade. The cages were for show: inside was the Zoological Society's current pride and joy, a year-old white tiger named Prince Charles, one of only fifty known white tigers in the world. Young Charley was the zoo's rarest and most valuable possession, but the thief hadn't attempted to steal him. Nobody in his right mind would try to make off with a frisky, five-hundred-pound tiger in the middle of the night.

Charley was asleep; so was his sister, a normally marked Bengal tiger named Whiskers. I looked at them for a few seconds, decided I wouldn't like to have to pay their food bill, and started to turn away.

Somebody was hurrying toward me, from over where the otter pool was located.

I could barely see him in the mist; he was just a moving black shape. I tensed a little, taking the flashlight out of my pocket, putting my cramped left hand on the walkie-talkie so I could use the thing if it looked like trouble. But it wasn't trouble. The figure called my name in a familiar voice, and when I put my flash on for a couple of seconds I saw that it was Sam Dettlinger.

"What's up?" I said when he got to me. "You're supposed to be over by the gorillas about now."

"Yeah," he said, "but I thought I saw something about fifteen minutes ago, out back by the cat grottoes."

"Saw what?"

"Somebody moving around in the bushes," he said. He tipped back his uniform cap, ran a gloved hand over his face to wipe away the thin film of moisture the fog had put there. He was in his forties, heavyset, owl-eyed, with carrot-colored hair and a mustache that looked like a dead caterpillar draped across his upper lip.

"Why didn't you put out a call?"

"I couldn't be sure I actually saw somebody and I didn't want to sound a false alarm; this damn fog distorts everything, makes you see things that aren't there. Wasn't anybody in the bushes when I went to check. It might have been a squirrel or something. Or just the fog. But I figured I'd better search the area to make sure."

"Anything?"

"No. Zip."

"Well, I'll make another check just in case."

"You want me to come with you?"

"No need. It's about time for your break, isn't it?"

He shot the sleeve of his coat and peered at his watch. "You're right, it's almost midnight—"

Something exploded onside the Lion House—a flat cracking noise that sounded like a gunshot.

Both Dettlinger and I jumped. He said, "What the hell was that?"

"I don't know. Come on!"

We ran the twenty yards or so to the front entrance. The noise had awakened Prince Charles and his sister; they were up and starting to prowl their cage as we rushed past. I caught hold of the door handle and tugged on it, but the lock was secure.

I snapped at Dettlinger, "Have you got a key?"

"Yeah, to all the buildings. . . ."

He fumbled his key ring out, and I switched on my flash to help him find the right key. From inside, there was cold dead silence; I couldn't hear anything anywhere else in the vicinity except for faint animal sounds lost in the mist. Dettlinger got the door unlocked, dragged it open. I crowded in ahead of him, across a short foyer and through another door that wasn't locked, into the building's cavernous main room.

A couple of the ceiling lights were on; we hadn't been able to tell from outside because the Lion House had no windows. The interior was a long rectangle with a terra-cotta tile floor, now-empty feeding cages along the entire facing wall and the near side wall, another set of entrance doors in the far side wall, and a kind of indoor garden full of tropical plants flanking the main entrance to the left. You could see all of the enclosure from two steps inside, and there wasn't anybody in it. Except—

"Jesus!" Dettlinger said. "Look!"

I was looking, all right. And having trouble accepting what I saw. A man lay sprawled on his back inside one of the cages diagonally to our right; there was a small glistening stain of blood on the front of his heavy coat and a revolver of some kind in one of his outflung hands. The small access door at the front of the cage was shut, and so was the sliding panel at the rear that let the big cats in and out at feeding time. In the pale light, I could see the man's face clearly: his teeth were bared in the rictus of death.

"It's Kirby," Dettlinger said in a hushed voice. "Sweet Christ, what—?"

I brushed past him and ran over and climbed the brass railing that fronted all the cages. The access door, a four-by-two-foot barred inset, was locked tight. I poked my nose between two of the bars, peering in at the dead man. Kirby, Al Kirby. The temporary night watchman the Zoo Commission had hired a couple of weeks ago. It looked as though he had been shot in the chest at close range; I could see where the upper middle of his coat had been scorched by the powder discharge.

My stomach jumped a little, the way it always does when I come face-to-face with violent death. The faint, gamy, big-cat smell that hung in the air didn't help it any. I turned toward Dettlinger, who had come up beside me.

"You have a key to this access door?" I asked him.

"No. There's never been a reason to carry one. Only the cat handlers have them." He shook his head in an awed way. "How'd Kirby get in there? What happened?"

"I wish I knew. Stay put for a minute."

I left him and ran down to the doors in the far side wall. They were locked. Could somebody have had time to shoot Kirby, get out through these doors, then relock them before Dettlinger and I busted in? It didn't seem likely. We'd been inside less than thirty seconds after we'd heard the shot.

I hustled back to the cage where Kirby's body lay. Dettlinger had backed away from it, around in front of the side-wall cages; he looked a little queasy now himself, as if the implications of violent death had finally registered on him. He had a pack of cigarettes in one hand, getting ready to soothe his nerves with some nicotine. But this wasn't the time or the place for a smoke; I yelled at him to put the things away, and he complied.

When I reached him I said, "What's behind these cages? Some sort of rooms back there, aren't there?"

"Yeah. Where the handlers store equipment and meat for the cats. Chutes, too, that lead out to the grottoes."

"How do you get to them?"

He pointed over at the rear side wall. "That door next to the last cage."

"Any other way in or out of those rooms?"

"No. Except through the grottoes, but the cats are out there."

I went around to the interior door he'd indicated. Like all the others, it was locked. I said to Dettlinger, "You have a key to this door?"

He nodded, got it out, and unlocked the door. I told him to keep watch out here, switched on my flashlight, and went on through. The flash beam showed me where the light switches were; I flicked them on and began a quick, cautious search. The door to one of the meat lockers was open, but nobody was hiding inside. Or anywhere else back there.

When I came out I shook my head in answer to Dettlinger's silent question. Then I asked him, "Where's the nearest phone?"

"Out past the grottoes, by the popcorn stand."

"Hustle out there and call the police. And while you're at it, radio Hammond to get over here on the double—"

"No need for that," a new voice said from the main entrance. "I'm already here."

I glanced in that direction and saw Gene Hammond, the other regular night watchman. You couldn't miss him; he was six-five, weighed in at a good two-fifty, and had a face like the back end of a bus. Disbelief was written on it now as he stared across at Kirby's body.

"Go," I told Dettlinger. "I'll watch things here."

"Right."

He hurried out past Hammond, who was on his way toward where I stood in front of the cage. Hammond said as he came up, "God—what happened?"

"We don't know yet."

"How'd Kirby get in there?"

"We don't know that either." I told him what we did know, which was not much. "When did you last see Kirby?"

"Not since the shift started at nine."

"Any idea why he'd have come in here?"

"No. Unless he heard something and came in to investigate. But he shouldn't have been in this area, should he?"

"Not for another half hour, no."

"Christ, you don't think that he—"

"What?"

"Killed himself," Hammond said.

"It's possible. Was he despondent for some reason?"

"Not that I know about. But it sure looks like suicide. I mean, he's got that gun in his hand, he's all alone in the building, all the doors are locked. What else could it be?"

"Murder," I said.

"How? Where's the person who killed him, then?"

"Got out through one of the grottoes, maybe."

"No way," Hammond said. "Those cats would maul anybody who went out among 'em—and I mean anybody; not even any of the handlers would try a stunt like that. Besides, even if somebody made it down into the moat, how would he scale that twenty-foot back wall to get out of it?"

I didn't say anything.

Hammond said, "And another thing: why would Kirby be locked in cage if it was murder?"

"Why would he lock himself in to commit suicide?"

He made a bewildered gesture with one of his big hands. "Crazy," he said. "The whole thing's crazy."

He was right. None of it seemed to make any sense at all.

I knew one of the homicide inspectors who responded to Dettlinger's call. His name was Branislaus and he was a pretty decent guy, so the preliminary questions-and-answers went fast and hassle-free. After which he packed Dettlinger and Hammond and me off to the zoo office while he and the lab crew went to work inside the Lion House.

I poured some hot coffee from my thermos, to help me thaw out a little, and then used one of the phones to get Lawrence Factor out of bed. He was paying my fee and I figured he had a right to know what had happened as soon as possible. He made shocked noises when I told him, asked a couple of pertinent questions, said he'd get out to Fleishhacker right away, and rang off.

An hour crept away. Dettlinger sat at one of the desks with a pad of paper and a pencil and challenged himself in a string of tick-tack-toe games. Hammond chain-smoked cigarettes until the air in there was blue with smoke. I paced around for the most part, now and then stepping out into the chill night to get some fresh air: all that cigarette smoke was playing merry hell with my lungs. None of us had much to say. We were all waiting to see what Branislaus and the rest of the cops turned up.

Factor arrived at one-thirty, looking harried and upset. It was the first time I had ever seen him without a tie and with his usually immaculate Robert Redford hairdo in some disarray. A patrolman accompanied him into the office, and judging from the way Factor glared at him, he had had some difficulty getting past the front gate. When the patrolman left I gave Factor a detailed account of what had taken place as far as I knew it, with embellishments from Dettlinger. I was just finishing when Branislaus came in.

Branny spent a couple of minutes discussing matters with Factor. Then he said he wanted to talk to the rest of us one at a time, picked me to go first, and herded me into another room.

The first thing he said was, "This is the screwiest shooting case I've come up against in twenty years on the force. What in bloody hell is going on here?"

"I was hoping maybe you could tell me."

"Well, I can't—yet. So far it looks like a suicide, but if that's it, it's a candidate for Ripley. Whoever heard of anybody blowing himself away in a lion cage at the zoo?"

"Any indication he locked himself in there?"

"We found a key next to his body that fits the access door in front."

"Just one loose key?"

"That's right."

"So it could have been dropped in there by somebody else after Kirby was dead and after the door was locked. Or thrown in through the bars from outside."

"Granted."

"And suicides don't usually shoot themselves in the chest," I said.

"Also granted, although it's been known to happen."

"What kind of weapon was he shot with? I couldn't see it too well from outside the cage, the way he was lying."

"Thirty-two Iver Johnson."

"Too soon to tell yet if it was his, I guess."

"Uh-huh. Did he come on the job armed?"

"Not that I know about. The rest of us weren't, or weren't supposed to be."

"Well, we'll know more when we finish running a check on the serial number," Branislaus said. "It was intact, so the thirty-two doesn't figure to be a Saturday night special."

"Was there anything in Kirby's pockets?"

"The usual stuff. And no sign of a suicide note. But you don't think it was suicide anyway, right?"

"No, I don't."

"Why not?"

"No specific reason. It's just that a suicide under those circumstances rings false. And so does a suicide on the heels of the thefts the zoo's been having lately."

"So you figure there's a connection between Kirby's death and the thefts?"

"Don't you?"

"The thought crossed my mind," Branislaus said dryly. "Could be the thief slipped back onto the grounds tonight, something happened before he had a chance to steal something, and he did for Kirby—I'll admit the possibility. But what were the two of them doing in the Lion House? Doesn't add up that Kirby caught the guy in there. Why would the thief enter it in the first place? Not because he was trying to steal a lion or a tiger, that's for sure."

"Maybe Kirby stumbled on him somewhere else, somewhere nearby. Maybe there was a struggle; the thief got the drop on Kirby, then forced him to let both of them into the Lion House with his key."

"Why?"

"To get rid of him where it was private."

"I don't buy it," Branny said. "Why wouldn't he just knock Kirby over the head and run for it?"

"Well, it could be he's somebody Kirby knew."

"Okay. But the Lion House angle is still too much trouble for him to go through. It would've been much easier to shove the gun into Kirby's belly and shoot him on the spot. Kirby's clothing would have muffled the sound of the shot; it wouldn't have been audible more than fifty feet away."

"I guess you're right," I said.

"But even supposing it happened the way you suggest, it *still* doesn't add up. You and Dettlinger were inside the Lion House thirty seconds after the shot, by your own testimony. You checked the side entrance doors almost immediately and they were locked; you looked around behind the cages and nobody was there. So how did the alleged killer get out of the building?"

"The only way he could have got out was through one of the grottoes in back."

"Only he *couldn't* have, according to what both Dettlinger and Hammond say."

I paced over to one of the windows—nervous energy—and looked out at the fog-wrapped construction site for the new monkey exhibit. Then I turned and said, "I don't suppose your men found anything in the way of evidence inside the Lion House?"

"Not so you could tell it with the naked eye."

"Or anywhere else in the vicinity?"

"No."

"Any sign of tampering on any of the doors?"

"None. Kirby used his key to get in, evidently."

I came back to where Branislaus was leaning hipshot against somebody's desk. "Listen, Branny," I said, "this whole thing is too screwball. Somebody's playing games here, trying to muddle our thinking—and that means murder."

"Maybe," he said. "Hell, probably. But how was it done? I can't come up with an answer, not even one that's believably far-fetched. Can you?"

"Not yet."

"Does that mean you've got an idea?"

"Not an idea; just a bunch of little pieces looking for a pattern."

He sighed. "Well, if they find it, let me know."

When I went back into the other room I told Dettlinger that he was next on the grill. Factor wanted to talk some more, but I put him off. Hammond was still polluting the air with his damned cigarettes, and I needed another shot of fresh air; I also needed to be alone for a while.

I put my overcoat on and went out and wandered past the cages where the smaller cats were kept, past the big open fields that the giraffes and rhinos called home. The wind was stronger and colder than it had been earlier; heavy gusts swept dust and twigs along the ground, broke the fog up into scudding wisps. I pulled my cap down over my ears to keep them from numbing.

The path led along to the concourse at the rear of the Lion House, where the open cat-grottoes were. Big, portable electric lights had been set up there and around the front so the police could search the area. A couple of patrolmen glanced at me as I approached, but they must have recognized me because neither of them came over to ask what I was doing there.

I went to the low, shrubberied wall that edged the middle cat-grotto. Whatever was in there, lions or tigers, had no doubt been aroused by all the activity; but they were hidden inside the dens at the rear. These grottoes had been newly renovated—lawns, jungly vegetation, small trees, everything to give the cats the illusion of their native habitat. The side walls separating this grotto from the other two were man-made rocks, high and unscalable. The moat below was fifty feet wide, too far for either a big cat or a man to jump; and the near moat wall was sheer and also unscalable from below, just as Hammond and Dettlinger had said. No way anybody could have got out of the Lion House through the grottoes, I thought. Just no way.

No way it could have been murder then. Unless—

I stood there for a couple of minutes, with my mind beginning, to open up. Then I hurried around to the front of the Lion House and looked at the main entrance for a time, remembering things. And then I knew.

Branislaus was in the zoo office, saying something to Factor, when I came back inside. He glanced over at me as I shut the door.

Branny," I said, "those little pieces I told you about a while ago finally found their pattern."

He straightened. "Oh? Some of it or all of it?"

"All of it, I think."

Factor said, "What's this about?"

"I figured out what happened at the Lion House tonight," I said. "Al Kirby didn't commit suicide: he was murdered. And I can name the man who killed him."

I expected a reaction, but I didn't get one beyond some widened eyes and opened mouths. Nobody said anything and nobody moved much. But you could feel the sudden tension in the room, as thick in its own intangible way as the layers of smoke from Hammond's cigarettes.

"Name him," Branislaus said.

But I didn't, not just yet. A good portion of what I was going to say was guesswork—built on deduction and logic, but still guesswork—and I wanted to choose my words carefully. I took off my cap, unbuttoned my coat, and moved away from the door, over near where Branny was standing.

He said, "Well? Who do you say killed Kirby?"

"The same person who stole the birds and other specimens. And I don't mean a professional animal thief, as Mr. Factor suggested when he hired me. He isn't an outsider at all; and he didn't climb the fence to get onto the grounds."

"No?"

"No. He was already in here on those nights and on this one because he works here as a night watchman. The man I'm talking about is Sam Dettlinger."

That got some reaction. Hammond said, "I don't believe it," and Factor said, "My God!" Branislaus looked at me, looked at Dettlinger, looked at me again—moving his head like a spectator at a tennis match.

The only one who didn't move was Dettlinger. He sat still at one of the desks, his hands resting easily on its blotter; his face betrayed nothing.

He said, "You're a liar," in a thin, hard voice.

"Am I? You've been working here for some time; you know the animals and which ones are endangered and valuable. It was easy for you to get into the buildings during your rounds: just use your key and walk right in. When you had the specimens you took them to some prearranged spot along the outside fence and passed them over to an accomplice."

"What accomplice?" Branislaus asked.

"I don't know. You'll get it out of him, Branny; or you'll find out some other way. But that's how he had to have worked it."

"What about the scratches on the locks?" Hammond asked. "The police told us the locks were picked—"

"Red herring," I said. "Just like Dettlinger's claim that he chased a stranger on the grounds the night the rattlers were stolen. Designed to cover up the fact that it was an inside job." I looked back at Branislaus. "Five'll get you ten Dettlinger's had some sort of locksmithing experience. It shouldn't take much digging to find out."

Dettlinger started to get out of his chair, thought better of it, and sat down again. We were all staring at him, but it did not seem to bother him much; his owl eyes were on my neck, and if they'd been hands I would have been dead of strangulation.

Without shifting his gaze, he said to Factor, "I'm going to sue this son of a bitch for slander. I can do that, can't I, Mr. Factor?"

"If what he says isn't true, you can," Factor said.

"Well, it isn't true. It's all a bunch of lies. I never stole anything. And I sure never killed Al Kirby. How the hell could I? I was with this guy, outside the Lion House, when Al died inside."

"No, you weren't," I said.

"What kind of crap is that? I was standing right next to you, we both heard the shot."

"That's right, we both heard the shot. And that's the first thing that put me onto you, Sam. Because we damned well shouldn't have heard it."

"No? Why not?"

"Kirby was shot with a thirty-two-caliber revolver. A thirty-two is a small gun; it doesn't make much of a bang. Branny, you remember saying to me a little while ago that if somebody had shoved that thirty-two into Kirby's middle, you wouldn't have been able to hear the pop more than fifty feet away? Well, that's right. But Dettlinger and I were a lot more than fifty feet from the cage where we found Kirby—twenty yards from the front entrance, thick stucco walls, a ten-foot foyer, and another forty feet or so of floor space to the cage. Yet we not only heard a shot, we heard it loud and clear."

Branislaus said, "So how is that possible?"

I didn't answer him. Instead I looked at Dettlinger and I said, "Do you smoke?"

That got a reaction out of him. The one I wanted: confusion. "What?"

"Do you smoke?"

"What kind of question is that?"

"Gene must have smoked half a pack since we've been in here, but I haven't seen you light up once. In fact, I haven't seen you light up the whole time I've been working here. So answer me, Sam—do you smoke or not?"

"No, I don't smoke. You satisfied?"

"I'm satisfied," I said. "Now suppose you tell me what it was you had in your hand in the Lion House, when I came back from checking the side doors?"

He got it, then—the way I'd trapped him. But he clamped his lips together and sat still.

"What are you getting at?" Branislaus asked me. "What did he have in his hand?"

"At the time I thought it was a pack of cigarettes; that's what it looked like from a distance. I took him to be a little queasy, a delayed reaction to finding the body, and I figured he wanted some nicotine to calm his nerves. But that wasn't it at all; he wasn't queasy, he was scared —because I'd seen what he had in his hand before he could hide it in his pocket."

"So what was it?"

"A tape recorder," I said. "One of those small battery-operated jobs they make nowadays, a white one that fits in the palm of the hand. He'd just picked it up from wherever he'd stashed it earlier—behind the bars in one of the other cages, probably. I didn't notice it there because it was so small and because my attention was on Kirby's body."

"You're saying the shot you heard was on tape?"

"Yes. My guess is, he recorded it right after he shot Kirby. Fifteen minutes or so earlier."

"Why did he shoot Kirby? And why in the Lion House?"

"Well, he and Kirby could have been in on the thefts together; they could have had some kind of falling-out, and Dettlinger decided to get rid of him. But I don't like that much. As a premeditated murder, it's too elaborate. No, I think the recorder was a spur-of-the-moment idea; I doubt if it belonged to Dettlinger, in fact. Ditto the thirty-two. He's clever, but he's not a planner, he's an improviser."

"If the recorder and the gun weren't his, whose were they? Kirby's?"

I nodded. "The way I see it, Kirby found out about Dettlinger pulling the thefts; saw him do the last one, maybe. Instead of reporting it, he did some brooding and then decided tonight to try a little shakedown. But Dettlinger's bigger and tougher than he was, so he brought the thirty-two along for protection. He also brought the recorder, the idea probably being to tape his conversation with Dettlinger, without Deftlinger's knowledge, for further blackmail leverage.

"He buttonholed Dettlinger in the vicinity of the Lion House and the two of them went inside to talk it over in private. Then something happened. Dettlinger tumbled to the recorder, got rough, Kirby pulled the gun, they struggled for it, Kirby got shot dead—that sort of scenario.

"So then Dettlinger had a corpse on his hands. What was he going to do? He could drag it outside, leave it somewhere, make it look like the mythical fence-climbing thief killed him; but if he did that he'd be running the risk of me or Hammond appearing suddenly and spotting him. Instead he got what he thought was a bright idea: he'd create a big mystery and confuse hell out of everybody, plus give himself a dandy alibi for the apparent time of Kirby's death.

"He took the gun and the recorder to the storage area behind the cages. Erased what was on the tape, used the fast-forward and the timer to run off fifteen minutes of tape, then switched to record and fired a second shot to get the sound of it on tape. I don't know for sure what he fired the bullet into; but I found one of the meat locker doors open when I searched back there, so maybe he used a slab of meat for a target. And then piled a bunch of other slabs on top to hide it until he could get rid of it later on. The police wouldn't be looking for a second bullet, he thought, so there wasn't any reason for them to rummage around in the meat.

"His next moves were to rewind the tape, go back out front, and stash the recorder—turned on, with the volume all the way up. That gave him fifteen minutes. He picked up Kirby's body . . . most of the blood from the wound had been absorbed by the heavy coat Kirby was wearing, which was why there wasn't any blood on the floor and why Dettlinger didn't get any on him. And why I didn't notice, fifteen minutes later, that it was starting to coagulate. He carried the body to the cage, put it inside with the thirty-two in Kirby's hand, relocked the access door—he told me he didn't have a key, but that was a lie—and then threw the key in with the body. But putting Kirby in the cage was his big mistake. By doing that he made the whole thing too bizarre. If he'd left the body where it was, he'd have had a better chance of getting away with it.

"Anyhow, he slipped out of the building without being seen and hid over by the otter pool. He knew I was due there at midnight, because of the schedule we'd set up; and he wanted to be with me when that recorded gunshot went off. Make me the cat's-paw, if you don't mind a little grim humor, for what he figured would be his perfect alibi.

"Later on, when I sent him to report Kirby's death, he disposed of the recorder. He couldn't have gone far from the Lion House to get rid of it; he made the call, and he was back within fifteen minutes. With any luck, his fingerprints will be on the recorder when your men turn it up.

"And if you want any more proof I'll swear in court I didn't smell cordite when we entered the Lion House; all I smelled was the gamy odor of jungle cats. I should have smelled cordite if that thirty-two had just been discharged. But it hadn't, and the cordite smell from the earlier discharges had already faded."

That was a pretty long speech and it left me dry-mouthed. But it had made its impression on the others in the room, Branislaus in particular. He asked Dettlinger, "Well? You have anything to say for yourself?"

"I never did any of those things he said—none of 'em, you hear?"

"I hear."

"And that's all I'm saying until I see a lawyer."

"You've got one of the best sitting next to you. How about it, Mr. Factor? You want to represent Dettlinger?"

"Pass," Factor said thinly. "This is one case where I'll be glad to plead bias."

Dettlinger was still strangling me with his eyes. I wondered if he would keep on proclaiming his innocence even in the face of stronger evidence than what I'd just presented. Or if he'd crack under pressure, as most amateurs do.

I decided he was the kind who'd crack eventually, and I quit looking at him and at the death in his eyes.

"Well, I was wrong about that much," I said to Kerry the following night. We were sitting in front of a log fire in her Diamond Heights apartment, me with a beer and her with a glass of wine, and I had just finished telling her all about it. "Dettlinger hasn't cracked and it doesn't look as if he's going to. The DA'll have to work for his conviction."

"But you were right about most of it?"

"Pretty much. I probably missed a few details; with Kirby dead, and unless Dettlinger talks, we may never know some of them for sure. But for the most part I think I got it straight."

"My hero," she said, and gave me an adoring look.

She does that sometimes—puts me on like that. I don't understand women, so I don't know why. But it doesn't matter. She has auburn hair and green eyes and a fine body; she's also smarter than I am—she works as an advertising copywriter—and she is stimulating to be around. I love her to pieces, as the boys in the back room used to say.

"The police found the tape recorder," I said. "Took them until late this morning, because Dettlinger was clever about hiding it. He'd buried it in some rushes inside the hippo pen, probably with the idea of digging it up again later on and getting rid of it permanently. There was one clear print on the fast-forward button—Dettlinger's."

"Did they also find the second bullet he fired?"

"Yep. Where I guessed it was: in one of the slabs of fresh meat in the storage locker."

"And did Dettlinger have locksmithing experience?"

"Uh-huh. He worked for a locksmith for a year in his mid-twenties. The case against him, even without a confession, is pretty solid."

"What about his accomplice?"

"Branislaus thinks he's got a line on the guy," I said. "From some things he found in Dettlinger's apartment. Man named Gerber—got a record of animal poaching and theft. I talked to Larry Factor this afternoon and he's heard of Gerber. The way he figures it, Dettlinger and Gerber had a deal for the specimens they stole with some collectors in Florida. That seems to be Gerber's usual pattern of operation anyway."

"I hope they get him too," Kerry said. "I don't like the idea of stealing birds and animals out of the zoo. It's . . . obscene, somehow."

"So is murder."

We didn't say anything for a time, looking into the fire, working on drinks.

"You know," I said finally, "I have a lot of sympathy for animals myself. Take gorillas, for instance."

"Why gorillas?"

"Because of their mating habits."

"What are their mating habits?"

I had no idea, but I made up something interesting. Then I gave her a practical demonstration.

No gorilla ever had it so good.

She was drinking a sweet almond liqueur that she took on the rocks. It tastes like dessert, but it's as strong as whiskey.

"He told me not to come," she said. "To the funeral. He said it was a matter of respect for the dead." She picked up her glass and stared into it. I've never known what people hope to see there, though it's a gesture I've performed often enough myself.

"Respect," she said. "What's he care about respect? I would have just been part of the office crowd; we both work at Tannahill; far as anyone there knows, we're just friends. And all we ever were is friends, you know."

"Whatever you say."

"Oh, shit," she said. "I don't mean I wasn't fucking him, for the Lord's sake. I mean it was just laughs and good times. He was married and he went home to Momma every night and that was jes' fine, because who in her right mind'd want Tommy Tillary around by the dawn's early light? Christ in the foothills, did I spill this or drink it?"

We agreed she was drinking them a little too fast. It was this fancy New York sweet-drink shit, she maintained, not like the bourbon she'd grown up on. You knew where you stood with bourbon.

I told her I was a bourbon drinker myself, and it pleased her to learn this. Alliances have been forged on thinner bonds than that, and ours served to propel us out of Armstrong's, with a stop down the block for a fifth of Maker's Mark—her choice—and a four-block walk to her apartment. There were exposed brick walls, I remember, and candles stuck in straw-wrapped bottles, and several travel posters from Sabena, the Belgian airline.

We did what grown-ups do when they find themselves alone together. We drank our fair share of the Maker's Mark and went to bed. She made a lot of enthusiastic noises and more than a few skillful moves, and afterward she cried some.

A little later, she dropped off to sleep. I was tired myself, but I put on my clothes and sent myself home. Because who in her right mind'd want Matt Scudder around by the dawn's early light?

Over the next couple of days, I wondered every time I entered Armstrong's if I'd run into her, and each time I was more relieved than disappointed when I didn't. I didn't encounter Tommy, either, and that, too, was a relief and in no sense disappointing.

Then, one morning, I picked up the *News* and read that they'd arrested a pair of young Hispanics from Sunset Park for the Tillary burglary and homicide. The paper ran the usual photo—two skinny kids, their hair unruly, one of them trying to hide his face from the camera, the other smirking defiantly, and each of them handcuffed to a broad-shouldered, grim-faced Irishman in a suit. You didn't need the careful caption to tell the good guys from the bad guys.

Sometime in the middle of the afternoon, I went over to Armstrong's for a hamburger and drank a beer with it. The phone behind the bar rang and Dennis put down the glass he was wiping and answered it. "He was here a minute ago," he said. "I'll see if he stepped out." He covered the mouthpiece with his hand and looked quizzically at me. "Are you still here?" he asked. "Or did you slip away while my attention was diverted?"

"Who wants to know?"

"Tommy Tillary."

You never know what a woman will decide to tell a man or how a man will react to it. I didn't want to find out, but I was better off learning over the phone than face-to-face. I nodded and took the phone from Dennis.

I said, "Matt Scudder, Tommy. I was sorry to hear about your wife."

"Thanks, Matt. Jesus, it feels like it happened a year ago. It was what, a week?"

"At least they got the bastards."

There was a pause. Then he said, "Jesus. You haven't seen a paper, huh?"

"That's where I read about it. Two Spanish kids."

"You didn't happen to see this afternoon's *Post*."

"No. Why, what happened? They turn out to be clean?"

"The two spicks. Clean? Shit, they're about as clean as the men's room in the Times Square subway station. The cops hit their place and found stuff from my house everywhere they looked. Jewelry they had descriptions of, a stereo that I gave them the serial number, everything. Monogrammed shit. I mean, that's how clean they were, for Christ's sake."

"So?"

"They admitted the burglary but not the murder."

"That's common, Tommy."

"Lemme finish, huh? They admitted the burglary, but according to them it was a put-up job. According to them, I hired them to hit my place. They could keep whatever they got and I'd have everything out and arranged for them, and in return I got to clean up on the insurance by over-reporting the loss."

"What did the loss amount to?"

"Shit, I don't know. There were twice as many things turned up in their apartment as I ever listed when I made out a report. There's things I missed a few days after I filed the report and others I didn't know were gone until the cops found them. You don't notice everything right away, at least I didn't, and on top of it, how could I think straight with Peg dead? You know?"

"It hardly sounds like an insurance setup."

"No, of course it wasn't. How the hell could it be? All I had was a standard homeowner's policy. It covered maybe a third of what I lost. According to them, the place was empty when they hit it. Peg was out."

"And?"

"And I set them up. They hit the place, they carted everything away, and I came home with Peg and stabbed her six, eight times, whatever it was, and left her there so it'd look like it happened in a burglary."

"How could the burglars testify that you stabbed your wife?"

"They couldn't. All they said was they didn't and she wasn't home when they were there, and that I hired them to do the burglary. The cops pieced the rest of it together."

"What did they do, take you downtown?"

"No. They came over to the house, it was early, I don't know what time. It was the first I knew that the spicks were arrested, let alone that they were trying to do a job on me. They just wanted to talk, the cops, and at first I talked to them, and then I started to get the drift of what they were trying to put onto me. So I said I wasn't saying anything more without my lawyer present, and I called him, and he left half his breakfast on the table and came over in a hurry, and he wouldn't let me say a word."

"And the cops didn't take you in or book you?"

"No."

"Did they buy your story?"

"No way. I didn't really tell 'em a story, because Kaplan wouldn't let me say anything. They didn't drag me in, because they don't have a case yet, but Kaplan says they're gonna be building one if they can. They told me not to leave town. You believe it? My wife's dead, the *Post* headline says, 'QUIZ HUSBAND IN BURGLARY MURDER,' and what the hell do they think I'm gonna do? Am I going fishing for fucking trout in Montana? 'Don't leave town.' You see this shit on television, you think nobody in real life talks this way. Maybe television's where they get it from."

I waited for him to tell me what he wanted from me. I didn't have long to wait.

"Why I called," he said, "is Kaplan wants to hire a detective. He figured maybe these guys talked around the neighborhood, maybe they bragged to their friends, maybe there's a way to prove they did the killing. He says the cops won't concentrate on that end if they're too busy nailing the lid shut on me."

I explained that I didn't have any official standing, that I had no license and filed no reports.

"That's okay," he insisted. "I told Kaplan what I want is somebody I can trust, somebody who'll do the job for me. I don't think they're gonna have any kind of a case at all, Matt, but the longer this drags on, the worse it is for me. I want it cleared up, I want it in the papers that these Spanish assholes did it all and I had nothing to do with anything. You name a fair fee and I'll pay it, me to you, and it can be cash in your hand if you don't like checks. What do you say?"

He wanted somebody he could trust. Had Carolyn from the Caroline told him how trustworthy I was?

What did I say? I said yes.

I met Tommy Tillary and his lawyer in Drew Kaplan's office on Court Street, a few blocks from Brooklyn's Borough Hall. There was a Syrian restaurant next door and, at the corner, a grocery store specializing in Middle Eastern imports stood next to an antique shop overflowing with stripped-oak furniture and brass lamps and bedsteads. Kaplan's office ran to wood paneling and leather chairs and oak file cabinets. His name and the names of two partners were painted on the frosted-glass door in old-fashioned gold-and-black lettering. Kaplan himself looked conservatively up-to-date, with a three-piece striped suit that was better cut than mine. Tommy wore his burgundy blazer and gray flannel trousers and loafers. Strain showed at the corners of his blue eyes and around his mouth. His complexion was off, too.

"All we want you to do," Kaplan said, "is find a key in one of their pants pockets, Herrera's or Cruz's, and trace it to a locker in Penn Station, and in the locker there's a foot-long knife with their prints and her blood on it."

"Is that what it's going to take?"

He smiled. "It wouldn't hurt. No, actually, we're not in such bad shape. They got some shaky testimony from a pair of Latins who've been in and out of trouble since they got weaned to Tropicana. They got what looks to them like a good motive on Tommy's part."

"Which is?"

I was looking at Tommy when I asked. His eyes slipped away from mine. Kaplan said, "A marital triangle, a case of the shorts, and a strong money motive. Margaret Tillary inherited a little over a quarter of a million dollars six or eight months ago. An aunt left a million two and it got cut up four ways. What they don't bother to notice is he loved his wife, and how many husbands cheat? What is it they say—ninety percent cheat and ten percent lie?"

"That's good odds."

"One of the killers, Angel Herrera, did some odd jobs at the Tillary house last March or April. Spring cleaning; he hauled stuff out of the basement and attic, a little donkeywork. According to Herrera, that's how Tommy knew him to contact him about the burglary. According to common sense, that's how Herrera and his buddy Cruz knew the house and what was in it and how to gain access."

"The case against Tommy sounds pretty thin."

"It is," Kaplan said. "The thing is, you go to court with something like this and you lose even if you win. For the rest of your life, everybody remembers you stood trial for murdering your wife, never mind that you won an acquittal.

"Besides," he said, "you never know which way a jury's going to jump. Tommy's alibi is he was with another lady at the time of the burglary. The woman's a colleague; they could see it as completely aboveboard, but who says they're going to? What they sometimes do, they decide they don't believe the alibi because it's his girlfriend lying for him, and at the same time they label him a scumbag for screwing around while his wife's getting killed."

"You keep it up," Tommy said, "I'll find myself guilty, the way you make it sound."

"Plus he's hard to get a sympathetic jury for. He's a big handsome guy, a sharp dresser, and you'd love him in a gin joint, but how much do you love him in a courtroom? He's a securities salesman, he's beautiful on the phone, and that means every clown who ever lost a hundred dollars on a stock tip or bought magazines over the phone is going to walk into the courtroom with a hard-on for him. I'm telling you, I want to stay the hell out of court. I'll win in court, I know that, or the worst that'll happen is I'll win on appeal, but who needs it? This is a case that shouldn't be in the first place, and I'd love to clear it up before they even go so far as presenting a bill to the grand jury."

"So from me you want—"

"Whatever you can find, Matt. Whatever discredits Cruz and Herrera. I don't know what's there to be found, but you were a cop and now you're private, and you can get down in the streets and nose around."

I nodded. I could do that. "One thing," I said. "Wouldn't you be better off with a Spanish-speaking detective? I know enough to buy a beer in a bodega, but I'm a long way from fluent."

Kaplan shook his head. "A personal relationship's worth more than a dime's worth of '*Me llamo Matteo y ¿como estd usted?*'"

"That's the truth," Tommy Tillary said. "Matt, I know I can count on you."

I wanted to tell him all he could count on was his fingers. I didn't really see what I could expect to uncover that wouldn't turn up in a regular police investigation. But I'd spent enough time carrying a shield to know not to push away money when somebody wants to give it to you. I felt comfortable taking a fee. The man was inheriting a quarter of a million, plus whatever insurance his wife had carried. If he was willing to spread some of it around, I was willing to take it.

So I went to Sunset Park and spent some time in the streets and some more time in the bars. Sunset Park is in Brooklyn, of course, on the borough's western edge, above Bay Ridge and south and west of Green-Wood Cemetery. These days, there's a lot of brown-stoning going on there, with young urban professionals renovating the old houses and gentrifying the neighborhood. Back then, the upwardly mobile young had not yet discovered Sunset Park, and the area was a mix of Latins and Scandinavians, most of the former Puerto Ricans, most of the latter Norwegians. The balance was gradually shifting from Europe to the islands, from light to dark, but this was a process that had been going on for ages and there was nothing hurried about it.

I talked to Herrera's landlord and Cruz's former employer and one of his recent girlfriends. I drank beer in bars and the back rooms of bodegas. I went to the local station house, I read the sheets on both of the burglars and drank coffee with the cops and picked up some of the stuff that doesn't get on the yellow sheets.

I found out that Miguelito Cruz had once killed a man in a tavern brawl over a woman. There were no charges pressed; a dozen witnesses reported that the dead man had gone after Cruz first with a broken bottle. Cruz had most likely been carrying the knife, but several witnesses insisted it had been tossed to him by an anonymous benefactor, and there hadn't been enough evidence to make a case of weapons possession, let alone homicide.

I learned that Herrera had three children living with their mother in Puerto Rico. He was divorced but wouldn't marry his current girlfriend because he regarded himself as still married to his ex-wife in the eyes of God. He sent money to his children when he had any to send.

I learned other things. They didn't seem terribly consequential then and they've faded from memory altogether by now, but I wrote them down in my pocket notebook as I learned them, and every day or so I duly reported my findings to Drew Kaplan. He always seemed pleased with what I told him.

I invariably managed a stop at Armstrong's before I called it a night. One night she was there, Carolyn Cheatham, drinking bourbon this time, her face frozen with stubborn old pain. It took her a blink or two to recognize me. Then tears started to form in the corners of her eyes, and she used the back of one hand to wipe them away.

I didn't approach her until she beckoned. She patted the stool beside hers and I eased myself onto it. I had coffee with bourbon in it and bought a refill for her. She was pretty drunk already, but that's never been enough reason to turn down a drink.

She talked about Tommy. He was being nice to her, he said. Calling up, sending flowers. But he wouldn't see her, because it wouldn't look right, not for a new widower, not for a man who'd been publicly accused of murder.

"He sends flowers with no card enclosed," she said. "He calls me from pay phones. The son of a bitch."

Billie called me aside. "I didn't want to put her out," he said, "a nice woman like that, shit-faced as she is. But I thought I was gonna have to. You'll see she gets home?"

I said I would.

I got her out of there and a cab came along and saved us the walk. At her place, I took the keys from her and unlocked the door. She half sat, half sprawled on the couch. I had to use the bathroom, and when I came back, her eyes were closed and she was snoring lightly.

I got her coat and shoes off, put her to bed, loosened her clothing and covered her with a blanket. I was tired from all that and sat down on the couch for a minute, and I almost dozed off myself. Then I snapped awake and let myself out.

I went back to Sunset Park the next day. I learned that Cruz had been in trouble as a youth. With a gang of neighborhood kids, he used to go into the city and cruise Greenwich Village, looking for homosexuals to beat up. He'd had a dread of homosexuality, probably flowing as it generally does out of a fear of a part of himself, and he stifled that dread by fag bashing.

"He still doan' like them," a woman told me. She had glossy black hair and opaque eyes, and she was letting me pay for her rum and orange juice. "He's pretty, you know, an' they come on to him, an' he doan' like it."

I called that item in, along with a few others equally earthshaking. I bought myself a steak dinner at the Slate over on Tenth Avenue, then finished up at Armstrong's, not drinking very hard, just coasting along on bourbon and coffee.

Twice, the phone rang for me. Once, it was Tommy Tillary, telling me how much he appreciated what I was doing for him. It seemed to me that all I was doing was taking his money, but he had me believing that my loyalty and invaluable assistance were all he had to cling to.

The second call was from Carolyn. More praise. I was a gentleman, she assured me, and a hell of a fellow all around. And I should forget that she'd been bad-mouthing Tommy. Everything was going to be fine with them.

I took the next day off. I think I went to a movie, and it may have been *The Sting*, with Newman and Redford achieving vengeance through swindling.

The day after that, I did another tour of duty over in Brooklyn. And the day after that, I picked up the *News* first thing in the morning. The headline was nonspecific, something like "KILL SUSPECT HANGS SELF IN CELL," but I knew it was my case before I turned to the story on page three.

Miguelito Cruz had torn his clothing into strips, knotted the strips together, stood his iron bedstead on its side, climbed onto it, looped his homemade rope around an overhead pipe, and jumped off the upended bedstead and into the next world.

That evening's six o'clock TV news had the rest of the story. Informed of his friend's death, Angel Herrera had recanted his original story and admitted that he and Cruz had conceived and executed the Tillary burglary on their own. It had been Miguelito who had stabbed the Tillary woman when she walked in on them. He'd picked up a kitchen knife while Herrera watched in horror. Miguelito always had a short temper, Herrera said, but they were friends, even cousins, and they had hatched their story to protect Miguelito. But now that he was dead, Herrera could admit what had really happened.

I was in Armstrong's that night, which was not remarkable. I had it in mind to get drunk, though I could not have told you why, and that was remarkable, if not unheard of. I got drunk a lot those days, but I rarely set out with that intention. I just wanted to feel a little better, a little more mellow, and somewhere along the way I'd wind up waxed.

I wasn't drinking particularly hard or fast, but I was working at it, and then somewhere around ten or eleven the door opened and I knew who it was before I turned around. Tommy Tillary, well dressed and freshly barbered, making his first appearance in Jimmy's place since his wife was killed.

"Hey, look who's here!" he called out, and grinned that big grin. People rushed over to shake his hand. Billie was behind the stick, and he'd no sooner set one up on the house for our hero than Tommy insisted on buying a round for the bar. It was an expensive gesture—there must have been thirty or forty people in there—but I don't think he cared if there were three or four hundred.

I stayed where I was, letting the others mob him, but he worked his way over to me and got an arm around my shoulders. "This is the man," he announced. "Best fucking detective ever wore out a pair of shoes. This man's money," he told Billie, "is no good at all tonight. He can't buy a drink; he can't buy a cup of coffee; if you went and put in pay toilets since I was last here, he can't use his own dime."

"The john's still free," Billie said, "but don't give the boss any ideas."

"Oh, don't tell me he didn't already think of it," Tommy said. "Matt, my boy, I love you. I was in a tight spot, I didn't want to walk out of my house, and you came through for me."

What the hell had I done? I hadn't hanged Miguelito Cruz or coaxed a confession out of Angel Herrera. I hadn't even set eyes on either man. But he was buying the drinks, and I had a thirst, so who was I to argue?

I don't know how long we stayed there. Curiously, my drinking slowed down even as Tommy's picked up speed. Carolyn, I noticed, was not present, nor did her name find its way into the conversation. I wondered if she would walk in—it was, after all, her neighborhood bar, and she was apt to drop in on her own. I wondered what would happen if she did.

I guess there were a lot of things I wondered about, and perhaps that's what put the brakes on my own drinking. I didn't want any gaps in my memory, any gray patches in my awareness.

After a while, Tommy was hustling me out of Armstrong's. "This is celebration time," he told me. "We don't want to sit in one place till we grow roots. We want to bop a little."

He had a car, and I just went along with him without paying too much attention to exactly where we were. We went to a noisy Greek club on the East Side, I think, where the waiters looked like Mob hit men. We went to a couple of trendy singles joints. We wound up somewhere in the Village, in a dark, beery cave.

It was quiet there, and conversation was possible, and I found myself asking him what I'd done that was so praiseworthy. One man had killed himself and another had confessed, and where was my role in either incident?

"The stuff you came up with," he said.

"What stuff? I should have brought back fingernail parings, you could have had someone work voodoo on them."

"About Cruz and the fairies."

"He was up for murder. He didn't kill himself because he was afraid they'd get him for fag bashing when he was a juvenile offender."

Tommy took a sip of scotch. He said, "Couple days ago, huge black guy comes up to Cruz in the chow line. 'Wait'll you get up to Green

Haven,' he tells him. 'Every blood there's gonna have you for a girlfriend. Doctor gonna have to cut you a brand-new asshole, time you get outa there.'"

I didn't say anything.

"Kaplan," he said. "Drew talked to somebody who talked to somebody, and that did it. Cruz took a good look at the idea of playin' drop the soap for half the jigs in captivity, and the next thing you know, the murderous little bastard was dancing on air. And good riddance to him."

I couldn't seem to catch my breath. I worked on it while Tommy went to the bar for another round. I hadn't touched the drink in front of me, but I let him buy for both of us.

When he got back, I said, "Herrera."

"Changed his story. Made a full confession."

"And pinned the killing on Cruz."

"Why not? Cruz wasn't around to complain. Who knows which one of 'em did it, and for that matter, who cares? The thing is, you gave us the lever."

"For Cruz," I said. "To get him to kill himself."

"And for Herrera. Those kids of his in Santurce. Drew spoke to Herrera's lawyer and Herrera's lawyer spoke to Herrera, and the message was, 'Look, you're going up for burglary whatever you do, and probably for murder; but if you tell the right story, you'll draw shorter time, and on top of that, that nice Mr. Tillary's gonna let bygones be bygones and every month there's a nice check for your wife and kiddies back home in Puerto Rico.'"

At the bar, a couple of old men were reliving the Louis-Schmeling fight, the second one, where Louis punished the German champion. One of the old fellows was throwing roundhouse punches in the air, demonstrating.

I said, "Who killed your wife?"

"One or the other of them. If I had to bet, I'd say Cruz. He had those little beady eyes; you looked at him up close and you got that he was a killer."

"When did you look at him up close?"

"When they came and cleaned the house, the basement, and the attic. Not when they came and cleaned me out; that was the second time."

He smiled, but I kept looking at him until the smile lost its certainty.

"That was Herrera who helped around the house," I said. "You never met Cruz."

"Cruz came along, gave him a hand."

"You never mentioned that before."

"Oh, sure I did, Matt. What difference does it make, anyway?"

"Who killed her, Tommy?"

"Hey, let it alone, huh?"

"Answer the question."

"I already answered it."

"You killed her, didn't you?"

"What are you, crazy? Cruz killed her and Herrera swore to it, isn't that enough for you?"

"Tell me you didn't kill her."

"I didn't kill her."

"Tell me again."

"I didn't fucking kill her. What's the matter with you?

"I don't believe you."

"Oh, Jesus," he said. He closed his eyes, put his head in his hands. He sighed and looked up and said, "You know, it's a funny thing with me. Over the telephone, I'm the best salesman you could ever imagine. I swear I could sell sand to the Arabs, I could sell ice in the winter, but face-to-face I'm no good at all. Why do you figure that is?"

"You tell me."

"I don't know. I used to think it was my face, the eyes and the mouth; I don't know. It's easy over the phone. I'm talking to a stranger, I don't know who he is or what he looks like, and he's not lookin' at me, and it's a cinch. Face-to-face, especially with someone I know, it's a different story." He looked at me. "If we were doin' this over the phone, you'd buy the whole thing."

"It's possible."

"It's fucking certain. Word for word, you'd buy the package. Suppose I was to tell you I did kill her, Matt. You couldn't prove anything. Look, the both of us walked in there, the place was a mess from the burglary, we got in an argument, tempers flared, something happened."

"You set up the burglary. You planned the whole thing, just the way Cruz and Herrera accused you of doing. And now you wriggled out of it."

"And you helped me—don't forget that part of it."

"I won't."

"And I wouldn't have gone away for it anyway, Matt. Not a chance. I'da beat it in court, only this way I don't have to go to court. Look, this is just the booze talkin', and we can forget it in the morning, right? I didn't kill her, you didn't accuse me, we're still buddies, everything's fine. Right?"

Blackouts are never there when you want them. I woke up the next day and remembered all of it, and I found myself wishing I didn't. He'd killed his wife and he was getting away with it. And I'd helped him. I'd taken his money, and in return I'd shown him how to set one man up for suicide and pressure another into making a false confession.

And what was I going to do about it?

I couldn't think of a thing. Any story I carried to the police would be speedily denied by Tommy and his lawyer, and all I had was the thinnest of hearsay evidence, my own client's own words when he and I both had a skinful of booze. I went over it for a few days, looking for ways to shake something loose, and there was nothing. I could maybe interest a newspaper reporter, maybe get Tommy some press coverage that wouldn't make him happy, but why? And to what purpose?

It rankled. But I would just have a couple of drinks, and then it wouldn't rankle so much.

Angel Herrera pleaded guilty to burglary, and in return, the Brooklyn DA's office dropped all homicide charges. He went upstate to serve five to ten.

And then I got a call in the middle of the night. I'd been sleeping a couple of hours, but the phone woke me and I groped for it. It took me a minute to recognize the voice on the other end.

It was Carolyn Cheatham.

"I had to call you," she said, "on account of you're a bourbon man and a gentleman. I owed it to you to call you."

"What's the matter?"

"He ditched me," she said, "and he got me fired out of Tannahill and Company so he won't have to look at me around the office. Once he didn't need me to back up his story, he let go of me, and do you know he did it over the phone?"

"Carolyn—"

"It's all in the note," she said. "I'm leaving a note."

"Look, don't do anything yet," I said. I was out of bed, fumbling for my clothes. "I'll be right over. We'll talk about it."

"You can't stop me, Matt."

"I won't try to stop you. We'll talk first, and then you can do anything you want."

The phone clicked in my ear.

I threw my clothes on, rushed over there, hoping it would be pills, something that took its time. I broke a small pane of glass in the downstairs door and let myself in, then used an old credit card to slip the bolt of her spring lock.

The room smelled of cordite. She was on the couch she'd passed out on the last time I saw her. The gun was still in her hand, limp at her side, and there was a black-rimmed hole in her temple.

There was a note, too. An empty bottle of Maker's Mark stood on the coffee table, an empty glass beside it. The booze showed in her handwriting and in the sullen phrasing of the suicide note.

I read the note. I stood there for a few minutes, not for very long, and then I got a dish towel from the Pullman kitchen and wiped the bottle and the glass. I took another matching glass, rinsed it out and wiped it, and put it in the drainboard of the sink.

I stuffed the note in my pocket. I took the gun from her fingers, checked routinely for a pulse, then wrapped a sofa pillow around the gun to muffle its report. I fired one round into her chest, another into her open mouth.

I dropped the gun into a pocket and left.

They found the gun in Tommy Tillary's house, stuffed between the cushions of the living-room sofa, clean of prints inside and out. Ballistics got a perfect match. I'd aimed for soft tissue with the round shot into her chest, because bullets can fragment on impact with bone. That was one reason I'd fired the extra shots. The other was to rule out the possibility of suicide.

After the story made the papers, I picked up the phone and called Drew Kaplan. "I don't understand it," I said. "He was free and clear; why the hell did he kill the girl?"

"Ask him yourself," Kaplan said. He did not sound happy. "You want my opinion, he's a lunatic. I honestly didn't think he was. I figured maybe he killed his wife, maybe he didn't. Not my job to try him. But I didn't figure he was a homicidal maniac."

"It's certain he killed the girl?"

"Not much question. The gun's pretty strong evidence. Talk about finding somebody with the smoking pistol in his hand, here it was in Tommy's couch. The idiot."

"Funny he kept it."

"Maybe he had other people he wanted to shoot. Go figure a crazy man. No, the gun's evidence, and there was a phone tip—a man called in the shooting, reported a man running out of there and gave a description that fitted Tommy pretty well. Even had him wearing that red blazer he wears, tacky thing makes him look like an usher at the Paramount."

"It sounds tough to square."

"Well, somebody else'll have to try to do it," Kaplan said. "I told him I can't defend him this time. What it amounts to, I wash my hands of him."

I thought of that when I read that Angel Herrera got out just the other day. He served all ten years because he was as good at getting into trouble inside the walls as he'd been on the outside.

Somebody killed Tommy Tillary with a homemade knife after he'd served two years and three months of a manslaughter stretch. I wondered at the time if that was Herrera getting even, and I don't suppose I'll ever know. Maybe the checks stopped going to Santurce and Herrera took it the wrong way. Or maybe Tommy said the wrong thing to somebody else and said it face-to-face instead of over the phone.

I don't think I'd do it that way now. I don't drink anymore, and the impulse to play God seems to have evaporated with the booze.

But then, a lot of things have changed. Billie left Armstrong's not long after that, left New York, too; the last I heard, he was off drink himself, living in Sausalito and making candles. I ran into Dennis the other day in a bookstore on lower Fifth Avenue full of odd volumes on yoga and spiritualism and holistic healing. And Armstrong's is scheduled to close the end of next month. The lease is up for renewal, and I suppose the next you know, the old joint'll be another Korean fruit market.

I still light a candle now and then for Carolyn Cheatham and Miguelito Cruz. Not often. Just every once in a while.

Eight Mile and Dequindre

by Loren D. Estleman

1

T HE CLIENT WAS A NO-SHOW, as four out of ten of them to be.
She had called me in the customary white heat, a woman with one
of those voices you hear in supermarkets and then thank God you're not
married, and arranged to meet me someplace not my office and not her
home. The bastard had been paying her the same alimony for the past
five years, she'd said, and she wanted a handle on his secret bank
accounts to prove he was making twice as much as when they split. In the
meantime she'd cooled down or the situation had changed or she'd
found a private investigator who worked even cheaper than I did,
leaving me to drink yellow coffee alone at a linoleum counter in a gray
cinder-block building on Dequindre at Eight Mile Road. I was just as
happy. Why I'd agreed to meet her at all had to do with a bank balance
smaller than my IQ, and since talking to her I'd changed my mind and
decided to refer her to another agency anyway. So I worked on my coffee
and once again considered taking on a security job until things got better.

A portable radio behind the counter was tuned to a Pistons game,
but the guy who'd poured my coffee, lean and young with butch-cut
red hair and a white apron, didn't look to be listening to it, whistling
while he chalked new prices on the blackboard menu on the wall next to
the cash register. Well, it was March and the Pistons were where they
usually were in the standings at that time and nobody in Detroit was
listening. I asked him what the chicken on a roll was like.

"Better than across the street," he said, wiping chalk off his hands
onto the apron.

Across the street was a Shell station. I ordered the chicken anyway; unless he skipped some lines it was too far down on the board for him to raise the price before I'd eaten it. He opened a stainless steel door over the sink and took the plastic off a breaded patty the color of fresh sawdust and slapped it hissing on the griddle.

We'd had the place to ourselves for a while, but then the pneumatic front door whooshed and sucked in a male customer in his thirties and a sport coat you could hear across the street, who cocked a hip onto a stool at the far end of the counter and asked for a glass of water.

"Anything to go with that?" asked Butch, setting an amber-tinted tumbler in front of him.

"No, I'm waiting for someone."

"Coffee, maybe."

"No, I want to keep my breath fresh."

"Oh. That kind of someone." He wiped his hands again. "It's okay for now, but if the place starts to fill up you'll have to order something, a Coke or something. You don't have to drink it."

"Sounds fair."

"This ain't a bus station."

"I can see that."

Nodding, Butch turned away and picked up a spatula and flipped the chicken patty and broke a roll out of plastic. The guy in the sport coat asked how the game was going, but Butch either didn't hear him or didn't want to. The guy gave up on him and glanced down the counter at me.

"You waiting for someone too?"

"I was," I said. "Now I'm waiting for that bird."

"Stood you up, huh? That's tough."

"I'm used to it."

He hesitated, then got down and picked up his glass and carried it to my end and climbed onto the stool next to mine. Up close he was about thirty, freckled, with a double chin starting and dishwater hair going thin in front. A triangle of white shirt showed between his belt buckle and the one button he had fastened on the jacket. He had prominent front teeth and looked a little like Howdy Doody. "This girl I'm waiting for would never stand anyone up," he said. "She's got manners."

"Yeah?"

"No, really. Looks too. Here's her picture." He took a fat curved wallet out of his hip pocket and showed me the head and torso of a blond in a red bandanna top, winking and grinning at the camera. She stank professional model.

"Nice," I said. "What's she do?"

"Waitress at the Peacock's Roost. That'll change when we're married. I don't want my wife to work."

"The girls in steel-rimmed glasses and iron pants will burn their bras on your lawn."

"To hell with them. Rena won't have anything to do with that kind. That's her name, Rena."

"I think it's dead now," I told Butch.

He landed the chicken patty on one half of the roll and planted the other half on top and put it on a china saucer and set the works on the linoleum. Howdy Doody finished putting away his wallet and stuck his right hand across his body in front of me. "Dave Tillet."

"Amos Walker." I shook the hand and picked up the sandwich. As it turned out I couldn't have done any worse across the street at the Shell station.

Tillet sipped his water. "That clock right?"

Butch looked up to see which clock he meant. There was only one in the place, advertising Stroh's beer on the wall behind the counter. "Give or take a minute."

"She ought to be here now. She's usually early."

"Maybe she stood you up after all," I said.

"Not Rena."

I ate the chicken and Tillet drank his water and the guy behind the counter picked up his chalk and resumed changing prices and didn't listen to the basketball game. I wiped my mouth with a cheesy paper napkin and asked Butch what the tariff was. He said, "Buck ninety-five." I got out my wallet.

"Maybe I better call her," said Tillet. "That phone working?"

Butch said it was. Tillet drained his glass and went to the pay telephone on the wall just inside the door. I paid for the sandwich and coffee. "Well, good luck," I told Tillet on my way past him.

"What? Yeah, thanks. You too." He was listening to the purring in the earpiece. I pushed on the glass door.

Two guys were on their way in and I stepped aside and held the door for them. They were wearing dark windbreakers and colorful knit caps and when they saw me they reached up with one hand apiece and rolled the caps down over their faces and the caps turned into ski masks. Their other hands were coming out of the slash pockets of the windbreakers and when I saw that I jumped back and let go of the door,

but the man closest to it caught it with his arm and stuck a long-barreled
.22 target pistol in my face while his partner came in past him and
lamped the place quickly and then put the .22's twin almost against
Tillet's noisy sport coat. Three flat reports slapped the air. Tillet's mouth
was open and he was leaning one shoulder against the wall and he
hadn't had time to start falling or even know he was shot when the guy
fired again into his face and then deliberately moved the gun and gave
him another in the ear. The guy's buddy wasn't watching. He was
looking at me through the eyeholes in his mask and his eyes were as flat
and gray as nickels on a pad. They held no more expression than the
empty blue hole also staring me in the face.

Then the pair left, Gray Eyes backing away with his gun still on me
while his partner walked swiftly to a brown Plymouth Volare and
around to the driver's side and got in and then Gray Eyes let himself in
the passenger's side and they were rolling before he got the door closed.

Tillet fell then, crumpling in on himself like a gas bag deflating, and
folded to the floor with no more noise than laundry makes skidding
down a chute. Very bright red blood leaked out of his ear and slid into a
puddle on the gray linoleum floor.

I ran out to the sidewalk in time to see the Plymouth take the corner.
Forget about the license number. I wasn't wearing a gun. I hardly ever
needed one to meet a woman in a diner.

When I went back in, the counterman was standing over Tillet's
body, wiping his hands over and over on his apron. His face was as pale
as the cloth. The telephone receiver swung from its cord and the
metallic purring on the other end was loud in the silence following the
shots. I bent and placed two fingers on Tillet's neck. Nothing was
happening in the big artery. I straightened, picked up the receiver,
worked the plunger, and dialed 911. Standing there waiting for
someone to answer I was sorry I'd eaten the chicken.

2

They sent an Adam and Eve team, a white man and a black woman in
uniform. You had to look twice at the woman to know she was a
woman. They hadn't gotten around to cutting uniforms to fit them, and
her tunic hung on her like a tarpaulin. Her partner had baby fat in his
cheeks and a puppy mustache. His face went stiff when he saw the
body. The woman might have been looking at a loose tile on the floor
for all her expression gave up. Just to kill time I gave them the story,

knowing I'd have to do it all over again for the plainclothes team. Butch was sitting on one of the customers' stools with his hands in his lap and whenever they looked at him he nodded in agreement with my details. The woman took it all down in shorthand.

The first string arrived ten minutes later. Among them was a black lieutenant, coarse-featured and heavy in the chest and shoulders, wearing a gray suit cut in heaven and a black tie with a silver diamond pattern. When he saw me he groaned.

"Hello, John," I said. "This is a hike north from headquarters."

John Alderdyce of Detroit homicide patted all his pockets and came up with an empty Lucky Strikes package. I gave him a Winston from my pack and took one for myself and lit them both. He squirted smoke and said, "I was eight blocks from here when I got the squeal. If I'd known you were back of it I'd have kept driving."

John and I had known each other a long time, a thing I admitted to a lot more often than he did. While I was recounting the last few minutes in the life of Dave Tillet, a police photographer came in and took pictures of the body from forty different angles and then a bearded black homicide sergeant I didn't know tugged on a pair of surgical gloves and knelt and started going through Tillet's clothes. Butch had recovered from his shock by this time and came over to watch. "Them gloves are to protect the fingerprints, right?" he asked.

"Wrong. Catch." The sergeant tossed him Tillet's wallet. Butch caught it against his chest. "It's wet."

"That's why the gloves."

Butch thought about it, then dropped the wallet quickly and mopped his hands on his apron.

"Can the crap," barked Alderdyce. "What's inside?"

Still chuckling, the sergeant picked up the wallet and went through the contents. He whistled. "Christ, it's full of C-notes. Eight, ten, twelve—this guy was carrying fifteen hundred bucks on his hip."

"What else?"

The celluloid windows gave up a Social Security card and a temporary driver's license, both made out to David Edward Tillet, and the picture of the blond.

"That Rena?" Alderdyce asked.

I nodded. "She waits tables at the Peacock's Roost, Tillet said."

Alderdyce told the sergeant to bag the wallet and its contents. To me: "You saw these guys before they pulled down their ski masks?"

"Not enough before. They were just guys' faces. I didn't much look at them till they went for the guns. The trigger was my height, maybe ten pounds to the good. His partner gave up a couple of inches, same build, gray eyes." I described the getaway car.

"Stolen," guessed the sergeant. He stood and slid a glassine bag containing the wallet into the side pocket of his coat.

Alderdyce nodded. "It was a market job. The girl was the finger. She's smoke by now. Dope?"

"That or numbers," said the sergeant. "He's a little pale for either one in this town, but the rackets are nothing if not an equal opportunity employer. Nobody straight carries cash anymore."

"I still owe a thousand on this building." Butch's upper lip was folded over his chin. "I guess I'd be dumb to pay it off now."

"The place is made," the sergeant told him.

"Yeah?" The counterman looked hopefully at Alderdyce, who grunted.

"The Machus Red Fox is booked into next year and has been ever since Hoffa caught his last ride from in front of it."

"Yeah?"

The lieutenant was still looking at me. "When can you come down and sign a statement?"

"Whenever it's ready. I'm not exactly swamped."

"Five o'clock, then." He paused. "Your part in this is finished, right?"

"When I work I get paid," I said.

"How come that doesn't comfort me?"

I said I'd see him at five.

The morgue wagon was just creaking its brakes in front when I came out into the afternoon sunlight and walked around the blue and white and a couple of unmarked units and a green Fiat to my heap. I was about to get in behind the wheel when I stopped and looked again at the Fiat. The girl Dave Tillet had called Rena was sitting in the driver's seat, staring at the blank cinder-block wall in front of the windshield.

3

I opened the door on the passenger side and got in next to her. She jumped in the seat and looked at me quickly. Her honey-colored hair was caught in a clasp behind her neck, below which a kind of ponytail hung down her back, and she was wearing a tailored navy suit over a cream-colored blouse open at the neck and jet buttons in her ears, but I recognized her large smoky eyes and the just slightly too-wide mouth that was built for grinning, although she wasn't grinning. The interior of the little car smelled of car and sandalwood.

She snatched up a blue bag from the seat and her hand vanished inside. I caught her wrist. She struggled, but I applied pressure and her face went white and she stopped struggling. I relaxed the hold, but just a little.

"Dave's dead," I said. "You can't help him now."

She said nothing. On "dead," her head jerked as if I'd smacked her. I went on.

"You don't want to be here when the cops come out. They've got your picture and they think you fingered Dave."

"That's stupid." Her voice came from just in back of her tongue. I didn't know how it was normally.

"It's not stupid. He was expecting you and got five slugs from a twenty-two. The cops know where you work and pretty soon they'll know where you live and when they find you they'll book you as a material witness and change it to accessory to the fact later."

"You talk like you're not one of them."

"Get real, lady. If I were we wouldn't be sitting here talking. On the other hand, if you set up Dave deliberately you wouldn't be here at all. It could just be you're someone who could use some help."

Her lips twisted. "And it could just be you're someone who could give it."

"We're talking," I reminded her. "I'm not hollering cop."

"Who the hell are you?"

I told her. Her lips twisted some more.

"A cheap snooper. I should have guessed it would be something like that."

I said, "It's a buyer's market. I don't set the price."

"What's the price?"

"Some truth. Not right now, though. Not here. Let's go somewhere."

"You go," she said. "I've got a pistol in this purse and when I pull the trigger it won't much matter whether it's inside or outside."

I didn't move. "Guns, everybody's got 'em. After a killer's screwed one in your face the rest aren't so scary."

We sat like that for a while, she with her hand in the purse and turned a little in the seat so that one silken knee showed under the hem of her pleated skirt while a cramp crawled across the palm I had clenched on her wrist. The morgue crew came out the front door of the diner wheeling a stretcher with a zipped bag full of Dave Tillet on it and folded the works into the back of the wagon. Rena didn't look at them. Finally I let go of her and got out one of my cards and a pen. I moved slowly to avoid attracting bullets.

"I'll just put my home address and telephone number on the back," I said, writing. "Open twenty-four hours. Just ring and ask for Amos. But do it before the cops get you or I'm just another spent shell."

She said nothing. I tucked the card under the mirror she had clamped to the sun visor on the passenger side and got out and into my crate and started the motor and swung out into the street and took off with my cape flying behind me.

4

I made some calls from the office, but none of the security firms or larger investigation agencies in town had anything to farm out. I bought myself a drink from the file drawer in the desk and when that was finished I bought myself another, and by then it was time to go to police headquarters at 1300 Beaubien, or just plain 1300 as it's known in town. The lady detective who announced me to John Alderdyce was too much detective not to notice the scotch on my breath but too much lady to mention it. Little by little they are changing things down there, but it's a slow process.

In John's office I gave my story again to a stenographer while Alderdyce and the bearded sergeant listened for variations. When the steno left to type up my statement I asked John what he'd found out.

"Tillet kept the books for Great Lakes Importers. Ever hear of it?"

"Front for the Mob."

"So you say. It's worth a slander suit if you say it in public, they're that well screened with lawyers and holding corporations." He broke open a fresh pack of Luckies and fired one up with a Zippo. I already had a Winston going. "Tillet rented a house in Southfield. A grand a month."

"Any grand jury investigations in progress?" I asked. "They're hard on the bookkeeping population."

He shook his head. "We got a call in to the feds, but even if they get back to us we'll still have to go up to the mountain to get any information out of those tight-mouthed clones. We're pinning our hopes on the street trade and this woman Rena. Especially her."

"What'd you turn on her?"

"She works at the Peacock's Roost like you said, goes by Rena Murrow. She didn't show up for the four PM shift today. She's got an apartment on Michigan and we have men waiting for her there, but she's empty tracks by now. Tillet's landlady says he's been away someplace on vacation. Lying low. Whoever wanted him out in the open got to Rena. By all accounts she is a woman plenty of scared accountants would break cover to meet."

"Maybe someone used her."

He grinned that tight grin that was always bad news for someone. "Your license to hunt dulcineas still valid?"

"Everyone needs a hobby," I said. "Stamps are sissy."

"Safer, though. According to the computer, this damsel has two priors for soliciting, but that was before she started bumming around with one Peter Venito. 'Known former associate,' it says in the printout. Computers have no romance in their circuits."

I smoked and thought. Peter Venito, born Pietro, had come up through the Licavoli Mob during Prohibition and during the old Kefauver Committee hearings had been identified as one of the five dons on the board of governors of that fraternal organization the Italian Anti-Defamation League would have us believe no longer exists.

"Venito's been dead four or five years," I said.

"Six. But his son Paul's still around and a slice off the old pizza. His secretary at Great Lakes Importers says he's in Las Vegas. Importing."

"Anything on the street soldiers?"

"Computer got a hernia sorting through gray eyes and the heights and builds you gave us. I'd go to the mugs but you say you didn't get a long enough hinge at them without their masks, so why go into golden time? Just sign the statement and give my eyes a rest from your ugly pan."

The stenographer had just returned with three neatly typewritten sheets. I read my words and wrote my name at the bottom.

"I have it on good authority I'm a heartbreaker," I told Alderdyce, handing him the sheets.

"What's a dulcinea, anyway?" asked the sergeant.

5

The shooting at Eight Mile and Dequindre was on the radio. They got my name and occupation right, anyway. I switched to a music station and drove through coagulating dusk to my little three-room house west of Hamtramck, where I put my key in a door that was already unlocked. I'd locked it when I left that morning.

I went back for the Luger I keep in a special compartment under the dash, and when I had a round in the chamber I sneaked up on the door with my back to the wall and twisted the knob and pushed the door open at arm's length. When no bullets tore through the opening I eased the gun and my face past the door frame. Rena was sitting in my one easy chair in the living room with a .32 Remington automatic in her right hand and a bottle of scotch and a half-full glass standing on the end table on the other side.

"I thought it might be you," she said. "That's why I didn't shoot."

"Thanks for the vote of confidence."

"You ought to get yourself a dead-bolt lock. I've known how to slip latches since high school."

"All they taught me was algebra." I waved the Luger. "Can we put up the artillery? It's starting to get silly."

She laid the pistol in her lap. I snicked the safety into place on mine and put it on the table near the door and closed the door behind me. She picked up her glass and sipped from it. "You buy good whiskey. Keyhole peeping must pay pretty good."

"That's my Christmas bottle."

"Your friends must like you."

"I bought it for myself." I went into the kitchen and got a glass and filled it from the bottle.

She said, "The cops were waiting for me at my place. One of them was smoking a pipe. I smelled it the minute I hit my floor."

"The world's full of morons. Cops come in for their share." I drank.

"What's it going to cost me to get clear of this?"

"How much you got?"

She glanced down at the blue bag wedged between her left hip and the arm of the chair. It was a nice hip, long and slim with the pleated navy skirt stretched taut over it. "Five hundred."

I shrugged.

"All of it?"

"It'd run you that and more to put breathing space between you and Detroit," I said. "It wouldn't buy you a day in any of the safe houses in town."

"What will I eat on?"

"On the rest of it. You knew damn well I'd set my price at whatever you said you had, so I figure you knocked it down by at least half."

She twisted her lips in that way she had and opened the bag and peeled three C-notes and four fifties off a roll that would choke a tuba. I accepted the bills and riffled through them and stuck the wad in my inside breast pocket.

"How's Paul?" I asked.

"He's in Vegas," she answered automatically. Then she looked up at me quickly and pursed her lips. I cut her off.

"The cops know about you and old Peter Venito, may he rest in peace. The word on the street is young Paul inherited everything."

"Not everything."

I was lighting a cigarette and so didn't bother to shrug. I flipped the match into an ashtray. "Dave Tillet."

"I liked Dave. He wasn't like the others that worked for Paul. He wanted to get out. He was all set to take the CPA exam in May."

"He didn't just like you," I said. "He was planning to marry you."

She raised her eyebrows. They were darker than her hair, two inverted commas over eyes that I saw now were ringed with red under her makeup. "I didn't know," she said quietly.

"Who dropped the dime on him?"

Now her face took on the hard sheen of polished metal. "All right, so you tricked me into admitting I knew Paul Venito. That doesn't mean I know the heavyweights he hires."

"You've answered my question. When a bookkeeper for the Mob starts making leaving noises, his employers start wondering where he's going with what he knows. What'd Venito do to get you to set up Dave?"

"I didn't set him up!"

I smoked and waited. In the silence she looked at the wall behind me and then at the floor and then at her hands on the purse in her lap and then she drained her glass and refilled it. The neck of the bottle jingled against the rim. She drank.

"Dave went into hiding a week ago because of some threats he said he got over his decision to quit," she said. "None of them came from Paul, but from his own fellow workers. He gave me a number where he could be reached and told me to memorize it and not write it down or give it to anyone else. I'd gone with Paul for a while after old Peter died and Paul knew I was seeing Dave and he came to my apartment yesterday and asked me where he could reach Dave. I wouldn't give him the number. He said he just wanted to talk to him and would I arrange a meeting without saying it would be with Paul. He was afraid Dave's fellow workers had poisoned him against the whole operation. He wanted to make Dave a cash offer to keep quiet about his, Paul's, activities and that if I cared for him and his future I'd agree to help. I said okay. It sounded like the Paul Venito I used to know," she added quickly. "He would spend thousands to avoid hurting someone; he said that was bad business and cost more in the long run."

"Who picked the spot?"

"Paul did. He called it neutral territory, halfway between Dave's place in Southfield and Paul's office downtown."

"It's also handy to expressways out of the city," I said. "So you set up the parley. Then what?"

"I called Paul's office today to ask him if I could sit in on the meeting. His secretary told me he left for Las Vegas last night. That's when I knew he had no intention of keeping his appointment, or of being anywhere near the place when whoever was keeping it for him went in to see Dave. I broke every law driving here, but—"

The metal sheen cracked apart then. She said, "Damn," and dug in her purse for a handkerchief. I watched her pawing blindly through the contents for a moment, then handed her mine. If it was an act it was sweet.

"Did anyone follow you here?" I asked.

She wiped her eyes, blew her nose as discreetly as a thing like that can be done, and looked up. Her cheeks were smeared blue-black. That was when I decided to believe her. You don't look like her and know how to turn the waterworks on and off without knowing how to keep your mascara from running too.

"I don't think so," she said. "I kept an eye out for cops and parked around the corner. Why?"

"Because if what you told me is straight, you're next on Venito's list of Things to Do Today. You're the only one who can connect him to that diner. Have you got a place to stay?"

"I guess one of the girls from the Roost could put me up."

"No, the cops will check them out. They'll hit all the hotels and motels too. You'd better stay here."

"Oh." She gave me her crooked smile. "That plus the five hundred, is that how it goes?"

"I'll toss you for the bed. Loser gets the couch."

"You don't like blondes?"

"I'm not sure I ever met one. But it has something to do with not going to the bathroom where you eat. Give me your keys and I'll stash your car in the garage. Cops'll have a BOL out on it by now."

She was reaching inside her purse when the door buzzer blew us a raspberry. Her hand went to the baby Remington. I touched a finger to my lips and pointed at the bedroom door. She got up clutching her purse and the gun and went into the bedroom and pushed the door shut, or almost. She left a crack. I retrieved my handkerchief stained with her makeup from the chair and put it in a pocket and picked up the Luger and said, "Who is it?"

"Alderdyce."

I opened the door. He glanced down at the gun as if it were a loose button on my jacket and walked around me into the living room. "Expecting trouble?"

"It's a way of life in this town." I safetied the Luger and returned it to the table.

"You alone?" He looked around.

"Who's asking, you or the department?"

He said nothing, circling the living room with his hands in his pockets. He stopped near the bedroom door and sniffed the air. "Nice cologne. A little feminine."

"Even detectives have a social life," I said.

"You couldn't prove it by me."

I killed my cigarette butt and fought the tug to reach for a replacement. "You didn't come all this way to do 'Who's on First' with me."

"We tracked down Paul Venito. I thought you'd want to know."

"In Vegas?"

He moved his large close-cropped head from side to side slowly. "At Detroit Metropolitan Airport. Stiff as a stick in the trunk of a stolen Oldsmobile."

6

The antique clock my grandfather bought for his mother knocked out the better part of a minute with no competition. I shook out my last Winston and smoothed it between my fingers. "Shot?"

"Three times with a twenty-two. Twice in the chest, once in the ear. Sound familiar?"

"Yeah." I speared my lips with the cigarette and lit up. "How long's he been dead?"

"That's up to the ME. Twelve hours anyway. He was a cold cut long before Tillet bought it."

"Which means what?"

He shook his head again. His coarse face was drawn in the light of the one lamp I had burning.

"My day rate's two-fifty," I said. "If you're talking about consulting."

"I'm talking about withholding evidence and obstruction of justice. The Murrow woman is getting to be important, and I think you know where she is."

I smoked and said nothing.

"It's this tingly feeling I get," he said. "Happens every time a case involves a woman and Amos Walker too."

"Christ, John, all I did was order the chicken on a roll."

"I hope that's all you did. I sure hope."

We watched each other. Suddenly he seized the knob and pushed open the bedroom door, scooping his police special out of his belt holster. I lunged forward, then held back. The room was empty.

He went inside and looked out the open window and checked the closet and got down in push-up position to peer under the bed. Rising, he holstered the .38 and dusted his palms off against each other. "Perfume's stronger in here," he observed.

"I told you I was a heartbreaker."

"Make sure that's all you're breaking."

"Is this where you threaten to trash my license?"

"That's up to the state police," he said. "What I can do is tank you and link your name to that diner shoot for the reporters until little old ladies in Grosse Pointe won't trust you to walk their poodles."

On that chord he left me. John and I had been friendly a long time. But no matter how long you are something, you are not that something a lot longer.

7

So far I had two corpses and no Rena Murrow. It was time to punt. I dialed Great Lakes Importers, Paul Venito's legitimate front, but there was no answer. Well, it was way past closing time; in an orderly society even the crooks keep regular hours. I thawed something out for supper and watched an old Kirk Douglas film on television and turned in.

The next morning was misty gray with the bitter-metal smell of rain in the air. I broke out the foul-weather gear and drove to the Great Lakes building on East Grand River.

The reception area, kept behind glass like expensive cigars in a tobacco shop, was oval shaped with passages spiking out from it, decorated in orange sherbet with a porcelain doll seated behind a curved desk. She wore a tight pink cashmere sweater and a black skirt slit to her ears.

"Amos Walker to see Mr. Venito," I said.

"I'm sorry. Mr. Venito's suffered a tragic accident." Her voice was honey over velvet. It would be.

"Who took his place?"

"That would be Mr. DeMarco. But he's very busy."

"I'll wait." I pulled a thermos bottle full of hot coffee out of the slash pocket of my trench coat and sat down on an orange couch across from her desk.

The porcelain doll lifted her telephone receiver and spoke into it. A few minutes later, two men in tailored blue suits came out of one of the passages and stood over me, and that was when the front crumbled.

"Position."

I wasn't sure which of them had spoken. They looked alike down to the scar tissue over their eyes. I screwed the top back on the thermos and stood and placed my palms against the wall. One of them kicked my feet apart and patted me down from tie to socks, removing my hat last and peering inside for atomic devices. I wasn't carrying. He replaced the hat.

"Okay, this way."

I accompanied them down the passage with a man on either side. We went through a door marked P. VENITO into an office the size of Hart Plaza with green wall-to-wall carpeting and one wall that was all glass, before which stood a tall man with a fringe of gray hair and a neat Vandyke beard. His suit was tan and clung like sunlight to his trim frame.

"Mr. Walker?" he said pleasantly. "I'm Fred DeMarco. I was Mr. Venito's associate. This is a terrible thing that's happened."

"More terrible for him than you," I said.

He cocked his head and frowned. "This office, you mean. It's just a room. Paul's father had it before him and someone will have it after me. I recognized your name from the news. Weren't you involved in the shooting of this Tillet person yesterday?"

I nodded. "If you call being a witness involved. But you don't have to call him 'this Tillet person.' He worked for you."

"He worked for Great Lakes Importers, like me. I never knew him. The firm employs many people, most of whom I haven't had the chance to meet."

"My information is he was killed because he was leaving Great Lakes and someone was afraid he'd peddle what he knew."

"We're a legitimate enterprise, Mr. Walker. We have nothing to hide. Tillet was let go. Our accounting department is handled mostly by computers now and he elected not to undergo retraining. Whatever he was involved with outside the firm that led to his death has nothing to do with Great Lakes."

"For someone who never met him you know a lot about Tillet," I said.

"I had his file pulled for the police."

"Isn't it kind of a big coincidence that your president and one of your bookkeepers should both be shot to death within a few hours of each other, and with the same caliber pistol?"

"The police were here again last night to ask that same question," DeMarco said. "My answer is the same. If, like Tillet, Paul had dangerous outside interests, they are hardly of concern here."

I got out a Winston and tapped it on the back of my hand. "You've been on the laundering end too long, Mr. DeMarco. You think you've gotten away from playing hardball. Just because you can afford a tailor and a better barber doesn't mean you aren't still Freddy the Mark, who came up busting heads for Peter Venito in the bad old days."

One of the blue suits backhanded the cigarette out of my mouth as I was getting set to light it. "Mr. DeMarco doesn't allow smoking."

"That's enough, Andy." DeMarco's tone was even. "I was just a boy when Prohibition ended, Walker. Peter took me in and almost adopted me. I learned the business and when I got back from the war and college I showed him how to modernize, cut expenses, and increase profits. For thirty years I practically ran the organization. Then Peter died and his son took over and I was back to running errands. But for the good of the firm I drew my pay and kept my mouth shut. We're legitimate now and I mean for it to stay that way. I wouldn't jeopardize it for the likes of Dave Tillet."

"I think you would do just that. You remember a time when no one quit the organization, and when Tillet gave notice and you found out young Paul had arranged to buy his silence instead of making dead sure of it, you took Paul out of the way and then slammed the door on Tillet."

"You're fishing, Walker."

"Why not? I've got Rena Murrow for bait."

The room got quiet. Outside the glass, fourteen floors down, traffic glided along Grand River with all the noise of fish swimming in an aquarium.

"She set up the meet with Tillet for Venito," I went on. "She can tie Paul to that diner at Eight Mile and Dequindre and with a little work the cops will tie you to that trunk at Metro Airport. She can finger your two button men. Looking down the wrong end of life in Jackson, they'll talk."

"Get him out of here," DeMarco snarled.

The blue suits came toward me. I got out of there. I could use the smoke anyway.

8

I was closing my front door behind me when Rena came out of the bedroom. She had fixed her makeup since the last time I had seen her, but she had on the same navy suit and it was starting to look like a navy suit she had had on for two days.

I said, "You remembered to relock the door this time."

She nodded. "I stayed in a motel last night. The cops haven't got to them all yet. But I couldn't hang around. They get suspicious when you don't have luggage."

"You can't stay here. I just painted a bull's-eye on my back for Fred DeMarco." I told her what I'd told him.

"I can't identify the men who killed Dave," she protested.

"Freddy the Mark doesn't know that." I lifted the telephone. "I'm getting you a cab ride to police headquarters and then I'm calling the cops. Things are going to get interesting as soon as DeMarco gets over his mad."

The doorbell buzzed. This time I didn't have to tell her. She went into the bedroom and I got my Luger off the table and opened the door on a man who was a little shorter than I, with gray eyes like nickels on a pad. He had traded his windbreaker for a brown leather jacket but it looked like the same .22 target pistol in his right hand. Without the ski mask he looked about my age, with streaks of premature gray in his neat brown hair.

I waved the Luger and said, "Mine's bigger."

"Old movie line," he said with a sigh. "Take a gander behind you."

70

That was an old movie line too. I didn't turn. Then someone gasped and I stepped back and moved my head just enough to get the corner of my eye working. A man a little taller than Gray Eyes, with black hair to his collar and a handlebar mustache, stood behind Rena this side of the bedroom door with a squat .38 planted against her neck. His other hand was out of sight and the way Rena was standing said he had her left arm twisted behind her back. He too had ditched his windbreaker and was in shirtsleeves. The lighter-caliber gun he had used on Tillet and probably on Paul Venito would be scrap by now.

It seemed I was the only one who needed a key to get into my house.

"Two beats one, Zorro." Gray Eyes's tone remained tired and I figured out that was his normal voice. He stepped over the threshold and leaned the door shut. "Let's have the Heine." He held out his free hand.

"Uh-uh," I said. "I give it to you and then you shoot us."

"You don't, we shoot the girl first. Then you."

"You'll do that anyway. This way maybe I shoot you too."

Mustache shifted his weight. Rena shrieked. My eyes flickered that way. Gray Eyes swept the barrel of the .22 across my face and grasped the end of the Luger. I fired. The report gulped up all the sound in the room. Mustache let go of Rena and swung the .38 my way. She knocked up his arm and red flame streaked ceilingward. Rena dived for her blue bag on the easy chair. Mustache aimed at her back. I swung the Luger, but Gray Eyes was still standing and fired the .22. Something plucked at my left bicep. The front window exploded then, and Mustache was lifted off his feet and flung backward against the wall, his gun flying. The nasty cracking report followed an instant later.

I looked at Gray Eyes, but he was down now, his gun still in his hand but forgotten, both hands clasped over his abdomen with the blood dark between his fingers. I relieved him of the weapon and put it with the Luger on the table. Rena was half-reclining in the easy chair with her skirt hiked up over one long leg and her .32 Remington in both hands pointing at Mustache dead on the floor. She hadn't fired.

"Walker?"

The voice was tinny and artificially loud. But I recognized it.

"We're all right, John," I called. "Put down that bullhorn and come in." I told Rena to drop the automatic. She obeyed, in a daze.

Alderdyce came in with his gun drawn and looked at the man still alive at his feet and across at the other man who wasn't and at Rena. I introduced them. "She didn't set up Tillet," I added. "Fred DeMarco bought the hit, not Venito. This one will get around to telling you that if you stop

71

gawking and call an ambulance before he's done bleeding into his belly."

"For you too, maybe." Alderdyce picked up the telephone. He'd seen me grasping my left arm. "Just a crease," I said. "Like in the cowboy pictures."

"You're lucky. I know you, Walker. It's your style to set yourself up as the goat to smoke out a guy like DeMarco. I had men watching the place and had you tailed to and from Great Lakes. When the girl broke in we loaded the neighborhood. Then these two showed—" He broke off and started speaking into the mouthpiece.

I said, "My timing was off. I'm glad yours was better."

The bearded black sergeant came in with some uniformed officers, one of whom carried a 30.06 rifle with a mounted scope. "Nice shooting," Alderdyce told him, hanging up. "What's your name?"

"Officer Carl Breen, Lieutenant." He spelled it.

"Okay."

I let go of my arm and wiped the blood off my hand with my handkerchief and got out my wallet, counting out two hundred and fifty dollars, which I held out to Rena. "My day rate's two-fifty."

She was sitting up now, looking at the money. "Why'd you ask for five hundred?"

"You had your mind made up about me. It saved a speech."

"Keep it. You earned it and a lot more than I can pay."

I folded the bills and stuck them inside the outer breast pocket of her navy jacket. "I'd just blow it on cigarettes and whiskey."

"Who's the broad?" demanded the sergeant.

I thought of telling him that's what a dulcinea was, but the joke was old. We waited for the ambulance.

The surviving gunman's name was Richard Bledsoe. He had two priors in the Detroit area for ADW, one conviction, and after he was released from the hospital into custody he turned state's evidence and convicted Fred DeMarco on two counts of conspiracy to commit murder. DeMarco's appeal is still pending. The dead man went by Austin Grant and had done seven years in San Quentin for second-degree homicide knocked down from murder one. The Detroit police worked a deal with the Justice Department and got Rena Murrow relocation and a new identity to shield her from DeMarco's friends. I never saw her again.

I never ate in Butch's diner again, either. These days you can't get in the place without a reservation.

Turn Away

by Ed Gorman

O N THURSDAY she was there again. (This was on a soap opera he'd picked up by accident looking for a western movie to watch because he was all caught up on his work.) Parnell had seen her Monday but not Tuesday then not Wednesday either. But Thursday she was there again. He didn't know her name, hell it didn't matter, she was just this maybe twenty-two twenty-three-year-old who looked a lot like a nurse from Enid, Oklahoma, he'd dated a couple of times (Les Elgart had been playing in the Loop) six seven months after returning from WWII.

Now this young look-alike was on a soap opera and he was watching.

A frigging soap opera.

He was getting all dazzled up by her, just as he had on Monday, when the knock came sharp and three times, almost like a code.

He wasn't wearing the slippers he'd gotten recently at Kmart so he had to find them, and he was drinking straight from a quart of Hamm's so he had to put it down. When you were the manager of an apartment building, even one as marginal as the Alma, you had to go to the door with at least a little "decorousness," the word Sergeant Meister, his boss, had always used back in Parnell's cop days.

It was 11:23 AM and most of the Alma's tenants were at work. Except for the ADC mothers who had plenty of work of their own kind what with some of the assholes down at Social Services, not to mention the sheer simple burden of knowing the sweet innocent little child you loved was someday going to end up just as blown-out and bitter and useless as yourself.

He went to the door, shuffling in his new slippers which he'd bought two sizes too big because of his bunions.

The guy who stood there was no resident of the Alma. Not with his razor-cut black hair and his three-piece banker's suit and the kind of melancholy in his pale blue eyes that was almost sweet and not at all violent. He had a fancy mustache spoiled by the fact that his pink lips were a woman's.

"Mr. Parnell?"

Parnell nodded.

The man, who was maybe thirty-five, put out a hand. Parnell took it, all the while thinking of the soap opera behind him and the girl who looked like the one from Enid, Oklahoma. (Occasionally he bought whack-off magazines but the girls either looked too easy or too arrogant so he always had to close his eyes anyway and think of somebody he'd known in the past.) He wanted to see her, fuck this guy. Saturday he would be sixty-one and about all he had to look forward to was a phone call from his kid up the Oregon coast. His kid, who, God rest her soul, was his mother's son and not Parnell's, always ran a stopwatch while they talked so as to save on the phone bill. Hi Dad Happy Birthday and It's Been Really Nice Talking to You. I-Love-You-Bye.

"What can I do for you?" Parnell said. Then as he stood there watching the traffic go up and down Cortland Boulevard in baking July sunlight, Parnell realized that the guy was somehow familiar to him.

The guy said, "You know my father."

"Jesus H. Christ—"

"—Bud Garrett—"

"—Bud. I'll be goddamned." He'd already shaken the kid's hand and he couldn't do that again so he kind of patted him on the shoulder and said, "Come on in."

"I'm Richard Garrett."

"I'm glad to meet you, Richard."

He took the guy inside. Richard looked around at the odds and ends of furniture that didn't match and at all the pictures of dead people and immediately put a smile on his face as if he just couldn't remember when he'd been so enchanted with a place before, which meant of course that he saw the place for the dump Parnell knew it to be.

"How about a beer?" Parnell said, hoping he had something besides the generic stuff he'd bought at the 7-Eleven a few months ago.

74

"I'm fine, thanks."

Richard sat on the edge of the couch with the air of somebody waiting for his flight to be announced. He was all ready to jump up. He kept his eyes downcast and he kept fiddling with his wedding ring. Parnell watched him. Sometimes it turned out that way. Richard's old man had been on the force with Parnell. They'd been best friends. Garrett, Sr., was a big man, six-three and fleshy but strong, a brawler and occasionally a mean one when the hootch didn't settle in him quite right. But his son . . . Sometimes it turned out that way. He was manly enough, Parnell supposed, but there was an air of being trapped in himself, of petulance, that put Parnell off.

Three or four minutes of silence went by. The soap opera ended with Parnell getting another glance of the young lady. Then a "CBS Newsbreak" came on. Then some commercials. Richard didn't seem to notice that neither of them had said anything for a long time. Sunlight made bars through the venetian blinds. The refrigerator thrummed. Upstairs but distantly a kid bawled.

Parnell didn't realize it at first, not until Richard sniffed, that Bud Garrett's son was either crying or doing something damn close to it.

"Hey, Richard, what's the problem?" Parnell said, making sure to keep his voice soft.

"My, my dad."

"Is something wrong?"

"Yes."

"What?"

Richard looked up with his pale blue eyes. "He's dying."

"Jesus."

Richard cleared his throat. "It's how he's dying that's so bad."

"Cancer?"

Richard said, "Yes. Liver. He's dying by inches."

"Shit."

Richard nodded. Then he fell once more into his own thoughts. Parnell let him stay there awhile, thinking about Bud Garrett. Bud had left the force on a whim that all the cops said would fail. He started a rent-a-car business with a small inheritance he'd come into. That was twenty years ago. Now Bud Garrett lived up in Woodland Hills and drove the big Mercedes and went to Europe once a year. Bud and Parnell had tried to remain friends but beer and champagne didn't mix. When the Mrs. had died Bud had sent a lavish display of flowers to the funeral and a note that Parnell knew to be sincere but they hadn't had any real contact in years.

"Shit," Parnell said again.

Richard looked up, shaking his head as if trying to escape the aftereffects of drugs. "I want to hire you."

"Hire me? As what?"

"You're a personal investigator aren't you?"

"Not anymore. I mean I kept my ticket—it doesn't cost that much to renew it—but hell I haven't had a job in five years." He waved a beefy hand around the apartment. "I manage these apartments."

From inside his blue pin-striped suit Richard took a sleek wallet. He quickly counted out five one-hundred-dollar bills and put them on the blond coffee table next to the stack of Luke Short paperbacks. "I really want you to help me."

"Help you do what?"

"Kill my father."

Now Parnell shook his head. "Jesus, kid, are you nuts or what?"

Richard stood up. "Are you busy right now?"

Parnell looked around the room again. "I guess not."

"Then why don't you come with me?"

"Where?"

When the elevator doors opened to let them out on the sixth floor of the hospital, Parnell said, "I want to be sure that you understand me."

He took Richard by the sleeve and held him and stared into his pale blue eyes. "You know why I'm coming here, right?"

"Right."

"I'm coming to see your father because we're old friends. Because I cared about him a great deal and because I still do. But that's the only reason."

"Right."

Parnell frowned. "You still think I'm going to help you, don't you?"

"I just want you to see him."

On the way to Bud Garrett's room they passed an especially good-looking nurse. Parnell felt guilty about recognizing her beauty. His old friend was dying just down the hall and here Parnell was worrying about some nurse.

Parnell went around the corner of the door. The room was dark. It smelled sweet from flowers and fetid from flesh literally rotting.

Then he looked at the frail yellow man in the bed. Even in the shadows you could see his skin was yellow.

"I'll be damned," the man said.

It was like watching a skeleton talk by some trick of magic.

Parnell went over and tried to smile his ass off but all he could muster was just a little one. He wanted to cry until he collapsed. You son of a bitch, Parnell thought, enraged. He just wasn't sure who he was enraged with. Death or God or himself—or maybe even Bud himself for reminding Parnell of just how terrible and scary it could get near the end.

"I'll be damned," Bud Garrett said again.

He put out his hand and Parnell took it. Held it for a long time.

"He's a good boy, isn't he?" Garrett said, nodding to Richard.

"He sure is."

"I had to raise him after his mother died. I did a good job, if I say so myself."

"A damn good job, Bud."

This was a big private room that more resembled a hotel suite. There was a divan and a console TV and a dry bar. There was a Picasso lithograph and a walk-in closet and a deck to walk out on. There was a double-sized water bed with enough controls to drive a spaceship and a big stereo and a bookcase filled with hardcovers. Most people Parnell knew dreamed of living in such a place. Bud Garrett was dying in it.

"He told you," Garrett said.

"What?" Parnell spun around to face Richard, knowing suddenly the worst truth of all.

"He told you."

"Jesus, Bud, you sent him, didn't you?"

"Yes. Yes, I did."

"Why?"

Parnell looked at Garrett again. How could somebody who used to have a weight problem and who could throw around the toughest drunk the barrio ever produced get to be like this. Nearly every time he talked he winced. And all the time he smelled. Bad.

"I sent for you because none of us is perfect," Bud said.

"I don't understand."

"He's afraid."

"Richard?"

"Yes."

"I don't blame him. I'd be afraid too." Parnell paused and stared at Bud. "You asked him to kill you, didn't you?"

"Yes. It's his responsibility to do it."

Richard stepped up to his father's bedside and said, "I agree with that, Mr. Parnell. It is my responsibility. I just need a little help is all."

"Doing what?"

"If I buy cyanide, it will eventually be traced to me and I'll be tried for murder. If you buy it, nobody will ever connect you with my father."

Parnell shook his head. "That's bullshit. That isn't what you want me for. There are a million ways you could get cyanide without having it traced back."

Bud Garrett said, "I told him about you. I told him you could help give him strength."

"I don't agree with any of this, Bud. You should die when it's your time to die. I'm a Catholic."

Bud laughed hoarsely. "So am I, you asshole." He coughed and said, "The pain's bad. I'm beyond any help they can give me. But it could go on for a long time." Then, just as his son had an hour ago, Bud Garrett began crying almost imperceptibly. "I'm scared, Parnell. I don't know what's on the other side but it can't be any worse than this." He reached out his hand and for a long time Parnell just stared at it but then he touched it.

"Jesus," Parnell said. "It's pretty fucking confusing, Bud. It's pretty fucking confusing."

Richard took Parnell out to dinner that night. It was a nice place. The tablecloths were starchy white and the waiters all wore shiny shoes. Candles glowed inside red glass.

They'd had four drinks apiece, during which Richard told Parnell about his two sons (six and eight respectively) and about the perils and rewards of the rent-a-car business and about how much he liked windsurfing even though he really wasn't much good at it.

Just after the arrival of the fourth drink, Richard took something from his pocket and laid it on the table.

It was a cold capsule.

"You know how the Tylenol Killer in Chicago operated?" Richard asked.

Parnell nodded.

"Same thing," Richard said. "I took the cyanide and put it in a capsule."

"Christ. I don't know about it."

"You're scared too, aren't you?"

"Yeah, I am."

Richard sipped his whiskey and soda. With his regimental striped tie he might have been sitting in a country club. "May I ask you something?"

"Maybe."

"Do you believe in God?"

"Sure."

"Then if you believe in God, you must believe in goodness, correct?"

Parnell frowned. "I'm not much of an intellectual, Richard."

"But if you believe in God, you must believe in goodness, right?"

"Right."

"Do you think what's happening to my father is good?"

"Of course I don't."

"Then you must also believe that God isn't doing this to him—right?"

"Right."

Richard held up the capsule. Stared at it. "All I want you to do is give me a ride to the hospital. Then just wait in the car down in the parking lot."

"I won't do it."

Richard signaled for another round.

"I won't goddamn do it," Parnell said.

By the time they left the restaurant Richard was too drunk to drive. Parnell got behind the wheel of the new Audi. "Why don't you tell me where you live? I'll take you home and take a cab from there."

"I want to go to the hospital."

"No way, Richard."

Richard slammed his fist against the dashboard. "You fucking owe him that, man!" he screamed.

Parnell was shocked, and a bit impressed, with Richard's violent side. If nothing else, he saw how much Richard loved his old man.

"Richard, listen."

Richard sat in a heap against the opposite door. His tears were dry ones, choking ones. "Don't give me any of your speeches." He wiped snot from his nose on his sleeve. "My dad always told me what a tough guy Parnell was." He turned to Parnell, anger in him again. "Well, I'm not tough, Parnell, and so I need to borrow some of your toughness so I can get that man out of his pain and grant him his one last fucking wish. *Do you goddamn understand me?*"

He smashed his fist on the dashboard again.

Parnell turned on the ignition and drove them away.

When they reached the hospital, Parnell found a parking spot and pulled in. The mercury vapor lights made him feel as though he were on Mars. Bugs smashed against the windshield.

"I'll wait here for you," Parnell said.

Richard looked over at him. "You won't call the cops?"

"No."

"And you won't come up and try to stop me?"

"No."

Richard studied Parnell's face. "Why did you change your mind?"

"Because I'm like him."

"Like my father?"

"Yeah. A coward. I wouldn't want the pain either. I'd be just as afraid."

All Richard said, and this he barely whispered, was "Thanks."

While he sat there Parnell listened to country-western music and then a serious political call-in show and then a call-in show where a lady talked about Venusians who wanted to pork her and then some salsa music and then a religious minister who sounded like Foghorn Leghorn in the old Warner Brothers cartoons.

By then Richard came back.

He got in the car and slammed the door shut and said, completely sober now, "Let's go."

Parnell got out of there.

They went ten long blocks before Parnell said, "You didn't do it, did you?"

Richard got hysterical. "You son of a bitch! You son of a bitch!"

Parnell had to pull the car over to the curb. He hit Richard once, a fast clean right hand, not enough to make him unconscious but enough to calm him down.

"You didn't do it, did you?"

"He's my father, Parnell. I don't know what to do. I love him so much I don't want to see him suffer. But I love him so much I don't want to see him die, either."

Parnell let the kid sob. He thought of his old friend Bud Garrett and what a good goddamn fun buddy he'd been and then he started crying, too.

When Parnell came down Richard was behind the steering wheel. Parnell got in the car and looked around the empty parking lot and said, "Drive."

"Any place especially?"

"Out along the East River road. Your old man and I used to fish off that little bridge there."

Richard drove them. From inside his sport coat Parnell took the pint of Jim Beam.

When they got to the bridge Parnell said, "Give me five minutes alone and then you can come over, okay?"

Richard was starting to sob again.

Parnell got out of the car and went over to the bridge. In the hot night you could hear the hydroelectric dam half a mile downstream and smell the fish and feel the mosquitoes feasting their way through the evening.

He thought of what Bud Garrett had said, "Put it in some whiskey for me, will you?"

So Parnell had obliged.

He stood now on the bridge looking up at the yellow circle of moon thinking about dead people, his wife and many of his WWII friends, the rookie cop who'd died of a sudden tumor, his wife with her rosary-wrapped hands. Hell, there was probably even a chance that nurse from Enid, Oklahoma, was dead.

"What do you think's on the other side?" Bud Garrett had asked just half an hour ago. He'd almost sounded excited. As if he were a farm kid about to ship out with the merchant marines.

"I don't know," Parnell had said.

"It scare you, Parnell?"

"Yeah," Parnell had said. "Yeah it does."

Then Bud Garrett had laughed. "Don't tell the kid that. I always told him that nothin' scared you."

Richard came up the bridge after a time. At first he stood maybe a hundred feet away from Parnell. He leaned his elbows on the concrete and looked out at the water and the moon. Parnell watched him, knowing it was all Richard, or anybody, could do.

Look out at the water and the moon and think about dead people and how you yourself would soon enough be dead.

Richard turned to Parnell then and said, his tears gone completely now, sounding for the first time like Parnell's sort of man, "You know, Parnell, my father was right. You're a brave son of a bitch. You really are."

Parnell knew it was important for Richard to believe that—that there were actually people in the world who didn't fear things the way most people did—so Parnell didn't answer him at all.

He just took his pint out and had himself a swig and looked some more at the moon and the water.

The Crooked Way

by Loren D. Estleman

YOU COULDN'T MISS THE INDIAN if you'd wanted to. He was sitting all alone in a corner booth, which was probably his idea, but he hadn't much choice because there was barely enough room in it for him. He had shoulders going into the next county and a head the size of a basketball, and he was holding a beer mug that looked like a shot glass between his callused palms. As I approached the booth he looked up at me—not very far up—through slits in a face made up of bunched ovals with a nose like the corner of a building. His skin was the color of old brick.

"Mr. Frechette?" I asked.

"Amos Walker?"

I said I was. Coming from him my name sounded like two stones dropping into deep water. He made no move to shake hands, but he inclined his head a fraction of an inch and I borrowed a chair from a nearby table and joined him. He had on a blue shirt buttoned to the neck, and his hair, parted on one side and plastered down, was blue-black without a trace of gray. Nevertheless he was about fifty.

"Charlie Stoat says you track like an Osage," he said. "I hope you're better than that. I couldn't track a train."

"How is Charlie? I haven't seen him since that insurance thing."

"Going under. The construction boom went bust in Houston just when he was expanding his operation."

"What's that do to yours?" He'd told me over the telephone he was in construction.

"Nothing worth mentioning. I've been running on a shoestring for years. You can't break a poor man."

I signaled the bartender for a beer and he brought one over. It was a workingman's hangout across the street from the Ford plant in Highland Park. The shift wasn't due to change for an hour and we had the place to ourselves. "You said your daughter ran away," I said, when the bartender had left. "What makes you think she's in Detroit?"

He drank off half his beer and belched dramatically. "When does client privilege start?"

"It never stops."

I watched him make up his mind. Indians aren't nearly as hard to read as they appear in books. He picked up a folded newspaper from the seat beside him and spread it out on the table facing me. It was yesterday's *Houston Chronicle*, with a banner:

BOYD MANHUNT MOVES NORTHEAST
Bandit's Van Found Abandoned in Detroit

I had read a related wire story in that morning's *Detroit Free Press*. Following the unassisted shotgun robberies of two savings and loan offices near Houston, concerned citizens had reported seeing twenty-two-year-old Virgil Boyd in Mexico and Oklahoma, but his green van with Texas plates had turned up in a city lot five minutes from where we were sitting. As of that morning, Detroit police headquarters was paved with feds and sun-crinkled out-of-state cops chewing toothpicks.

I refolded the paper and gave it back. "Your daughter's taken up with Boyd?"

"They were high school sweethearts," Frechette said. "That was before Texas Federal foreclosed on his family's ranch and his father shot himself. She disappeared from home after the first robbery. I guess that makes her an accomplice to the second."

"Legally speaking," I agreed, "if she's with him and it's her idea. A smart DA would knock it down to harboring if she turned herself in. She'd probably get probation."

"She wouldn't do that. She's got some crazy idea she's in love with Boyd."

"I'm surprised I haven't heard about her."

"No one knows. I didn't report her missing. If I had, the police would have put two and two together and there'd be a warrant out for her as well."

I swallowed some beer. "I don't know what you think I can do that the cops and the FBI can't."

"I know where she is."

I waited. He rotated his mug. "My sister lives in Southgate. We don't speak. She has a white mother, not like me, and she takes after her in looks. She's ashamed of being half Osage. First chance she had, she married a white man and got out of Oklahoma. That was before I left for Texas, where nobody knows about her. Anyway she got a big settlement in her divorce."

"You think Boyd and your daughter will go to her for a getaway stake?"

"They won't get it from me, and he didn't take enough out of Texas Federal to keep a dog alive. Why else would they come here?"

"So if you know where they're headed, what do you need me for?"

"Because I'm being followed and you're not."

The bartender came around to offer Frechette a refill. The big Indian shook his head and he went away.

"Cops?" I said.

"One cop. J. P. Ahearn."

He spaced out the name as if spelling a blasphemy. I said I'd never heard of him.

"He'd be surprised. He's a commander with the Texas state police, but he thinks he's the last of the Texas Rangers. He wants Boyd bad. The man's a bloodhound. He doesn't know about my sister, but he did his homework and found out about Suzie and that she's gone, not that he could get me to admit she isn't away visiting friends. I didn't see him on the plane from Houston. I spotted him in the airport here when I was getting my luggage."

"Is he alone?"

"He wouldn't share credit with Jesus for saving a sinner." He drained his mug. "When you find Suzie I want you to set up a meeting. Maybe I can talk sense into her."

"How old is she?"

"Nineteen."

"Good luck."

"Tell me about it. My old man fell off a girder in Tulsa when I was sixteen. Then I was fifty. Well, maybe one meeting can't make up for all the years of not talking after my wife died, but I can't let her throw her life away for not trying."

"I can't promise Boyd won't sit in on it."

"I like Virgil. Some of us cheered when he took on those bloodsuckers. He'd have gotten away with a lot more from that second job if he'd shot this stubborn cashier they had, but he didn't. He wouldn't hurt a horse or a man."

"That's not the way the cops are playing it. If I find him and don't report it I'll go down as an accomplice. At the very least I'll lose my license."

"All I ask is that you call me before you call the police." He gave me a high school graduation picture of a pretty brunette he said was Suzie. She looked more Asian than American Indian. Then he pulled a checkbook out of his hip pocket and made out a check to me for fifteen hundred dollars.

"Too much," I said.

"You haven't met J. P. Ahearn yet. My sister's name is Harriett Lord." He gave me an address on Eureka. "I'm at the Holiday Inn down the street, room seven-sixteen."

He called for another beer then and I left. Again he didn't offer his hand. I'd driven three blocks from the place when I spotted the tail.

The guy knew what he was doing. In a late-model tan Buick he gave me a full block and didn't try to close up until we hit Woodward, where traffic was heavier. I finally lost him in the grand circle downtown, which confused him just as it does most people from the greater planet earth. The Indians who settled Detroit were being farsighted when they named it the Crooked Way. From there I took Lafayette to I-75 and headed downriver.

Harriett Lord lived in a tall white frame house with blue shutters and a large lawn fenced by cedars that someone had bullied into cone shape. I parked in the driveway, but before leaving the car I got out the unlicensed Luger I keep in a pocket under the dash and stuck it in my pants, buttoning my coat over it. When you're meeting someone they tell you wouldn't hurt a horse or a man, arm yourself.

The bell was answered by a tall woman around forty, dressed in a khaki shirt and corduroy slacks and sandals. She had high cheekbones and slightly olive coloring that looked more like sun than heritage and her short hair was frosted, further reducing the Indian effect. When she confirmed that she was Harriett Lord I gave her a card and said I was working for her brother.

Her face shut down. "I don't have a brother. I have a half brother, Howard Frechette. If that's who you're working for, tell him I'm unavailable." She started to close the door.

"It's about your niece Suzie. And Virgil Boyd."

"I thought it would be."

I looked at the door and got out a cigarette and lit it. I was about to knock again when the door opened six inches and she stuck her face through the gap. "You're not with the police?"

"We tolerate each other on the good days, but that's it."

She glanced down. Her blue mascara gave her eyelids a translucent look. Then she opened the door the rest of the way and stepped aside. I entered a living room done all in beige and white and sat in a chair upholstered in eggshell chintz. I was glad I'd had my suit cleaned.

"How'd you know about Suzie and Boyd?" I used a big glass ashtray on the Lucite coffee table.

"They were here last night." I said nothing. She sat on the beige sofa with her knees together. "I recognized him before I did her. I haven't seen her since she was four, but I take a Texas paper and I've seen his picture. They wanted money. I thought at first I was being robbed."

"Did you give it to them?"

"Aid a fugitive? Family responsibility doesn't cover that even if I felt any. I left home because I got sick of hearing about our proud heritage. Howard wore his Indianness like a suit of armor, and all the time he resented me because I could pass for white. He accused me of being ashamed of my ancestry because I didn't wear my hair in braids and hang turquoise all over me."

"He isn't like that now."

"Maybe he's mellowed. Not toward me, though, I bet. Now his daughter comes here asking for money so she and her desperado boyfriend can go on running. I showed them the door."

"I'm surprised Boyd went."

"He tried to get tough, but he's not very big and he wasn't armed. He took a step toward me and I took two steps toward him and he grabbed Suzie and left. Some Jesse James."

"I heard his shotgun was found in the van. I thought he'd have something else."

"If he did, he didn't have it last night. I'd have noticed, just as I notice you have one."

I unbuttoned my coat and resettled the Luger. I was getting a different picture of "Mad Dog" Boyd from the one the press was painting. "The cops would call not reporting an incident like that being an accessory," I said, squashing out my butt.

"Just because I don't want anything to do with Howard doesn't mean I want to see my niece shot up by a SWAT team."

"I don't suppose they said where they were going."

"You're a good supposer."

I got up. "How did Suzie look?"

"Like an Indian."

I thanked her and went out.

I had a customer in my waiting room. A small angular party crowding sixty wearing a tight gray three-button suit, steel-rimmed glasses, and a tan snap-brim hat squared over the frames. His crisp gray hair was cut close around large ears that stuck out, and he had a long sharp jaw with a sour mouth slashing straight across. He stood up when I entered. "Walker?" It was one of those bitter pioneer voices.

"Depends on who you are," I said.

"I'm the man who ought to arrest you for obstructing justice."

"I'll guess. J. P. Ahearn."

"Commander Ahearn."

"You're about four feet short of what I had pictured."

"You've heard of me." His chest came out a little.

"Who hasn't?" I unlocked the inner office door. He marched in, slung a look around, and took possession of the customer's chair. I sat down behind the desk and reached for a cigarette without asking permission. He glared at me through his spectacles.

"What you did downtown today constitutes fleeing and eluding."

"In Texas, maybe. In Michigan there has to be a warrant out first. What you did constitutes harassment in this state."

"I don't have official status here. I can follow anybody for any reason or none at all."

"Is this what you folks call a Mexican standoff?"

"I don't approve of smoking," he snapped.

"Neither do I, but some of it always leaks out of my lungs." I blew some at the ceiling and got rid of the match. "Why don't let's stop circling each other and get down to why you're here?"

"I want to know what you and the Indian talked about."

"I'd show you, but we don't need the rain."

He bared a perfect set of dentures, turning his face into a skull. "I ran your plate with the Detroit police. I have their complete cooperation in this investigation. The Indian hired you to take money to Boyd to get him and his little Osage slut to Canada. You delivered it after you left the bar and lost me. That's aiding and abetting and accessory after the fact of armed robbery. Maybe I can't prove it, but I can make a call and tank you for forty-eight hours on suspicion."

"Eleven."

He covered up his store-boughts. "What?"

"That's eleven times I've been threatened with jail," I said. "Three of those times I wound up there. My license has been swiped at fourteen times, actually taken away once. Bodily harm—you don't count bodily harm. I'm still here, six feet something and one hundred eighty pounds of incorruptible PI with a will of iron and a skull to match. You hard guys come and go like phases of the moon."

"Don't twist my tail, son. I don't always rattle before I bite."

"What's got you so hot on Boyd?"

You could have cut yourself on his jaw. "My daddy helped run Parker and Barrow to ground in '34. His daddy fought Geronimo and chased John Wesley Hardin out of Texas. My son's a Dallas city patrolman, and so far I don't have a story to hand him that's a blister on any of those. I'm retiring next year."

"Last I heard Austin was offering twenty thousand for Boyd's arrest and conviction."

"Texas Federal has matched it. Alive or dead. Naturally, as a duly sworn officer of the law I can't collect. But you being a private citizen—"

"What's the split?"

"Fifty-fifty."

"No good."

"Do you know what the pension is for a retired state police commander in Texas? A man needs a nest egg."

"I meant it's too generous. You know as well as I do those rewards are never paid. You just didn't know I knew."

He sprang out of his chair. There was no special animosity in his move; that would be the way he always got up.

"Boyd won't get out of this country even if you did give him money," he snapped. "He'll never get past the border guards."

"So go back home."

"Boyd's *mine*."

The last word ricocheted. I said, "Talk is he felt he had a good reason to stick up those savings and loans. The company was responsible for his father's suicide."

"If he's got the brains God gave a mad dog he'll turn himself in to me before he gets shot down in the street or kills someone and winds up getting the needle in Huntsville. And his squaw right along with him." He took a shabby wallet out of his coat and gave me a card. "That's my number at the Houston post. They'll route your call here. If you're so concerned for Boyd you'll tell me where he is before the locals gun him down."

"Better you than some stranger, that it?"

"Just keep on twisting, son. I ain't in the pasture yet."

After he left, making as much noise in his two-inch cowboy heels as a cruiserweight, I called Barry Stackpole at the *Detroit News*.

"Guy I'm after is wanted for robbery, armed," I said, once the small talk was put away. "He ditched his gun and then his stake didn't come through and now he'll have to cowboy a job for case dough. Where would he deal a weapon if he didn't know anybody in town?"

"Emma Chaney."

"Ma? I thought she'd be dead by now."

"She can't die. The Detroit cops are third in line behind Interpol and customs for her scalp and they won't let her until they've had their crack." He sounded pleased, which he probably was. Barry made his living writing about crime and when it prospered he did, too.

"How can I reach her?"

"Are you suggesting I'd know where she is and not tell the authorities? Got a pencil?"

I tried the number as soon as he was off the line. On the ninth ring I got someone with a smoker's wheeze. "Uh-huh."

"The name's Walker," I said. "Barry Stackpole gave me this number."

The voice told me not to go away and hung up. Five minutes later the telephone rang.

"Barry says you're okay. What do you want?"

"Just talk. It isn't cheap like they say."

After a moment the voice gave me directions. I hung up not knowing if it was male or female.

It belonged to Ma Chaney, who greeted me at the door of her house in rural Macomb County wearing a red Japanese kimono with green parrots all over it. The kimono could have covered a Toyota. She was a five-by-five chunk with marcelled orange hair and round black eyes embedded in her face like nail heads in soft wax. A cigarette teetered on her lower lip. I followed her into a parlor full of flowered chairs and sofas and pregnant lamps with fringed shades. A long strip of pimply blond youth in overalls and no shirt took his brogans off the coffee table and stood up when she barked at him. He gaped at me, chewing gum with his mouth open.

"Mr. Walker, Leo," Ma wheezed. "Leo knew my Wilbur in Ypsi. He's like another son to me."

Ma Chaney had one son in the criminal ward at the Forensic Psychiatry Center in Ypsilanti and another on Florida's death row. The FBI was looking for the youngest in connection with an armored car robbery in Kansas City. The whole brood had come up from Kentucky when Old Man Chaney got a job on the line at River Rouge and stayed on after he was killed in a propane tank explosion. Now Ma, the daughter of a Hawkins County gunsmith, made her living off the domestic weapons market.

"You said talk ain't cheap," she said, when she was sitting in a big overstuffed rocker. "How cheap ain't it?"

I perched on the edge of a hard upright with doilies on the arms. Leo remained standing, scratching himself. "Depends on whether we talk about Virgil Boyd," I said.

"What if we don't?"

"Then I won't take up any more of your time."

"What if we do?"

"I'll double what he's paying."

She coughed. The cigarette bobbed. "I got a business to run. I go around scratching at rewards I won't have no customers."

"Does that mean Boyd's a customer?"

"Now, why'd that Texas boy want to come to Ma? He can deal hisself a shotgun at any Kmart."

"He can't show his face in the legal places and being new in town he doesn't know the illegal ones. But he wouldn't have to ask around too much to come up with your name. You're less selective than most."

"You don't have to pussyfoot around old Ma. I don't get a lot of second-timers on account of I talk for money. My boy Earl in Florida needs a new lawyer. But I only talk after, not before. I start setting up customers I won't get no first-timers."

"I'm not even interested in Boyd. It's his girlfriend I want to talk to. Suzie Frechette."

"Don't know her." She rocked back and forth. "What color's your money?"

Before leaving Detroit I'd cashed Howard Frechette's check. I laid fifteen hundred dollars on the coffee table in twenties and fifties. Leo straightened up a little to look at the bills. Ma resumed rocking. "It ain't enough."

"How much is enough?"

"If I was to talk to a fella named Boyd, and if I was to agree to sell him a brand new Ithaca pump shotgun and a P-thirty-eight still in the box, I wouldn't sell them for less than twenny-five hunnert. Double twenny-five hunnert is five thousand."

"Fifteen hundred now. Thirty-five hundred when I see the girl."

"I don't guarantee no girl."

"Boyd then. If he's come this far with her he won't leave her behind."

She went on rocking. "They's a white barn a mile north on this road. If I was to meet a fella named Boyd, there's where I might do it. I might pick eleven o'clock."

"Tonight?"

"I might pick tonight. If it don't rain."

I got up. She stopped rocking.

"Come alone," she said. "Ma won't."

On the way back to town I filled up at a corner station and used the pay telephone to call Howard Frechette's room at the Holiday Inn. When he started asking questions I gave him the number and told him to call back from a booth outside the motel.

"Ahearn's an anachronism," he said ten minutes later. "I doubt he taps phones."

"Maybe not, but motel operators have big ears."

"Did you talk to Suzie?"

"Minor setback," I said. "Your sister gave her and Boyd the boot and no money."

"Tight bitch."

"I know where they'll be tonight, though. There's an old auto court on Van Dyke between Twenty-one and Twenty-two Mile in Macomb County, the Log Cabin Inn. Looks like it sounds." I was staring at it across the road. "Midnight. Better give yourself an hour."

He repeated the information.

"I'm going to have to tap you for thirty-five hundred dollars," I said. "The education cost."

"I can manage it. Is that where they're headed?"

"I hope so. I haven't asked them yet."

I got to my bank just before closing and cleaned out my savings and all but eight dollars in my checking account. I hoped Frechette was good for it. After that I ate dinner in a restaurant and went to see a movie about a one-man army. I wondered if he was available.

The barn was just visible from the road, a moonlit square at the end of a pair of ruts cut through weeds two feet high. It was a chill night in early spring and I had on a light coat and the heater running. I entered a dip that cut off my view of the barn, then bucked up over a ridge and had to stand the Chevy on its nose when the lamps fell on a telephone pole lying across the path. A second later the passenger's door opened and Leo got in.

He had on a mackinaw over his overalls and a plaid cap. His right hand was wrapped around a large-bore revolver and he kept it on me, held tight to his stomach, while he felt under my coat and came up with the Luger. "Drive." He pocketed it.

I swung around the end of the pole and braked in front of the barn, where Ma was standing with a Coleman lantern. She was wearing a man's felt hat and a corduroy coat with sleeves that came down to her fingers. She signaled a cranking motion and I rolled down the window.

"Well, park it around back," she said. "I got to think for you, too?"

I did that and Leo and I walked back. He handed Ma the Luger and she looked at it and put it in her pocket. She raised the lantern then and swung it from side to side twice.

We waited a few minutes, then were joined by six feet and two hundred and fifty pounds of red-bearded young man in faded denim jacket and jeans carrying a rifle with an infrared scope. He had come from the direction of the road.

"Anybody following, Mason?" asked Ma.

He shook his head and I stared at him in the lantern light. He had small black eyes like Ma's with no shine in them. This would be Mace Chaney, for whom the FBI was combing the western states for the Kansas armored car robbery.

"Go on in and warm yourself," Ma said. "We got some time."

He opened the barn door and went inside. It had just closed when two headlamps appeared down the road. We watched them approach and slow for the turn onto the path. Ma, lighting a cigarette off the lantern, grunted.

"Early. Young folks all got watches and they can't tell time."

Leo trotted out to intercept the car. A door slammed. After a pause the lamps swung around the fallen telephone pole and came up to the barn, washing us all in white. The driver killed the lamps and engine and got out. He was a small man in his early twenties with short brown hair and stubble on his face. His flannel shirt and khaki pants were both in need of cleaning. He had scant eyebrows that were almost invisible in that light, giving him a perennially surprised look. I'd seen that look in Frechette's *Houston Chronicle* and in both Detroit papers.

"Who's he?" He was looking at me.

I had a story for that, but Ma piped up. "You ain't paying to ask no questions. Got the money?"

"Not all of it. A thousand's all Suzie could get from the sharks."

"The deal's two thousand."

"Keep the P-thirty-eight. The shotgun's all I need."

Ma had told me twenty-five hundred; but I was barely listening to the conversation. Leo had gotten out on the passenger's side, pulling with him the girl in the photograph in my pocket. Suzie Frechette had done up her black hair in braids and she'd lost weight, but her dark eyes and coloring were unmistakable. With that hairstyle and in a man's work shirt and jeans and boots with western heels she looked more like an Indian than she did in her picture.

Leo opened the door and we went inside. The barn hadn't been used for its original purpose for some time, but the smell of moldy hay would remain as long as it stood. It was lit by a bare bulb swinging from a frayed cord and heated by a barrel stove in a corner. Stacks of cardboard cartons reached almost to the rafters, below which Mace Chaney sat with his legs dangling over the edge of the empty loft, the rifle across his knees.

Ma reached into an open carton and lifted out a pump shotgun with the barrel cut back to the slide. Boyd stepped forward to take it. She swung the muzzle on him. "Show me some paper."

He hesitated, then drew a thick fold of bills from his shirt pocket and laid it on a stack of cartons. Then she moved to cover me. Boyd watched me add thirty-five hundred to the pile.

"What's *he* buying?"

Ma said, "You."

"Cop!" He lunged for the shotgun. Leo's revolver came out. Mace drew a bead on Boyd from the loft. He relaxed.

I was looking at Suzie. "I'm a private detective hired by your father. He wants to talk to you."

"He's here?" She touched Boyd's arm.

He tensed. "It's a damn cop trick!"

"You're smarter than that," I said. "You had to be, to pull those two jobs and make your way here with every cop between here and Texas looking for you. If I were one, would I be alone?"

"Do your jabbering outside." Ma reversed ends on the shotgun for Boyd to take. He did so and worked the slide.

"Where's the shells?"

"That's your headache. I don't keep ammo in this firetrap." That was a lie, or some of those cartons wouldn't be labeled C-4 Explosives. But you don't sell loaded guns to strangers.

Suzie said, "Virgil, you never load them anyway."

"Shut up."

"Your father's on his way," I said. "Ten minutes, that's all he wants."

"Come on." Boyd took her wrist.

"Stay put."

This was a new voice. Everyone looked at Leo, standing in front of the door with his gun still out.

"Leo, what in the hell—"

"Ma, the Luger."

She shut her mouth and took my gun out of her right coat pocket and put it on the carton with the money. Then she backed away.

"Throw 'er down, Mace." He covered the man in the loft, who froze in the act of raising the rifle. They were like that for a moment.

"Mason," Ma said.

His shoulders slumped. He snapped on the safety and dropped the rifle eight feet to the earthen floor.

"You, too, Mr. Forty Thousand Dollar Reward," Leo said. "Even empty guns give me the jumps."

Boyd cast the shotgun onto the stack of cartons with a violent gesture.

"That's nice. I cut that money in half if I got to put a hole in you."

"That reward talk's just PR," I said. "Even if you get Boyd to the cops they'll probably arrest you, too, for dealing in unlicensed firearms."

"Like hell. I'm through getting bossed around by fat old ladies. Let's go, Mr. Reward."

"No!" screamed Suzie.

An explosion slapped the walls. Leo's brows went up, his jaw dropping to expose the wad of pink gum in his mouth. He looked down at the spreading stain on the bib of his overalls and fell down on top of his gun. He kicked once.

Ma was standing with a hand in her left coat pocket. A finger of smoking metal poked out of a charred hole. "Dadgum it, Leo," she said, "this coat belonged to my Calvin, rest his soul."

I was standing in front of the Log Cabin Inn's deserted office when Frechette swung a rented Ford into the broken paved driveway. He unfolded himself from the seat and loomed over me.

"I don't think anyone followed me," he said. "I took a couple of wrong turns to make sure."

"There won't be any interruptions, then. The place has been closed a long time."

I led him to one of the log bungalows in back. Boyd's Plymouth, stolen from the same lot where he'd left the van, was parked alongside it facing out. We knocked before entering.

All of the furniture had been removed except a metal bedstead with sagging springs. The lantern we had borrowed from Ma Chaney hung hissing from one post. Suzie was standing next to it. "Papa." She didn't move. Boyd came out of the bathroom with the shotgun. The Indian took root.

"Man said you had money for us," Boyd said.

"It was the only way I could get him to bring Suzie here," I told Frechette.

"I won't pay to have my daughter killed in a shoot-out."

"Lying bastard!" Boyd swung the shotgun my way. Frechette backhanded him, knocking him back into the bathroom. I stepped forward and tore the shotgun from Boyd's weakened grip.

"Empty," I said. "But it makes a good club."

Suzie had come forward when Boyd fell. Frechette stopped her with an arm like a railroad gate. "Take Dillinger for a walk while I talk to my daughter," he said to me.

I stuck out a hand, but Boyd slapped it aside and got up. His right eye was swelling shut. He looked at the Indian towering a foot over him, then at Suzie, who said, "It's all right. I'll talk to him."

We went out. A porch ran the length of the bungalow. I leaned the shotgun against the wall and trusted my weight to the railing. "I hear you got a raw deal from Texas Federal."

"My old man did." He stood with his hands rammed deep in his pockets, watching the pair through the window. "He asked for a two-month extension on his mortgage payment, just till he brought in his crop. Everyone gets extensions. Except when Texas Federal wants to sell the ranch to a developer. He met the dozers with a shotgun. Then he used it on himself."

"That why you use one?"

"I can't kill a jackrabbit. It used to burn up my old man."

"You'd be out in three years if you turned yourself in."

"To you, right? Let you collect that reward." He was still looking through the window. Inside, father and daughter were gesturing at each other frantically.

"I didn't say to me. You're big enough to walk into a police station by yourself."

"You don't know Texas Federal. They'd hire their own prosecutor, see I got life, make an example. I'll die first."

"Probably, the rate you're going."

He whirled on me. The parked Plymouth caught his eye. "Just who the hell are you? And why'd you—" He jerked his chin toward the car.

I got out J. P. Ahearn's card and gave it to him. His face lost color.

"You work for that headhunter?"

"Not in this life. But in a little while I'm going to call that number from the telephone in that gas station across the road."

He lunged for the door. I was closer and got in his way. "I don't know how you got this far with a head that hot," I said. "For once in your young life listen. You might get to like it."

He listened.

"This is Commander Ahearn! I know you're in there, Boyd. I got a dozen men here and if you don't come out we'll shoot up the place!"

Neither of us had heard them coming, and with the moon behind a cloud the thin, bitter voice might have come from anywhere. This time Boyd won the race to the door. He had the reflexes of a deer.

"Kill the light!" I barked to Frechette. "Ahearn beat me to it. He must have followed you after all."

We were in darkness suddenly. Boyd and Suzie had their arms around each other. "We're cornered," he said. "Why didn't that old lady have shells for that gun?"

"We just have to move faster, that's all. Keep him talking. Give me a hand with this window." The last was for Frechette, who came over and worked his big fingers under the swollen frame.

"There's a woman in here!" Boyd shouted.

"Come on out and no one gets hurt!" Ahearn sounded wired. The window gave with a squawking wrench.

"One minute, Boyd. Then we start blasting!"

I hoped it was enough. I slipped out over the sill.

"The car! Get it!"

The Plymouth's engine turned over twice in the cold before starting. The car rolled forward and began picking up speed down the incline toward the road. Just then the moon came out, illuminating the man behind the wheel, and the night came apart like mountain ice breaking up, cracking and splitting with the staccato rap of handgun fire and the deeper boom of riot guns. Orange flame scorched the darkness. Slugs whacked the car's sheet metal and shattered the windshield. Then a red glow started to spread inside the vehicle and fists of yellow flame battered out the rest of the windows with a *whump* that shook the ground. The car rolled for a few more yards while the shooters, standing now and visible in the light of the blaze, went on pouring lead into it until it came to a stop against a road sign. The flame towered twenty feet above the crackling wreckage.

I approached Ahearn, standing in the overgrown grass with his shotgun dangling, watching the car burn. He jumped a little when I spoke. His glasses glowed orange.

"He made a dash, just like you wanted."

"If you think I wanted this you don't know me," he said. "Save it for the six o'clock news."

"What the hell are you doing here, anyway?"

"Friend of the family. Can I take the Frechettes home or do you want to eat them here?"

He cradled the shotgun. "We'll just go inside together."

We found Suzie sobbing in her father's arms. The Indian glared at Ahearn. "Get the hell out of here."

"He was a desperate man," Abeam said. "You're lucky the girl's alive."

"I said get out or I'll ram that shotgun down your throat."

He got out. Through the window I watched him rejoin his men. There were five, not a dozen as he'd claimed. Later I learned that three of them were off-duty Detroit cops and he'd hired the other two from a private security firm.

I waited until the fire engines came and Ahearn was busy talking to the firefighters, then went out the window again and crossed to the next bungalow, set farther back where the light of the flames didn't reach. I knocked twice and paused and knocked again. Boyd opened the door a crack.

"I'm taking Suzie and her father back to Frechette's motel for looks. Think you can lie low here until we come back in the morning for the rent car?"

"What if they search the cabins?"

"For what? You're dead. By the time they find out that's Leo in the car, if they ever do, you and Suzie will be in Canada. Customs won't be looking for a dead bandit. Give everyone a year or so to forget what you look like and then you can come back. Not to Texas, though, and not under the name Virgil Boyd."

"Lucky the gas tank blew."

"I've never had enough luck to trust to it. That's why I put a box of C-four in Leo's lap. Ma figured it was a small enough donation to keep her clear of a charge of felony murder."

"I thought you were some kind of corpse freak." He still had the surprised look. "You could've been killed starting that car. Why'd you do it?"

"The world's not as complicated as it looks," I said. "There's always a good and a bad side. I saw Ahearn's."

"You ever need anything," he said.

"If you do things right I won't be able to find you when I do." I shook his hand and returned to the other bungalow.

A week later, after J. P. Ahearn's narrow, jug-eared features had made the cover of *People*, I received an envelope from Houston containing a bonus check for a thousand dollars signed by Howard Frechette. He'd repaid the thirty-five hundred I'd given Ma before going home. That was the last I heard from any of them. I used the money to settle some old bills and had some work done on my car so I could continue to ply my trade along the Crooked Way.

The Killing Man

by Mickey Spillane

SOME DAYS HANG OVER MANHATTAN like a huge pair of unseen pincers slowly squeezing the city until you can hardly breathe. A low growl of thunder echoed up the cavern of Fifth Avenue, and I looked up to where the sky started at the seventy-first floor of the Empire State Building. I could smell the rain. It was the kind that hung above the orderly piles of concrete until it was soaked with dust and debris, and when it came down, it wasn't rain at all but the sweat of the city.

When I reached my corner, I crossed against the light and ducked into the ground-level arcade of my office building. It wasn't often that I bothered coming in on Saturdays, but my client couldn't make it any time other than noon today, and from what Velda had told me, he was representing some pretty big interests. I punched my button and rode the elevator up to the eighth floor.

On an ordinary day, the corridor would have been filled with the early-lunch crowd, but now the emptiness gave the place an eerie feeling, as though I were a trespasser and hidden eyes were watching me. Except that I was the only one there, and the single sign of life was the light behind my office door.

I turned the knob, pushed the door open, and just stood there a second because something was wrong, sure as hell wrong, and the silence was as loud as a wild scream. I had the .45 in my hand and I crouched and edged to one side, listening, waiting, watching.

Velda wasn't at her desk. Her pocketbook sat there, and a paper cup of coffee had spilled over and stained the sheaf of papers before dripping to the floor. And I didn't have to move far before I saw her body crumpled up against the wall, half of her face a bloody mass of clotted blood that seeped from under her hair.

The door to my office was partially open and there was somebody still in there, sitting at my desk, part of his arm clearly visible. I couldn't play it smart. I had to explode and ram through the door in a blind fury, ready to blow somebody into a death full of bloody, flying parts. . . . Then I stopped, my breath caught in my throat, because it had already been done.

The guy sitting there had been taped to my chair, his body immobilized. The wide splash of adhesive tape across his mouth had immobilized his voice, too, but all the horror that had happened was still there in his glazed, dead eyes that stared at hands whose fingertips had been amputated at the first knuckle and lay in neat order on the desktop. A dozen knife slashes had cut open the skin of his face and chest, and his clothes were a sodden mass of congealed blood.

But the thing that had killed him was the note spike I kept my expense receipts on. Somebody had slipped them all off the six-inch steel nail, positioned it squarely in the middle of the guy's forehead, and pounded it home with the bronze paperweight that held my folders down.

I ran back to Velda. Her pulse was weak, but it was there, and when I lifted her hair, there was a huge hematoma above her ear, the skin split wide from the vicious swelling of it. Her breathing was shallow and her vital signs weren't good. I grabbed her coat off the rack, draped it around her, stood up and forced the rage to leave me, then found the number in my phone book and dialed it.

The nurse said, "Dr. Reedey's office."

"Meg, this is Mike Hammer," I told her. "Burke in?"

"Yes, but—"

"Listen, call an ambulance and get a stretcher up here right away and get Burke to come up now. Velda's been hurt badly."

While she dialed, she said, "Don't move her. I'll send the doctor right up. Keep her warm and—" I hung up in midsentence.

Pat Chambers wasn't home, but his message service said he could be reached at his office. The sergeant at the switchboard answered, took my name, put me through, and when Pat said, "Captain Chambers," I told him to get to my office with a body bag. I wasn't about to waste time with explanations while Velda could be dying right beside me.

Her skin was clammy and her pulse was getting weaker. The

frustration I felt was the kind you get in a dream when you can't run fast enough away from some terror that is chasing you. And now I had to stay here and watch Velda slip away from life while some bastard was out there getting farther and farther away all the time.

There were hands around my shoulders that yanked me away from her, and Burke said, "Come on, Mike, let me get to her."

I almost swung on him before I realized who he was. When he saw my face, he said, "You all right?"

After a moment, I said, "I'm all right," and moved back out of the way.

Burke Reedey was a doctor who had come out of the slaughter of Vietnam with all the expertise needed to handle an emergency like this. He and his nurse moved swiftly and the helpless feeling I had before abated and I moved the desk to give him room, trying not to listen to their comments. There was something in their tone of voice that had a desperate edge to it. Almost on cue, the ambulance attendants arrived, visibly glad to see a doctor there ahead of them, and carefully, they got Velda onto the stretcher and out of the office, Burke going with them.

"What happened, Mike?" asked Meg.

"I don't know yet." I pointed to the door of my office. "Go look in there."

A worried look touched her eyes and she walked to the door and opened it. I didn't think old-time nurses could gasp like that. Her hand went to her mouth and I saw her head shake in horror. "Mike . . . you didn't mention—"

"He's dead. Velda wasn't. The cops will take care of that one."

She backed away from the door, turned and looked at me. "That's the first . . . deliberate murder . . . I've ever seen." Slowly, very slowly, her eyes widened.

I shook my head. "No, I didn't do it, Meg. Whoever hit Velda did that, too."

The relief in her expression was plain. "Do you know why?"

"Not yet."

When she left, I walked over to the miniature bar by the window and picked up a glass. Hell, this was no time to take a drink. I put the glass back and went into my office.

The dead guy was still looking at his mutilated hands, seemingly ignoring the spike driven into his skull until the ornamental base of it indented his skin. The glaze over his eyes seemed thicker.

I heard the front door open and Pat shouted my name. I called back, "In here."

Pat was a cop who had seen it all. This one was just another on his list. But the kill wasn't what disturbed him. It was where it had happened. He turned to the uniform at the door. "Anybody outside?"

"Only our people. They're shortstopping everybody at the elevators."

"Good, keep everybody out for five minutes. Our guys, too."

"Got it," the cop said and turned away.

"Let's talk," Pat said.

It didn't take long. "I was to meet a prospective client at noon in my office. Velda went ahead to open up and get some other work out of the way. I walked in a few minutes before twelve and found her on the floor and the guy dead."

"And you touched nothing?"

"Not in here, Pat. I wasn't about to wait for you to show before I got a doctor for Velda."

Pat looked at me with the same old look.

"Okay," he said. His eyes looked tired. "Let's get our guys in here."

While the photographer shot the corpse from all angles and did close-ups on the mutilation, Pat and I went into Velda's office, where the plainclothes officers were dusting for prints and vacuuming the area for any incidental evidence. Pat had already jotted down what I had told him. Now he said, "Give me the entire itinerary of your day, Mike. Start from when you got up this morning, and I'll check everything out while it's fresh."

"I got up at seven. I showered, dressed and went down to the deli for some rolls, picked up the paper, went back to the apartment, ate, read the news, and took off for the gym."

"Which one?"

"Bing's Gym. I got to the office a few minutes before twelve and walked into . . . this." I waved my hand at the room. "Burke Reedey will give you the medical report on Velda and the ME will be able to pinpoint the time of death pretty well, so don't get me mixed up in suspect status."

Pat finished writing, tore a leaf out of the pad, and closed the book. He called one of the detectives over and handed him the slip, telling him to check out all the details of my story. "Let's just keep straight with the system, buddy. Face it you're not one of its favorite people."

Pat bent over and examined the body carefully. His arm brushed the dead man's coat and pushed it open. Sticking up out of the shirt pocket was a Con Edison bill folded in half. When Pat straightened it out, he looked at the name and said, "Anthony DiCica." He held it out for me to look at. "You know him, Mike?"

"Never saw him before."

"DiCica was an enforcer for the New York Mob. He was a suspect in four homicides, never got tapped for any of them, and gained a reputation of being a pretty efficient workman."

"Then?"

"Simple. Somebody cracked his skull open in a street brawl and he came all unraveled. He was in a hospital and left with severely impaired mental faculties."

"Who sponsored him?"

"Nobody took him in. He remembered very little of his past, but he could handle uncomplicated things."

"What's the tag line, Pat?"

"He could have made enemies. Somebody saw him and came after him."

"In my office?"

"Okay, Mike, who would want you dead?"

"Nobody I can think of."

"Hell, somebody wants you even better than dead. They want you all chopped up and with a spike through your head. Somebody had a business engagement with you at noon, got here early, took out Velda and didn't have to wait for you because there was a guy in your office he thought was you and he nailed that poor bastard instead."

"I've thought of that," I said.

I picked up the phone and called the building super. I told him I needed the place cleaned up and what had happened. He said he'd do it personally. I thanked him and hung up.

Pat said, "Let's go get something to eat. You'll feel better. Then we'll go to the hospital."

"I don't want to eat. I'll tell you what you can do, though."

"What's that?"

"Station a cop at her door. Somebody missed Velda, and they may want another go when they find out what happened."

Pat had called ahead, and the cop at Velda's door looked at my ID and let me in. The hospital room was in a deep gloom, only a small night-light on the wall, making it possible to see the outlines of the bed and the equipment. When the door snicked shut, I picked up the straight-backed chair by the sink, went to the bed, and sat down beside her.

Velda. Beautiful, gorgeous Velda. Those deep brown eyes and that full, full mouth. Shimmering auburn hair that fell in a pageboy around her shoulders.

Now her face was a bloated black-and-blue mask on one side, one eye totally closed under the bulbous swelling, the other a flat slit. Her hair was gone around the bandaged area and her upper lip was twice its normal size.

I put my hand over hers and whispered, "Damn it, kitten. . . ." Then her wrist moved and her fingers squeezed mine gently. "Are you . . . all right?" she asked me softly.

"I'm fine, honey, I'm okay. Now, don't talk. Just take it easy. All I want is to be here with you. That's enough."

I just sat there, and in a minute, she said, "I can . . . listen, Mike. Please tell me . . . what happened."

I played it back without building it up. I didn't tell her the details of the kill and hinted that it was strictly the work of a nut, but she knew better.

Under my fingers, I could feel her pulse. It was steady. Her hand squeezed mine again. "They came in . . . very fast. One had a hand over his face . . . and he was . . . swinging at me . . . with the other. I . . . never saw a face at all." Remembering it hadn't excited her. The pulse rate hadn't changed.

I said, "Okay, honey, that's enough. You're supposed to take it real easy awhile."

But she insisted, "Mike . . .

"What, kitten?"

"If the police . . . ask questions . . ."

I knew what she was thinking. In her mind, she had already put it on a case basis and filed it for immediate activity.

"Play sick," I said.

Until she made a statement, everything was up in the air. She was still alive, so there was a possibility that she could have seen the killers. They couldn't afford any witness at all, but if they tried to erase her, they'd be sitting ducks themselves. From here on, there would be a solid cover on the hospital room. The killers were going to sweat a little more now.

I thought I saw the good corner of her mouth twitch in a smile, and again, I got the small finger squeeze. "Be careful," she said. Her voice was barely audible and she was slipping back into a sleep once more. "I want . . . you back."

Her fingers loosened and her hand slipped out of mine. She didn't hear me when I said, "I want you back, too, baby."

Outside the door, a cop said, "How is she?"

"Making it." He was a young cop, this one. He still had that determined look. He had the freshness of youth, but his eyes told me he had seen plenty of street work since he left the academy. "Did Captain Chambers tell you what this is about?" I asked.

"Only that it was heavy. The rest I got through the grapevine."

"It's going to get rougher," I said. "Don't play down what you're doing."

He grinned at me. "Don't worry, Mike, I'm not jaded yet."

"Take care of my girl in there, will you?"

His face suddenly went serious. "You got it, Mike."

Downstairs, another shift was coming on, fresh faces in white uniforms replacing the worn-out platoon that had gone through a rough offense on the day watch. The interns looked too young to be doctors, but they already had the wear and tear of their profession etched into them. One had almost made it to the door when the hidden PA speaker brought him up short, and with an expression of total fatigue, he shrugged and went back inside.

I cut around the little groups and pushed my way through the outside door. The rain had stopped, but the night was clammy, muting the street sounds and diffusing the light of the buildings. Nights like this stank. There were no incoming taxis and it was a two-block walk to where they might cruise by. There was no other choice, so I went down to the street.

I thought the little guy in the oddball suit who shuffled up to me on the street outside my apartment was another panhandler. He peered at me, a grin twisting his mouth, and said, "Remember me? I'm Ambrose."

"Ambrose who?"

"How many people with a name like that you know? From Charlie the Greek's place, man. Charlie says he wants you to give him a call."

"Why?"

"Beats me, man. He just told me to tell you that. And the sooner the better. It's important."

I told him okay, handed him two bucks, and watched him scuttle away. When I got upstairs, I dug out the old phone book, looked up the Greek's place, and called Charlie. His raspy voice started chewing me out for not stopping by the past six months, and when he was finished, he said, "There's a gent that wants to meet with you, Mike."

Charlie was an old-fashioned guy. When he said gent, it was with quotation marks around it, printed in red. Any gent would be somebody in the chain of command that led to the strange avenues of what they deny is organized crime. He wasn't connected; he was simply a useful tool in the underworld apparatus.

"He got a name, Charlie?"

"Sure, I guess. But I don't know it."

"What's the deal?"

"Like tonight. Can you make it down here tonight?"

I looked at my watch. "Okay, give me thirty. You think I need some backup?"

"Naw. This guy's clean."

"Tell him to sit at the bar."

"You got it, Mike."

The Greek's place was just a run-down old saloon in a neighborhood that was going under the wrecker's ball little by little. Half of the places had been abandoned, but Charlie's joint was near the corner, got a regular trade and a lot of daytime transients, but from four to seven every evening, the gay crowd took over like a swing shift, then left abruptly and everything went back to sloppy normalcy.

A pair of old biddies were sipping beer at the end of the bar and right in the center was a middle-aged portly guy in a dark suit having a highball. His eyes had picked me up in the back bar when I'd come in and we didn't have to be introduced. He waved Charlie over. I said, "Canadian Club and ginger," then we picked up the drinks and went to a table across the room.

"Appreciate your coming," he said.

"No trouble. What's happening?"

"There are some people interested in Tony DiCica's death."

"Pretty messy subject. You know what happened to him?"

He bobbed his head. "Tough."

"Yeah. He sure as hell messed up my office. But that's not what you want to know. Let's get something squared away here. You guys don't give a shit whether DiCica is dead or alive, do you?" I snarled.

"Couldn't care less."

"You mean unless he told my secretary what you wanted."

After thinking about it, he acknowledged the point. "Something like that."

I said, "You know, I don't give a rat's ass what Tony had. I don't have it and she doesn't either."

"Some people aren't going to look at it that way," he told me. "Until they are absolutely satisfied, you're going to have a problem."

"There's one hell of a hole in your presentation, fella," I said. "Tony's been running loose a long time. If he had something, why didn't they get it from him when he was alive?"

"You know about Tony's history?"

"I know."

"If you guess the answer, I'll tell you if it's right."

Hell, there could be only one answer. I said, "Tony had something he could hang somebody with." The guy kept watching me. "He had permanent amnesia after getting his head bashed in and didn't remember having it or putting it somewhere." The eyes were still on mine. The story line started to open up now. "Just lately, he said or did something that might have indicated a sudden return of memory." The eyes narrowed and I knew I had it.

When he put his drink away in two quick swallows, he rolled the empty glass between his fingers a moment and said, "A week ago, he suddenly recognized somebody—he called him by his right name."

"Then he relapsed into amnesia again?"

"Nobody knows that."

"So?"

"You have your fingers in all kinds of shit. You move with the clean guys and you go with the dirty ones just as easy. Nobody likes to mess with you because you've blown a few asses off with that cannon of yours and you got buddies up in Badgeville, where it counts. So you'd be just the kind of guy Tony DiCica would run to with a story that would keep his head on his shoulders."

"Crazy," I said.

"He went to your office to arrange something with you. Before you got there, somebody showed up and did the job, expecting to walk away with the information. He didn't have it on him."

This thing was really coming back at me. "Okay, what's my part?"

"He is your client, Mr. Hammer. He told you all in return for an escape route you were to furnish."

"That's a lot of bullshit, you know."

A gesture of his hands meant it didn't make any difference. "You see, as far as certain people are concerned, you're in until they say you're out. The information Tony had can be worth a lot of money and can cause a lot of killing. One way or another, they expect to get it back."

"What happens if the cops get it first?"

"Nobody really expects that to happen," he said. He pulled his cuff back and looked at his watch.

I took one more sip of my drink and stood up. "I guess somebody wants me to talk."

"Certain people are giving you a few days to make a decision."

I could feel my lips pulling back in controlled anger and knew it wasn't a nice grin at all. I pulled the .45 out and watched his eyes go blank until I flipped out the clip and fingered a shell loose. I handed it to him. "Give them that," I said.

"What's this supposed to mean?"

"They'll know," I told him.

I called Pat the next day. "What have you got on DiCica?"

"Interesting history. I'm going off duty. How about a beer?"

"How can you go off duty? It's afternoon."

"I'm the boss, that's how."

"I'll meet you downtown."

Over the beer, Pat told me about Anthony DiCica. He had a listing of all his arrests, convictions that were a laugh, and the victims he was suspected of killing. Every dead guy was involved in the Mob scene, and two of them were really big-time. Those two had been hit simultaneously while they were eating in a small Italian restaurant. DiCica, after shooting both parties in the head twice, made off with an envelope that had been seen on the table by a waiter. Following the hit, there had been an ominous quiet in the city for a week, then several other persons in the organization died. It was two weeks later that Anthony DiCica's head collided with a pipe in a street brawl.

"They went a little overboard in bringing him in and cracked his skull. After that, he was no good to anybody. They still needed his goods and had to wait for him to come out of his memory loss before they could move. . . ."

Pat lifted his beer and made a silent toast. "We really took his place apart, you know."

"No, I didn't know. What did you find?"

"Zilch. There were no hiding places. We even tried the cellar area. If he had anything at all, it's someplace else. End of case. It died with Anthony."

"The hell it did," I said. "Somebody in the organization thinks DiCica suddenly remembered and dropped his secret on me."

"Brother!"

I nodded. "The bastards as much as said it's my ass if I don't produce."

"Shake you up?"

"I've been in the business too long, kiddo. I just get more cautious and keep my forty-five on half cock."

He watched me, frowning, grouping his thoughts. "That mutilation of DiCica could have been a message to you, then."

"It's beginning to look like it," I said.

"What do you do now?"

"See how far I can go before I touch a trip wire."

"You don't give a damn, do you?" he said.

"About what?"

"Anything at all. You don't want any backup, no protection . . . you want to be out there all alone like a first-class idiotic target."

I shrugged.

"There's a lot more of them than there are of you."

I watched him and waited.

He finally said, "They know how you are, Mike. You're leaving yourself wide open."

I felt a tight grin stretch across my lips and said, "That's the trip wire I set out."

They knew me at the hospital but wanted to see my ID anyway. The cop at the door scanned my PI ticket and driver's license, checking my face against the photo before letting me into Velda's room.

"Hey, kid," I said softly. In the dim light, I saw her head turn slowly and knew she was awake. They had propped her up, the sheet lying lightly across her breasts, her arms outside it. The facial swelling had lessened, but the discoloration still put a dark shadow on her face. One eye still was closed and I knew smiling wasn't easy.

"Do I look terrible?"

I let out a small laugh and walked to the bed. "I've seen you when you looked better." I took her hand in mine and let the warmth of her seep into me. Inside, I could feel a madness clawing at my guts, scratching at my mind because somebody had done this to her. They had taken soft beauty and a loving body and tried to smash it into a lifeless hulk because it was there and killing was the simple way of moving it.

"Mike, don't," she said.

I sucked my breath in, held it, then eased out. I was squeezing her hand too hard and relaxed my fingers. "Everything okay, kitten?"

"Yes. They are taking care of me." She tilted her head up. "What's happening?"

I filled her in with some of the general information, but she stopped me. She wanted details, so I gave them to her.

I put my hands on the mattress and bent down so my face was close to hers. Her tongue slipped between her lips, wetting them, and as my mouth touched hers, she closed one eye. A kiss is strange. It's a living thing, a communication, a whole wild emotion expressed in a simple moist touch and, when her tongue barely met mine, a silent explosion. We felt, we tasted, then, satisfied, we separated.

"You know what you do to me?" I asked.

She smiled.

"Now I'm as horny as hell and I can't go out in the hall like this. Not yet."

"You can kiss me again while you're waiting."

"No. I'll need a cold shower if I do." I stood up, still feeling her mouth on mine. "I'll be back tomorrow, kitten."

Her smile was crooked and her eye laughed. "What are you going to do with . . . that?" she asked me.

"Hold my hat over it," I told her.

I had the cabby drop me at the corner and picked up a late-evening paper at the kiosk. There was a mist in the air and the streetlights had a soft glow around them and lighted windows in the apartments were gently blurred. It was the kind of night that dampened street sounds and put a dull slick on the pavement.

The doorman at my place generally paced under the marquee, but tonight I couldn't blame him for staying inside. I hugged the side of the building out of the wind, moved around the garbage pails outside the areaway that ran to the rear, and saw the feet inside the glass doors as the guy jumped me from behind.

Damn.

One arm grabbed me around the throat and a fist was ready to slam into my kidneys, but I was twisting and dropping at the same time, so fast that the fucker lost his rhythm and went down with me. His arm came loose and he rolled free, and I forgot all about him because the other one had come out of the hallway with a sap in his hand, ready to lay my skull open. I let the swing go past my face and threw a right smack into his nose, saw his head snap back, then put another into his gut.

Everything was working right. The guy behind me came off the sidewalk thinking he had me nailed. I didn't want any broken knuckles. I just drove my fist into his neck under his chin and didn't wait to see what would happen. The boy with the sap was still standing there, nose stunned, blood all over his face but not out of it.

You don't have to waste any skin on guys like that. I kicked him in the balls, and the pain-instinct reaction was so fast he nearly locked onto my foot. His mouth made silent screaming motions and he went down on his knees, his supper foaming out of his mouth.

I went inside. The doorman was just coming out of it, a lump already growing on the side of his head. "Can you hear me, Jeff?" I said.

He grimaced, his eyes opened and he nodded. "That bastard . . ."

"I have them outside. You give the cops a call."

"Yeah. Damn right."

The big guy I had rapped in the throat was trying to get away. He was on all fours, scratching toward the car at the curb. I took out the .45, let him hear me jack a shell into the chamber, and he stopped cold. That old army automatic can have a deadly sound to it. I walked over to him, knelt down, and poked the muzzle against his head.

"Who sent you?"

He shook his head.

I thumbed the hammer back. That sound, the double click, was even deadlier.

"We . . . was to . . . rough you up." His voice was hardly understandable.

"Who sent you?"

His head dropped, spit ran out of his mouth, and he shook his head again.

"Why?" I asked him. I kept the tone nasty.

All the big slob had in his eyes was fear. "You sent . . . the guys . . . a bullet."

I heard the siren of a squad car coming up Third Avenue. "How much did they pay you?"

"Five hundred . . . each."

"Asshole," I said. I eased the hammer back on half cock and took the rod away from his head. A grand for a mugging meant that the victim would be wary and dangerous, and these two slobs hadn't given it a thought. I gave him a kick in the side and told him to get over beside his buddy. I didn't have to tell him twice.

Wheels squealing, a car turned at the corner and the floodlight hit me while it was still rolling. The cameraman came out, turning film, a girl in a flapping trench coat right behind him, giving into a hand mike a rapid, detailed description of what was going on, and I even let New York City's favorite on-the-spot TV team catch me giving the guy another boot just for the hell of it.

When the squad car got there, I identified myself, gave a statement, and let the doorman fill in the rest. The two guys had waited near the curb nearly an hour, spotted me at the corner, then one had gone in, grabbed the doorman, then waited until the other had jumped me to lay a sap on his head before joining the fun. Luckily, the sweatband of the doorman's uniform cap had softened the blow. Both of the clowns had knives in their pockets along with the old standbys, brass knuckles and a blackjack. It took one radio call to get an ID on them and they were shoved, handcuffed, into the rear of the squad car.

Enough of the crowd had collected to make it an interesting spot in the late news coming up, and the reporter said, "Any further comment on this, Mr. Hammer?"

At least she'd remembered my name.

"They just tried to mug the wrong guy," I said. Then I winked into the lens and walked away.

Upstairs, I called Pat. I ran through the story again, then added, "It's all coming back to DiCica, buddy. They're making sure I know they're watching."

"You don't scare them, Mike."

"If they think I have access to what Anthony had, I can sure shake them up. What have you got?"

"Something extremely interesting. My boys came up with another lead, an old dealer who is straight now and doesn't want his name mentioned in any way. You're right. It all comes back to when DiCica shot those two gang leaders and picked up that envelope."

"And you know what was in it?"

"Yes. Directions."

"To what?"

"A truckload of cocaine."

"Do you realize how much stuff that is?"

"In dollars, the street value is incredible. Anyway, it came up via Route Ninety-five into the New York area. The trailer was delivered to a depot in Brooklyn, all the paperwork completed, and the next day, another tractor signed for it, hauled it out, and it hasn't been seen to this day."

"But somebody would know where the cargo went to."

"Sure," Pat said. "The drivers would have known."

"So they were the only ones who knew?"

"Why not? The fewer the better. They picked their own hiding spot for the shipment, made up a map, and delivered it to the bosses. On the way out, they were followed by hit men and taken out in a supposed accident. The bosses didn't want anybody knowing where the stuff went. Unfortunately, they were in line for a hit themselves that night. And DiCica got the map."

"Tell me something. How much is the street value of the junk today?"

He told me. I let out a low whistle. Nine-digit figures are understandable. When they reach ten, it's almost unbelievable.

"Mike, unless we find that cargo, nothing will ever end."

"Are you checking out all the leads?"

"The trailer would take a certain-size building to be concealed in. We're working on the assumption that something was bought, rather than leased. By now, taxes would be owing, and if anything matches, we'll be on it."

"You don't have that much time."

"Any other options?"

"A lot of luck."

Sickness and injury never stop in the big city. It was a bloody night in the emergency room, spatters of red on the walls, trails stringing along the floors, smeared where feet had skidded in its sticky viscosity. The walking wounded were crowded by stretchers and wheelchairs and my shortcut to Velda's floor was blocked.

When I reached her floor, I pushed through the steel fire door into the corridor and the wave of quiet was a soft kiss of relief. The nurse's desk was to my left, the white tip of the attendant's hat bobbing behind the counter. Someplace, a phone rang and was answered. Halfway down the hall, a uniformed officer was standing beside a chair, his back against the wall, reading a paper.

The nurse didn't look up, so I went by her. Two of the rooms I passed had their doors open, and in a half-lit room, I could see the forms of the patients, deep in sleep. The next two doors were closed and so was Velda's.

Until I was ten feet away, the cop didn't give me a tumble, then he turned and scowled at me. This was a new one on the night shift and he pulled back his sleeve and gave a deliberate look at his wristwatch, as if to remind me of the time.

I said, "Everything okay?"

For a second, the question seemed to confuse him. Then he nodded. "Sure," he replied. "Of course."

All I could do was nod back, like it was stupid of me to ask, and I let him go back to leaning against the wall. At the desk, the nurse glanced up. She recognized me and smiled. "Mr. Hammer, good evening."

"How's my doll doing?"

"Just fine, Mr. Hammer. Dr. Reedey was in twice today. Her bandages have been changed and one of the nurses has even helped her with cosmetics."

"Is she moving around?"

"Oh, no. The doctor wants her to have complete bed rest for now. It will be several days before she'll be active at all." She stopped, suddenly realizing the time herself. "Aren't you a little early?"

"I hope not." Something was bothering me. Something was grating at me and I didn't know what it was. "Nothing out of order on the floor?"

She seemed surprised. "No, everything is quite calm, fortunately."

A small timer on her desk pinged and she looked at her watch. "I'll be back in a few minutes, Mr. Hammer. . . ."

Now I knew what the feeling was. That cop had looked at his watch, too, and his was a Rolex Oyster, a big, fat, expensive watch street cops don't wear on duty. But the real kicker was his shoes. They were regulation black, but they were wing tips. The son of a bitch was a phony, but his rod would be for real and whatever was going down would be just as real.

I said, "How long has that cop been on her door?"

"Oh . . . he came in about fifteen minutes ago."

It was two hours too soon for a shift change.

"Did you see the other one check out?"

"Well, no, but he could have gone—"

"They always take the elevators down, don't they?"

She nodded, consternation showing in her eyes. She got the picture all at once and asked calmly, "What shall I do?"

"Give me the phone and you beat it. Don't look back. Do things the way you always do."

She patted her hair in place, went around the counter, and stepped on down the hall. She didn't look back. I pulled her call sheet over where I could see it and dialed hospital security. The phone rang eight times and nobody answered. I dialed the operator and she tried. Finally she said, "I'll put their code on, sir. The guards must be making their rounds."

Or they're laid out on their backs someplace.

Overhead, the call bell started to ping out a quiet code every few seconds.

I hung up and dialed Pat's office. I said, "Pat, I have no time for talk. I'm at the hospital and everything's breaking loose. There's a phony cop at the door, so the real officer is down somewhere. They're going to try to snatch Velda. Get some cars up here and no sirens. They smell cops and they'll kill her."

"They moving now?"

I heard wheels rolling on the tile and squinted around the wall. Coming out of the last door down on the right was an empty gurney pushed by a man in an orderly's clothes. "They're moving, Pat. Shake your ass."

I hung up and stepped out into the corridor, whistling between my teeth. The guy pushing the gurney stopped and started playing with the mattress. I pushed the button on the elevator, looked down at the cop who was watching me, and waved. The phony cop waved back.

When the elevator halted, I got in, let the doors close, and pushed the Stop button. I stood there, hoping the guy pushing the gurney wouldn't notice the lights over the door standing still. The rubber tires thumped a little louder, passed the elevator, and when I didn't hear them any longer, I pushed the Open button and stared out into the corridor. I took my hat off, dropped it on the floor, and yanked the .45 out of the holster. There was a shell in the chamber and the hammer was on half cock. I thumbed it back all the way and looked down the corridor.

The guy in the orderly's clothes was standing there with an AK-47 automatic rifle cradled in his arms, watching both ends of the hallway. His stance was low, and when he swung, his coat flopped open and it looked like he was wearing upper-body armor. The gurney was sticking out of Velda's door. She was strapped onto the carrier. The man in the uniform came out of her room, a police-service .38 in one hand and one hell of a big bruiser of an automatic in the other. Unless I got some backup, I was totally outgunned and no way could I close in on them without putting Velda's life on the line.

A quiet little code still pinged from the hall bell. Security still hadn't answered.

No wasted moves this time. The pair moved the gurney away from me and I knew they were headed toward the other bank of elevators. The phony orderly had draped a sheet over the gun on his arm. The uniform had hidden the automatic but had placed the .38 on the gurney next to Velda.

I stepped back into the car, let the doors close, pushed the first-floor button, and hoped nobody tried to get on. Like all hospital elevators, this one took forever to pass each level, and before it stopped, I picked my hat up and held it over my .45. When it reached the first floor, I stepped out. This time, I didn't run. The gurney would be moving at proper walking speed, seemingly going through a normal routine, and as long as I hurried, I could meet it outside the building. There was no way this play could be stopped without some kind of shooting, and I didn't want anybody else in the way.

They came out of the elevator just as I stepped outside, and now I felt better. They had turned toward the walkway door and I was waiting out there in the dark. There were only a few seconds to look around for their probable course and find cover. The walkway curved down to the street, but the parking places were filled with off-street overnighters, and the cars there couldn't handle a limp patient. Unless they had planned on a mobile van or a station wagon, any transportation would have to be farther down the line, out of sight from where I was standing.

I moved on down the walk, reached the parked cars, and got into the street behind them. The doors of the hospital swung inward. The guy in the orderly uniform came out first, the AK-47 under his arm, still covered. He never took his eyes off the area in front of him, pulling the gurney forward with one hand while the other man pushed from behind.

The gurney finally slid through the doors and now the phony cop had the oversized automatic in his hand.

I let them pass me, crouching down behind the cars, and when they were about ten feet in front of me, I kept pace with their movements.

A car turned up the road, momentarily lighting the area. It swept over the gurney, but the two went on in a normal manner. I stepped between the parked cars and let it pass. It was a civilian car with a woman at the wheel. It seemed like an hour had passed, but it had been only a few minutes.

Hell, the traffic was light. A squad car could have been here by now. Another set of lights turned up and a truck dropped down a gear and lumbered up the hill. I moved down two car lengths, still staying close, still silently swearing at the frustrating delays in emergency police actions. A car made a U-turn at the hospital and came toward me from the other direction, and only when it got past me did a raucous blast from the loud-hailer yell, "Freeze, police!" and the power lights from the truck turned night into day, blinding the two men in the glare.

Everything happened so quickly that there was a hesitancy in the movements the men made. The phony orderly wasted one second trying to strip the sheet from the AK-47 and a pair of rapid blasts took him down and out. The phony cop jammed himself down in a crouch and his gun came up to shoot through the bottom of the gurney. He was out of the others' sight but not out of mine, and I squeezed off a single round that took him in the shoulder and spun him around like a rag doll.

I was standing and had my hands over my head so the cops wouldn't take me out with a wild shot, figuring me for the other side. Pat came running up, a snub-nosed .38 in his fist, and said, "You okay, Mike?"

"No sweat." I took my hands down in time to yell and point behind Pat, and he turned and fired at the phony cop, who was about to let go at the gurney again. Pat put one into the side of his head, blowing his brains all over the sidewalk. They all came out one side, so his face was gory but still recognizable.

The area was cordoned off so fast no spectators had a chance to get near the bodies. Two cops took the gurney out to the truck and lifted it into the back, and the lady cop from the first car got in with Velda and the truck lurched ahead, made a turn in the street, and headed west.

Pat took my arm and hustled me toward his own marked cruiser that was close by. I said, "Where did you guys come from?"

"Come on, pal, I alerted this team as soon as you headed over here." He yanked a portable radio from his pocket and said into it, "Charlie squad, what do you have?"

There was a click and a hum, and a flat voice answered with, "One officer down in the patient's room, Captain. We have a doctor here who says he was sapped, then drugged. There are two syringes on the bed table, both empty."

"Is the officer okay?"

"Vital signs okay, doc says."

I tapped Pat on the shoulder. "Tell him to check the last room down the hall on the right."

He passed the message on, and a minute later, the receiver hummed and the voice said, "Got a nurse down in there, too, Captain. She got the same treatment. The patient who was there is gone."

"He sure is," Pat told him.

As we got into the car, the radio came alive again. Pat barked a go-ahead, and the cop on the other end said, "Captain, four hospital-security guys just got here. They answered a call in the basement and wound up locked in a storeroom."

"Good. Get a statement from them."

"Roger, Captain."

He turned the key and put the car in gear. Up ahead, the truck was turning the corner and he leaned on the gas to catch up to it. "Mind telling me where we're going?" I asked.

"For tonight, you're going fancy. I'm putting you up in my apartment. We'll hold you there overnight and get you squared away tomorrow. If you weren't a friend, I'd slap you in a prison ward to keep you out of trouble."

"Did you get a good look at the guy you shot?"

"I got a good look at both of them."

"Make 'em?"

He yanked the wheel, going around a car and pulling up directly behind the truck. "The slob playing cop was Nolo Abberniche. He started out as a kid with the Costello bunch. That bastard has knocked off a half dozen guys and all he has is three arrests on petty offenses."

"You seem to have a good line on him."

"Plenty of fliers, nationwide inquiries. Pal, you are traveling in some pretty heavy company. That other guy was Marty Santino. He's another hit man, but he likes fancy jobs. This one was right up his alley."

"Who's paying for it, Pat?"

"That died with those hoods. You know damn well we won't find anything to tie them in directly with any of the Mob boys."

"Beautiful," I said. "We wait for them to make another run on us."

"Not this time, Mike."

"What's that supposed to mean?" I asked him.

"Simple, pal. We have the location of the truck. It's in a barn on a farm north of Lake Hopatcong, New Jersey, on Route Ninety-four, just before Hamburg. Because it's an interstate operation, the FBI can get on this from their local offices a lot faster. And we're taking you and Velda out of the action. You're too important as witnesses and possible targets to be exposed during the mop-up. I know damn well you're not going to let her out of your sight, so we're setting both of you up at a safe house of our choosing. Any objections?"

"No."

"Good. I thought you'd do it my way for once. You'll be covering Velda and we'll be covering both of you, just in case. It may seem redundant, but we don't want to take any chances. Once we haul in that trailer, I expect things will quiet down."

"Things are never quiet around me, Pat. You should know that by now."

"Just shoulder the piece, Mike. You've had your revenge."

Out of the corner of my eye, I caught Pat grinning at me. We both laughed, while the buildings of the city passed by.

Final Resting Place

by Marcia Muller

THE VOICES OF THE WELL-DRESSED LUNCH CROWD reverberated off the chromium and Formica of Max's Diner. Busy waiters made their way through the room, trays laden with meat loaf, mashed potatoes with gravy, and hot turkey sandwiches. The booths and tables and counter seats of the trendy restaurant—one of the forerunners of San Francisco's fifties revival—were all taken, and a sizable crowd awaited their turn in the bar. What I waited for was Max's famous onion rings, along with the basket of sliders—little burgers—I'd just ordered.

I was seated in one of the window booths overlooking Third Street with Diana Richards, an old friend from college. Back in the seventies, Diana and I had shared a dilapidated old house a few blocks from the UC Berkeley campus with a fluctuating group of anywhere from five to ten other semi-indigent students, but nowadays we didn't see much of each other. We had followed very different paths since graduation: She'd become a media buyer with the city's top ad agency, drove a new Mercedes, and lived graciously in one of the new condominium complexes near the financial district; I'd become a private investigator with a law cooperative, drove a beat-up MG, and lived chaotically in an old cottage that was constantly in the throes of renovation. I still liked Diana, though—enough that when she'd called that morning and asked to meet with me to discuss a problem, I'd dropped everything and driven downtown to Max's.

Milk shakes—the genuine article—arrived. I poured a generous dollop into my glass from the metal shaker. Diana just sat there, staring out at the passersby on the sidewalk. We'd exchanged the usual small talk while waiting for a table and scanning the menu ("Have you heard from any of the old gang?" "Do you still like your job?" "Any interesting men in your life?"), but then she'd grown uncharacteristically silent. Now I sipped and waited for her to speak.

After a moment she sighed and turned her yellow eyes toward me. I've never known anyone with eyes so much like a cat's; their color always startles me when we meet to renew our friendship. And they are her best feature, lending her heart-shaped face an exotic aura and perfectly complementing her wavy light brown hair.

She said, "As I told you on the phone, Sharon, I have a problem."

"A serious one?"

"Not serious, so much as . . . nagging."

"I see. Are you consulting me on a personal or a professional basis?"

"Professional, if you can take on something for someone who's not an All Souls client." All Souls is the legal cooperative where I work; our clients purchase memberships, much as they would in a health plan, and pay fees that are scaled to their incomes.

"Then you actually want to hire me?"

"I'd pay whatever the going rate is."

I considered. At the moment my regular caseload was exceptionally light. And I could certainly use some extra money; I was in the middle of a home-repair crisis that threatened to drain my checking account long before payday. "I think I can fit it in. Why don't you tell me about the problem."

Diana waited while our food was delivered, then began: "Did you know that my mother died two months ago?"

"No, I didn't. I'm sorry."

"Thanks. Mom died in Cabo San Lucas, at this second home she and my father have down there. Dad had the cause of death hushed up, she'd been drinking a lot and passed out and drowned in the hot tub."

"God."

"Yes." Diana's mouth pulled down grimly. "It was a horrible way to go. And so unlike my mother. Dad naturally wanted to keep it from getting into the papers, so it wouldn't damage his precious reputation."

The bitterness and thinly veiled anger in her voice brought me a vivid memory of Carl Richards: a severe, controlling man, chief executive with a major insurance company. When we'd been in college, he and his wife, Teresa, had crossed the Bay Bridge from San Francisco once a month to take Diana and a few of her friends to dinner. The evenings were not great successes; the restaurants the Richardses chose were too elegant for our preferred jeans and T-shirts, the conversations stilted to the point of strangulation. Carl Richards made no pretense of liking any of us; he used the dinners as a forum for airing his disapproval of the liberal political climate at Berkeley, and boasted that he had refused to pay more than Diana's basic expenses because she'd insisted on enrolling there. Teresa Richards tried hard, but her ineffectual social flutterings reminded me of a bird trapped in a confined space. Her husband often mocked what she said, and it was obvious she was completely dominated by him. Even with the nonwisdom of nineteen, I sensed they were a couple who had grown apart, as the man made his way in the world and the woman tended the home fires.

Diana plucked a piece of fried chicken from the basket in front of her, eyed it with distaste, then put it back. I reached for an onion ring.

"Do you know what the San Francisco Memorial Columbarium is?" she asked.

I nodded. The columbarium was the old Odd Fellows mausoleum for cremated remains, in the Inner Richmond district. Several years ago it had been bought and restored by the Neptune Society—a sort of All Souls of the funeral industry, specializing in low-cost cremations and interments, as well as burials at sea.

"Well, Mom's ashes are interred there, in a niche on the second floor. Once a week, on Tuesdays, I have to consult with a major client in South San Francisco, and on the way back I stop in over the noon hour and . . . visit. I always take flowers—carnations, they were her favorite. There's a little vaselike thing attached to the wall next to the niche where you can put them. There were never any other flowers in it until three weeks ago. But then carnations, always white ones with a dusting of red, started to appear."

I finished the onion ring and started in on the little hamburgers. When she didn't go on, I said, "Maybe your father left them."

"That's what I thought. It pleased me, because it meant he missed her and had belatedly come to appreciate her. But I had my monthly dinner with him last weekend." She paused, her mouth twisting ruefully. "Old habits die hard. I suppose I do it to keep up the illusion we're a family. Anyway, at dinner I mentioned how glad I was he'd taken to visiting the columbarium, and he said he hadn't been back there since the interment."

The man certainly didn't trouble with sentiment, I thought. "Well, what about another relative? Or a friend?"

"None of our relatives live in the area, and I don't know of any close friend Mom might have had. Social friends, yes. The wives of other executives at Dad's company, the neighbors on Russian Hill, the ladies she played bridge with at her club. But no one who would have cared enough to leave flowers."

"So you want me to find out who is leaving them."

"Yes."

"Why?"

"Because since they've started appearing it's occurred to me that I never really knew my mother. I loved her, but in my own way I dismissed her almost as much as my father did. If Mom had that good a friend, I want to talk with her. I want to see my mother through the eyes of someone who did know her. Can you understand that?"

"Yes, I can," I said, thinking of my own mother. I would never dismiss Ma—wouldn't dare dismiss the hundred-and-five-pound dynamo who warms and energizes the McCone homestead in San Diego—but at the same time I didn't really know much about her life, except as it related to Pa and us kids.

"What about the staff at the columbarium?" I asked. "Could they tell you anything?"

"The staff occupy a separate building. There's hardly ever anyone in the mausoleum, except for occasional visitors, or when they hold a memorial service."

"And you've always gone on Tuesday at noon?"

"Yes."

"Are the flowers you find there fresh?"

"Yes. And that means they'd have to be left that morning, since the columbarium's not open to visitors on Monday."

"Then it means this friend goes there before noon on Tuesdays."

"Yes. Sometime after nine, when it opens."

"Why don't you just spend a Tuesday morning there and wait for her?"

"As I said, I have regular meetings with a major client then. Besides, I'd feel strange, just approaching her and asking to talk about Mom. It would be better if I knew something about her first. That's why I thought of you. You could follow her, find out where she lives and something about her. Knowing a few details would make it easier for me."

I thought for a moment. It was an odd request, something she really didn't need a professional investigator for, and not at all the kind of job I'd normally take on. But Diana was a friend, so for old times' sake . . .

"Okay," I finally said. "Today's Monday. I'll go to the columbarium at nine tomorrow morning and check it out."

Tuesday dawned gray, with a slowly drifting fog that provided the perfect backdrop for a visit to the dead. Foghorns moaned a lament as I walked along Loraine Court, a single block of pleasant stucco homes that dead-ended at the gates of the park surrounding the columbarium. The massive neoclassical building loomed ahead of me, a poignant reminder of the days when the Richmond district was mostly sand dunes stretching toward the sea, when San Franciscans were still laid to rest in the city's soil. That was before greed gripped the real-estate market in the early decades of the century, and developers decided the limited acreage was too valuable to be wasted on cemeteries. First cremation was outlawed within the city, then burials, and by the late 1930s the last bodies were moved south to the necropolis of Colma. Only the columbarium remained, protected from destruction by the Homestead Act.

When I'd first moved to the city I'd often wondered about the verdigrised copper dome that could be glimpsed when driving along Geary Boulevard, and once I'd detoured to investigate the structure it topped. What I'd found was a decaying rotunda with four small wings jutting off. Cracks and water stains marred its facade; weeds grew high around it; one stained-glass window had buckled with age. The neglect it had suffered since the Odd Fellows had sold it to an absentee owner some forty years before had taken its full toll. But now I saw the building sported a fresh coat of paint: a medley of lavender, beige, and subdued green highlighted its ornate architectural details. The lawn was clipped, the surrounding fir trees pruned, the names and dates on the exterior niches newly lettered and easily readable. The dome still had a green patina, but somehow it seemed more appropriate than shiny copper.

As I followed the graveled path toward the entrance, I began to feel as if I were suspended in a shadow world between the past and the present. A block away Geary was clogged with cars and trucks and buses, but here their sounds were muted. When I looked to my left I could see the side wall of the Coronet Theater, splattered with garish, chaotic graffiti; but when I turned to the right, my gaze was drawn to the rich colors and harmonious composition of a stained-glass window. The modern-day city seemed to recede, leaving me not unhappily marooned on this small island in time.

The great iron doors to the building stood open, inviting visitors. I crossed a small entry and stepped into the rotunda itself. Tapestry-cushioned straight chairs were arranged in rows there, and large floral offerings stood next to a lectern, probably for a memorial service. I glanced briefly at them and then allowed my attention to be drawn upward, toward the magnificent round stained-glass window at the top of the dome. All around me soft, prismatic light fell from it and the other windows.

The second and third floors of the building were galleries—circular mezzanines below the dome. The interior was fully as ornate as the exterior and also freshly painted, in restful blues and white and tans and gilt that highlighted the bas-relief flowers and birds and medallions. As I turned and walked toward an enclosed staircase to my left, my heels clicked on the mosaic marble floor; the sound echoed all around me. Otherwise the rotunda was hushed and chill; as near as I could tell, I was the only person there.

Diana had told me I would find her mother's niche on the second floor, in the wing called Kepheus—named, as the others were, after one of the four Greek winds. I climbed the curving staircase and began moving along the gallery. The view of the rotunda floor, through railed archways that were banked with philodendrons, was dizzying from this height; the wall opposite the arches was honeycombed with niches. Some of them were covered with plaques engraved with people's names and dates of birth and death; others were glass-fronted and afforded a view of the funerary urns. Still others were vacant, a number marked with red tags—meaning, I assumed, that the niche had been sold.

I found the name Kepheus in sculpted relief above an archway several yards from the entrance to the staircase. Inside was a smallish room—no more than twelve by sixteen feet—containing perhaps a hundred niches. At its front were two marble pillars and steps leading up to a large niche containing a coffin-shaped box; the ones on the walls to either side of it were backed with stained-glass windows. Most of the other niches were smaller and contained urns of all types—gold, silver, brass, ceramics. Quickly I located Teresa Richards's: at eye level near the entry, containing a simple jar of hand-thrown blue pottery. There were no flowers in the metal holder attached to it.

Now what? I thought, shivering from the sharp chill and glancing around the room. The reason for the cold was evident: part of the leaded-glass skylight was missing. Water stains were prominent on the vaulted ceiling and walls; the pillars were chipped and cracked. Diana had mentioned that the restoration work was being done piecemeal, because the Neptune Society—a profit-making organization—was not eligible for funding usually available to those undertaking projects of historical significance. While I could appreciate the necessity of starting on the ground floor and working upward, I wasn't sure I would want my final resting place to be in a structure that—up here, at least—reminded me of Dracula's castle.

And then I thought, Just listen to yourself. It isn't as if you'd be peering through the glass of your niche at your surroundings! And just think of being here with all the great San Franciscans—Adolph Sutro, A. P. Hotaling, the Stanfords and Folgers and Magnins. Of course, it isn't as if you'd be creeping out of your niche at night to hold long, fascinating conversations with them, either. . . .

I laughed aloud. The sound seemed to be sucked from the room and whirled in an inverted vortex toward the dome. Quickly I sobered and considered how to proceed. I couldn't just be standing here when Teresa Richards's friend paid her call—if she paid her call. Better to move about on the gallery, pretending to be a history buff studying the niches out there.

I left the Kepheus Room and walked around the gallery, glancing at the names, admiring the more ornate or interesting urns, peering through archways. Other than the tapping of my own heels on the marble, I heard nothing. When I leaned out and looked down at the rotunda floor, then up at the gallery above me, I saw no one. I passed a second staircase, wandered along, glanced to my left, and saw familiar marble pillars. . . .

What is this? I wondered. How far have I walked? Surely I'm not already back where I started.

But I was. I stopped, puzzled, studying what I could discern of the columbarium's layout.

It was a large building, but by virtue of its imposing architecture it seemed even larger. I'd had the impression I'd only traveled partway around the gallery, when in reality I'd made the full circle.

I ducked into the Kepheus Room to make sure no flowers had been placed in the holder at Teresa Richards's niche during my absence. Disoriented as I'd been, it wouldn't have surprised me to find that someone had come and gone. But the little vase was still empty.

Moving about, I decided, was a bad idea in this place of illusion and filtered light. Better to wait in the Kepheus Room, appearing to pay my respects to one of the other persons whose ashes were interred there.

I went inside, chose a niche belonging to someone who had died the previous year, and stood in front of it. The remains were those of an Asian man—one of the things I'd noticed was the ethnic diversity of the people who had chosen the columbarium as their resting place—and his urn was of white porcelain, painted with one perfect, windblown tree. I stared at it, trying to imagine what the man's life had been, its happiness and sorrows. And all the time I listened for a footfall.

After a while I heard voices, down on the rotunda floor. They boomed for a moment, then there were sounds as if the tapestried chairs were being rearranged. Finally all fell as silent as before. Fifteen minutes passed. Footsteps came up the staircase, slow and halting. They moved along the gallery and went by. Shortly after that there were more voices, women's, that came close and then faded.

Was it always this deserted? I wondered. Didn't anyone visit the dead who rested all alone?

More sounds again, down below. I glanced at my watch, was surprised to see it was ten-thirty.

Footsteps came along the gallery—muted and squeaky this time, as if the feet were shod in rubber soles. Light, so light I hadn't heard them on the staircase. And close, coming through the archway now.

I stared at the wind-bent tree on the urn, trying to appear reverent, oblivious to my surroundings.

The footsteps stopped. According to my calculations, the person who had made them was now in front of Teresa Richards's niche.

For a moment there was no sound at all. Then a sigh. Then noises as if someone was fitting flowers into the little holder. Another sigh. And more silence.

After a moment I shifted my body ever so slightly. Turned my head. Strained my peripheral vision.

A figure stood before the niche, head bowed as if in prayer. A bunch of carnations blossomed in the holder—white, with a dusting as red as blood. The figure was clad in a dark blue windbreaker, faded jeans, and worn athletic shoes. Its hands were clasped behind its back.

It wasn't the woman Diana had expected I would find. It was a man, slender and tall, with thinning gray hair. And he looked very much like a grieving lover.

At first I was astonished, but then I had to control the urge to laugh at Diana's and my joint naïveté. A friend of mine has coined a phrase for that kind of childlike thinking: "teddy bears in the brain." Even the most cynical of us occasionally falls prey to it, especially when it comes to relinquishing the illusion that our parents—while they may be flawed—are basically infallible. Almost everyone seems to have difficulty setting that idea aside, probably because we fear that acknowledging their human frailty will bring with it a terrible and final disappointment. And that, I supposed, was what my discovery would do to Diana.

But maybe not. After all, didn't this mean that someone had not only failed to dismiss Teresa Richards, but actually loved her? Shouldn't Diana be able to take comfort from that?

Either way, now was not the time to speculate. My job was to find out something about this man. Had it been the woman I'd expected, I might have felt free to strike up a conversation with her, mention that Mrs. Richards had been an acquaintance. But with this man, the situation was different: he might be reluctant to talk with a stranger, might not want his association with the dead woman known. I would have to follow him, use indirect means to glean my information.

I looked to the side again; he stood in the same place, staring silently at the blue pottery urn. His posture gave me no clue as to how long he would remain there. As near as I could tell, he'd given me no more than a cursory glance upon entering, but if I departed at the same time he did, he might become curious. Finally I decided to leave the room and wait on the opposite side of the gallery. When he left, I'd take the other staircase and tail him at a safe distance.

I went out and walked halfway around the rotunda, smiling politely at two old ladies who had just arrived laden with flowers. They stopped at one of the niches in the wall near the Kepheus Room and began arguing about how to arrange the blooms in the vase, in voices loud enough to raise the niche's occupant. Relieved that they were paying no attention to me, I slipped behind a philodendron on the railing and trained my eyes on the opposite archway. It was ten minutes or more before the man came through it and walked toward the staircase.

I straightened and looked for the staircase on this side. I didn't see one.

That can't be! I thought, then realized I was still a victim of my earlier delusion. While I'd gotten it straight as to the distance around the rotunda and the number of small wings jutting off it, I hadn't corrected my false assumption that there were two staircases instead of one.

I hurried around the gallery as fast as I could without making a racket. By the time I reached the other side and peered over the railing, the man was crossing toward the door. I ran down the stairs after him.

Another pair of elderly women were entering. The man was nowhere in sight. I rushed toward the entry, and one of the old ladies glared at me. As I went out, I made mental apologies to her for offending her sense of decorum.

There was no one near the door, except a gardener digging in a bed of odd, white-leafed plants. I turned left toward the gates to Loraine Court. The man was just passing through them. He walked unhurriedly, his head bent, hands shoved in the pockets of his windbreaker.

I adapted my pace to his, went through the gates, and started along the opposite sidewalk. He passed the place where I'd left my MG and turned right on Anza Street. He might have parked his car there, or he could be planning to catch a bus or continue on foot. I hurried to the corner, slowed, and went around it.

The man was unlocking the door of a yellow VW bug three spaces down. When I passed, he looked at me with that blank, I'm-not-really-seeing-you expression that we city dwellers adopt as protective coloration. His face was thin and pale, as if he didn't spend a great deal of time outdoors; he wore a small beard and mustache, both liberally shot with gray. I returned the blank look, then glanced at his license plate and consigned its number to memory.

"It's a man who's been leaving the flowers," I said to Diana. "Gordon DeRosier, associate professor of art at SF State. Fifty-three years old. He owns a home on Ninth Avenue, up the hill from the park in the area near Golden Gate Heights. Lives alone; one marriage, ended in divorce eight years ago, no children. Drives a 1979 VW bug, has a good driving record. His credit's also good—he pays his bills in full, on time. A friend of mine who teaches photography at State says he's a likable enough guy, but hard to get to know. Shy, doesn't socialize. My friend hasn't heard of any romantic attachments."

Diana slumped in her chair, biting her lower lip, her yellow eyes troubled. We were in my office at All Souls—a big room at the front of the second floor, with a bay window that overlooks the flat Outer Mission district. It had taken me all afternoon and used up quite a few favors to run the check on Gordon DeRosier; at five Diana had called wanting to know if I'd found out anything, and I'd asked her to come there so I could report my findings in person.

Finally she said, "You, of course, are thinking what I am. Otherwise you wouldn't have asked your friend about this DeRosier's romantic attachments."

I nodded, keeping my expression noncommittal.

"It's pretty obvious, isn't it?" she added. "A man wouldn't bring a woman's favorite flowers to her grave three weeks running if he hadn't felt strongly about her."

"That's true."

She frowned. "But why did he start doing it now? Why not right after her death?"

"I think I know the reason for that: he's probably done it all along, but on a different day. State's summer class schedule just began; DeRosier is probably free at different times than he was in the spring."

"Of course." She was silent a moment, then muttered, "So that's what it came to."

"What do you mean?"

"My father's neglect. It forced her to turn to another man." Her eyes clouded even more, and a flush began to stain her cheeks. When she continued, her voice shook with anger. "He left her alone most of the time, and when he was there he ignored or ridiculed her. She'd try so hard—at being a good conversationalist, a good hostess, an interesting person—and then he'd just laugh at her efforts. The bastard!"

"Are you planning to talk with Gordon DeRosier?" I asked, hoping to quell the rage I sensed building inside her.

"God, Sharon, I can't. You know how uncomfortable I felt about approaching a woman friend of Mom's. This . . . the implications of this make it impossible for me."

"Forget it, then. Content yourself with the fact that someone loved her."

"I can't do that, either. This DeRosier could tell me so much about her."

"Then call him up and ask to talk."

"I don't think . . . Sharon, would you—"

"Absolutely not."

"But you know how to approach him tactfully, so he won't resent the intrusion. You're so good at things like that. Besides, I'd pay you a bonus."

Her voice had taken on a wheedling, pleading tone that I remembered from the old days. I recalled one time when she'd convinced me that I really wanted to get out of bed and drive her to Baskin-Robbins at midnight for a gallon of pistachio ice cream. And I don't even like ice cream much, especially pistachio.

"Diana—"

"It would mean so much to me."

"Dammit—"

"Please."

I sighed. "All right. But if he's willing to talk with you, you'd better follow up on it."

"I will, I promise."

Promises, I thought. I knew all about promises. . . .

"We met when she took an art class from me at State," Gordon DeRosier said. "An oil-painting class. She wasn't very good. Afterward we laughed about that. She said she was always taking classes in things she wasn't good at, trying to measure up to her husband's expectations."

"When was that?"

"Two years ago last April."

Then it hadn't been a casual affair, I thought.

We were seated in the living room of DeRosier's small stucco house on Ninth Avenue. The house was situated at the bottom of a dip in the road, and the evening fog gathered there; the branches of an overgrown plane tree shifted in a strong wind and tapped at the front window. Inside, however, all was warm and cozy. A fire burned on the hearth, and DeRosier's paintings—abstracts done in reds and blues and golds—enhanced the comfortable feeling. He'd been quite pleasant when I'd shown up on his doorstep, although a little puzzled because he remembered seeing me at the columbarium that morning. When I'd explained my mission, he'd agreed to talk with me and graciously offered me a glass of an excellent zinfandel.

I asked, "You saw her often after that?"

"Several times a week. Her husband seldom paid any attention to her comings and goings, and when he did, she merely said she was pursuing her art studies."

"You must have cared a great deal about her."

"I loved her," he said simply.

"Then you won't mind talking with her daughter?"

"Of course not. Teresa spoke of Diana often. Knowing her will be a link to Teresa—something more tangible than that urn I visit every week."

I found myself liking Gordon DeRosier. In spite of his ordinary appearance, there was an impressive dignity about the man, as well as a warmth and genuineness. Perhaps he could become a friend to Diana, someone who would make up in part for losing her mother before she really knew her.

He seemed to be thinking along the same lines, because he said, "It'll be good to finally meet Diana. All the time Teresa and I were together I'd wanted to, but she was afraid Diana wouldn't accept the situation. And then at the end, when she'd decided to divorce Carl, we both felt it was better to wait until everything was settled."

"She was planning to leave Carl?"

He nodded. "She was going to tell him that weekend, in Cabo San Lucas, and move in here the first of the week. I expected her to call on Sunday night, but she didn't. And she didn't come over as she'd promised she would on Monday. On Tuesday I opened the paper and found her obituary."

"How awful for you!"

"It was pretty bad. And I felt so . . . shut out. I couldn't even go to her memorial service—it was private. I didn't even know how she had died—the obituary merely said 'suddenly.'"

"Why didn't you ask someone? A mutual friend? Or Diana?"

"We didn't have any mutual friends. Perhaps that was the bond between us; neither of us made friends easily. And Diana . . . I didn't see any reason for her ever to know about her mother and me. It might have caused her pain, colored her memories of Teresa."

"That was extremely caring of you."

He dismissed the compliment with a shrug and asked, "Do you know how she died? Will you tell me, please?"

I related the circumstances. As I spoke DeRosier shook his head as if in stunned denial.

When I finished, he said, "That's impossible."

"Diana said something similar—how unlike her mother it was. I gather Teresa didn't drink much—"

"No, that's not what I mean." He rose and began to pace, extremely agitated now. "Teresa did drink too much. It started during all those years when Carl alternately abused her and left her alone. She was learning to control it, but sometimes it would still control her."

"Then I imagine that's what happened that weekend down in Cabo. It would have been a particularly stressful time, what with having to tell Carl she was getting a divorce, and it's understandable that she might—"

"That much is understandable, yes. But Teresa would not have gotten into that hot tub—not willingly."

I felt a prickly sense of foreboding. "Why not?"

"Teresa had eczema, a severe case, lesions on her wrists and knees and elbows. She'd suffered from it for years, but shortly before her death it had spread and become seriously aggravated. Water treated with chemicals, as it is in hot tubs and swimming pools, makes eczema worse and causes extreme pain."

"I wonder why Diana didn't mention that."

"I doubt she knew about it. Teresa was peculiar about illness—it stemmed from having been raised a Christian Scientist. Although she wasn't religious anymore, she felt physical imperfection was shameful and wouldn't talk about it."

"I see. Well, about her getting into the hot tub—don't you think since she was drunk, she might have anyway?"

"No. We had a discussion about hot tubs once, because I was thinking of installing one here. She told me not to expect her to use it, that she had tried the one in Cabo just once. Not only had it aggravated her skin condition, but it had given her heart palpitations, made her feel she was suffocating. She hated that tub. If she really did drown in it, she was put in against her will. Or after she passed out from too much alcohol."

"If that was the case, I'd think the police would have caught on and investigated."

DeRosier laughed bitterly. "In Mexico? When the victim is the wife of a wealthy foreigner with plenty of money to spread around, and plenty of influence?" He sat back down, pressed his hands over his face, as if to force back tears. "When I think of her there, all alone with him, at his mercy . . . I never should have let her go. But she said the weekend was planned, that after all the years she owed it to Carl to break the news gently." His fist hit the arm of the chair. "Why didn't I stop her?"

"You couldn't know." I hesitated, trying to find a flaw in his logic. "Mr. DeRosier, why would Carl Richards kill his wife? I know he's a proud man, and conscious of his position in the business and social communities, but divorce really doesn't carry any stigma these days."

"But a divorce would have denied him the use of Teresa's money. Carl had done well in business, and they lived comfortably. But the month before she died, Teresa inherited a substantial fortune from an uncle. The inheritance was what made her finally decide to leave Carl; she didn't want him to get his hands on it. And, as she told me in legalese, she hadn't commingled it with what she and Carl held jointly. If she divorced him immediately, it wouldn't fall under the community property laws."

I was silent, reviewing what I knew about community property and inheritances. What Teresa had told him was valid—and it gave Carl Richards a motive for murder.

DeRosier was watching me. "We could go to the police. Have them investigate."

I shook my head. "It happened on foreign soil; the police down there aren't going to admit they were bribed, or screwed up, or whatever happened. Besides, there's no hard evidence."

"What about Teresa's doctor? He could substantiate that she had severe eczema and wouldn't have gotten into that tub voluntarily."

"That's not enough. She was drunk; drunks do irrational things."

"Teresa wasn't an irrational woman, drunk or sober. Anyone who knew her would agree with me."

"I'm sure they would. But that's the point: You knew her the police didn't."

DeRosier leaned back, deflated and frustrated. "There's got to be some way to get the bastard."

"Perhaps there is," I said, "through some avenue other than the law."

"How do you mean?"

"Well, consider Carl Richards: He's very conscious of his social position, his business connections. He's big on control. What if all of that fell apart—either because he came under suspicion of murder or if he began losing control because of psychological pressure?"

DeRosier nodded slowly. "He is big on control. He dominated Teresa for years, until she met me."

"And he tried to dominate Diana. With her it didn't work so well."

"Diana . . ." DeRosier half rose from his chair.

"What about her?"

"Shouldn't we tell her what we suspect? Surely she'd want to avenge her mother somehow. And she knows her father and his weak points far better than you or I."

I hesitated, thinking of the rage Diana often displayed toward Carl Richards. And wondering if we wouldn't be playing a dangerous game by telling her. Would her reaction to our suspicions be a rational one? Or would she strike out at her father, do something crazy? Did she really need to know any of this? Or did she have a right to the knowledge? I was ambivalent: On the one hand, I wanted to see Carl Richards punished in some way; on the other, I wanted to protect my friend from possible ruinous consequences. DeRosier's feelings were anything but ambivalent, however; he waited, staring at me with hard, glittering eyes. I knew he would embark on some campaign of vengeance, and there was nothing to stop him from contacting Diana if I refused to help. Together their rage at Richards might flare out of control, but if I exerted some sort of leavening influence . . .

After a moment I said, "All right, I'll call Diana and ask her to come over here. But let me handle how we tell her."

It was midnight when I shut the door of my little brown-shingled cottage and leaned against it, sighing deeply. When I'd left Gordon DeRosier's house, Diana and he still hadn't decided what course of action to pursue in regard to Carl Richards, but I felt certain it would be a sane and rational one.

A big chance, I thought. That's what you took tonight. Did you really have a right to gamble with your friend's life that way? What if it had turned out the other way?

But then I pictured Diana and Gordon standing in the doorway of his house when I'd left. Already I sensed a bond between them, knew that they'd forged a united front against a probable killer. Old Carl would get his, one way or the other.

Maybe their avenging Teresa's death wouldn't help her rest more easily in her niche at the columbarium, but it would certainly salve the pain of the two people who remembered and loved her.

Dust Devil

by Nancy Pickard

THE FATHER OF THE CHILD pulled back the vertical blinds that hung at the window of his law office, and stared at the merciless sky that glared back at him from above downtown Kansas City. The sun was a branding iron, scorching the Midwest wherever its rays touched the earth. In this, the hottest August on record, the temperature had broken one hundred degrees for twenty-one days running. Newspapers warned parents not to leave their children or pets in cars, the city pools were so full a person couldn't dive under water without hitting somebody's legs, in airless rooms old people died for lack of fans.

The private investigator who was seated in the room inquired, "Look like it could rain?"

The man at the window, Chad Peters, didn't bother to answer the question that was on everybody's lips. He wasn't looking for rain. He was looking for his three-month-old son, Brook.

"My wife stole him from the hospital," Peters said, as if the private investigator hadn't spoken.

"Your wife's name?"

"Diane." His voice was hard and cracked, like the scorched earth, and it shook with a rage that rivaled the heat of the drought. "Diane Peters. If she's still using my name. If not, she might use her maiden name, Brewer. Diane Brewer. She was going to abort, but I got a court order preventing her from doing it. By the time her lawyers got that reversed, she was too far along in her pregnancy. And then what does she do, she steals the baby she didn't want to begin with. I'm the one who wanted the baby, not her. My son Brook wouldn't be alive if it weren't for me. I don't even know if he is still alive. . . ." He let the blinds fall, plunging his office into artificial coolness and light, and he turned his face away.

The private investigator watched him. He judged Chad Peters to be around forty years old, already a full partner with his name on the door. Peters was tall, slim, a good-looking man, but not likable in his grief; he held himself upright and rigid as a dam, as if afraid that if somebody touched him it would poke a hole in his defenses, and all of his emotions would come rushing out in a drowning flood. The private investigator didn't like him, but he felt sorry for him, all the same. Losing a child to the other parent, that was tough on anybody. When the man had himself under control once again, he looked back at the private investigator. Peters's eyes were red-rimmed, but his flushed cheeks were dry, as if the heat of his anger had dried his tears before they could fall.

"Find them for me," he said. "I'll give you your advance, and expenses, and whatever it costs beyond that, but I'll tell you, the last investigator I hired took my money and ran with it. I never heard from him again after the first couple of phone calls. What I figure is that he found her, and that Diane talked him into letting her go. She's capable of that. Diane would screw an ax murderer if she thought it would hurt me somehow." His glance at the private investigator was aggressive, offensive. "How do I know you won't screw me, too?"

"You don't, but I won't."

Peters shrugged, as if he were past the point of expecting any good to come of anything. "What's your name again?"

"Ken, Mr. Peters. I'm Ken Meredith."

"I can't remember anything anymore. I don't know where to tell you to look, either. I'll give you the names of her family and friends, everything I gave the other guy, I'll give you any information you need, and I'll warn you as I warned him—"

Meredith cocked his head, always interested in warnings.

"Diane is nuts. She's an overgrown flower child, a twenty-seven-year-old hippie who's too young even to know what that means. She didn't want me, she didn't want our child. Too conventional. Too bourgeois. Of course, she also didn't want to use birth control pills while we were married," he said, bitterly. "Too much risk of cancer, she said. You run a greater risk of getting run over by a truck on the highway, I said. It's not your body, she said. Which is the same thing she said when I stopped her from having the abortion. It may not be my body, I said, but it's sure as hell my child. I don't know how far she'll go to spite me, but . . ." Peters shook his head. "I'm afraid. . . ."

"Of what, exactly?"

"That Diane will abandon my son. Or kill him."

"Kill her own child?"

There was a moment of silence, and then Peters said, "What do you think abortion is, Mr. Meredith?"

"What do I do when I find them?"

"Call me, but not if it means letting her out of your sight. If you so much as suspect that she'll run with him again, then take him."

"Steal the baby, just grab him? I can't—"

Peters interrupted him. "She has no rights."

Meredith was not convinced, but he thought of something else that settled the argument for him. "Okay, but it'll cost a lot more if I have to do it that way."

"Of course." The father of the child pulled back a slat of the vertical blinds and stared outside again. Meredith could barely hear his next words. "Everything costs more than you think it will."

The grandmother of the child, on the father's side, showed the private investigator her son's baby book.

"This is Chad as a baby, I'm showing you this because he looked just like my grandson. I got to see Brook in the hospital before she stole him away. Brook is a beautiful baby, just like his daddy was—look at all of that dark hair! I remember the doctor joking, he said, 'Mrs. Peters, if we'd given him a haircut, you wouldn't have had to have a C-section!' Take this picture with you, Mr. Meredith. If you find a baby who looks like this, it's Brook." She was a young and pretty grandmother, and she gazed at him with sad hope in her eyes. "Maybe you could have some copies made? Put them up in truck stops, or something?"

"Where do you think she took him, Mrs. Peters?"

She sighed, and he watched the hope fade from her eyes as the breath escaped from her mouth. "If there were still such a thing as a Haight-Ashbury, she would have taken him there. She was so strange and emotional all the time, Mr. Meredith, I always suspected she must be on drugs. I don't know why Chad married her, although she's pretty, I'd have to say that she's very pretty. Chad always wanted a family, especially children. That could be one reason he married a woman so much younger than he is. And maybe he thought she was fun for a while, so much younger and freer in her behavior, you know."

She was working her wedding band, rubbing it up and down on her finger. Her eyes filled and her voice cracked on her next words.

"I think my worst fear is that she'll sell him, for money, for drugs."

"She isn't a very responsible person," her best friend confided to the private investigator as they sat together in her kitchen drinking sun tea from an iced pitcher she had set on the table between them. "I told the other guy that, too. I'll be straight with you, like I was with him. I love her like a sister, but she was always a little crazy. Like she'd fall for these guys, and she'd just move in with them after one date! Crazy. Nobody does that anymore. It's not . . . responsible. AIDS, and herpes and serial killers and all that. You can't trust people like you used to. But Diane always trusted everybody." Her mouth twisted into an expression of wry bitterness. "At least she did until she met Chad. He taught her that there are people in this world you can only trust to use you. He's like that, incredibly controlling. You'll do things Chad's way, or else. Diane was always so flaky, she must have looked like somebody he could mold, you know? Like turn her into this sweet, obedient little wife." The best friend looked up at Meredith, and laughed. "Boy, was he wrong."

"Why didn't she want to have the baby?"

"Why should she?"

"What?"

"I said, why should she want to have one?"

"I don't know. I thought every woman did."

"No." She didn't say it in an unfriendly way, but just as a statement of fact. He felt a little amazed at that.

"Then why did she keep it and run away with it?"

Her best friend smiled. "He was really cute."

"The baby? Is that the reason, because he was so cute?"

"I don't know, it could be. You probably think she's a bad person because she didn't want to have a baby and because she wanted to abort it. But she isn't. She didn't love Chad and she didn't want to have a baby, especially with him, that's all. You could say that when she met her baby, she fell for him." Her best friend grinned. "I told you, she was always falling in love at first sight. So just because she didn't want him before doesn't mean she might not want him when he got here. Sure, she ran away with him, but it wouldn't be the first time she ran off with some guy."

Ken Meredith found himself feeling very confused, as if he'd wandered into a thicket of femaleness where he was lost without a map. He thought of the first PI, and pictured him running off with nutty Diane Peters and her baby. She'd keep him around only until they spent the money, that's what she'd do, and then she'd split again. Although, if she was half as good-looking as her pictures, maybe that wasn't such a bad way for a guy to make a fool of himself, even if it was just for just a little while. Meredith felt like laughing. The heat was getting to him, he decided. He sucked an ice cube into his mouth, to chill himself back into reality.

"But she took him away from his father," he said, talking around the melting cube.

"Well, of course," her best friend said, and then leaned forward to add patiently, as though to someone slow and stupid, "Chad's a lawyer, you know. Chad got custody, in the divorce settlement, and Diane gave up all visitation rights, because she didn't think she wanted the baby. He would have taken the baby away from her forever."

"The baby she didn't want, right?"

"Before. Not after." She screwed up her face so that she looked very intense, as if she were trying to convince him of something. "Mr. Meredith, can you imagine how it'd feel if other people made you grow a baby inside of you?" She touched her hands to her abdomen. "It'd be horrible." Her long fingernails scraped the fabric of her yellow shorts. "You'd feel like you wanted to tear it out of you with your bare hands."

"Then why didn't she just go ahead and abort it?"

"Chad told her he'd send her to prison."

Meredith doubted that could happen, but he wasn't sure, so he just said, "Where'd she go with the baby?"

The best friend leaned back, and grinned again. "I'm going to tell you?"

Meredith sighed. He wondered if the other PI had also felt like strangling this woman, if she had said that to him, too.

"No, really," she said, quickly, as if sensing that she'd gone too far. "Honestly, I don't know, although it's true that I wouldn't tell you if I did. But I don't, really."

"What's she using for money?"

The best friend shrugged. "From the divorce. And she's got a car, she could go a long way." The last phrase was accompanied by a swift, sly glance, as if she hoped to persuade him that it was useless to look.

"Mr. Peters is afraid she might abandon the baby."

She looked angry. "No way."

"His mother thinks she might sell the baby for drugs."

That produced a laugh. "Yeah, right."

"But you said yourself that she's irresponsible."

She rubbed her nose and thought about it. "I guess . . . I guess what I'm afraid of is that she won't have the sense to keep him out of this heat. What if she goes into a grocery store, or something, and she leaves him sleeping in her car? You know what she said to me one time? She said, I don't see why you couldn't just leave a baby in the house for ten minutes while you ran to the grocery store. Can you believe that? My God, I told her, in ten minutes—less than that—a house could burn down!" The best friend nibbled on her lower lip. "What if Diane does something dumb like that? He could . . . die. . . ." She looked up at him, the laughter gone. "Okay. Well, I don't know where she went, but she loves nature. She always wanted to live on a farm, out in the country. You might look there."

He thought of all of the Midwest, most of it countryside, all of it baking under the 104-degree sun, and he shook his head, and smiled. "You couldn't be a little more specific?"

"Well, you might try the Flint Hills," she said. "Diane thinks it's beautiful out there." The best friend shuddered. "Gives me the creeps, all that open space."

"Thanks," he said, getting up. By advising him to "try the Flint Hills," she had narrowed it down to only about a couple of million acres of open country.

"How'd you get to be a private eye?" she asked him.

Abruptly, he sat down again. The best friend was attractive and he was divorced and loathe to go out into the hundred-plus heat again. "I ought to warn you that I'm not really a very nice person," he said, surprising both of them. "What I do, sometimes it's shitty, like spying on unsuspecting people, like that. You might think, well, if a husband's playing around, he's got it coming, but you might be surprised to find out that he's the nice one, and the wife who hired me, she's the bitch. Or maybe it's the husband who hired me and he's a jerk, and his wife, the one I'm following around, she's okay. But I'm working for whoever's paying me, that's the bottom line for me."

"You think Chad's a jerk?" she asked him, smiling a little.

"No, no, I didn't say that. You wouldn't have a beer, would you?"

Ken Meredith figured that the first investigator had also gotten a line on the possibility that the mother and child were hiding in the Flint Hills. According to Peters, the first guy had made his last report from a Rodeway Inn on I-35 at Emporia. Said he was following a lead. Meredith had laughed to himself when he heard that: sure, we're all following leads, even when we're sitting on our butts in air-conditioned motel rooms watching HBO. What the first guy had followed was the money, Meredith figured, and he'd followed it right on down the road.

In the first couple of days after getting the job from Chad Peters, Meredith followed his usual routine for disappearances: no moving violations had been issued to her in the three months she had been gone; she wasn't running up any credit card bills; if she was working, which he doubted, because of the infant, Social Security didn't show any sign of it yet. She had been the assistant manager of a health food store in Kansas City, and he doubted there were many of those in the meat-and-potatoes country of the Flint Hills. If she had been traveling alone, she might have been one of those adults who was nearly impossible to locate because she didn't want to be found. But as long as she kept the baby with her, he thought he had a chance of finding her. Babies needed diapers. And checkups and shots from doctors, maybe even medicine she'd have to buy from a pharmacy.

It was over one hundred degrees for the twenty-fourth day in a row when he drove southwest out of Kansas City. Even though he'd kept his car in his garage overnight, it didn't cool down enough to be comfortable until he reached Olathe. He wore a short-sleeved shirt and a tie, and his suit coat hung on a hanger in the backseat. On his way out of town, he stopped at a Kmart on Shawnee Mission Parkway and bought a car seat, a baby bottle, some formula, and a pacifier, just in case.

The farther south he drove, the farther away from city sprinklers and garden hoses, the drier and browner the state looked. When he stopped outside of Ottawa for an iced tea, he fancied he could smell the earth smoldering, heating up like a compost heap, slowly incinerating itself, smelling of dead baked grass and garbage. Meredith thought to himself: if we don't get rain soon, we'll be toast by September.

At the edge of the beginning of the Flint Hills, he started asking questions. He showed photographs of Diane and Brook to people working in the hospitals, pediatricians' offices, and drugstores in Emporia. When that netted him nothing, he drove deeper into the Flint Hills themselves, where the cattle listlessly swished flies with their tails at dry water holes.

He wished Diane had been deeply religious, so that he might have stood a chance of locating her through one of the many little churches that dotted the region. But unless you counted an interest in astrology, Diane wasn't religious, her husband had said, with a certain bitter wryness. If only she'd been Catholic, Chad Peters had said, and opposed to abortion, she'd have saved them all a lot of trouble. Just for the hell of it, and because you never knew where the oddest facts might lead you, Meredith bought a cheap horoscope book in a drugstore and looked up the Peterses' birth dates in an astrology book: Diane was an Aries and Chad was a Scorpio. The baby was a Cancer. The private investigator was amused to see that, according to the descriptions in the astrology book, it was no wonder that "flighty, passionate" Aries couldn't stay married to "cynical Scorpio." As for the baby, when he read that Cancers were supposed to love family, home, and hearth, he thought: fat chance for this child.

In Council Groves, near the site of a tree stump where there was a plaque commemorating the fact that General George Custer had rested there with his troops before charging on toward Little Big Horn, Meredith stopped at a grocery store for cigarettes.

More out of habit than hope, he showed the photographs to the clerk who checked him out.

"Oh yeah, I seen her, she come in here for diapers one time."

Meredith nearly laughed out loud. Wasn't it always the way that he found what he wanted when he wasn't really looking. All those nurses, all those pharmacists he'd quizzed, and none of them as helpful as this skinny girl with pimples standing beside the cash register and behind the jar of beef jerky. He could have reached across the *People* magazines and kissed her.

Still, he was afraid to hope for much; after all, Diane could have stopped here once before driving on to Texas, or New Mexico, or even old Mexico, for God's sake. But the clerk decided that yes, the woman with the baby had been back a second time. And then Meredith found a Texaco station where they'd changed a tire for her, and then a volunteer at a thrift shop recalled that a young woman looking like Diane's picture had purchased some baby clothes a few weeks ago. But it was at another grocery store, on the main street, that he made the discovery that settled the issue for him: about a month previously Diane had purchased several hundred dollars' worth of canned goods, diet Cokes, and other imperishables.

That told him she was staying around there, somewhere within driving vicinity of Council Groves. To figure out where, he sought the help of the sheriff.

The sheriff showed Ken Meredith a map of the county and pointed out to him the locations of empty and abandoned buildings. "If she's not staying with friends someplace, or if somebody hasn't taken her in, then my bet is that she's holed up with the baby in one of these vacant places," the sheriff said. "Some of them are in falling-down condition, I mean she'd have to be crazy for sure to live in one of them, but one or two of them are nice places that belong to absentee landowners. Like this ranch—" He penciled an X on a thin line of road on the map. "I suppose she could be camped out, but I think somebody'd notice her, where they wouldn't necessarily if she kept inside of one of these old barns or houses."

By the time he was finished at the sheriff's office, Ken Meredith had a map and a list of rural addresses and directions on how to get to each place. He also had instructions to include the sheriff's office in any action he might be forced to take that might require legal, possibly armed, assistance.

It was easy, he thought, as he got back into his car, when you knew how to do it. He was so damned hot, though, and annoyed at this woman for running away and causing him so much aggravation in such miserable weather. He pictured himself spending the next days driving for miles over dirt and gravel roads, raising clouds of brown dust. What if his car overheated out in the middle of nowhere? What if he busted an oil pan or a tire?

Meredith could almost sympathize with the other private investigator for taking off with the money and saying to hell with the selfish bitch.

The mother of the child climbed the hill behind the cabin every day, sometimes carrying Brook to the top in a papoose sack strapped to her back, other times climbing alone while the baby napped in the cabin. The hill was her Indian lookout, where she'd found an arrowhead that she wore around her neck on a string like an amulet.

The cabin she called her "safe" house. When she'd found it, it was empty except for a broken-leg table and a leftover wooden stool. Diane had cleaned its filthy kitchen, the bathroom, and all the rest of it. There she settled in with Brook, stocking the cupboards with the pans, food, and supplies she purchased after she fled from the hospital, making beds on the floor for both of them out of stolen hospital blankets and thrift store sheets.

Nobody bothered them. Sometimes she longed for the sound of traffic, for a telephone, and especially for a television. At those moments, she felt ashamed of her weakness. Then she reminded herself that she loved the cabin, its isolation, the eerie quiet, the pitch-dark nights that made her feel as if she were as courageous as the early prairie mothers.

She even loved the drought.

It seemed, on some days, to evaporate her, so that she felt as if she'd disappeared entirely. On other days, it baked her into a calm, stolid passivity that felt like endurance.

"We're blessed," she whispered to the baby. "Thank the stars for these blessings, my little one."

The two of them, mother and child, had themselves and Diane's full breasts and canned goods in the cupboards and the cabin and the enveloping, comforting heat. During the days, she felt safe. But at night, waves of emotion—love, hate, fear—swept over Diane like terrifying, psychedelic waves of shimmering, pulsating heat.

One day after lunch, in the third month of their disappearance, when the baby was asleep in the cabin, Diane climbed to the top of the hill. The brown grass, hard and prickly as straight pins, crackled under her tennis shoes so that she felt as if she were climbing a tinfoil mountain.

As she climbed, the sun felt like a warm body pressed against her, sweating against her, and it filled her with a different, but very familiar, kind of longing. At the top, she stripped out of her halter top, her jeans, her panties, even her shoes. Stepping carefully on the flint pebbles and the grass that cut her feet, she stood on the hilltop, feeling like a tiny, invisible speck of life in an immense, dying landscape.

She could see no one.

No one could see her.

She lifted her arms above her head, so her hair fell down her back, and she closed her eyes and faced the sun. She hummed, the sort of tuneless song she thought an Indian woman might have hummed, a propitiation, and a prayer of gratitude to the sun.

The heat embraced her.

After a moment, she turned her face away from the sun and opened her eyes.

Down the dirt lane, dust was moving.

A deer? Diane lowered her arms to her sides, smiling at the thought of a deer—perhaps the antlered stag she had seen—and herself alone on the prairie, two natural creatures in a wilderness. . . .

The dust moved, and cleared, and she saw a man walking down the dirt road.

The shock of seeing a human being on the lane was so great that for a moment she didn't move. Then she dropped to the ground, wincing as the sharp grass and rocks bit her bare skin. Frantic with haste and fear, she worked herself back into the halter, jeans, and shoes, leaving the panties where they lay. When she looked up again, the man was closer, walking without any sound she could hear, keeping to the shade of the cottonwood trees, but coming steadily, as if he had a purpose in mind.

From behind the old tractor, with shaking hands and racing heart, she observed him.

He was tall, thin, with straight brown hair that shone when the sun hit it, as if it were greasy. The man wore city shoes and cheap-looking trousers and a short-sleeved blue shirt, opened three buttons at the neck so that his white T-shirt showed beneath it. He kept to the shadows, walking with his eyes on his shoes, except that every few seconds, he glanced up at the cabin. He didn't look at the top of the hill. Was that because he had already spied her there?

"Who are you?" she whispered, her mouth gone as dry as the ground around her.

With a single long stride, the man stepped out from the shade of the cottonwoods and began the long walk up the driveway. Diane strained to hear the sound of gravel under his shoes. Why would a stranger walk up her gravel drive in the middle of the broiling day? There were many possible reasons, but only one likely one. She stared at him so hard her eyes squinted to slits in the sun, as if she were trying to probe through that long skull into the reasons he held in his brain, as if she were trying to will him away, away! He had a long, tired face, and he looked angry, as if the heat had provoked him.

She watched him walk up the two steps to the back door.

Now he stood between her and the baby, and she felt it acutely. The three of them were in a line now—Diane crouching at the top of the rise, the stranger at the door, and the baby sleeping in the cabin.

Ken Meredith cupped his hands, making binoculars out of them, and peered through the window that was set into the back door of the little cabin. He couldn't see into the dark interior, so he drew back and walked around the house, trying to look into the other windows. But they were all curtained against the sun. Or against somebody looking in them, and maybe seeing something hidden in there?

Instead of knocking, he placed his hand on the door knob.

"What are you doing!"

Startled, he turned quickly and looked toward the sound of the woman's voice. He saw her now, standing at the top of the rise behind the cabin. At first, he thought he was hallucinating in the heat, because what he thought he saw was a wild-haired, copper-skinned Indian woman above him. But then he saw that it was Diane Peters, all right, and that she was holding a good-sized rock in her right hand.

He held his hands high, open wide, to display innocence.

He had the unnerving feeling of having aroused something ancient and primitive from deep within the Flint Hills of the prairie. He was not normally an introspective man, or even a sensitive one, but Meredith knew fear when he saw it, and raw, dangerous fury.

He put down his hands, easily, appeasingly.

"Ran out of gas, ma'am. Use your phone?"

His heart beat twice before she said, "You'll have to go somewhere else."

The private investigator pretended to slump against the back door screen. "I don't think I can," he called tiredly up to her, and smiled as charmingly as he knew how. "Ma'am, I've already walked about five miles in these darned shoes, and if I don't get a drink of water, I'm going to die right here on your stoop. Please, if you could even make the call for me, I'll leave, and wait back down the road for the tow truck."

"I thought you said you ran out of gas."

He coughed into his hands before he squinted up at her again. "I don't know for sure that's the problem, ma'am. Could be a dead battery, or maybe it's just this heat that killed it, you know how cars are, they're like us people, can't take too much pressure." He smiled again, inviting her to smile down, to climb down the hill to him.

Instead, she shifted her weight, lifting the rock for a moment as she did so.

Instinctively, Meredith stepped back, though he tried to disguise the movement as meaningless and as casual as a man shaking dirt out of his shoe. But he knew that she had seen it and recognized that no man with just an empty gas tank on his mind would move so quickly, so defensively.

"Go away," she said in a tough voice.

He pursed his lips, as if he were thinking that over, but then he shook his head at her, almost sadly, as if he were disappointed in her.

The man suddenly cocked his head toward the cabin.

Oh my God, Diane thought, he's heard the baby.

One of his hands disappeared from her view, and she realized he was opening the cabin door.

Through the open windows, filtered through the curtains and the dusty screens, came the crying sounds of a baby waking up. The man shot her a look that had cunning in it. Quickly, he turned his back on her and faced the door.

"No!" Diane screamed. "Stay out of there!"

She ran down the hill at him, and reached the stoop just as he was about to shut the door in her face. Diane shoved her weight at the door, forcing it open.

"Damn, lady!"

The door pushed Meredith backward, and he was laughing a little, as though in astonishment at her strength. "Now hold on, Diane, let's just talk about this. . . ." His arms flew up to protect his head as she flung herself at him with the rock. "Your husband's got a right to see his baby. . . ."

The baby began to wail in the bedroom.

"No!" She brought the rock down on the side of Meredith's face. Blood ran into his eyes, blinding him, and then into his open, astonished mouth, choking him. "No, no, no!" With every scream, she struck him, until he slumped to the floor.

Her hands lost their strength, and the rock fell out of them. The man was still breathing.

After a moment, Diane stepped over him.

She washed her hands at the sink, and then ran to the screaming baby. With the stranger out of her sight, around the bend of the L-shaped room, she nursed Brook back to tranquility.

"I will never let anyone take you away from me."

She whispered it over and over, in a singsong, like a lullaby. The idea had come to her as she had lain in her own blood on the delivery table, the very moment they placed at her breast the baby that Chad had forced her to bear, and which he would force her to give up forever. She had stared at the tiny face and thought: this is what Chad wants more than anything else in the world. And suddenly she had known what to do. She would take the baby. By running away with the child, she could make Chad suffer every day for the rest of his life. Lying on the delivery table with the baby in her arms, filled with hatred for her ex-husband, Diane had felt a stirring of love for the child, as unexpected as a lily floating in a pool of acid. She also experienced an orgasmic-like rush of the vicious, soul-deep satisfaction of perfect revenge. She vowed: no one will ever take this child away from me.

Nobody. Ever.

While the baby kicked his legs happily on the cabin floor, Diane pulled the unconscious man deep into the cold, damp darkness of the storm cellar where the other man's body lay, and then she walked out and bolted the door. This time, she didn't take his wallet to see what his name was, or how old he was, or to see if he had any pictures in his wallet of a wife or little children. This time she didn't want to know anything about him, not even if he carried a private investigator's license, like the first one. She did remove his keys, however, and then set out walking until she found his car a half mile down the road. She drove it into the same barn where her own car was stored, and then abandoned the vehicles to the owls and rats. Back at the cabin, Diane scrubbed the linoleum floor, while her jeans and halter top soaked in cold water in the sink.

In the morning, the baby giggled at the sight of the deer in the pasture.

The drought carried on into September.

In Kansas City, Chad Peters hired a third private eye, this one a former cop by the name of Ed Banks.

In the country, every day after lunch, Diane climbed the rise behind the house. The heat was such that she began taking her clothes off inside the cabin and going naked into the afternoon. The sun baked her skin to brown and warmed the milk in her heavy breasts.

At the top of the rise, she raised her arms to the sun, her hair fell down her back like an Indian blanket, and she closed her eyes. When she opened them, she gazed down, looking for dust devils blowing up the long dirt road.

Mary, Mary, Shut the Door

by Benjamin M. Schutz

ENZO SCOLARI MOTORED INTO MY OFFICE and motioned me to sit. What the hell, I sat. He pulled around to the side of my desk, laced his fingers in his lap, and sized me up.

"I want to hire you, Mr. Haggerty," he announced.

"To do what, Mr. Scolari?"

"I want you to stop my niece's wedding."

"I see. And why is that?"

"She is making a terrible mistake, and I will not sit by and let her do it."

"Exactly what kind of mistake is she making?"

"She knows nothing about him. They just met. She is infatuated, nothing more. She knows nothing about men. Nothing. The first one to pay any attention to her and she wants to get married."

"You said they just met. How long ago, exactly?" Just a little reality check.

"Two weeks. Can you believe it? Two weeks. And I just found out about it yesterday. She brought him to the house last night. There was a party and she introduced him to everyone and told us she was going to marry him. How can you marry someone you've known for two weeks? That's ridiculous. It's a guarantee of failure and it'll break her heart. I can't let that happen."

"Mr. Scolari, I'm not sure we can help you with this. Your niece may be doing something foolish, but she has a right to do it. I understand your concern for her well-being, but I don't think you need a detective, maybe a priest or a therapist. We don't do premarital background checks. Our investigations are primarily criminal."

"The crime just hasn't happened yet, Mr. Haggerty. My niece may be a foolish girl, but he isn't. He knows exactly what he's doing."

"And what is that?"

"He's taking advantage of her naïveté, her innocence, her fears, her loneliness, so he can get her money. That's a crime, Mr. Haggerty."

And a damn hard one to prove. "What are you afraid of, Mr. Scolari? That he'll kill her for her money? That's quite a leap from an impulsive decision to marry. Do you have any reason to think that this guy is a killer?"

He straightened up and gave that one some thought. Enzo Scolari was wide and thick with shoulders so square and a head so flat he could have been a candelabra. His snow-white eyebrows and mustache hung like awnings for his eyes and lips.

"No. Not for that. But I can tell he doesn't love Gina. Last night I watched him. Every time Gina left his side his eyes went somewhere else. A man in love, his eyes follow his woman everywhere. No, he's following the maid or Gina's best friend. Gina comes back and he smiles like she's the sunrise. And she believes it.

"He spent more time touching the tapestries than he did holding her hand. He went through the house like a creditor, not a guest. No, he doesn't want Gina, he wants her money. You're right, murder is quite a step from that, but there are easier ways to steal. Gina is a shy, quiet woman who has never had to make any decisions for herself. I don't blame her for that. My sister, God rest her soul, was terrified that something awful would happen to Gina and she tried to protect her from everything. It didn't work. My sister was the one who died and it devastated the girl. Now Gina has to live in the world and she doesn't know how. If this guy can talk her into marrying him so quickly, he'll have no trouble talking her into letting him handle her money."

"How much money are we talking about here?"

"Ten million dollars, Mr. Haggerty." Scolari smiled, having made his point. People have murdered or married for lots less.

"How did she get all this money?"

"It's in a trust for her. A trust set up by my father. My sister and I each inherited half of Scolari Enterprises. When she died, her share went to Gina as her only child."

"This trust, who manages it?"

"I do, of course."

Of course. Motive number two just came up for air. "So, where's the problem? If you control the money, this guy can't do anything."

"I control the money as trustee for my sister. I began that when Gina was still a little girl. Now she is of age and can control the money herself if she wants to."

"So you stand to lose the use of ten million dollars. Have I got that right?"

Scolari didn't even bother to debate that one with me. I liked that. I'll take naked self-interest over the delusions of altruism any day.

"If they've just met, how do you know that this guy even knows that your niece has all this money?"

Scolari stared at me, then spat out his bitter reply. "Why else would he have pursued her? She is a mousy little woman, dull and plain. She's afraid of men. She spent her life in those fancy girls' schools where they taught her how to set the table. She huddled with her mother in that house, afraid of everything. Well, now she is alone and I think she's latched onto the first person who will rescue her from that."

"Does she know how you feel?"

He nodded. "Yes, she does. I made it very clear to her last night."

"How did she take it?"

"She told me to mind my own business." Scolari snorted. "She doesn't even know that that's what I'm doing. She said she loved him and she was going to marry him, no matter what."

"Doesn't sound so mousy to me. She ever stand up to you before?"

"No, never. On anything else, I'd applaud it. But getting married shouldn't be the first decision you ever make."

"Anyone else that might talk to her that she'd listen to?"

"No. She's an only child. Her father died when she was two in the same explosion that killed my father and took my legs. Her mother died in an automobile accident a little over a year ago. I am a widower myself and Gina was never close to my sons. They frightened her as a little girl. They were loud and rough. They teased her and made her cry." Scolari shrugged as if boys would be boys. "I did not like that and would stop it whenever I caught them, but she was such a timid child, their cruelty sprouted whenever she was around. There is no other family."

I picked up the pipe from my desk, stuck it in my mouth, and chewed on it. A glorified pacifier. Kept me from chewing up the inside of my mouth, though. Wouldn't be much of a stretch to take this one on. What the hell, work is work.

"Okay, Mr. Scolari, we'll take the case. I want you to understand that we can't and we won't stop her wedding. There are guys who will do that, and I know who they are, but I wouldn't give you their names. We'll do a background check on this guy and see if we can find something that'll change her mind or your mind. Maybe they really love each other. That happens, you know. This may be a crazy start, but I'm not sure that's a handicap. What's the best way to run a race when you don't know where the finish is?" I sure didn't have an answer and Scolari offered none.

"Mr. Haggerty, I am not averse to taking a risk, but not a blind one. If there's information out there that will help me calculate the odds, then I want it. That's what I want you to get for me. I appreciate your open mind, Mr. Haggerty. Perhaps you will change my mind, but I doubt it."

"Okay, Mr. Scolari. I need a description of this guy, his name and anything else you know about him. First thing Monday morning, I'll assign an investigator and we'll get on this."

"That won't do, Mr. Haggerty. You need to start on this immediately, this minute."

"Why is that?"

"Because they flew to St. Mary's this morning to get married."

"Aren't we a little late, then?"

"No. You can't apply for a marriage license on St. Mary's until you've been on the island for two days."

"How long to get the application approved?"

"I called the embassy. They say it takes three days to process the application. I'm looking into delaying that, if possible. Once it's issued they say most people get married that day or the next."

"So we've got what, five or six days? Mr. Scolari, we can't run a complete background check in that period of time. Hell, no one can. There just isn't enough time."

"What if you put everyone you've got on this, round the clock?"

"That gets you a maybe and just barely that. He'd have to have a pimple on his backside the size of Mount Rushmore for us to find it that fast. If this guy's the sneaky, cunning opportunist that you think he is, then he's hidden that, maybe not perfectly, but deep enough that six days won't turn it up. Besides, I can't put everyone on this, we've got lots of other cases that need attention."

"So hire more staff, give them the other cases, and put everyone else on this. Money is no object, Mr. Haggerty. I want you to use all your resources on this."

My jaw hurt from clamping on the dead pipe. Scolari was old enough to make a foolish mistake. I told him it was a long shot at best. What more could I tell him? When did I become clairvoyant, and know how things would turn out? Suppose we did find something, like three dead ex-wives? Right! Let's not kid ourselves—all the staff for six days—round the clock—that's serious money. What was it Rocky said? When you run a business, money's always necessary but it's never sufficient. Don't confuse the two and what you do at the office won't keep you up at night.

I sorted everything into piles and then decided. "All right, Mr. Scolari, we'll do it. I can't even tell you what it'll cost. We'll bill you at our hourly rates plus all the expenses. I think a reasonable retainer would be thirty thousand dollars."

He didn't even blink. It probably wasn't a week's interest on ten million dollars.

"There's no guarantee that we'll find anything, Mr. Scolari, not under these circumstances. You'll know that you did everything you could, but that's all you'll know for sure."

"That's all you ever know for sure, Mr. Haggerty."

I pulled out a pad to make some notes. "Do you know where they went on St. Mary's?"

"Yes. A resort called the Banana Bay Beach Hotel. I have taken the liberty of registering you there."

"Excuse me." I felt like something under his front wheel.

"The resort is quite remote and perched on the side of a cliff. I have been assured that I would not be able to make my way around. I need you to be my legs, my eyes. If your agents learn anything back here, someone has to be able to get that information to my niece. Someone has to be there. I want that someone to be you, Mr. Haggerty. That's what I'm paying for. Your brains, your eyes, your legs, to be there because I can't."

I stared at Scolari's withered legs and the motorized wheelchair he got around in. More than that he had money, lots of money. And money's the ultimate prosthetic.

"Let's start at the top. What's his name?"

The island of St. Mary's is one of lush green mountains that drop straight into the sea. What little flat land there is, is on the west coast, and that's where almost all the people live. The central highlands and peaks are still wild and pristine.

My plane banked around the southern tip of the island and headed toward one of those flat spots, the international airport. I flipped through the file accumulated in those few hours between Enzo Scolari's visit and my plane's departure. While Kelly, my secretary, made travel arrangements I called everyone into the conference room and handed out jobs. Clancy Hopper was to rearrange caseloads and hire temporary staff to keep the other cases moving. Del Winslow was to start investigating our man Derek Marshall. We had a name, real or otherwise, an address, and a phone number. Del would do the house-to-house with the drawing we made from Scolari's description. Larry Burdette would be smilin' and dialin'. Calling every computerized data base we could access to get more information. Every time Marshall's name appeared he'd take the information and hand it to another investigator to verify every fact and then backtrack each one by phone or in person until we could re-create the life of Derek Marshall. Our best chance was with the St. Mary's Department of Licenses. To apply for a marriage license Marshall had to file a copy of his passport, birth certificate, decrees of divorce if previously married, death certificate if widowed, and proof of legal name change, if any. If the records were open to the public, we'd get faxed copies or I'd go to the offices myself and look at them personally. I took one last look at the picture of Gina Dalesandro and then the sketch of Derek Marshall, closed the file, and slipped it into my bag as the runway appeared outside my window.

I climbed out of the plane and into the heat. A dry wind moved the heat around me as I walked into the airport. I showed my passport and had nothing to declare. They were delighted to have me on their island. I stepped out of the airport and the cab master introduced me to my driver. I followed him to a battered Toyota, climbed into the front seat, and stowed my bag between my feet. He slammed the door and asked where to.

"Banana Bay Beach Hotel," I said as he turned the engine on and pulled out.

"No problem."

"How much?" We bounced over a sleeping policeman.

"Eighty ecee."

Thirty-five dollars American. "How far is it?"

"Miles or time?"

"Both."

"Fifteen miles. An hour and a half."

I should have gotten out then. If the road to hell is paved at all, then it doesn't pass through St. Mary's. The coast road was a lattice of potholes winding around the sides of the mountains. There were no lanes, no lights, no signs, and no guardrails. The sea was a thousand feet below and we were never more than a few inches from visiting it.

Up and down the hills, there were blue bags on the trees. "What are those bags?" I asked.

"Bananas. The bags keep the insects away while they ripen."

I scanned the slopes and tried to imagine going out there to put those bags on. Whoever did it, they couldn't possibly be paying him enough. Ninety minutes of bobbing and weaving on those roads like a fighter on the ropes and I was exhausted from defying gravity. I half expected to hear a bell to end the trip as we pulled up to the resort.

I checked in, put my valuables in a safe-deposit box, took my key and information packet, and headed up the hill to my room. Dinner was served in about an hour. Enough time to get oriented, unpack, and shower.

My room overlooked the upstairs bar and dining area and below that the beach, the bay, and the surrounding cliffs. I had a thatched-roof veranda with a hammock and clusters of flamboyant and chenille red-hot cattails close enough to pluck. The bathroom was clean and functional. The bedroom large and sparely furnished. Clearly, this was a place where the attractions were outdoors and rooms were for sleeping in. The mosquito netting over the bed and the coils on the dresser were not good signs. It was the rainy season and Caribbean mosquitoes can get pretty cheeky. In Antigua one caught me in the bathroom and pulled back the shower curtain like he was Norman Bates.

I unpacked quickly and read my information packet. It had a map of the resort, a list of services, operating hours, and tips on how to avoid common problems in the Caribbean such as sunburn, being swept out to sea, and a variety of bites, stings, and inedible fruits. I familiarized myself with the layout and took out the pictures of Gina and Derek. Job one was to find them and then tag along unobtrusively until the home office gave me something to work with.

I showered, changed, and lay down on the bed to wait for dinner. The best time to make an appearance was midway through the meal. Catch the early birds leaving and the stragglers on their way in.

Around eight-thirty, I sprayed myself with insect repellent, slipped my keys into my pocket, and headed down to dinner. The schedule said that it would be a barbecue on the beach.

At the reception area I stopped and looked over the low wall to the beach below. Scolari was right, he wouldn't be able to get around here. The rooms jutted out from the bluff and were connected by a steep roadway. However, from this point on, the hillside was a precipice. A staircase wound its way down to the beach. One hundred and twenty-six steps, the maid said.

I started down, stopping periodically to check the railing. There were no lights on the trail. Late at night, a little drunk on champagne, a new bride could have a terrible accident. I peered over the side at the concrete roadway below. She wouldn't bounce and she wouldn't survive.

I finished the zigzagging descent and noted that the return trip would be worse.

Kerosene lamps led the way to the beach restaurant and bar. I sat on a stool, ordered a yellowbird, and turned to look at the dining area. Almost everyone was in couples, the rest were families. All white, mostly Americans, Canadians, British, and German. At least that's what the brochure said.

I sipped my drink and scanned the room. No sign of them. No problem, the night was young even if I wasn't. I had downed a second drink when they came in out of the darkness. Our drawing of Marshall was pretty good. He was slight, pale, with brown hair parted down the middle, round-rimmed tortoiseshell glasses, and a deep dimpled smile he aimed at the woman he gripped by the elbow. He steered her between the tables as if she had a tiller.

They took a table and I looked about to position myself. I wanted to be able to watch Marshall's face and be close enough to overhear them without looking like it. One row over and two up a table was coming free. I took my drink from the bar and ambled over. The busboy cleared the table and I took a long sip from my drink and set it down.

Gina Dalesandro wore a long flower-print dress. Strapless, she had tan lines where her bathing suit had been. She ran a finger over her ear and flipped back her hair. In profile she was thin-lipped, hook-nosed, and high-browed. Her hand held Marshall's, and then, eyes on his, she pulled one to her and kissed it. She moved from one knuckle to the next, and when she was done she took a finger and slowly slid it into her mouth.

"Gina, please, people will look," he whispered.

"Let them," she said, smiling around his finger.

Marshall pulled back and flicked his eyes around. My waitress had arrived and I was ordering when he passed over me. I had the fish chowder, the grilled dolphin with stuffed christophine, and another drink.

Gina picked up Marshall's hand and held it to her cheek and said something soothing because he smiled and blew her a kiss. They ordered and talked in hushed tones punctuated with laughter and smiles. I sat nearby, watching, waiting, her uncle's gargoyle in residence.

When dessert arrived, Gina excused herself and went toward the ladies' room. Marshall watched her go. I read nothing in his face or eyes. When she disappeared into the bathroom, his eyes wandered around the room, but settled on no one. He locked in on her when she reappeared and led her back to the table with his eyes. All in all it proved nothing.

We all enjoyed the banana cake and coffee and after a discreet pause I followed them back toward the rooms. We trudged silently up the stairs, past the bar and the reception desk, and back into darkness. I kept them in view as I went toward my room and saw that they were in room 7, two levels up and one over from me. When their door clicked closed, I turned around and went back to the activities board outside the bar. I scanned the list of trips for tomorrow to see if they had signed up for any of them. They were down for the morning trip to the local volcano. I signed aboard and went to arrange a wake-up call for the morning.

After a quick shower, I lit the mosquito coils, dialed the lights way down, and crawled under the netting. I pulled the phone and my book inside, propped up the pillows, and called the office. For his money, Scolari should get an answer. He did.

"Franklin Investigations."

"Evening, Del. What do we have on Derek Marshall?"

"Precious little, boss, that's what."

"Well, give it to me."

"Okay, I canvassed his neighborhood. He's the invisible man. Rented apartment. Manager says he's always on time with the rent. Nothing else. I missed the mailman, but I'll catch him tomorrow. See if he can tell me anything. Neighbors know him by sight. That's about it. No wild parties. Haven't seen him with lots of girls. One thought he was seeing this one particular woman but hasn't seen her around in quite a while."

"How long has he been in the apartment?"

"Three years."

"Manager let you look at the rent application?"

"Leo, you know that's confidential. I couldn't even ask for that information."

"We prosper on the carelessness of others, Del. Did you ask?"

"Yes, and he was offended and indignant."

"Tough shit."

"Monday morning we'll go through court records and permits and licenses for the last three years, see if anything shakes out."

"Neighbors tell you anything else?"

"No, like I said, they knew him by sight, period."

"You find his car?"

"Yeah. Now that was a gold mine. Thing had stickers all over it."

"Such as?"

"Bush-Quayle. We'll check him out with Young Republican organizations. Also, Georgetown Law School."

"You run him through our directories?"

"Yeah, nothing. He's either a drone or modest."

"Call Walter O'Neil, tonight. Give him the name, see if he can get a law firm for the guy, maybe even someone who'll talk about him."

"Okay. I'm also going over to the school tomorrow, use the library, look up yearbooks, et cetera. See if we can locate a classmate. Alumni affairs will have to wait until Monday."

"How about NCIC?"

"Clean. No warrants or arrests. He's good or he's tidy."

"Anything else on the car?"

"Yeah, a sticker for something called Ultimate Frisbee. Nobody here knows anything about it. We're trying to track down an association for it, find out where it's played, then we'll interview people."

"Okay. We've still got three, maybe four days. How's the office doing? Are the other cases being covered?"

"Yeah, we spread them around. Clancy hired a couple of freelancers to start next week. Right now, me, Clancy, and Larry are pulling double shifts on this. Monday when the offices are open and the databases are up, we'll probably put the two new guys on it."

"Good. Any word from the St. Mary's registrar's office?"

"No. Same problem there. Closed for the weekend. Won't know anything until Monday."

"All right. Good work, Del." I gave him my number. "Call here day or night with anything. If you can't get me directly, have me paged. I'll be out tomorrow morning on a field trip with Marshall and Gina, but I should be around the rest of the day."

"All right. Talk to you tomorrow."

I slipped the phone under the netting. Plumped the pillows and opened my book. Living alone had made me a voracious reader, as if all my other appetites had mutated into a hunger for the words that would make me someone else, put me somewhere else, or at least help me to sleep. The more I read, the harder it was to keep my interest. Boredom crept over me like the slow death it was. I was an old jaded john needing ever kinkier tricks just to get it up, or over with. Pretty soon nothing would move me at all. Until then, I was grateful for Michael Malone and the jolts and length of *Time's Witness*.

I woke up to the telephone's insistent ring, crawled out of bed, and thanked the front desk for the call. A chameleon darted out from under the bed and headed out the door. "Nice seeing you," I called out, and hoped he'd had a bountiful evening keeping my room an insect-free zone. I dressed and hurried down to breakfast.

After a glass of soursop, I ordered saltfish and onions with bakes and lots of coffee. Derek and Gina were not in the dining room. Maybe they'd ordered room service, maybe they were sleeping in and wouldn't make it. I ate quickly and kept checking my watch while I had my second cup of coffee. Our driver had arrived and was looking at the activities board. Another couple came up to him and introduced themselves. I wiped my mouth and left to join the group. Derek and Gina came down the hill as I checked in.

Our driver told us that his name was Wellington Bramble and that he was also a registered tour guide with the Department of the Interior. The other couple climbed into the back of the van, then Derek and Gina in the middle row. I hopped in up front, next to Wellington, turned, and introduced myself.

"Hi, my name is Leo Haggerty."

"Hello, I'm Derek Marshall and this is my fiancée, Gina Dalesandro."

"Pleasure to meet you."

Derek and Gina turned and we were all introduced to Tom and Dorothy Needham of Chicago, Illinois.

Wellington stuck his head out the window and spoke to one of the maids. They spoke rapidly in the local patois until the woman slapped him across the forearm and waved a scolding finger at him.

He engaged the gears, pulled away from the reception area, and told us that we would be visiting the tropical rain forests that surround the island's active volcano. All this in perfect English, the language of strangers and for strangers.

Dorothy Needham asked the question on all of our minds. "How long will we be on this road to the volcano?"

Wellington laughed. "Twenty minutes, ma'am, then we go inland to the volcano."

We left the coast road and passed through a gate marked ST. MARY'S ISLAND CONSERVANCY—DEVIL'S CAULDRON VOLCANO AND TROPICAL RAIN FOREST. I was first out and helped the women step down into the muddy path. Wellington lined us up and began to lead us through the jungle, calling out the names of plants and flowers and answering questions.

There were soursop trees, lime trees, nutmeg, guava, bananas, coconuts, cocoa trees, ginger lilies, lobster-claw plants, flamboyant and hibiscus, impression fern, and chenille red-hot cattails. We stopped on the path at a large fern. Wellington turned and pointed to it.

"Here, you touch the plant, right here," he said, pointing at Derek, who eyed him suspiciously. "It won't hurt you."

Derek reached out a finger and touched the fern. Instantly the leaves retracted and curled in on themselves.

"That's Mary, Mary, Shut the Door. As you can see, a delicate and shy plant indeed."

He waved us on and we followed. Gina slipped an arm through Derek's and put her head on his shoulder. She squeezed him once.

"Derek, you know I used to be like that plant. Before you came along. All closed up and frightened if anybody got too close. But not anymore. I am so happy," she said, and squeezed him again.

Other than a mild self-loathing, I was having a good time, too. We came out of the forest and were on the volcano. Wellington turned to face us.

"Ladies and gentlemen, please listen very carefully. We are on top of an active volcano. There is no danger of an eruption, because there is no crust, so there is no pressure buildup. The last eruption was over two hundred years ago. That does not mean that there is no danger here. You must stay on the marked path at all times and be very careful on the sections that have no guardrail. The water in the volcano is well over three hundred degrees Fahrenheit; should you stumble and fall in, you would be burned alive. I do not wish to alarm you unreasonably, but a couple of years ago we did lose a visitor, so please be very careful. Now follow me."

We moved along, single file and well spaced through a setting unlike any other I'd ever encountered. The circular top of the volcano looked like a wound on the earth. The ground steamed and smoked and nothing grew anywhere. Here and there black water leaked out of crusty patches like blood seeping from under a scab. The smell of sulfur was everywhere.

I followed Derek and Gina and watched him stop a couple of times and test the railings before he let her proceed. Caution, Derek? Or a trial run?

We circled the volcano and retraced our path back to the van. As promised, we were back at the hotel twenty minutes later. Gina was flushed with excitement and asked Derek if they could go back again. He thought that was possible, but there weren't any other guided tours this week, so they'd have to rent a car and go themselves. I closed my eyes and imagined her by the side of the road, taking a picture perhaps, and him ushering her through the foliage and on her way to eternity.

We all went in for lunch and ate separately. I followed them back to their room and then down to the beach. They moved to the far end of the beach and sat facing away from everyone else. I went into the bar and worked my way through a pair of long necks.

A couple in the dining room was having a spat, or maybe it was a tiff. Whatever, she called him a *schwein* and really tagged him with an open forehand to the chops. His face lit up redder than a baboon's ass.

She pushed back her chair, swung her long blond hair in an about-face, and stormed off. I watched her go, taking each step like she was grinding out a cigarette under her foot. Made her hips and butt do terrible things.

I pulled my eyes away when I realized I had company. He was leering at me enthusiastically.

I swung around slowly. "Yes?"

It was one of the local hustlers who patrolled the beach, as ubiquitous and resourceful as the coconuts that littered the sand.

"I seen you around, man. Y'all alone. That's not a good thin', man. I was thinkin' maybe you could use some company. Someone to share paradise wit'. Watcha say, man?"

I shook my head. "I don't think so."

He frowned. "I know you ain't that way, man. I seen you watch that blond with the big ones. What'sa matter? What you afraid of?" He stopped and tried to answer that one for me. "She be clean, man. No problem."

When I didn't say anything, he got pissed. "What is it then? You don't fuck strange, man?"

"Watch my lips, bucko. I'm not interested. Don't make more of it than there is."

He sized me up and decided I wasn't worth the aggravation. Spinning off his stool, he called me something in patois. I was sure it wasn't "sir."

I found a free lounge under a *bohio* and kept an eye on Derek and Gina. No sooner had I settled in than Gina got up and headed across the cocoa-colored volcanic sands to the beach bar. She was a little pink around the edges. Probably wouldn't be out too long today. Derek had his back to me, so I swiveled my head to keep her in sight. She sat down and one of the female staff came over and began to run a comb through her hair. Cornrowing. She'd be there for at least an hour. I ordered a drink from a wandering waiter, closed my eyes, and relaxed.

Gina strolled back, her hair in tight little braids, each one tipped with a series of colored beads. She was smiling and kicking up little sprays of water. I watched her take Derek by the hands and pull him up out of his chair. She twirled around and shook her head back and forth, just to watch the braids fly by. They picked up their snorkels and fins and headed for the water. I watched to see which way they'd go. The left side of the bay had numerous warning signs about the strong current including one on the point that said TURN BACK—NEXT STOP PANAMA.

They went right and so did I. Maybe it was a little fear, maybe it was love, but she held on to his hand while they hovered over the reef. I went farther out and then turned back so I could keep them in sight. The reef was one of the richest I'd ever been on and worthy of its reputation as one of the best in the Caribbean.

I kept my position near the couple, moving when they did, just like the school of squid I was above. They were in formation, tentacles tucked in, holding their position by undulating the fins on each lateral axis. When the school moved, they all went at once and kept the same distance from each other. I drifted off the coral to a bed of sea grass. Two creatures were walking through the grass. Gray-green, with knobs and lumps everywhere, they had legs and wings! They weren't toxic-waste mutants, just the flying gurnards. I dived down on them and they spread their violet wings and took off.

When I surfaced, Derek and Gina were heading in. I swam downstream from them and came ashore as they did. Gina was holding her side and peeking behind her palm. Derek steadied her and helped get her flippers off.

"I don't know what it was, Derek. It just brushed me and then it felt like a bee sting. It really burns," Gina said.

I wandered by and said, "Looks like a jellyfish sting. When did it happen?"

"Just a second ago." They answered in unison.

"Best thing for that is papaya skins. Has an enzyme that neutralizes the toxin. The beach restaurant has plenty of them. They keep it just for things like this. You better get right over, though. It only works if you apply it right away."

"Thanks. Thanks a lot," Derek said, then turned to help Gina down the beach. "Yes, thank you," she said over his shoulder. "You're welcome," I said to myself, and went to dry off.

I sat at the bar, waiting for dinner and playing backgammon with myself. Derek and Gina came in and went to the bar to order. Her dress was a swirl of purple, black, and white and matched the color of the beads in her hair. Derek wore lime green shorts and a white short-sleeved shirt. Drinks in hand, they walked over to me. I stood up, shook hands, and invited them to join me.

"That tip of yours was a lifesaver. We went over to the bar and got some papaya on it right away. I think the pain was gone in maybe five minutes. How did you know about it?" Gina asked.

"I've been stung myself before. Somebody told me about it. Now I tell you. Word of mouth."

"Well, we're very grateful. We're getting married here on the island and I didn't want anything to mess this time up for us," Derek said.

I raised my glass in a toast. "Congratulations to you. This is a lovely place to get married. When is the ceremony?" I asked, sipping my drink.

"Tomorrow," Gina said, running her arm through Derek's. "I'm so excited."

I nearly drowned her in rerouted rum punch but managed to turn away and choke myself instead. I pounded my chest and waved off any assistance.

"Are you okay?" Derek asked.

"Yes, yes, I'm fine," I said as I got myself under control. Tomorrow? How the hell could it be tomorrow? "Sorry. I was trying to talk when I was drinking. Just doesn't work that way."

Derek asked if he could buy me another drink and I let him take my glass to the bar.

"I read the tourist brochure about getting married on the island. How long does it take for them to approve an application? They only said that you have to be on the island for two days before you can submit an application."

Gina leaned forward and touched my knee. "It usually takes two or three days, but Derek found a way to hurry things up. He sent the papers down early to the manager here and he agreed to file them for us as if we were on the island. It'll be ready tomorrow morning and we'll get married right after noon."

"That's wonderful. Where will the ceremony be?" My head was spinning.

"Here at the hotel. Down on the beach. They provide a cake, champagne, photographs, flowers. Would you join us afterward to celebrate?"

"Thank you, that's very kind. I'm not sure that I'll still be here, though. My plane leaves in the afternoon, and you know with that ride back to the airport, I might be gone. If I'm still here, I'd be delighted."

Derek returned with drinks and sat close to Gina and looped an arm around her.

"Honey, I hope you don't mind, but I invited Mr. Haggerty to join us after the ceremony." She smiled anxiously.

"No, that sounds great, love to have you. By the way, it sounded like you've been to the islands before. This is our first time. Have you ever gone scuba diving?" Derek was all graciousness.

"Yeah, are you thinking of trying it?"

"Maybe, they have a course for beginners tomorrow. We were talking about taking the course and seeing if we liked it," he said.

"I'm a little scared. Is it really dangerous?" Gina asked.

Absolutely lethal. Russian roulette with one empty chamber. Don't do it. Wouldn't recommend it to my worst enemy.

"No, not really. There are dangers if you're careless, and they're pretty serious ones. The sea is not very forgiving of our mistakes. But if you're well trained and maintain some respect for what you're doing, it's not all that dangerous."

"I don't know. Maybe I'll just watch you do it, Derek."

"Come on, honey. You really liked snorkeling. Can you imagine how much fun it would be if you didn't have to worry about coming up for air all the time?" Derek gave Gina a squeeze. "And besides, I love the way you look in that new suit."

I saw others heading to the dining room and began to clean up the tiles from the board.

"Mr. Haggerty, would you—" Gina began.

"I'm sure we'll see Mr. Haggerty again, Gina. Thanks for your help this afternoon," Derek said, and led her to the dining room.

I finished my drink and took myself to dinner. After that, I sat and watched them dance to the *shak-shak* band. She put her head on his shoulder and molded her body to his. They swayed together in the perfect harmony only lovers and mothers and babies have.

They left that way, her head on his shoulder, a peaceful smile on her lips. I could not drink enough to cut the ache I felt and went to bed when I gave up trying.

Del was in when I called and gave me the brief bad news.

"The mailman was a dead end. I went over to the school library and talked to teachers and students. So far, nobody's had anything useful to tell us. I've got a class list and we're working our way through it. Walt did get a lead on him, though. He's a junior partner in a small law firm, a 'boutique' he called it."

"What kind of law?" Come on, say tax and estate.

171

"Immigration and naturalization."

"Shit. Anything else?"

"Yeah, he's new there. Still don't know where he came from. We'll try to get some information from the partners first thing in the morning."

"It better be first thing. Our timetable just went out the window. They're getting married tomorrow at noon."

"Jesus Christ, that puts the screws to us. We'll only have a couple of hours to work with."

"Don't remind me. Is that it?"

"For right now. Clancy is hitting bars looking for people that play this 'Ultimate Frisbee' thing. He's got a sketch with him. Hasn't called in yet."

"Well, if he finds anything, call me no matter what time it is. I'll be around all morning tomorrow. If you don't get me direct, have me paged, as an emergency. Right now we don't have shit."

"Hey, boss, we just ran out of time. I'm sure in a couple of days we'd have turned something up."

"Maybe so, Del, but tomorrow around noon somebody's gonna look out over their heads and ask if anybody has anything to say or forever hold your peace. I don't see myself raising my hand and asking for a couple of more days, 'cause we're bound to turn something up."

"We did our best. We just weren't holding very good cards is all."

"Del, we were holding shit." I should have folded when Scolari dealt them.

I hung up and readied my bedroom to repel all boarders. Under the netting, I sat and mulled over my options. I had no reason to stick my nose into Gina's life. No reason at all to think that Derek was anything but the man she'd waited her whole life for. Her happiness was real, though. She was blossoming under his touch. I had seen it. And happiness is a fragile thing. Who was I to cast a shadow on hers? And without any reason. Tomorrow was a special day for her. How would she remember it? How would I?

I woke early from a restless night and called the office. Nothing new. I tried Scolari's number and spoke briefly to him. I told him we were out of time and had nothing of substance. I asked him a couple of questions and he gave me some good news and some bad. There was nothing else to do, so I went down to see the betrothed.

They were in the dining room holding hands and finishing their coffee. I approached and asked if I could join them.

"Good morning, Mr. Haggerty. Lovely day, isn't it?" Gina said, her face aglow.

I settled into the chair and decided to smack them in the face with it. "Before you proceed with your wedding, I have some news for you."

They sat upright and took their hands, still joined, off the table.

"Gina's uncle, Enzo Scolari, wishes me to inform you that he has had his attorneys activate the trustee's discretionary powers over Miss Dalesandro's portion of the estate so that she cannot take possession of the money or use it in any fashion without his consent. He regrets having to take this action, but your insistence on this marriage leaves him no choice."

"You son of a bitch. You've been spying on us for that bastard," Derek shouted, and threw his glass of water at me. I sat there dripping while I counted to ten. Gina had gone pale and was on the verge of tears. Marshall stood up. "Come on, Gina, let's go. I don't want this man anywhere near me." He leaned forward and stabbed a finger at me. "I intend to call your employer, Mr. Scolari, and let him know what a despicable piece of shit I think he is, and that goes double for you." He turned away. "Gina, are you coming?"

"Just a second, honey," she whispered. "I'll be along in just a second." Marshall crashed out of the room, assaulting chairs and tables that got in his way.

"Why did you do this to me? I've waited my whole life for this day. To find someone who loves me and wants to live with me and to celebrate that. We came here to get away from my uncle and his obsessions. You know what hurts the most? You reminded me that my uncle doesn't believe that anyone could love me for myself. It has to be my money. What's so wrong with me? Can you tell me that?" She was starting to cry and wiped at her tears with her palms. "Hell of a question to be asking on your wedding day, huh? You do good work, Mr. Haggerty. I hope you're proud of yourself."

I'd rather Marshall had thrown acid in my face than the words she hurled at me. "Think about one thing, Miss Dalesandro. This way you can't lose. If he doesn't marry you now, you've avoided a lot of heartache and maybe worse. If he does, knowing this, then you can relax knowing it's you and not your money. The way I see it, either way you can't lose. But I'm sorry. If there had been any other way, I'd have done it."

"Yes, well, I have to go, Mr. Haggerty." She rose, dropped her napkin on the table, and walked slowly through the room, using every bit of dignity she could muster.

I spent the rest of the morning in the bar waiting for the last act to unfold.

At noon, Gina appeared in a long white dress. She had a bouquet of flowers in her hands and was trying hard to smile. I sipped some anesthetic and looked away. No need to make it any harder now. I wasn't sure whether I wanted Marshall to show up or not.

Derek appeared at her side in khaki slacks and an embroidered white shirt. What will be, will be. They moved slowly down the stairs. I went to my room, packed, and checked out. By three o'clock I was off the island and on my way home.

It was almost a year later when Kelly buzzed me on the intercom to say that a Mr. Derek Marshall was here to see me.

"Show him in."

He hadn't changed a bit. Neither one of us moved to shake hands. When I didn't invite him to sit down, he did anyway. "What do you want, Marshall?"

"You know, I'll never forget that moment when you told me that Scolari had altered the trust. Right there in public. I was so angry that you'd try to make me look bad like that in front of Gina and everyone else. It really has stayed with me. And here I am, leaving the area. I thought I'd come by and return the favor before I left."

"How's Gina?" I asked with a veneer of nonchalance over trepidation.

"Funny you should ask. I'm a widower, you know. She had a terrible accident about six months ago. We were scuba diving. It was her first time. I'd already had some courses. I guess she misunderstood what I'd told her and she held her breath coming up. Ruptured a lung. She was dead before I could get her to shore."

I almost bit through my pipe stem. "You're a real piece of work, aren't you? Pretty slick, death by misinformation. Got away with it, didn't you?"

"The official verdict was accidental death. Scolari was beside himself, as you can imagine. There I was, sole inheritor of Gina's estate, and according to the terms of the trust her half of the grandfather's money was mine. It was all in Scolari stock, so I made a deal with the old man. He got rid of me and I got paid fifty percent more than the shares were worth."

"You should be careful, Derek, that old man hasn't got long to live. He might decide to take you with him."

"That thought has crossed my mind. So I'm going to take my money and put some space between him and me."

Marshall stood up to leave. "By the way, your bluff wasn't half-bad. It actually threw me there for a second. That's why I tossed the water on you. I had to get away and do some thinking, make sure I hadn't overlooked anything. But I hadn't."

"How did you know it was a bluff?" You cocky little shit.

Marshall pondered that a moment. "It doesn't matter. You'll never be able to prove this. It's not on paper anywhere. While I was in law school I worked one year as an unpaid intern at the law firm handling the estate of old man Scolari, the grandfather. This was when Gina's mother died. I did a turn in lots of different departments. I read the documents when I was xeroxing them. That's how I knew the setup. Her mother's share went to Gina. Anything happens to her and the estate is transferred according to the terms of Gina's will. An orphan, with no siblings. That made me sole inheritor, even if she died intestate. Scolari couldn't change the trust or its terms. Your little stunt actually convinced Gina of my sincerity. I wasn't in any hurry to get her to write a will and she absolutely refused to do it when Scolari pushed her on it.

"Like I said, for a bluff it wasn't half-bad. Gina believed you, but I think she was the only one who didn't know anything about her money. Well, I've got to be going, got a plane to catch." He smiled at me like he was a dog and I was his favorite tree.

It was hard to resist the impulse to threaten him, but a threat is also a warning and I had no intention of playing fair. I consoled myself with the fact that last time I only had two days to work with. Now I had a lifetime. When I heard the outer door close, I buzzed Kelly on the intercom.

"Yes, Mr. Haggerty?"

"Reopen the file on Derek Marshall."

Benjamin M. Schutz

ACKNOWLEDGMENTS

I'd like to thank the following people for their contributions to this story: Joyce Huxley of Scuba St. Lucia for her information on hyperbaric accidents; Michael and Alison Weber of Charlottesville for the title and good company, and John Cort and Rebecca Barbetti for including us in their wedding celebration and tales of "the spork" among other things.

The Merciful Angel of Death

by Lawrence Block

"People come here to die, Mr. Scudder. They check out of hospitals, give up their apartments, and come to Caritas. Because they know we'll keep them comfortable here. And they know we'll let them die."

Carl Orcott was long and lean, with a long sharp nose and a matching chin. Some gray showed in his fair hair and his strawberry blond mustache. His facial skin was stretched tight over his skull, and there were hollows in his cheeks. He might have been naturally spare of flesh, or worn down by the demands of his job. Because he was a gay man in the last decade of a terrible century, another possibility suggested itself. That he was HIV-positive. That his immune system was compromised. That the virus that would one day kill him was already within him, waiting.

"Since an easy death is our whole reason for being," he was saying, "it seems a bit much to complain when it occurs. Death is not the enemy here. Death is a friend. Our people are in very bad shape by the time they come to us. You don't run to a hospice when you get the initial results from a blood test, or when the first purple K-S lesions show up. First you try everything, including denial, and everything works for a while, and finally nothing works, not the AZT, not the pentamidine, not the Louise Hay tapes, not the crystal healing. Not even the denial. When you're ready for it to be over, you come here and we see you out." He smiled thinly. "We hold the door for you. We don't boot you through it."

"But now you think—"

"I don't know what I think." He selected a briar pipe from a walnut stand that held eight of them, examined it, sniffed its bowl. "Grayson Lewes shouldn't have died," he said. "Not when he did. He was doing very well, relatively speaking. He was in agony, he had a CMV infection that was blinding him, but he was still strong. Of course he was dying, they're all dying, everybody's dying, but death certainly didn't appear to be imminent."

"What happened?"

"He died."

"What killed him?"

"I don't know." He breathed in the smell of the unlit pipe. "Someone went in and found him dead. There was no autopsy. There generally isn't. What would be the point? Doctors would just as soon not cut up AIDS patients anyway, not wanting the added risk of infection. Of course most of our general staff are seropositive, but even so you try to avoid unnecessary additional exposure. Quantity could make a difference, and there could be multiple strains. The virus mutates, you see." He shook his head. "There's such a great deal we still don't know."

"There was no autopsy."

"No. I thought about ordering one."

"What stopped you?"

"The same thing that keeps people from getting the antibody test. Fear of what I might find."

"You think someone killed Lewes."

"I think it's possible."

"Because he died abruptly. But people do that, don't they? Even if they're not sick to begin with. They have strokes or heart attacks."

"That's true."

"This happened before, didn't it? Lewes wasn't the first."

He smiled ruefully. "You're good at this."

"It's what I do."

"Yes." His fingers were busy with the pipe. "There have been a few unexpected deaths. But there would be, as you've said. So there was no real cause for suspicion. There still isn't."

"But you're suspicious."

"Am I? I guess I am."

"Tell me the rest of it, Carl."

"I'm sorry," he said. "I'm making you drag it out of me, aren't I?

Grayson Lewes had a visitor. She was in his room for twenty minutes, perhaps half an hour. She was the last person to see him alive. She may have been the first person to see him dead."

"Who is she?"

"I don't know. She's been coming here for months. She always brings flowers, something cheerful. She brought yellow freesias the last time. Nothing fancy, just a five-dollar bunch from the Korean on the corner, but they do brighten a room."

"Had she visited Lewes before?"

He shook his head. "Other people. Every week or so she would turn up, always asking for one of our residents by name. It's often the sickest of the sick that she comes to see."

"And then they die?"

"Not always. But often enough so that it's been remarked upon. Still, I never let myself think that she played a causative role. I thought she had some instinct that drew her to your side when you were circling the drain." He looked off to the side. "When she visited Lewes, someone joked that we'd probably have his room available soon. When you're on staff here, you become quite irreverent in private. Otherwise you'd go crazy."

"It was the same way on the police force."

"I'm not surprised. When one of us would cough or sneeze, another might say, 'Uh-oh, you might be in line for a visit from Mercy.' "

"Is that her name?"

"Nobody knows her name. It's what we call her among ourselves. The Merciful Angel of Death. Mercy, for short."

A man named Bobby sat up in bed in his fourth-floor room. He had short gray hair and a gray brush mustache and a gray complexion bruised purple here and there by Kaposi's sarcoma. For all the ravages of the disease, he had a heartbreakingly youthful face. He was a ruined cherub, the oldest boy in the world.

"She was here yesterday," he said.

"She visited you twice," Carl said.

"Twice?"

"Once last week and once three or four days ago."

"I thought it was one time. And I thought it was yesterday." He frowned. "It all seems like yesterday."

"What does, Bobby?"

"Everything. Camp Arrowhead. 'I Love Lucy.' The moon shot. One enormous yesterday with everything crammed into it, like his closet. I don't remember his name but he was famous for his closet."

"Fibber McGee," Carl said.

"I don't know why I can't remember his name," Bobby said languidly. "It'll come to me. I'll think of it yesterday."

I said, "When she came to see you—"

"She was beautiful. Tall, slim, gorgeous eyes. A flowing dove-gray robe, a bloodred scarf at her throat. I wasn't sure if she was real or not. I thought she might be a vision."

"Did she tell you her name?"

"I don't remember. She said she was there to be with me. And mostly she just sat there, where Carl's sitting. She held my hand."

"What else did she say?"

"That I was safe. That no one could hurt me anymore. She said—"

"Yes?"

"That I was innocent," he said, and he sobbed and let his tears flow.

He wept freely for a few moments, then reached for a Kleenex. When he spoke again his voice was matter-of-fact, even detached. "She was here twice," he said. "I remember now. The second time I got snotty, I really had the rag on, and I told her she didn't have to hang around if she didn't want to. And she said I didn't have to hang around if I didn't want to.

"And I said, right, I can go tap-dancing down Broadway with a rose in my teeth. And she said, no, all I have to do is let go and my spirit will soar free. And I looked at her, and I knew what she meant."

"And?"

"She told me to let go, to give it all up, to just let go and go to the light. And I said—this is strange, you know?"

"What did you say, Bobby?"

"I said I couldn't see the light and I wasn't ready to go to it. And she said that was all right, that when I was ready the light would be there to guide me. She said I would know how to do it when the time came. And she talked about how to do it."

"How?"

"By letting go. By going to the light. I don't remember everything she said. I don't even know for sure if all of it happened, or if I dreamed part of it. I never know anymore. Sometimes I have dreams and later they feel like part of my personal history. And sometimes I look back at my life and most of it has a veil over it, as if I never lived it at all, as if it were nothing but a dream."

Back in his office Carl picked up another pipe and brought its blackened bowl to his nose. He said, "You asked why I called you instead of the police. Can you imagine putting Bobby through an official interrogation?"

"He seems to go in and out of lucidity."

He nodded. "The virus penetrates the blood-brain barrier. If you survive the K-S and the opportunistic infections, the reward is dementia. Bobby is mostly clear, but some of his mental circuits are beginning to burn out. Or rust out, or clog up, whatever it is that they do."

"There are cops who know how to take testimony from people like that."

"Even so. Can you see the tabloid headlines? MERCY STRIKES AIDS HOSPICE. We have a hard enough time getting blood as it is. You know, whenever the press happens to mention how many dogs and cats the SPCA puts to sleep, donations drop to a trickle. Imagine what would happen to us."

"Some people would give you more."

He laughed. "'Here's a thousand dollars—kill ten of 'em for me.' You could be right."

He sniffed at the pipe again. I said, "You know, as far as I'm concerned you can go ahead and smoke that thing."

He stared at me, then at the pipe, as if surprised to find it in his hand. "There's no smoking anywhere in the building," he said. "Anyway, I don't smoke."

"The pipes came with the office?"

He colored. "They were John's," he said. "We lived together. He died . . . God, it'll be two years in November. It doesn't seem that long."

"I'm sorry, Carl."

"I used to smoke cigarettes, Marlboros, but I quit ages ago. But I never minded his pipe smoke, though. I always liked the aroma. And now I'd rather smell one of his pipes than the AIDS smell. Do you know the smell I mean?"

"Yes."

"Not everyone with AIDS has it but a lot of them do, and most sickrooms reek of it. You must have smelled it in Bobby's room. It's an unholy musty smell, a smell like rotted leather. I can't stand the smell of leather anymore. I used to love leather, but now I can't help associating it with the stink of gay men wasting away in fetid airless rooms.

"And this whole building smells that way to me. There's the stench of disinfectant over everything. We use tons of it, spray and liquid. The virus is surprisingly frail, it doesn't last long outside the body; but we leave as little as possible to chance, and so the rooms and halls all smell of disinfectant. But underneath it, always, there's the smell of the disease itself."

He turned the pipe over in his hands. "His clothes were full of the smell. John's. I gave everything away. But his pipes held a scent I had always associated with him, and a pipe is such a personal thing, isn't it, with the smoker's toothmarks in the stem." He looked at me. His eyes were dry, his voice strong and steady. There was no grief in his tone, only in the words themselves. "Two years in November, though I swear it doesn't seem that long, and I use one smell to keep another at bay. And, I suppose, to bridge the gap of years, to keep him a little closer to me." He put the pipe down. "Back to cases. Will you take a careful but unofficial look at our Angel of Death?"

I said I would. He said I'd want a retainer, and opened the top drawer of his desk. I told him it wouldn't be necessary.

"But isn't that standard for private detectives?"

"I'm not one, not officially. I don't have a license."

"So you told me, but even so—"

"I'm not a lawyer, either," I went on, "but there's no reason why I can't do a little pro bono work once in a while. If it takes too much of my time I'll let you know, but for now let's call it a donation."

The hospice was in the Village, on Hudson Street. Rachel Bookspan lived five miles north in an Italianate brownstone on Claremont Avenue. Her husband, Paul, walked to work at Columbia University, where he was an associate professor of political science. Rachel was a freelance copy editor, hired by several publishers to prepare manuscripts for publication. Her specialties were history and biography.

She told me all this over coffee in her book-lined living room. She talked about a manuscript she was working on, the biography of a woman who had founded a religious sect in the late nineteenth century. She talked about her children, two boys, who would be home from school in an hour or so. Finally she ran out of steam and I brought the conversation back to her brother, Arthur Fineberg, who had lived on Morton Street and worked downtown as a librarian for an investment firm. And who had died two weeks ago at the Caritas Hospice.

"How we cling to life," she said. "Even when it's awful. Even when we yearn for death."

"Did your brother want to die?"

"He prayed for it. Every day the disease took a little more from him, gnawing at him like a mouse, and after months and months and months of hell it finally took his will to live. He couldn't fight anymore. He had nothing to fight with, nothing to fight for. But he went on living all the same."

She looked at me, then looked away. "He begged me to kill him," she said.

I didn't say anything.

"How could I refuse him? But how could I help him? First I thought it wasn't right but then I decided it was his life, and who had a better right to end it if he wanted to? But how could I do it? How?

"I thought of pills. We don't have anything in the house except Midol for cramps. I went to my doctor and said I had trouble sleeping. Well, that was true enough. He gave me a prescription for a dozen Valium. I didn't even bother getting it filled. I didn't want to give Artie a handful of tranquilizers. I wanted to give him one of those cyanide capsules the spies always had in World War Two movies. You bite down and you're gone. But where do you go to get something like that?"

She sat forward in her chair. "Do you remember that man in the Midwest who unhooked his kid from a respirator? The doctors wouldn't let the boy die and the father went into the hospital with a gun and held everybody at bay until his son was dead. I think that man was a hero."

"A lot of people thought so."

"God, I wanted to be a hero! I had fantasies. There's a Robinson Jeffers poem about a crippled hawk and the narrator puts it out of its misery. 'I gave him the lead gift,' he says. Meaning a bullet, a gift of lead. I wanted to give my brother that gift. I don't have a gun. I don't even believe in guns. At least I never did. I don't know what I believe in anymore.

"If I'd had a gun, could I have gone in there and shot him? I don't see how. I have a knife, I have a kitchen full of knives, and believe me, I thought of going in there with a knife in my purse and waiting until he dozed off and then slipping the knife between his ribs and into his heart. I visualized it, I went over every aspect of it, but I didn't do it. My God, I never even left the house with a knife in my bag."

She asked if I wanted more coffee. I said I didn't. I asked her if her brother had had other visitors, and if he might have made the same request of one of them.

"He had dozens of friends, men and women who loved him. And yes, he would have asked them. He told everybody he wanted to die. As hard as he fought to live, for all those months, that's how determined he became to die. Do you think someone helped him?"

"I think it's possible."

"God, I hope so," she said. "I just wish it had been me."

"I haven't had the test," Aldo said. "I'm a forty-four-year-old gay man who led an active sex life since I was fifteen. I don't have to take the test, Matthew. I assume I'm seropositive. I assume everybody is."

He was a plump teddy bear of a man, with black curly hair and a face as permanently buoyant as a smile button. We were sharing a small table at a coffeehouse on Bleecker, just two doors from the shop where he sold comic books and baseball cards to collectors.

"I may not develop the disease," he said. "I may die a perfectly respectable death due to overindulgence in food and drink. I may get hit by a bus or struck down by a mugger. If I do get sick I'll wait until it gets really bad, because I love this life, Matthew, I really do. But when the time comes I don't want to make local stops. I'm gonna catch an express train out of here."

"You sound like a man with his bags packed."

"No luggage. Travelin' light. You remember the song?"

"Of course."

He hummed a few bars of it, his foot tapping out the rhythm, our little marble-topped table shaking with the motion. He said, "I have pills enough to do the job. I also have a loaded handgun. And I think I have the nerve to do what I have to do, when I have to do it." He frowned, an uncharacteristic expression for him. "The danger lies in waiting too long. Winding up in a hospital bed too weak to do anything, too addled by brain fever to remember what it was you were supposed to do. Wanting to die but unable to manage it."

"I've heard there are people who'll help."

"You've heard that, have you?"

"One woman in particular."

"What are you after, Matthew?"

"You were a friend of Grayson Lewes. And of Arthur Fineberg. There's a woman who helps people who want to die. She may have helped them."

"And?"

"And you know how to get in touch with her."

"Who says?"

"I forget, Aldo."

The smile was back. "You're discreet, huh?"

"Very."

"I don't want to make trouble for her."

"Neither do I."

"Then why not leave her alone?"

"There's a hospice administrator who's afraid she's murdering people. He called me in rather than start an official police inquiry. But if I don't get anywhere—"

"He calls the cops." He found his address book, copied out a number for me. "Please don't make trouble for her," he said. "I might need her myself."

I called her that evening, met her the following afternoon at a cocktail lounge just off Washington Square. She was as described, even to the gray cape over a long gray dress. Her scarf today was canary yellow. She was drinking Perrier, and I ordered the same.

She said, "Tell me about your friend. You say he's very ill."

"He wants to die. He's been begging me to kill him but I can't do it."

"No, of course not."

"I was hoping you might be able to visit him."

"If you think it might help. Tell me something about him, why don't you."

I don't suppose she was more than forty-five, if that, but there was something ancient about her face. You didn't need much of a commitment to reincarnation to believe she had lived before. Her facial features were pronounced, her eyes a graying blue. Her voice was pitched low, and along with her height it raised doubts about her sexuality. She might have been a sex change, or a drag queen. But I didn't think so. There was an Eternal Female quality to her that didn't feel like parody.

I said, "I can't."

"Because there's no such person."

"I'm afraid there are plenty of them, but I don't have one in mind." I told her in a couple of sentences why I was there. When I'd finished she let the silence stretch, then asked me if I thought she could kill anyone. I told her it was hard to know what anyone could do.

She said, "I think you should see for yourself what it is that I do."

She stood up. I put some money on the table and followed her out to the street.

We took a cab to a four-story brick building on Twenty-second Street west of Ninth. We climbed two flights of stairs, and the door opened when she knocked on it. I could smell the disease before I was across the threshold. The young black man who opened the door was glad to see her and unsurprised by my presence. He didn't ask my name or tell me his.

"Kevin's so tired," he told us both. "It breaks my heart."

We walked through a neat, sparsely furnished living room and down a short hallway to a bedroom, where the smell was stronger. Kevin lay in a bed with its head cranked up. He looked like a famine victim, or someone liberated from Dachau. Terror filled his eyes.

She pulled a chair up to the side of his bed and sat in it. She took his hand in hers and used her free hand to stroke his forehead. You're safe now, she told him. You're safe, you don't have to hurt anymore, you did all the things you had to do. You can relax now, you can let go now, you can go to the light.

"You can do it," she told him. "Close your eyes, Kevin, and go inside yourself and find the part that's holding on. Somewhere within you there's a part of you that's like a clenched fist, and I want you to find that part and be with that part. And let go. Let the fist open its fingers. It's as if the fist is holding a little bird, and if you open up the hand the bird can fly free. Just let it happen, Kevin. Just let go."

He was straining to talk, but the best he could do was make a sort of cawing sound. She turned to the black man, who was standing in the doorway. "David," she said, "his parents aren't living, are they?"

"I believe they're both gone."

"Which one was he closest to?"

"I don't know. I believe they're both gone a long time now."

"Did he have a lover? Before you, I mean."

"Kevin and I were never lovers. I don't even know him that well. I'm here 'cause he hasn't got anybody else. He had a lover."

"Did his lover die? What was his name?"

"Martin."

"Kevin," she said, "you're going to be all right now. All you have to do is go to the light. Do you see the light? Your mother's there, Kevin, and your father, and Martin—"

"Mark!" David cried. "Oh, God, I'm sorry, I'm so stupid, it wasn't Martin, it was Mark, Mark, that was his name."

"That's all right, David."

"I'm so damn stupid—"

"Look into the light, Kevin," she said. "Mark is there, and your parents, and everyone who ever loved you. Matthew, take his other hand. Kevin, you don't have to stay here anymore, darling. You did everything you came here to do. You don't have to stay. You don't have to hold on. You can let go, Kevin. You can go to the light. Let go and reach out to the light—"

I don't know how long she talked to him. Fifteen, twenty minutes, I suppose. Several times he made the cawing sound, but for the most part he was silent. Nothing seemed to be happening, and then I realized that his terror was no longer a presence. She seemed to have talked it away. She went on talking to him, stroking his brow and holding his hand, and I held his other hand. I was no longer listening to what she was saying, just letting the words wash over me while my mind played with some tangled thought like a kitten with yarn.

Then something happened. The energy in the room shifted and I looked up, knowing that he was gone.

"Yes," she murmured. "Yes, Kevin. God bless you, go on, you rest. Yes."

"Sometimes they're stuck," she said. "They want to go but they can't. They've been hanging on so long, you see, that they don't know how to stop."

"So you help them."

"If I can."

"What if you can't? Suppose you talk and talk and they still hold on?"

"Then they're not ready. They'll be ready another time. Sooner or later everybody lets go, everybody dies. With or without my help."

"And when they're not ready—"

"Sometimes I come back another time. And sometimes they're ready then."

"What about the ones who beg for help? The ones like Arthur Fineberg, who plead for death but aren't physically close enough to it to let go?"

"What do you want me to say?"

"The thing you want to say. The thing that's stuck in your throat, the way his own unwanted life was stuck in Kevin's throat. You're holding on to it."

"Just let it go, eh?"

"If you want."

We were walking somewhere in Chelsea, and we walked a full block now without either of us saying a word. Then she said, "I think there's a world of difference between assisting someone verbally and doing anything physical to hasten death."

"So do I."

"And that's where I draw the line. But sometimes, having drawn that line—"

"You step over it."

"Yes. The first time I swear I acted without conscious intent. I used a pillow, I held it over his face and—" She breathed deeply. "I swore it would never happen again. But then there was someone else, and he just needed help, you know, and—"

"And you helped him."

"Yes. Was I wrong?"

"I don't know what's right or wrong."

"Suffering is wrong," she said, "unless it's part of His plan, and how can I presume to decide if it is or not? Maybe people can't let go because there's one more lesson they have to learn before they move on. Who the hell am I to decide it's time for somebody's life to end? How dare I interfere?"

"And yet you do."

"Just once in a while, when I just don't see a way around it. Then I do what I have to do. I'm sure I must have a choice in the matter, but I swear it doesn't feel that way. It doesn't feel as though I have any choice at all." She stopped walking, turned to look at me. She said, "Now what happens?"

"Well, she's the Merciful Angel of Death," I told Carl Orcott. "She visits the sick and dying, almost always at somebody's invitation. A friend contacts her, or a relative."

"Do they pay her?"

"Sometimes they try to. She won't take any money. She even pays for the flowers herself." She'd taken Dutch iris to Kevin's apartment on Twenty-second Street. Blue, with yellow centers that matched her scarf.

"She does it pro bono," he said.

"And she talks to them. You heard what Bobby said. I got to see her in action. She talked the poor son of a bitch straight out of this world and into the next one. I suppose you could argue that what she does comes perilously close to hypnosis, that she hypnotizes people and convinces them to kill themselves psychically, but I can't imagine anybody trying to sell that to a jury."

"She just talks to them."

"Uh-huh. 'Let go, go to the light.' "

" 'And have a nice day.' "

"That's the idea."

"She's not killing people?"

"Nope. Just letting them die."

He picked up a pipe. "Well, hell," he said, "that's what we do. Maybe I ought to put her on staff." He sniffed the pipe bowl. "You have my thanks, Matthew. Are you sure you don't want some of our money to go with it? Just because Mercy works pro bono doesn't mean you should have to."

"That's all right."

"You're certain?"

I said, "You asked me the first day if I knew what AIDS smelled like."

"And you said you'd smelled it before. Oh."

I nodded. "I've lost friends to it. I'll lose more before it's over. In the meantime I'm grateful when I get the chance to do you a favor. Because I'm glad this place is here, so people have a place to come to."

Even as I was glad she was around, the woman in gray, the Merciful Angel of Death. To hold the door for them, and show them the light on the other side. And, if they really needed it, to give them the least little push through it.

The Necessary Brother

by Brendan DuBois

I STILL HAVE THE PROBLEM of last evening's phone call on my mind as I wait for Sarah to finish her shower this Thursday holiday morning in November. From my vantage point on the bed I see that the city's weather is overcast, and I wonder if snow flurries will start as I begin the long drive that waits for me later in the morning. The bedroom is large and is in the corner of the building, with a balcony that overlooks Central Park. I pause between the satin sheets and wait, my hands folded behind my head, as the shower stops and Sarah ambles out. She smiles at me and I smile back, feeling effortless in doing that, for we have no secrets from each other, no worries or frets about what the future may bring. That was settled months ago, in our agreement when we first met, and our arrangement works for both of us.

She comes over, toweling her long blond hair with a thick white towel, smile still on her face, a black silk dressing gown barely covering her model's body. As she clambers on the bed and straddles me, she drops the towel and leans forward, enveloping me in her damp hair, nuzzling my neck.

"I don't see why you have to leave, Carl," she says, in her breathless voice that can still make my head turn. "And I can't believe you're driving. That must be at least four hours away. Why don't you fly?"

"It's more like five," I say, idly caressing her slim hips. "And I'm driving because flying is torture this time of year, and I want to travel alone."

She gently bites me on the neck and then sits back, her pale blue eyes laughing at me. With her long red fingernails she idly traces the scars along my side and chest, and then touches the faint ones on my arms where I had the tattoos removed years ago. When we first met and first

191

made love, Sarah was fascinated by the marks on my body, and it's a fascination that has grown over the months. At night, during our loveplay, she will sometimes atop and touch a scar and demand a story, and sometimes I surprise her by telling her the truth.

"And why are you going?" she asks. "We could have a lot of fun here today, you and me. Order up a wonderful meal. Watch the parades and old movies. Maybe even catch one of the football games."

I reach up and stroke her chin. "I'm going because I have to. And because it's family."

She makes a face and gets out of bed, drawing the gown closer to her. "Hah. Family. Must be some family to make you drive all that way. But I don't understand you, not at all. You hardly ever talk about them, Carl. Not ever. What's the rush? What's the reason?"

I shrug. "Because they're family. No other reason."

Sarah tosses the towel at my head and says in a joking tone, "You're impossible, and I'm not sure why I put up with you."

"Me too," I say, and I get up and go into the steamy bathroom as she begins to dive into the walk-in closet that belongs to her.

I stay in the shower for what seems hours, luxuriating in the hot and steamy water, remembering the times growing up in Boston Falls when showers were rationed to five minutes apiece because of the creaky hot water that could only stand so much use every cold day. Father had to take his shower before going to the mills, and Brad was next because he was the oldest. I was fortunate, being in the middle, for our youngest brother, Owen, sometimes ended up with lukewarm water, if that. And Mother, well, we never knew when she bathed. It was a family secret.

I get out and towel myself down, enjoying the feel of the warm heat on my lean body as I enter the bedroom. Another difference. Getting out of the shower used to mean walking across cold linoleum, grit on your feet as you got dressed for school. Now it means walking into a warm and carpeted bedroom, my clothes laid out neatly on my bed. I dress quickly, knowing I will have to move fast to avoid the traffic for the day's parade. I go out to the kitchen overlooking the large and dark sunken living room, and Sarah is gone, having left breakfast for me on the marbletop counter. The day's *Times* is there, folded, and I stand and eat the scrambled eggs, toast, and bacon, while drinking a large glass of orange juice and a cup of coffee.

When I unfold the *Times* a note falls out. It's in Sarah's handwriting. *Do have a nice trip*, it says. *I've called down to Raphael. See you when you get back. Yours, S.*

Yours. Sarah has never signed a note or a letter to me that says love. Always it's "yours." That's because Sarah tells the truth.

I wash the dishes and go into the large walk-in closet near the door that leads out to the hallway. I select a couple of heavy winter jackets, and from a combination-lock box similar to a fuse box, take out a Bianchi shoulder holster, a 9mm Beretta, and two spare magazines. I slide on the holster and pull a wool cardigan on and leave and take the elevator down, whistling as I do so.

Out on the sidewalk by the lobby Raphael nods to me as I step out into the brisk air, his doorkeeper's uniform clean and sharp. My black Mercedes is already pulled up, engine purring, faint tendrils of exhaust eddying up into the thick, cold air. Raphael smiles and touches his cap with a brief salute. There is an old knife scar on his brown cheek, and though still a teenager, he has seen some things that could give me the trembling wake-ups at two AM. In addition to his compensation from the building, I pay Raphael an extra hundred a week to keep his eyes open for me. The doorkeepers in this city open and close lots of doors, and they also open and close a lot of secrets, and that's a wonderful resource for my business.

Raphael walks with me and opens the door. "A cold morning, Mr. Curtis. Are you ready for your drive?"

I slip a folded ten-dollar bill into his white-gloved hand, and it disappears effortlessly. "Absolutely. Trunk packed?"

"That it is," he says as I toss the two winter coats onto the passenger's seat and buckle up in the warm interior. I always wear seat-belts, a rule that, among others, I follow religiously. As he closes the doer, Raphael smiles again and says, *"Vaya con Dios,"* and since the door is shut, I don't reply. But I do smile in return and he goes back to his post.

I'm about fifteen minutes into my drive when I notice the thermos bottle on the front seat, partially covered by the two coats I dumped there. At a long stoplight I unscrew the cap and smell the fresh coffee, then take a quick drink and decide Raphael probably deserves a larger Christmas bonus this year.

As I drive I listen to my collection of classical music CDs. I can't tell you the difference between an opus and a symphony, a quartet or a movement, or who came first, Bach or Beethoven. But I do know what I like, and classical music is something that just seems to settle into my soul, like hot honey traveling into a honeycomb. I have no stomach for, nor interest in, what passes as modern music. When I drive I start at one end of my CD collection and in a month or so I get to the other end, and then start again.

The scenery as I go through the busy streets and across the numbered highways on my way to Connecticut is an urban sprawl of dead factories, junkyards, tenements, vacated lots, and battered cars with bald tires. Not a single pedestrian I see looks up. They all stare at the ground, as if embarrassed at what is around them, as if made shy by what has become of their country. I'm not embarrassed. I'm somewhat amused. It's the hard lives in that mess that give me my life's work.

I drive on, humming along to something on the CD that features a lot of French horns.

Through Connecticut I drive in a half-daze, listening to the music, thinking over the phone call of the previous night and the unique problem that it poses for me. I knew within seconds of hanging up the telephone what my response would be, but it still troubles me. Some things are hard to confront, especially when they're personal. But I have no choice. I know what I must do and that gives me some comfort, but not enough. Not nearly enough.

While driving along the flat asphalt and concrete of the Connecticut highways, I keep my speed at an even sixty miles per hour, conscious of the eager state police who patrol these roads. Radar detectors are still illegal in this state and the police here seem to relish their role as adjuncts to the state's tax collection department. They have the best unmarked cars in the region, and I am in no mood to tempt them as I drive, drive along.

Only once do I snap out of my reverie, and that's when two Harley-Davidson motorcycles rumble by, one on each side, the two men squat and burly in their low seats, long hair flapping in the breeze, goggles hiding their eyes, their denim vests and leather jackets looking too thin for this weather, their expressions saying they don't particularly care. The sight brings back some sharp memories: the wind in my face, the throb of the engine against my thighs, the almost Zen-like sense of traveling at high speed, just inches away from the asphalt and only seconds away from serious injury or death, and the certainty and comfort of what those motored bikes meant. Independence. Willing companions. Some sharp and tight actions. I almost sigh at the pleasurable memory. I have not ridden a motorcycle for years, and I doubt that I ever will again.

I'm busy with other things.

Somewhere in Massachusetts the morning and midmorning coffee I have drunk has managed to percolate through my kidneys and is demanding to be released, and after some long minutes I see a sign that marks a rest area. As I pull into the short exit lane I see a smaller sign that in one line sums up the idiocy of highway engineering: No Sanitary Facilities. A rest area without a rest room. Why not.

There's a tractor-trailer parked at the far end of the lot, and the driver is out, slouched by the tires, examining something. Nearly a dozen cars have stopped and it seems odd to me that so many drivers have pulled over in this empty rest area. All this traffic, all these weary drivers, at this hour of this holiday morning?

I walk past the empty picnic tables, my leather boots crunching on the two or three inches of snow, when a man comes out from behind a tree. He's smoking a cigarette and he's shivering, and his knee-length leather coat is open, showing jeans and a white T-shirt. His blond hair is cut quite short, and he's to the point: "Looking for a date?"

The number of parked and empty cars now makes sense and I feel slightly foolish. I nod at the man and say, "Nope. Just looking for an empty tree," and keep on going. Some way to spend a holiday.

I find my empty tree and as I relieve myself against the pine trunk, I hear footsteps approach. I zip up and turn around and two younger men are there. One has a moustache and the other a beard, and both are wearing baseball caps with the bills pointed to the rear. Jeans, short black leather jackets, and sneakers mark their dress code. I smile and say, "No thanks, guys. I'm all set," as I walk away from the tree.

The one with the scraggly moustache laughs. "You don't understand, faggot. We're not all set."

Now they both have knives out, and the one with the beard says, "Turn over your wallet, 'fore we cut you where it counts."

I hold up my empty hands and say, "Jeez, no trouble, guys." I reach back and in a breath or two, my Beretta is in my hand, pointing at the two men. Their pasty-white faces deflate, like day-old balloons losing air, and I give them my best smile. They back up a few steps but I shake my head, and they stop, mouths still open in shock.

"Gee," I say. "Now I've changed my mind. I guess I'm not all set. Both knives, toss them behind you."

The knives are thrown behind them, making clattering noises as they strike tree branches and trunks before hitting the ground. The two young men turn again, arms held up, and the bearded one's hands are shaking.

"Very good," I say. I move the Beretta back and forth, scanning, so that one of the two is always covered. "Next I want those pants off and your wallets on the ground, and your jackets. No arguing."

The one with the moustache says, "You can't—"

I cock the hammer back on the Beretta. The noise sounds like a tree branch cracking from too much snow and ice.

"You don't listen well," I say. "No arguing."

The two slump to the ground and in a matter of moments the clothing is in a pile, and then they stand up again. Their arms go back up. One of the two—the one with the moustache—was not wearing any underwear and he is shriveled with cold and fear. Their legs are pasty white and quivering and I feel no pity whatsoever. I say, "Turn around, kneel down, and cross your ankles. Now."

They do as they're told, and I can see their bodies flinch as their bare skin strikes the snow and ice. I swoop down and pick up the clothing and say, "Move in the next fifteen minutes and you'll disappear, just like that."

I toss the clothing on the hood of my car and pull out a set of car keys and two wallets. From the wallets I take out a bundle of bills in various denominations, and I don't bother counting it. I just shove it into my pants pocket, throw everything into the car, and drive off.

After a mile I toss out the pants and jackets, and another mile after that, I toss out the car keys and wallets.

Too lenient, perhaps, but it is a holiday.

Ninety minutes later I pull over on a turn-off spot on Route 3, overlooking Boston Falls, the town which gave me the first years of my life. By now a light snow is falling and I check my watch. Ten minutes till one. Perfect timing. Mother always has her Thanksgiving dinner at three PM, and I'll be on time, with a couple of free hours for chitchat and time for some other things. I lean against the warm hood of the Mercedes and look at the mills and buildings of the town below me. Self-portrait of the prodigal son returning, I think, and what would make the picture perfect would be a cigarette in my hand, thin gray smoke curling above my head, as I think great thoughts.

But I haven't smoked in years, and the thoughts I think aren't great, they're just troubled.

I wipe some snow off the fender of the car. The snow is small and dry, and whispers away with no problem.

A few minutes later I pull up to 74 Wall Street, the place where I grew up, a street with homes lining it on either side. The house is a small Cape Cod which used to be a bright red and now suffers a covering of tan vinyl siding. In my mind's eye, this house is always red. It's surrounded by a chain-link fence that Father put up during the few years of retirement he enjoyed before dying ("All my life, all I wanted was a fence to keep those goddamn dogs in the neighborhood from pissing on my shrubs, and now I'm going to get it."). I hope he managed to enjoy it before coughing up his lungs at Manchester Memorial. Father never smoked a cigarette in his life, but the air in those mills never passed through a filter on its journey to his lungs. Parked in front of the house is the battered tan Subaru that belongs to my younger brother Owen and the blue Ford pickup truck that is owned by older brother Brad.

On Owen's Subaru there is a sticker on the rear windshield for the Society for the Protection of New Hampshire Forests, and on Brad's Ford is a sticker for the Manchester Police Benevolent Society. One's life philosophy, spelled out in paper and gummed labels. The rear windshield of my Mercedes is empty. They don't make stickers for what I do or believe in.

Getting out of the car, I barely make it through the front door of the house before I'm assaulted by sounds, smells, and a handful of small children in the living room. The smells are of turkey and fresh bread, and most of the sounds come from the children yelling, "Uncle Carl! Uncle Carl!" as they jump around me. There are three of them—all girls—and they belong to Brad and his wife Deena: Carey, age twelve;

Corinne, age nine; and the youngest, Christine, age six. All have blond hair in various lengths and they grasp at me, saying the usual kid things of how much they miss me, what was I doing, would I be up here long, and of course, their favorite question:

"Uncle Carl, did you bring any presents?"

Brad is standing by the television set in the living room, a grimace pretending to be a smile marking his face. Deena looks up to him, troubled, and then manages a smile for me and that's all I need. I toss my car keys to Carey, the oldest.

"In the trunk," I say, "and there's also one for your cousin."

The kids stream outside and then my brother Owen comes in from the kitchen holding his baby son Todd, and he's followed by his wife Jan, and Mother. Owen tries to say something, but Mother barrels by and gives me the required hug, kiss, and why-don't-you-call-me-more look. Mother's looking fine, wearing an apron that one of us probably gave her as a birthday gift a decade or two ago, and her eyes are bright and alive behind her glasses. Most of her hair is gray and is pulled back in a bun, and she's wearing a floral print dress.

"My, you are looking sharp as always, Carl," she says admiringly, turning to see if Owen and Brad agree, and Owen smiles and Brad pretends to be watching something on television. Jan looks at me and winks, and I do nothing in return.

Mother goes back into the kitchen and I follow her and get a glass of water. When she isn't looking I reach up to a shelf and pull down a sugar bowl that contains her "mad money." I shove in the wad that I liberated earlier this day, and I return the bowl to the shelf, just in time to help stir the gravy.

As she works about the stove with me Owen comes in, still holding his son Todd, and Jan is with him. Owen sits down, looking up at me, holding the baby and its bottle, and it gurgles with what seems to be contentment. Owen's eyes are shiny behind his round, wire-rimmed glasses, and he says, "How are things in New York?"

"Cold," I say. "Loud. Dirty. The usual stuff."

Owen laughs and Jan joins in, but there's a different sound in her laugh. Owen is wearing a shapeless gray sweater and tan chinos, while Jan has on designer jeans and a buttoned light pink sweater that's about one button too many undone. Her brown hair is styled and shaped, and I can tell from her eyes that the drink in her hand isn't the first of the day.

"Maybe so," she says, "but at least it isn't boring, like some places people are forced to live."

Mother pretends to be busy about the stove and Owen is still smiling, though his eyes have faltered, as if he has remembered some old debt unpaid. I give Jan a sharp look and she just smiles and drinks, and I say to Owen, "How's the reporting?"

He shrugs, gently moving Todd back and forth. "The usual. Small-town stuff that doesn't get much coverage. But I've been thinking about starting a novel, nights when I get home from meetings. Something about small towns and small-town corruption."

Jan clicks her teeth against her glass. "Maybe your brother can help you. With some nasty ideas."

I finish off my water and walk past her. "Oh, I doubt that very much," I say, and I go into the living room, hearing the sound of Jan's laughter as I go.

The three girls have come back and the floor is a mesa of shredded paper and broken boxes, as they ooh and aah over their gifts. There's a mix of clothing and dolls, the practical and the playful, because I know to the penny how much my older brother Brad makes each year and his budget is prohibitively tight.

His wife Deena is on the floor, playing with the girls, and she gives me a happy nod as I come in and sit down on the couch. She is a large woman and has on black stretch pants and a large blue sweater. I find that the more I get to know Deena, the more I like her. She comes from a farm family and makes no bones about having dropped out of high school at age sixteen. Though she's devoted utterly and totally to my brother, she also has a sharp rural way of looking at things, and though I'm sure Brad has told her many awful stories about me, she has also begun to trust her own feelings. I think she likes me, though I know she would never admit that to Brad.

Brad is sitting in an easy chair across the way, intent on looking at one of the Thanksgiving Day parades. He's wearing sensible black shoes, gray slacks, and an orange sweater, and pinned to one side is a turkey button, probably given to him by one of his daughters. Brad has a thin moustache and his black hair is slicked back, for he started losing it at age sixteen. He looks all right, though there's a roll of fat beginning to swell about his belly.

"How's it going, Brad?" I ask, sending out the first peace feeler.

"Oh, not bad," he says, eyes not leaving the screen.

"Detective work all right? Got any interesting cases you're working on?"

"Unh hunh," and he moves a glass of what looks like milk from one hand to the other.

"Who do you think will win the afternoon game?" I try again.

He shrugs. "Whoever has the best team, I imagine."

Well. Deena looks up again, troubled, and I just give her a quiet nod, saying with my look that everything's all right, and then I get up from the couch and go outside and get my winter coats and overnight bag and bring them back inside. I drop them off upstairs in the tiny room that used to be my bedroom so many years and memories ago, and then I look into a mirror over a battered bureau and say, "Time to get to work," and that makes me laugh. For the first time in a long time I'm working gratis.

I go downstairs to the basement, switching on the overhead fluorescents, which click-click-hum into life. Father's old workbench is in one corner, and dumped near the workbench is a pile of firewood for the living room fireplace. The rest of the basement is taken up with boxes, old bicycles, and a washer and drier. The basement floor is concrete and relatively clean. I go upstairs fast, taking two steps at a time. Brad is in the living room, with his three girls, trying to show some enthusiasm for the gifts I brought. I call out to him and he looks up.

"Yeah?" he says.

"C'mere," I say, excitement tingeing my voice. "You won't believe what I found."

He pauses for a moment, as if debating with himself whether he should ever trust his younger brother, and I think his cop curiosity wins out, for he says, "'Suse me," to his daughters and ambles over.

"What's going on?" he says in that flat voice I think cops learn at their service academy.

"Downstairs," I say. "I was poking around and behind Father's workbench there's an old shoebox. Brad, it looks like your baseball card collection, the one Mother thought she tossed away."

For the first time I get a reaction out of Brad and a grin pops into life. "Are you sure?"

"Sure looks like it to me. C'mon down and take a look."

Brad brushes by me and thunders downstairs on the plain wooden steps, and I follow close behind, saying, "You've got to stretch across the table and really take a close look, Brad, but I think it's them."

He says, "My God, it's been almost twenty years since I've seen them. Think of how much money they could be worth . . ."

In front of the workbench Brad leans over, casting his head back and forth, his orange sweater rising up, treating me to a glimpse of his bare back and the top of his hairy buttocks, and he says, "Carl, I don't see—"

And with that I pick up a piece of firewood and pound it into the back of his skull.

Brad makes a coughing sound and falls on top of the workbench, and I kick away his legs and he swears at me and in a minute or two of tangled struggle, he ends up on his back. I straddle his chest, my knees digging into his upper arms, a forearm pressed tight against his throat, and he gurgles as I slap his face with my free hand.

"Do I have your attention, older brother?"

He curses some more and struggles, and I press in again with my forearm and replay the slapping. I'm thankful that no one from upstairs has heard us. I say, "Older brother, I'm younger, faster, and stronger, and we need to talk; if you'll stop thrashing around, we'll get somewhere."

Another series of curses, but then he starts gurgling louder and nods, and I ease up on the forearm and say, "Just how stupid do you have to be before you stop breathing, Brad?"

"What the hell are you doing, you maniac?" he demands, his voice a loud whisper. "I'm gonna have you arrested for assault, you no-good—"

I lean back with the forearm and he gurgles some more and I say, "Listen once, and listen well, older brother. I got a phone call last night from an old friend saying my police-detective brother is now in the pocket of one Bill Sutler. You mind telling me how the hell that happened?"

His eyes bug out and I pull back my forearm and he says, "I don't know what the hell you're talking about, you lowlife biker."

Two more slaps to the face. "First, I'm no biker and you know it. Second, I'm talking about Bill Sutler, who handles the numbers and other illegal adventures for this part of this lovely state. I'm talking about an old friend I can trust with my life telling me that you now belong to this charming gentleman. Now. Let's stop dancing and start talking, shall we?"

Brad's eyes are piggish and his face is red, his slick black hair now a tangle, and I'm preparing for another struggle or another series of denials, and then it's like a dam that has been ruptured, a wall that has been breached, for I feel his body loosen underneath me, and he turns his face. "Shit," he whispers.

"Gambling?" I ask.

He just nods. "How much?" I ask again.

"Ten K," he says. "It's the vig that's killing me, Carl, week after week, and now, well, now he wants more than just money."

"Of course," I say, leaning back some. "Information: Tip-offs. Leads on some investigations involving him and his crew."

Brad looks up and starts talking and I slap him again, harder, and I lean back into him and say in my most vicious tone, "Where in hell have you been storing your brains these past months, older brother? Do you have even the vaguest idea of what you've gotten yourself into? Do you think a creature like Bill Sutler is going to let you go after a couple of months? Of course not, and if he ever gets arrested by the state or the feds, he's going to toss you up for a deal so fast you'll think the world is spinning backwards."

He tries to talk but I keep plowing on. "Then let's take it from there, after you get turned over. Upstairs is a woman who loves you so much she'd probably go after this Sutler guy with her bare hands if she could, and you have three daughters who think you're the best daddy in the Western Hemisphere. Not to mention a woman who thinks you're the good son, the successful one, and a younger brother who wishes he could be half the man you pretend you are. Think of how they'll all do, how they'll live, when they see you taken away to the state prison in orange overalls."

By now Brad is silently weeping, the tears rolling down his quivering cheeks, and I feel neither disgust nor pity. It's what I expected, what I planned for, and I say, "Then think about what prison will be like, you, a cop, side by side with some rough characters who would leap at a chance to introduce you to some hard loving. Do I have your attention now, older brother? Do I?"

He's weeping so much that he can only nod, and then I get off his chest and stand up and he rolls over, in a fetal position, whispering faint obscenities, over and over again, and I don't mind since they're not aimed at me.

"Where does this guy Sutler live?" I ask.

"Purmort," he says.

"Get up," I say. "I'm going to pay him a visit, and you're going to help."

Brad sits up, snuffling, and leans back against the wooden workbench. "You're going to see him? Now? An hour before Thanksgiving dinner? You're crazy, even for a biker."

I shrug, knowing that I will be washing my hands momentarily. They look clean, but right now they feel quite soiled. "He'll talk to me, and you're going to back me up, because I'm saving your sorry ass this afternoon."

Brad looks suspicious. "What does that mean?"

"You'll find out, soon enough."

Before Brad can say anything, the door upstairs opens up and Deena calls down, "Hey, you guys are missing the parade."

I look at Brad and he's rubbing at his throat. I reply to Deena, "So we are, so we are."

Fifteen minutes later I pull into Founder's Park, near the Bellamy River, in an isolated section of town. Of course it's deserted on this special day and I point out an empty park bench, near two snow-covered picnic tables. "Go sit there and contemplate your sorry life."

"What?"

"I said, get out there and contemplate your sorry life. I'm going to talk to this Sutler character alone."

"But—"

"I'm getting you out of trouble today, older brother, and all I ask from you is one thing. That you become my alibi. Anything comes up later today or next week that has to do with me, you're going to swear as a gentleman and a police officer that the two of us were just driving around at this time of the day, looking at the town and having some fond recollections before turkey dinner. Understand?"

Brad looks stubborn for a moment and says, "It's cold out there."

I reach behind me and pull out the thermos bottle that Raphael had packed for me, so many hours and places ago. "Here. I freshened it up at the house a while ago, before we left. Go out there and sit and I'll be back."

That same stubborn look. "Why are you doing this for me?"

I lean over him and open the door. "Not for you. For the family. Get out, will you? I don't want to be late."

At last he steps out and walks over to the park bench, the thermos bottle in his humiliated hands, and he sits down and stares out at the frozen river. He doesn't look my way as I pull out and head to Purmort.

I've parked the Mercedes on a dirt road that leads into an abandoned gravel pit, and I have a long wool winter coat on over my cardigan sweater. The air is still and some of the old trees still have coverings of snow looking like plastic casts along the branches. There's a faint maze of animal tracks in the snow, and I recognize the prints of a rabbit and a squirrel. I'm leaning against the front hood of the Mercedes as a black Ford Bronco ambles up the dirt path. It parks in front of my car and I feel a quick tinge of unease: I don't like having my escape routes blocked, and then the unease grows as two men get out of the Bronco. I had only been expecting one.

The man on the right moves a bit faster than his companion and I figure that he's Bill Sutler. My guess is correct, and it is he who begins to chatter at me.

"Let me start off by saying I don't like you already for two reasons," he says in a gravelly tone that's either come from throat surgery or too many cigarettes at an early age. He's just a few inches shorter than me, and though his black hair is balding, he has a long strip at the back tied in a ponytail. Fairly fancy for this part of the state. His face is slightly pockmarked with old acne scars, and he has on a bright blue ski jacket with the obligatory tattered ski passes hanging from the zipper. Jeans and dull orange construction boots finish off his ensemble.

"Why's that?" I say, arms and legs crossed, still leaning against the warm hood of my Mercedes, my boots in the snow cover.

"Because you pulled me out of my house on Thanksgiving, and because of your license plates," he says, pointing to the front of my Mercedes, talking fast, his entire face seemingly squinting at me. "You're from New York, and I hate guys from New York who think they can breeze in here and throw their weight around. You're in my woods now, guy, and I don't care what games you've played back on your crappy island. We do things different up here."

His companion has stepped away from the passenger's side of the

Bronco and is keeping watch on me. He seems a bit younger but he's considerably more bulky, with a tangle of curly hair and a thick beard. He's wearing an army fatigue coat and the same jeans/boot combination that Sutler is sporting. I note that the right pocket of his coat is sagging some, from the weight of something inside.

I nod over to the second man. "That your muscle, along to keep things quiet?"

Sutler turns his head for a moment. "That there's Kelly, and he's here because I want him here. I tell him to leave, he'll leave. I tell him to break every finger on your hands, he'd do that, too. So let's leave him out of things right now. Talk. You got me here, what do you want?"

I rub at my chin. "I want something that you have. I want Brad Curtis's *cojones*, and I understand you have them in your pocket."

Sutler smirks. "That I do. What's your offer?"

This just might be easy. "In twenty-four hours, I settle his gambling debt," I say. "I also put in a word to a couple of connected guys, and some extra business gets tossed your way. You get your money, you get some business, and I get what I want. You also never have any contact or dealings with him again, any time in the future."

"You're a relation, right?"

I nod. "His brother."

"Younger or older?"

"Younger."

Sutler smirks again, and I decide I don't like the look. "Isn't that sweet. Well, look at this, younger brother. The answer is no."

I cock my head. "Is that a real no, or do you want a counter offer? If it's a counter offer, mention something. I'm sure I can be reasonable."

He laughs and rocks back on his heels a bit and says, "Little one, this isn't a negotiation. The answer is no."

"Why?"

That stops him for a moment, and there's a furtive gesture from his left hand, and Kelly steps a bit closer. "Because I already told you," he says. "I don't like you New York guys, and I don't trust you. Sure, you'd probably pay off the money, but everything else you say is probably crap. You think I'm stupid? Well, I think you're stupid, and here's why. I got something good in that nitwit detective, and you and your New York friends aren't going to take it away. I got him and my work here on my own, and I don't need your help. Understand?"

"Are you sure?"

Another laugh. "You think I'm giving up a detective on the largest police force in this state for you? The stuff he can feed me is pure gold, little one, and it's gonna set me for life. There's nothing you have that can match that. Nothing."

He gestures again. "And I'm tired of you, and I'm tired of this crap. I'm going back home."

"Me too," I say, and I slide my hand into the cardigan, pull out my Beretta, and blow away Kelly's left knee.

Kelly is on the ground, howling, and the echo of the shot is still bouncing about the hills as I slam the Beretta into the side of Sutler's head. He falls, and I stride over to Kelly. Amid his thrashings on the now-bloody snow, I grab a .357 revolver from his coat and toss it into the woods. In a matter of heartbeats I'm back to Sutler, who's on the ground, fumbling to get into his ski jacket. I kick him solidly in the crotch. He yelps and then I'm on him, the barrel of the Beretta jamming into his lips until he gags and has a couple of inches of the oily metal in his mouth. His eyes are very wide and there's a splotch of blood on his left cheek. I take a series of deep breaths, knowing that I want my voice cool and calm.

"About sixty seconds ago I was interested in negotiating with you, but now I've lost interest. Do you understand? If you do, nod your head, but nod it real slow. It's cold and my fingers are beginning to get numb."

His eyes are tearing and he nods, just like I said. "Very good," I say, trying to place a soothing tone in my voice. "I came here in a good mood, in a mood to make a deal that could help us both, and all you've done since we've met is insult me. Do you think I got up early this morning and drove half the day so a creature like you can toss insults my way? Do you?"

Though I didn't explain to him the procedure for shaking his head, Sutler shows some initiative and gently shakes it. Kelly, some yards away, is still groaning and occasionally crying. I ignore him because I want to, and I think Sutler is ignoring him because he has to.

"Now," I continue. "If you had some random brain cells in that sponge between your ears, I think you would have figured out that because this matter involves my brother, I might have a personal interest in what was going on. But you were too stupid to realize that, correct?"

Another nod of the head, and saliva and blood is beginning to drip down the barrel of the Beretta. "So instead of accepting a very generous offer, you said no and insulted me. So you left me no choice. I had to show you how serious I was, and I had to make an impression."

I gesture over to the sobbing hulk of his companion. "Take a look at Kelly if you can. I don't know the man, I have nothing against him, and if the two of us had met under different circumstances, we might have become friends."

Well, I doubt that, but I keep my doubts to myself. I am making a point. "But I had to make an example," I continue, "and in doing so, I've just crippled Kelly for life. Do you understand that? His knee is shattered and he'll never walk well again for the next thirty or forty years of his life because of your ill manners and stubbornness. Now. You having rejected my offer, here's my counteroffer. Are you now interested?"

Another nod, a bit more forceful. "Good. Here it is. You forget the gambling debt. You forget you ever knew my brother, and you take poor Kelly here to a hospital and tell them that he was shot in a hunting accident or something. I don't care. And if you ever bother my brother or his family, any time in the future, I'll come back."

I poke the Beretta in another centimeter or two, and Sutler groans. "Then I'll find out who counts most in your life—your mother, your wife, your child, for all I know—and I'll do the same thing to them that I did to Kelly. Oh, I could make it permanent, but a year or two after the funeral, you usually get on with life. Not with this treatment. The person suffers in your presence, for decades to come, because of you. Now. Is the deal complete?"

Sutler closes his teary eyes and nods, and I get up, wiping the Beretta's barrel on his ski jacket. Sutler is grimacing and the crotch of his pants is wet and steaming in the cold. Kelly is curled up on his side, weeping, his left leg a bloody mess, and I take a step back and gently prod Sutler with my foot.

"Move your Bronco, will you?" I ask politely.

My brother's face is a mix of anger and hope as he climbs back into my Mercedes, rubbing his hands from the cold. His face and ears are quite red.

"Well?" he asks.

"Piece of cake," I say, and I drive back to the house.

Dinner is long and wonderful, and I have a sharp appetite and eat well, sitting at the far end of the table. My nieces good-naturedly fight over the supposed honor of sitting next to me, which makes Mother and Deena laugh, and even Brad attempts a smile or two. I stuff myself and we regale each other with stories of holidays and Christmases and Thanksgivings past, and Owen bounces Todd on his knee as Jan smiles to herself and sips from one glass of wine and then another.

I feel good belonging here with them. Though I know that none of them quite knows who I am or what I do, it's still a comfortable feeling. It's like nothing else I experience, ever, and I cherish it.

Later, I take a nap in my old bedroom, and feeling greasy from the day's exertions and the long meal, I take a quick shower, remembering a lot of days and weeks and years gone past as I climb into the tiny stall. It seems fairly humorous that I am in this house taking a weak and lukewarm shower after having remembered this creaky bathroom earlier this morning, back at my Manhattan home. That explains why I am smiling when I go back into my old bedroom, threadbare light green towel wrapped around my waist, and I find Jan there, waiting for me, my brother Owen's wife.

Her eyes are aglitter and her words are low and soft, but there's a hesitation there, as if she realizes she has been drinking for most of the day and she has to be careful in choosing each noun and verb. She's standing by an old bureau, jean-encased hip leaning up against the wood, and she has something in her hands.

"Look at this, will you," she says. "Found it up here while I was waiting for you."

I step closer and I can smell the alcohol on her breath, and I also smell something a bit earthier. I try not to sigh, seeing the eager expression on her face. I take her offering and turn it over. It's an old color photograph, and it shows a heavyset man with a beard and long hair in a ponytail sitting astride a black Harley-Davidson motorcycle. He's wearing the obligatory jeans and leather vest. His arms are tattooed. The photo is easily a decade old, and in those years the chemicals on the print have faded and mutated, so that there's an eerie yellow glow about everything, as if the photo were taken at a time when volcanic ash was drifting through the air.

I look closely at the photo and then hand it back to my sister-in-law. About the only thing I recognize about the person is the eyes, for it's the only thing about me that I've not changed since that picture was taken.

"That's really you, isn't it?" she asks, that eager tone in her voice still there. With her in my old room, everything seems crowded.

There's a tiny closet, the bureau, a night table, and lumpy bed with thin blankets and sheets. A window about the size of a pie plate looks out to the pale green vinyl siding of the house next door.

"Yes, that's me," I say. "Back when I was younger and dumber."

She licks her lips. "Asking questions about you of Owen is a waste of time, and your mother and Brad aren't much help either. You were a biker, right?"

I nod. "That's right."

"What was it like, Carl?" she asks, moving a few inches closer to me. I know I should feel embarrassed, standing in my old bedroom with my sister-in-law, just wearing a towel, but I'm not sure what I feel. I just know it's not embarrassment. So instead of debating the point, I answer her question.

"It was like moving to a different country and staying at home, all at the same time," I say. "There was an expression, something about being free and being a citizen. Being free meant the bike and your friends and whatever money you had for gas and food, and the time to travel anywhere you wanted, anytime, with no one to stop you, feeling the wind in your hair and face. Being a citizen meant death, staying at home, paying taxes, and working a forty-hour week. That's what it was like."

She gives me a sharp-toothed smile. "You almost make it sound like a Boy Scout troop. Way your older brother talks, I figure you've been in trouble."

I shrug. "Comes with the territory. It's something you get used to. Being free means you run into a lot of different people, and sometimes their tempers are short and their memories are long. Sometimes you do some work for some money that wouldn't look good on a job application form."

"So that explains the scars?" she asks.

"Yeah, I guess it does."

"So why did you change? What happened? From the picture, I can tell you've had your tattoos taken off."

I look around and see that my clothes are still on the bed where I left them. "I got tired of having my life depend on other people. Thing is, you run with a group, the group can sometimes pull you down. What the group accomplishes can come back at night and break your windows, or gnaw on your leg. And I didn't want to become a citizen. So I chose a bit of each world and made my own, and along the way I changed my look."

"And what do you do now? Everyone says consulting work, but they always have an uncomfortable look on their face when they mention that, like they have gas or something. So what's your job?"

I pause and say, "Systems engineer."

Her eyes blink in amusement. "A what?"

"Systems engineer. Sometimes a system needs an outside pressure or force to make a necessary change or adjustment. That's what I do. I'm an independent contractor."

"Sounds very exciting," she says, arching an eyebrow this time. "You should talk some to your younger brother. Maybe pass some of that excitement along. Or maybe you're the brother who got it all in this family."

I now feel an aching sorrow for Owen, and I try not to think of what their pillow talk must be like at night. "Guess you have to work with what you've got."

"Unh-hunh," she says. "Look, you must be getting cold. Are you going to get dressed, or what?"

I decide she wants a show, or wants something specific to happen, so I say, "Or what, I suppose." I turn to the bed and drop the towel and get dressed, and I hear a hush of breath coming from her. After the underwear, pants, and boots, I turn, buttoning my shirt, and she's even closer and I reach to her and she comes forward, lips wet, and then I strike out and put a hand around her throat. And I squeeze.

"Jan," I say, stepping forward and looking into her eyes, "you and I are about to come to an agreement, do you understand?"

"What are you doing, you—" and I squeeze again, and she makes a tiny yelping sound, and her nostrils begin to flare as she tries to breathe harder. She starts to flail with her hands and I grab one hand and press her against the bureau. It shakes and she tries to kick, but I'm pushing at her at an uncomfortable angle, and she can't move.

"This won't take long, but I ask that you don't yell. You try to yell and I'll squeeze hard enough to make you black out. Do you understand? Try blinking your eyes."

She blinks, tears forming in her eyes. My mind plays with a few words and then I say, "Owen and my family mean everything to me. Everything. And right now, by accident of marriage and the fact of my brother's love, you're part of this family. But not totally. My mother and Owen and even Brad come before you. You're not equal in my eyes, do you understand?"

She moves her head a bit, and I'm conscious that I might have to take another shower when I'm finished. "So that's where I'm coming from when I tell you this: I don't care if you love my brother or hate my brother, but I do demand this. That you show him respect. He deserves that. Stay with him or leave him tonight, I don't care. But don't toss yourself to those random men that manage to cross your path, especially ones related to him. If you can't stand being with him, leave, but do it with dignity. Show him respect or I'll hurt you, Jan."

"You're hurting me now," she whispers.

"No, I'm not," I explain. "I'm not hurting you. I'm getting your attention. In an hour you'll be just fine, but in a hundred years you're always going to remember this conversation in this dingy bedroom. Am I right?"

She nods and I say, "So we've reached an understanding. Agreed?"

Another nod and I let her go and back away, and Jan rubs at her throat and coughs. Then she whispers a dark series of curses and leaves, slamming the door behind her, and what scares me is that she isn't crying, not one tear, not one sign of regret or fear.

I finish getting dressed, trying not to think of Owen.

Despite a lumpy bed and too-silent surroundings of Boston Falls, I sleep fairly well that night, with none of those disturbing dreams of loud words and sharp actions that sometimes bring me awake. I get up with the sun and slowly walk through the living room to the kitchen. Sprawled across the carpeted floor in sleeping bags are my three nieces—Carey, Corinne, and Christine—and their shy innocence and the peacefulness of their slight breathing touches something inside of me that I wasn't sure even existed anymore.

Mother is in the kitchen and I give her a brief hug and grab a cup of coffee. I try not to grimace as I sip the brew; Mother, God bless her, has never made a decent cup of coffee in her life. I've been dressed since getting up and Mother is wearing a faded blue bathrobe, and as she stirs a half-dozen eggs in a mixing bowl she looks over at me through her thick glasses and says, "I'm not that dumb, you know."

I gamely try another sip of coffee. "I've always known that, ever since you found my collection of girlie magazines when I was in high school."

"Bah," she says, stirring the whisk harder. "I knew you had those for a while, and I knew boys always get curious at that age. I didn't mind much until your younger brother Owen was snooping around. Then I couldn't allow it. He was too young."

She throws in a bit of grated cheese and goes back to the bowl and says, "Are you all right, Carl?"

"Just fine."

"I wonder," she says. "Yesterday you were roaming around here like a panther at the zoo, and then you and Brad go off for a mysterious trip. You said it was just a friendly trip, but the two of you haven't been friends for years. You do something bad out there?"

I think about Kelly with the shattered leg and Bill Sutler with his equally ruined day, and I say, "Yeah, I suppose so."

Her voice is sharp. "Was it for Brad?"

Even Mother probably can see the surprise on my face, so I say, "Yes, it was for Brad."

"You hurt someone?"

I nod. "But he deserved it, Mom."

Then she puts down her utensils and wipes her hands on her apron and says, "That's what you do for a living, isn't it, Carl? You hurt people."

Right then I wish the coffee tasted better, for I could take a sip and gain a few seconds for a response, but Mother is looking right through me and I say, "You're absolutely right."

She sighs. "But yesterday was for Brad. And the money you send me, and the gifts for your nieces, and everything else, all comes from your job. Hurting people."

"That's right."

Mother goes back to the eggs, starts whisking again with the wire beater, and says, "I've known that for a very long time, ever since you claimed you quit being a biker. I just knew you went on to something different, something probably even worse, though you certainly dressed better and looked clean."

She looks over again. "Thank you for the truth, Carl. And I'll never ask you again, you can believe that. Just tell me that what you do is right, and that you're happy."

So I tell her what she wants to hear, and she gives me another hug, and then there's some noise as the kids get up.

And then after breakfast it's time to go, and though Jan hangs back and says nothing, the kids are all over me, as is Mother, and even Deena—Brad's wife—gives me a peck on the cheek. Owen shakes my hand and I tell him to call me, anytime, making sure that Jan has heard me. And then there's the surprise, as Brad shakes my hand for the first time in a very long year or five.

"Thanks," he says. "And, um, well, come by sometime. The girls do miss you."

With that one sentence playing in my mind, I drive for over an hour, not bothering with the music on my CD player, for I'm hearing louder music in my head.

Later that night I'm in my large sunken tub, a small metal pitcher of vodka martinis on the marble floor. Sarah is in the tub with me, suds up to her lovely and full chest, and her hair is drawn up around her head, making her look like a Gibson Girl from the turn of the century. I talk for some minutes and she laughs a few times and then reaches out with a wet and soapy foot and caresses my side. Like myself, she's holding a glass full of ice cubes and clear liquid.

"Only a guy like you, Carl, could travel hours to your family's home on a holiday weekend and bring your work with you," she says.

I sink a bit in the tub, feeling the hot water relax my back muscles. It had snowed some on the way back, and I'm still a bit tense from the drive.

"It wasn't work," I say. "It was a favor, a family thing."

"Mmmm," she says, sipping from her glass. "So that makes it all right?"

I shrug. "It just makes it, I guess."

"A worthwhile trip, then?"

"Very," I say, drinking from my own glass, enjoying the slightly oily bite of the drink. She sighs again and says, "You never really answered me, you know."

I close my eyes and say, "I didn't know I owed you an answer."

She nudges me with her foot. "Brute. From Thursday morning. When I asked you why you went there. And all you could say was family. Is that it, Carl? Truly?"

I know the true answer, which is that the little group of people in that tiny town are the only thing I have that is not bought or paid for in blood, and that keeping that little tie alive and well is important, very important to me. For if that tie were broken, then whatever passes for a human being in me would shrivel up and rot away, and I could not allow that. That is the truth, but I don't feel like debating philosophy tonight.

So I say, "Haven't you heard the expression?"

"What's that?"

I raise my drink to her in a toast. "Even the bad can do good."

Sarah makes a face and tosses the drink's contents at me, and then water starts slopping over onto the floor, and the lovely evening gets even lovelier, and there's no more talk of family and obligations, which is just fine.

Lucky Penny

by Linda Barnes

LIEUTENANT MOONEY MADE ME dish it all out for the record. He's a good cop, if such an animal exists. We used to work the same shift before I decided—wrongly—that there was room for a lady PI in this town. Who knows? With this case under my belt, maybe business'll take a 180-degree spin, and I can quit driving a hack.

See, I've already written the official report for Mooney and the cops, but the kind of stuff they wanted: date, place, and time, cold as ice and submitted in triplicate, doesn't even start to tell the tale. So I'm doing it over again, my way.

Don't worry, Mooney. I'm not gonna file this one.

The Thayler case was still splattered across the front page of the *Boston Globe.* I'd soaked it up with my midnight coffee and was puzzling it out—my cab on automatic pilot, my mind on crime—when the mad tea party began.

"Take your next right, sister. Then pull over, and douse the lights. Quick!"

I heard the bastard all right, but it must have taken me thirty seconds or so to react. Something hard rapped on the cab's dividing shield. I didn't bother turning around. I hate staring down gun barrels.

I said, "Jimmy Cagney, right? No, your voice is too high. Let me guess, don't tell me—"

"Shut up!"

"*Kill* the lights, *turn off* the lights, okay. But *douse* the lights? You've been tuning in too many old gangster flicks."

"I hate a mouthy broad," the guy snarled. I kid you not.

"Broad," I said. "Christ! *Broad?* You trying to grow hair on your balls?"

"Look, I mean it, lady!"

"Lady's better. Now you wanna vacate my cab and go rob a phone booth?" My heart was beating like a tin drum, but I didn't let my voice shake, and all the time I was gabbing at him, I kept trying to catch his face in the mirror. He must have been crouching way back on the passenger side. I couldn't see a damn thing.

"I want all your dough," he said.

Who can you trust? This guy was a spiffy dresser: charcoal gray three-piece suit and rep tie, no less. And picked up in front of the swank Copley Plaza. I looked like I needed the bucks more than he did, and I'm no charity case. A woman can make good tips driving a hack in Boston. Oh, she's gotta take precautions, all right. When you can't smell a disaster fare from thirty feet, it's time to quit. I pride myself on my judgment. I'm careful. I always know where the police checkpoints are, so I can roll my cab past and flash the old lights if a guy starts acting up. This dude fooled me cold.

I was ripped. Not only had I been conned, I had a considerable wad to give away. It was near the end of my shift, and like I said, I do all right. I've got a lot of regulars. Once you see me, you don't forget me—or my cab.

It's gorgeous. Part of my inheritance. A '59 Chevy, shiny as new, kept on blocks in a heated garage by the proverbial dotty old lady. It's the pits of the design world. Glossy blue with those giant chromium fins. Restrained decor: just the phone number and a few gilt curlicues on the door. I was afraid all my old pals at the police department would pull me over for minor traffic violations if I went whole hog and painted "CARLOTTA'S CAB" in ornate script on the hood. Some do it anyway.

So where the hell were all the cops now? Where are they when you need 'em?

He told me to shove the cash through that little hole they leave for the passenger to pass the fare forward. I told him he had it backwards. He didn't laugh. I shoved bills.

"Now the change," the guy said. Can you imagine the nerve?

I must have cast my eyes up to heaven. I do that a lot these days.

"I mean it." He rapped the plastic shield with the shiny barrel of his gun. I checked it out this time. Funny how big a little .22 looks when it's pointed just right.

I fished in my pockets for change, emptied them.

"Is that all?"

"You want the gold cap on my left front molar?" I said.

"Turn around," the guy barked. "Keep both hands on the steering wheel. High."

I heard jingling, then a quick intake of breath.

"Okay," the crook said, sounding happy as a clam, "I'm gonna take my leave—"

"Good. Don't call this cab again."

"Listen!" The gun tapped. "You cool it here for ten minutes. And I mean frozen. Don't twitch. Don't blow your nose. Then take off."

"Gee, thanks."

"Thank *you*," he said politely. The door slammed.

At times like that, you just feel ridiculous. You know the guy isn't going to hang around waiting to see whether you're big on insubordination. *But*, he might. And who wants to tangle with a .22 slug? I rate pretty high on insubordination. That's why I messed up as a cop. I figured I'd give him two minutes to get lost. Meantime I listened.

Not much traffic goes by those little streets on Beacon Hill at one o'clock on a Wednesday morn. Too residential. So I could hear the guy's footsteps tap along the pavement. About ten steps back, he stopped. Was he the one in a million who'd wait to see if I turned around? I heard a funny kind of whooshing noise. Not loud enough to make me jump, and anything much louder than the ticking of my watch would have put me through the roof. Then the footsteps patted on, straight back and out of hearing.

One minute more The only saving grace of the situation was the location: District One. That's Mooney's district. Nice guy to talk to.

I took a deep breath, hoping it would have an encore, and pivoted quickly, keeping my head low. Makes you feel stupid when you do that and there's no one around.

I got out and strolled to the corner, stuck my head around a building kind of cautiously. Nothing, of course.

I backtracked. Ten steps, then whoosh. Along the sidewalk stood one of those new "Keep Beacon Hill Beautiful" trash cans, the kind with the swinging lid. I gave it a shove as I passed. I could just as easily have kicked it; I was in that kind of funk.

Whoosh, it said, just as pretty as could be.

Breaking into one of those trash cans is probably tougher than busting into your local bank vault. Since I didn't even have a dime left to fiddle the screws on the lid, I was forced to deface city property. I got the damn thing open and dumped the contents on somebody's front lawn, smack in the middle of a circle of light from one of those ritzy Beacon Hill gas street lamps.

Halfway through the whiskey bottles, wadded napkins, and beer cans, I made my discovery. I was being thorough. If you're going to stink like garbage anyway, why leave anything untouched, right? So I was opening all the brown bags—you know, the good old brown lunch-and-bottle bags—looking for a clue. My most valuable find so far had been the moldy rind of a bologna sandwich. Then I hit it big: one neatly creased brown bag stuffed full of cash.

To say I was stunned is to entirely underestimate how I felt as I crouched there, knee-deep in garbage, my jaw hanging wide. I don't know what I'd expected to find. Maybe the guy's gloves. Or his hat, if he'd wanted to get rid of it fast in order to melt back into anonymity. I pawed through the rest of the debris fast. My change was gone.

I was so befuddled I left the trash right on the front lawn. There's probably still a warrant out for my arrest.

District One headquarters is off the beaten path, over on New Sudbury Street. I would have called first, if I'd had a dime.

One of the few things I'd enjoyed about being a cop was gabbing with Mooney. I like driving a cab better, but face it, most of my fares aren't scintillating conversationalists. The Red Sox and the weather usually covers it. Talking to Mooney was so much fun, I wouldn't even consider dating him. Lots of guys are good at sex, but conversation—now there's an art form.

Mooney, all six-foot-four, two-hundred-and-forty linebacker pounds of him, gave me the glad eye when I waltzed in. He hasn't given up trying. Keeps telling me he talks even better in bed.

"Nice hat," was all he said, his big fingers pecking at the typewriter keys.

I took it off and shook out my hair. I wear an old slouch cap when I drive to keep people from saying the inevitable. One jerk even misquoted Yeats at me: "Only God, my dear, could love you for yourself alone and not your long red hair." Since I'm seated when I drive, he missed the chance to ask me how the weather is up here. I'm six-one in my stocking feet and skinny enough to make every inch count twice. I've got a wide forehead, green eyes, and a pointy chin. If you want to be nice about my nose, you say it's got character.

Thirty's still hovering in my future. It's part of Mooney's past.

I told him I had a robbery to report and his dark eyes steered me to a chair. He leaned back and took a puff of one of his low-tar cigarettes. He can't quite give 'em up, but he feels guilty as hell about 'em.

When I got to the part about the bag in the trash, Mooney lost his sense of humor. He crushed a half-smoked butt in a crowded ashtray.

"Know why you never made it as a cop?" he said.

"Didn't brown-nose enough."

"You got no sense of proportion! Always going after crackpot stuff!"

"Christ, Mooney, aren't you interested? Some guy heists a cab, at gunpoint, then tosses the money. Aren't you the least bit *intrigued*?"

"I'm a cop, Ms. Carlyle. I've got to be more than intrigued. I've got murders, bank robberies, assaults—"

"Well, excuse me. I'm just a poor citizen reporting a crime. Trying to help—"

"Want to help, Carlotta? Go away." He stared at the sheet of paper in the typewriter and lit another cigarette. "Or dig me up something on the Thayler case."

"You working that sucker?"

"Wish to hell I wasn't."

I could see his point. It's tough enough trying to solve any murder, but when your victim is *the* Jennifer (Mrs. Justin) Thayler, wife of the famed Harvard Law prof, and the society reporters are breathing down your neck along with the usual crime-beat scribblers, you got a special kind of problem.

"So who did it?" I asked.

Mooney put his size twelves up on his desk. "Colonel Mustard in the library with the candlestick! How the hell do I know? Some scumbag housebreaker. The lady of the house interrupted his haul. Probably didn't mean to hit her that hard. He must have freaked when he saw all the blood, 'cause he left some of the ritziest stereo equipment this side of heaven, plus enough silverware to blind your average hophead. He snatched most of old man Thayler's goddamn idiot art works, collections, collectibles—whatever the hell you call 'em—which ought to set him up for the next few hundred years, if he's smart enough to get rid of them."

"Alarm system?"

"Yeah, they had one. Looks like Mrs. Thayler forgot to turn it on. According to the maid, she had a habit of forgetting just about anything after a martini or three."

"Think the maid's in on it?"

"Christ, Carlotta. There you go again. No witnesses. No fingerprints. Servants asleep. Husband asleep. We've got word out to all the fences here and in New York that we want this guy. The pawnbrokers know the stuff's hot. We're checking out known art thieves and shady museums—"

"Well, don't let me keep you from your serious business," I said, getting up to go. "I'll give you the collar when I find out who robbed my cab."

"Sure," he said. His fingers started playing with the typewriter again.

"Wanna bet on it?" Betting's an old custom with Mooney and me.

"I'm not gonna take the few piddling bucks you earn with that ridiculous car. "

"Right you are, boy. I'm gonna take the money the city pays you to be unimaginative! Fifty bucks I nail him within the week."

Mooney hates to be called "boy." He hates to be called "unimaginative." I hate to hear my car called ridiculous. We shook hands on the deal. Hard.

Chinatown's about the only chunk of Boston that's alive after midnight, I headed over to Yee Hong's for a bowl of won ton soup.

The service was the usual low-key, slow-motion routine. I used a newspaper as a shield; if you're really involved in the *Wall Street Journal*, the casual male may think twice before deciding he's the answer to your prayers. But I didn't read a single stock quote. I tugged at strands of my hair, a bad habit of mine. Why would somebody rob me and then toss the money away?

Solution Number One he didn't. The trash bin was some mob drop, and the money I'd found in the trash had absolutely nothing to do with the money filched from my cab. Except that it was the same amount—and that was too big a coincidence for me to swallow.

Two: the cash I'd found was counterfeit and this was a clever way of getting it into circulation. Nah. Too baroque, entirely. How the hell would the guy know I was the pawing-through-the-trash type? And if this stuff was counterfeit, the rest of the bills in my wallet were too.

Three: it was a training session. Some fool had used me to perfect his robbery technique. Couldn't he learn from TV like the rest of the crooks?

Four: it was a frat hazing. Robbing a hack at gunpoint isn't exactly in the same league as swallowing goldfish.

I closed my eyes.

My face came to a fortunate halt about an inch above a bowl of steaming broth. That's when I decided to pack it in and head for home. Won ton soup is lousy for the complexion.

I checked out the log I keep in the Chevy, totaled my fares. $4.82 missing, all in change. A very reasonable robbery.

By the time I got home, the sleepiness had passed. You know how it is: one moment you're yawning, the next your eyes won't close. Usually happens when my head hits the pillow; this time I didn't even make it that far. What woke me up was the idea that my robber hadn't meant to steal a thing. Maybe he'd left me something instead. You know, something hot, cleverly concealed. Something he could pick up in a few weeks, after things cooled off.

I went over that back seat with a vengeance, but I didn't find anything besides old Kleenex and bent paper clips. My brainstorm wasn't too clever after all. I mean, if the guy wanted to use my cab as a hiding place, why advertise by pulling a five-and-dime robbery?

I sat in the driver's seat, tugged my hair, and stewed. What did I have to go on? The memory of a nervous thief who talked like a B movie and stole only change. Maybe a mad tollbooth collector.

I live in a Cambridge dump. In any other city, I couldn't sell the damned thing if I wanted to. Here, I turn real-estate agents away daily. The key to my home's value is the fact that I can hoof it to Harvard Square in five minutes. It's a seller's market for tarpaper shacks within walking distance of the Square. Under a hundred thou only if the plumbing's outside.

It took me a while to get in the door. I've got about five locks on it. Neighborhood's popular with thieves as well as gentry. I'm neither. I inherited the house from my weird Aunt Bea, all paid for. I consider the property taxes my rent, and the rent's getting steeper all the time.

I slammed my log down on the dining room table. I've got rooms galore in that old house, rent a couple of them to Harvard students, I've got my own office on the second floor. But I do most of my work at the dining room table. I like the view of the refrigerator.

I started over from square one. I called Gloria. She's the late night dispatcher for the Independent Taxi Owners Association. I've never seen her, but her voice is as smooth as mink oil and I'll bet we get a lot of calls from guys who just want to hear her say she'll pick 'em up in five minutes.

"Gloria, it's Carlotta."

"Hi, babe. You been pretty popular today."

"Was I popular at one thirty-five this morning?"

"Huh?"

"I picked up a fare in front of the Copley Plaza at one thirty-five. Did you hand that one out to all comers or did you give it to me solo?"

"Just a sec." I could hear her charming the pants off some caller in the background. Then she got back to me.

"I just gave him to you, babe. He asked for the lady in the '59 Chevy. Not a lot of those on the road."

"Thanks, Gloria,"

"Trouble?" she asked.

"Is mah middle name," I twanged. We both laughed and I hung up before she got a chance to cross-examine me.

So. The robber wanted my cab. I wished I'd concentrated on his face instead of his snazzy clothes. Maybe it was somebody I knew, some jokester in mid-prank. I killed that idea; I don't know anybody who'd pull a stunt like that, at gunpoint and all. I don't want to know anybody like that.

Why rob my cab, then toss the dough.

I pondered sudden religious conversion. Discarded it. Maybe my robber was some perpetual screw-up who'd ditched the cash by mistake.

Or. . . . Maybe he got exactly what he wanted. Maybe he desperately desired my change.

Why?

Because my change was special, valuable beyond its $4.82 replacement cost.

So how would somebody know my change was valuable? Because he'd given it to me himself, earlier in the day.

"Not bad," I said out loud. "Not bad." It was the kind of reasoning they'd bounced me off the police force for, what my so-called "superiors" termed the "fevered product of an overimaginative mind."

I leapt at it because it was the only explanation I could think of. I do like life to make some sort of sense.

I pored over my log. I keep pretty good notes: where I pick up a fare, where I drop him, whether he's a hailer or a radio call.

First, I ruled out all the women. That made the task slightly less impossible. Sixteen suspects down from thirty-five, Then I yanked my hair and stared at the blank white porcelain of the refrigerator door. Got up and made myself a sandwich: ham, swiss cheese, salami, lettuce and tomato, on rye. Ate it. Stared at the porcelain some more until the suspects started coming into focus.

Five of the guys were just plain fat and one was decidedly on the hefty side; I'd felt like telling them all to walk. Might do them some good, might bring on a heart attack. I crossed them all out. Making a thin person look plump is hard enough; it's damn near impossible to make a fatty look thin.

Then I considered my regulars: Jonah Ashley, a tiny blond Southern gent; musclebound "just-call-me-Harold" at Longfellow Place; Dr. Homewood getting his daily ferry from Beth Israel to MGH; Marvin of the gay bars; and Professor Dickerman, Harvard's answer to Berkeley's sixties radicals.

I crossed them all off. I could see Dickerman holding up the First Filthy Capitalist Bank, or disobeying civilly at Seabrook, even blowing up an oil company or two. But my mind boggled at the thought of the great liberal Dickerman robbing some poor cabbie. It would be like Robin Hood joining the Sheriff of Nottingham on some particularly rotten peasant swindle. Then they'd both rape Maid Marian and go off pals together.

Dickerman was a lousy tipper. That ought to be a crime.

So what did I have? Eleven out of sixteen guys cleared without leaving my chair. Me and Sherlock Holmes, the famous armchair detectives.

I'm stubborn; that was one of my good cop traits. I stared at that log till my eyes bugged out. I remembered two of the five pretty easily; they were handsome and I'm far from blind. The first had one of those elegant bony faces and far-apart eyes. He was taller than my bandit. I'd ceased eyeballing him when I'd noticed the ring on his left hand; I never fuss with the married kind. The other one was built, a weight-lifter. Not an Arnold Schwarzenegger extremist, but built. I think I'd have noticed that bod on my bandit. Like I said, I'm not blind.

That left three.

Okay. I closed my eyes. Who had I picked up at the Hyatt on Memorial Drive? Yeah, that was the salesman guy, the one who looked so uncomfortable that I'd figured he'd been hoping to ask his cabbie for a few pointers concerning the best skirt-chasing areas in our fair city. Too low a voice. Too broad in the beam.

The log said I'd picked up a hailer in Kenmore Square when I'd let out the salesman. Ah yes, a talker. The weather, mostly. Don't you think it's dangerous for you to be driving a cab? Yeah, I remembered him, all right: a fatherly type, clasping a briefcase, heading to the financial district. Too old.

Down to one. I was exhausted but not the least bit sleepy. All I had to do was remember who I'd picked up on Beacon near Charles. A hailer. Before five o'clock which was fine by me because I wanted to be long gone before rush hour gridlocked the city. I'd gotten onto Storrow and taken him along the river into Newton Center. Dropped him off at the BayBank Middlesex, right before closing time. It was coming back. Little nervous guy. Pegged him as an accountant when I'd let him out at the bank. Measly, undernourished soul. Skinny as a rail, stooped, with pits left from teenage acne.

Shit. I let my head sink down onto the dining room table when I realized what I'd done. I'd ruled them all out, every one. So much for my brilliant deductive powers.

I retired to my bedroom, disgusted. Not only had I lost $4.82 in assorted alloy metals, I was going to lose fifty to Mooney. I stared at myself in the mirror, but what I was really seeing was the round hole at the end of a .22, held in a neat gloved hand.

Somehow, the gloves made me feel better. I'd remembered another detail about my piggybank robber. I consulted the mirror and kept the recall going. A hat. The guy wore a hat. Not like my cap, but like a hat out of a forties gangster flick. I had one of those: I'm a sucker for hats. I plunked it on my head, jamming my hair up underneath—and I drew in my breath sharply.

A shoulder-padded jacket, a slim build, a low slouched hat. Gloves. Boots with enough heel to click as he walked away. Voice? High.

Breathy, almost whispered. Not unpleasant. Accentless. No Boston "R."

I had a man's jacket and a couple of ties in my closet. Don't ask. They may have dated from as far back as my ex-husband, but not necessarily so. I slipped into the jacket, knotted the tie, tilted the hat down over one eye.

I'd have trouble pulling it off. I'm skinny, but my build is decidedly female. Still, I wondered—enough to traipse back downstairs, pull a chicken leg out of the fridge, go back to the log, and review the feminine possibilities. Good thing I did.

Everything clicked. One lady fit the bill exactly: mannish walk and clothes, tall for a woman. And I was in luck. While I'd picked her up in Harvard Square, I'd dropped her at a real address, a house in Brookline. 782 Mason Terrace, at the top of Corey Hill.

JoJo's garage opens at seven. That gave me a big two hours to sleep.

I took my beloved car in for some repair work it really didn't need yet and sweet-talked JoJo into giving me a loaner. I needed a hack, but not mine. Only trouble with that Chevy is it's too damn conspicuous.

I figured I'd lose way more than fifty bucks staking out Mason Terrace. I also figured it would be worth it to see old Mooney's face.

She was regular as clockwork, a dream to tail. Eight-thirty-seven every morning, she got a ride to the Square with a next-door neighbor. Took a cab home at five-fifteen. A working woman. Well, she couldn't make much of a living from robbing hacks and dumping the loot in the garbage.

I was damn curious by now. I knew as soon as I looked her over that she was the one, but she seemed so blah, so normal. She must have been five seven or eight, but the way she stooped, she didn't look tall. Her hair was long and brown with a lot of blonde in it, the kind of hair that would have been terrific loose and wild, like a horse's mane. She tied it back with a scarf. A brown scarf. She wore suits. Brown suits. She had a tiny nose, brown eyes under pale eyebrows, a sharp chin. I never saw her smile. Maybe what she needed was a shrink, not a session with Mooney. Maybe she'd done it for the excitement. God knows if I had her routine, her job, I'd probably be dressing up like King Kong and assaulting skyscrapers.

See, I followed her to work. It wasn't even tricky. She trudged the same path, went in the same entrance to Harvard Yard, probably walked the same number of steps every morning. Her name was Marcia Heidegger and she was a secretary in the admissions office of the College of Fine Arts.

I got friendly with one of her co-workers.

There was this guy typing away like mad at the desk in her office. I could just see him from the side window. He had grad student written all over his face. Longish wispy hair. Gold-rimmed glasses. Serious. Given to deep sighs and bright velour V-necks. Probably writing his thesis on "Courtly Love and the Theories of Chrétien de Troyes."

I latched onto him at Bailey's the day after I'd tracked Lady Heidegger to her Harvard lair.

Too bad Roger was so short. Most short guys find it hard to believe that I'm really trying to pick them up. They look for ulterior motives. Not the Napoleon type of short guy; he assumes I've been waiting years for a chance to dance with a guy who doesn't have to bend to stare down my cleavage. But Roger was no Napoleon. So I had to engineer things a little.

I got into line ahead of him and ordered, after long deliberation, a BLT on toast. While the guy made it up and shoved it on a plate with three measly potato chips and a sliver of pickle you could barely see, I searched through my wallet, opened my change purse, counted out silver, got to $1.60 on the last five pennies. The counterman sang out: "That'll be a buck eighty-five." I pawed through my pockets, found a nickel, two pennies. The line was growing restive. I concentrated on looking like a damsel in need of a knight, a tough task for a woman over six feet.

Roger (I didn't know he was Roger then) smiled ruefully and passed over a quarter. I was effusive in my thanks. I sat at a table for two, and when he'd gotten his tray (ham-and-cheese and a strawberry ice cream soda), I motioned him into my extra chair.

He was a sweetie. Sitting down, he forgot the difference in our height, and decided I might be someone he could talk to. I encouraged him. I hung shamelessly on his every word. A Harvard man, imagine that. We got around slowly, ever so slowly, to his work at the admissions office. He wanted to duck it and talk about more important issues, but I persisted. I'd been thinking about getting a job at Harvard, possibly in admissions. What kind of people did he work with? Where they congenial? What was the atmosphere like? Was it a big office? How many people? Men? Women? Any soul-mates? Readers? Or just, you know, office people?

According to him, every soul he worked with was brain dead.

I had to be more obvious. I interrupted a stream of complaint with, "Gee, I know somebody who works for Harvard. I wonder if you know her."

"It's a big place," he said, hoping to avoid the whole endless business.

"I met her at a party. Always meant to look her up." I searched through my bag, found a scrap of paper and pretended to read Marcia Heidegger's name off it.

"Marcia? Geez, I work with Marcia. Same office."

"Do you think she likes her work? I mean I got some strange vibes from her." I said I actually said "strange vibes" and he didn't laugh his head off. People in the Square say things like that and other people take them seriously.

His face got conspiratorial, of all things, and he leaned closer to me.

"You want it, I bet you could get Marcia's job."

"You mean it?" What a compliment—a place for me among the brain dead.

"She's gonna get fired if she doesn't snap out of it."

"Snap out of what?"

"It was bad enough working with her when she first came over. She's one of those crazy neat people, can't stand to see papers lying on a desktop, you know? She almost threw out the first chapter of my thesis!"

I made a suitable horrified noise and he went on.

"Well, you know, about Marcia, it's kind of tragic. She doesn't talk about it."

But he was dying to.

"Yes?" I said, as if he needed egging on.

He lowered his voice. "She used to work for Justin Thayler over at the law school, that guy in the news, whose wife got killed. You know, her work hasn't been worth shit since it happened. She's always on the phone, talking real soft, hanging up if anybody comes in the room. I mean, you'd think she was in love with the guy or something, the way she—"

I don t remember what I said. For all I know, I may have volunteered to type his thesis. But I got rid of him somehow and then I scooted around the corner of Church Street and found a pay phone and dialed Mooney.

"Don't tell me,' he said "Somebody mugged you but they only took your trading stamps."

"I have just one question for you, Moon."

"I accept. A June wedding, but I'll have to break it to Mother gently."

"Tell me what kind of junk Justin Thayler collected."

I could hear him breathing into the phone.

"Just tell me," I said, "for curiosity's sake."

"You onto something, Carlotta?"

"I'm curious, Mooney. And you're not the only source of information in the world."

"Thayler collected Roman stuff: Antiques. And I mean old. Artifacts, statues—"

"Coins?"

"Whole mess of them."

"Thanks."

"Carlotta—"

I never did find out what he was about to say because I hung up. Rude, I know. But I had things to do. And it was better Mooney shouldn't know what they were, because they came under the heading of illegal activities.

When I knocked at the front door of the Mason Terrace house at ten AM the next day, I was dressed in dark slacks, a white blouse, and my old police department hat. I looked very much like the guy who reads your gas meter. I've never heard of anyone being arrested for impersonating the gas man. I've never heard of anyone really giving the gas man a second look. He fades into the background and that's exactly what I wanted to do.

I knew Marcia Heidegger wouldn't be home for hours. Old Reliable had left for the Square at her usual time, precise to the minute. But I wasn't one hundred percent sure Marcia lived alone. Hence the gas man. I could knock on the door and check it out.

Those Brookline neighborhoods kill me. Act sneaky and the neighbors call the cops in twenty seconds, but walk right up to the front door, knock, talk to yourself while you're sticking a shim in the crack of the door, let yourself in, and nobody does a thing. Boldness is all.

The place wasn't bad. Three rooms, kitchen and bath, light and airy. Marcia was incredibly organized, obsessively neat, which meant I had to keep track of where everything was and put it back just so. There was no clutter in the woman's life. The smell of coffee and toast lingered, but if she'd eaten breakfast she'd already washed, dried, and put away the dishes. The morning paper had been read and tossed in the trash. The mail was sorted in one of those plastic accordion files. I mean she folded her underwear like origami.

Now coins are hard to look for. They're small; you can hide 'em anywhere. So this search took me one hell of a long time. Nine out of ten women hide things that are dear to them in the bedroom They keep their finest jewelry closest to the bed, sometimes in the nightstand, sometimes right under the mattress. That's where I started.

Marcia had a jewelry box on top of her dresser. I felt like hiding it for her. She had some nice stuff and a burglar could have made quite a haul with no effort.

The next favorite place for women to stash valuables is the kitchen. I sifted through her flour. I removed every Kellogg's Rice Krispie from the giant economy-sized box—and returned it. I went through her place like no burglar ever will. When I say thorough, I mean thorough.

I found four odd things. A neatly squared pile of clippings from the *Globe* and the *Herald*, all the articles about the Thayler killing. A manila envelope containing five different safe deposit box keys. A Tupperware container full of superstitious junk, good luck charms mostly, the kind of stuff I'd never have associated with a straight arrow like Marcia: rabbits' feet galore, a little leather bag on a string that looked like some kind of voodoo charm, a pendant in the shape of a cross surmounted by a hook, and, I swear to God, a pack of worn tarot cards. Oh yes, and a .22 automatic, looking a lot less threatening stuck in an ice cube tray. I took the bullets; the loaded gun threatened a defenseless box of Breyers' mint chocolate chip ice cream.

I left everything else just the way I'd found it and went home. And tugged my hair. And stewed. And brooded. And ate half the stuff in the refrigerator, I kid you not.

At about one in the morning, it all made blinding, crystal-clear sense.

The next afternoon, at five-fifteen, I made sure I was the cabbie who picked up Marcia Heidegger in Harvard Square. Now cab stands have the most rigid protocol since Queen Victoria; you do not grab a fare out of turn or your fellow cabbies are definitely not amused. There was nothing for it but bribing the ranks. This bet with Mooney was costing me plenty.

I got her. She swung open the door and gave the Mason Terrace number. I grunted, kept my face turned front, and took off.

Some people really watch where you're going in a cab, scared to death you'll take them a block out of their way and squeeze them for an extra nickel. Others just lean back and dream. She was a dreamer, thank God. I was almost at District One headquarters before she woke up.

"Excuse me," she said polite as ever. "That's Mason Terrace in *Brookline*."

"Take the next right, pull over and douse your lights," I said in a low Bogart voice. My imitation was not that good, but it got the point across. Her eyes widened and she made an instinctive grab for the door handle.

"Don't try it lady," I Bogied on. "You think I'm dumb enough to take you in alone? There s a cop car behind us, just waiting for you to make a move."

Her, hand froze. She was a sap for movie dialogue.

"Where's the cop?" was all she said on the way up to Mooney's office,

"What cop?"

"The one following us."

"You have touching faith in our law enforcement system," I said.

She tried a bolt, I kid you not. I've had experience with runners a lot trickier than Marcia. I grabbed her in approved cop hold number three and marched her into Mooney's office.

He actually stopped typing and raised an eyebrow, an expression of great shock for Mooney.

"Citizen's arrest," I said.

"Charges?"

"Petty theft. Commission of a felony using a firearm." I rattled off a few more charges, using the numbers I remembered from cop school.

"This woman is crazy," Marcia Heidegger said with all the dignity she could muster.

"Search her," I said. "Get a matron in here. I want my $4.82 back."

Mooney looked like he agreed with Marcia's opinion of my mental state. He said, "Wait up, Carlotta. You'd have to be able to identify that $4.82 as yours. Can you do that? Quarters are quarters. Dimes are dimes."

"One of the coins she took was quite unusual," I said. "I'm sure I'd be able to identify it."

"Do you have any objection to displaying the change in your purse?" Mooney said to Marcia. He got me mad the way he said it, like he was humoring an idiot.

"Of course not," old Marcia said, cool as a frozen daiquiri.

"That's because she's stashed it somewhere else, Mooney," I said patiently. "She used to keep it in her purse, see. But then she goofed. She handed it over to a cabbie in her change. She should have just let it go, but she panicked because it was worth a pile and she was just babysitting it for someone else. So when she got it back, she hid it somewhere. Like in her shoe. Didn't you ever carry your lucky penny in your shoe?"

"No," Mooney said. "Now, Miss—"

"Heidegger," I said clearly. "Marcia Heidegger. She used to work at Harvard Law School." I wanted to see if Mooney picked up on it, but he didn't. He went on: "This can be taken care of with a minimum of fuss. If you'll agree to be searched by—"

"I want to see my lawyer," she said.

"For $4.82?" he said. "It'll cost you more than that to get your lawyer up here."

"Do I get my phone call or not?"

Mooney shrugged wearily and wrote up the charge sheet. Called a cop to take her to the phone.

He got JoAnn, which was good. Under cover of our old-friend-long-time-no-see greetings, I whispered in her ear.

"You'll find it fifty well spent," I said to Mooney when we were alone.

"I don't think you can make it stick."

"We'll see, won't we?"

JoAnn came back, shoving Marcia slightly ahead of her. She plunked her prisoner down in one of Mooney's hard wooden chairs and turned to me, grinning from ear to ear.

"Got it?" I said. "Good for you."

"What's going on?" Mooney said.

"She got real clumsy on the way to the pay phone," JoAnn said. "Practically fell on the floor. Got up with her right hand clenched tight. When we got to the phone, I offered to drop her dime for her. She wanted to do it herself. I insisted and she got clumsy again. Somehow this coin got kicked clear across the floor."

She held it up. The coin could have been a dime, except the color was off: warm, rosy gold instead of dead silver. How I missed it the first time around I'll never know.

"What the hell is that?" Mooney said.

"What kind of coins were in Justin Thayler's collection?" I asked. Roman?„

Marcia jumped out of the chair, snapped her bag open and drew out her little .22. I kid you not. She was closest to Mooney and she just stepped up to him and rested it above his left ear. He swallowed, didn't say a word. I never realized how prominent his Adam's apple was. JoAnn froze, hand on her holster.

Good old reliable, methodical Marcia. Why, I said to myself, *why* pick today of all days to trot your gun out of the freezer? Did you read bad luck in your tarot cards? Then I had a truly rotten thought. What if she had two guns? What if the disarmed .22 was still staring down the mint chip ice cream?

"Give it back," Marcia said. She held out one hand, made an impatient waving motion.

"Hey, you don't need it, Marcia," I said. "You've got plenty more. In all those safe-deposit boxes."

"I'm going to count to five—" she began.

"Were you in on the murder from Day One? You know, from the planning stages?" I asked. I kept my voice low, but it echoed off the walls of Mooney's tiny office. The hum of everyday activity kept going in the main room. Nobody noticed the little gun in the well-dressed lady's hand. "Or did you just do your beau a favor and hide the loot after he iced his wife? In order to back up his burglary tale? I mean, if Justin Thayler really wanted to marry you, there is such a thing as divorce. Or was old Jennifer the one with the bucks?"

"I want that coin," she said softly. "Then I want the two of you"—she motioned to JoAnn and me—"to sit down facing that wall. If you yell, or do anything before I'm out of the building, I'll shoot this gentleman. He's coming with me."

"Come on, Marcia," I said, "put it down. I mean, look at you. A week ago you just wanted Thayler's coin back. You didn't want to rob my cab, right? You just didn't know how else to get your good luck charm back with no questions asked. You didn't do it for money, right? You did it for love. You were so straight you threw away the cash. Now here you are with a gun pointed at a cop—"

"Shut up!"

I took a deep breath and said, "You haven't got the style, Marcia. Your gun's not even loaded."

Mooney didn't relax a hair. Sometimes I think the guy hasn't ever believed a word I've said to him. But Marcia got shook. She pulled the barrel away from Mooney's skull and peered at it with a puzzled frown. JoAnn and I both tackled her before she got a chance to pull the trigger. I twisted the gun out of her hand. I was almost afraid to look inside.

Mooney stared at me and I felt my mouth go dry and a trickle of sweat worm its way down my back.

I looked.

No bullets. My heart stopped fibrillating, and Mooney actually cracked a smile in my direction.

So that's all. I sure hope Mooney will spread the word around that I helped him nail Thayler. And I think he will; he's a fair kind of guy. Maybe it'll get me a case or two. Driving a cab is hard on the backside, you know?

Dying in the Post-War World

by Max Allan Collins

1

L IFE WAS PRETTY MUCH PERFECT.
I had a brand-new brown-brick GI Bill bungalow in quietly
suburban Lincolnwood; Peggy, my wife since December of last year,
was ripely pregnant; I'd bribed a North Side car dealer into getting one
of the first new Plymouths; and I'd just moved the A-1 Detective
Agency into the prestigious old Rookery Building in the Loop.

True, business was a little slow—a good share of A-1's trade, over
the years, has been divorce work, and nobody was getting divorced
right now. It was July of 1947, and former soldiers and their blushing
brides were still fucking, not fighting, but that would come. I was
patient. In the meantime, there were plenty of credit checks to run.
People were spending dough, chasing after their post—war dreams.

Sunlight was filtering in through the sheer curtains of our little
bedroom, teasing my beautiful wife into wakefulness. I was already up
–it was a quarter to eight, and I tried to be in to work by nine (when
you're the boss, punctuality is optional). I was standing near the bed,
snugging my tie, when Peg looked up at me through slits.

"I put the coffee on," I said. "I can scramble you some eggs, if you
like. Fancier than that, you're your own."

"What time is it?" She sat up; the covers slid down the slope of her
tummy. Her swollen breasts poked at the gathered top of her
nightgown.

I told her the time, even though a clock was on the nightstand nearby.
She swallowed thickly. Blinked. Peg's skin was pale, translucent; a

faint trail of freckles decorated a pert nose. Her eyebrows were thick, her eyes big and violet. Without make-up, her dark brown curly locks a mess, seven months pregnant, first thing in the morning, she was gorgeous.

She, of course, didn't think so. She had told me repeatedly, for the last two months—when her pregnancy had begun to make itself blatantly obvious—that she looked hideous and bloated. Less than ten years ago, she'd been an artist's model; just a year ago, she'd been a smartly dressed young businesswoman. Now, she was a pregnant housewife, and not a happy one.

That was why I'd been making breakfast for the last several weeks.

Out in the hall, the phone rang.

"I'll get it," I said.

She nodded; she was sitting on the bed, easing her swollen feet into pink slippers, a task she was approaching with the care and precision of a bomb-squad guy removing a detonator.

I got it on the third ring. "This is Heller," I said.

"Nate . . . this is Bob."

I didn't recognize the voice, but I recognized the tone: desperation, with some despair mixed in.

"Bob . . . ?"

"Bob Keenan," the tremulous voice said.

"Oh! Bob." And I immediately wondered why Bob Keenan, who was just a passing acquaintance, would be calling me at home, first thing in the morning. Keenan was a friend and client of an attorney I did work for, and I'd had lunch with both of them, at Binyon's, around the corner from my old office on Van Buren, perhaps four times over the past six months. That was the extent of it.

"I hate to bother you at home . . . but something . . . something *awful*'s happened. You're the only person I could think of who can help me. Can you come, straight-away?"

"Bob, do you want to talk about this?"

"Not on the phone! Come right away. Please?"

That last word was a tortured cry for help.

I couldn't turn him down. Whatever was up, this guy was hurting. Besides which, Keenan was well off—he was one of the top administrators at the Office of Price Administration. So there might be some dough in it.

"Sure," I said. "I'll be right there."

He gave me the address of his home, and I wrote it down and hung up; went out in the kitchen, where Peg sat in her white terry cloth bathrobe, staring over her black coffee.

"Can you fix yourself something, honey?" I asked. "I'm going to have to skip breakfast."

Peg looked at me hollow-eyed.

"I want a divorce," she said.

I swallowed. "Well, maybe I do have time to fix you a little breakfast."

She looked at me hard. "I'm not kidding, Nate. I want a divorce."

I nodded. Sighed, and said, "We'll talk about it later."

She looked away. Sipped her coffee. "Let's do that," she said.

I slipped on my suit coat and went out into the bright, sunny day. Birds were chirping. From down the street came the gentle whir of a lawn mower. It would be hot later, but right now it was pleasant, even a little cool.

The dark blue Plymouth was at the curb and I went to it. Well, maybe this wasn't all bad: maybe this meant A-1's business would be picking up, now that divorce had finally come home from the war.

2

The house—mansion, really—had been once belonged to a guy named Murphy who invented the bed of the same name, one of which I had slept in many a night, back when my office and my apartment were one and the same. But the rectangular cream-color brick building, wearing its jaunty green hat of a roof, had long ago been turned into a two-family dwelling.

Nonetheless, it was an impressive residence, with a sloping lawn and a twin-pillared entrance, just a block from the lake on the far North Side. And the Keenan family had a whole floor to themselves, the first, with seven spacious rooms. Bob Keenan was doing all right, with his OPA position.

Only right now he wasn't doing so good.

He met me at the front door; in shirtsleeves, no tie, his fleshy face long and pale, eyes wide with worry. He was around forty years of age, but something, this morning, had added an immediate extra ten years.

"Thank you, Nate," he said, grasping my hand eagerly, "thank you for coming."

"Sure, Bob," I said.

He ushered me through the nicely but not lavishly furnished apartment like a guy with the flu showing a plumber where the busted toilet was.

"Look in here," he said, and he held his palm out. I entered what was clearly a child's room, a little girl's room. Pink floral wallpaper, a graceful tiny wooden bed, slippers on the rug nearby, sheer feminine curtains, a toy chest on which various dolls sat like sweetly obedient children.

I shrugged. "What . . . ?"

"This is JoAnn's room," he said, as if that explained it.

"Your little girl?"

He nodded. "The younger of my two girls. Jane's with her mother in the kitchen."

The bed was unmade; the window was open. Lake wind whispered in.

"Where's JoAnn, Bob?" I asked.

"Gone," he said. He swallowed thickly. "Look at this."

He walked to the window; pointed to a scrap of paper on the floor. I walked there, knelt. I did not pick up the greasy scrap of foolscap. I didn't have to, to read the crudely printed words there:

"Get $20,000 Ready & Waite for Word. Do Not Notify FBI or Police. Bills in 5's and 10's. Burn this for her safty!"

I stood and sucked in some air; hands on hips, I looked into Bob Keenan's wide, red, desperate eyes and said, "You haven't called the cops?"

"No. Or the FBI. I called you."

Sounding more irritable than I meant to, I said, "For Christ's sake, why?"

"The note said no police. I needed help. I may need an intermediary. I sure as hell need somebody who knows his way around this kind of thing."

I gestured with open, raised palms, like a mime making a wall. "Don't touch anything. Have you touched anything?"

"No. Not even the note."

"Good. Good." I put my hand on his shoulder. "Now, just take it easy, Bob. Let's go sit in the living room."

I walked him in there, hand never leaving his shoulder.

"Okay," I said gently, "why exactly did you call *me*?"

He was next to me on the couch, sitting slumped, staring downward, legs apart, hands clasped. He was a big man—not fat: big.

He shrugged. "I knew you worked on the Lindbergh case."

Yeah, and hadn't *that* worked out swell.

"I was a cop, then," I said. "I was the liaison between the Chicago PD and the New Jersey authorities. And that was a long time ago."

"Well, Ken mentioned it once."

"Did you call Ken before you called me? Did he suggest you call me?"

Ken was the attorney who was our mutual friend and business associate.

"No. Nate . . . to be quite frank with you, I called because, well . . . you're supposed to be connected."

I sighed. "I've had dealings with the Outfit from time to time, but I'm no gangster, Bob, and even if I was . . . "

"I didn't mean that! If you were a gangster, do you think I would have called you?"

"I'm not understanding this, Bob."

His wife, Norma, entered the room tentatively; she was a pretty petite woman in a floral print dress that was like a darker version of the wallpaper in her little girl's room. Her pleasant features were distorted; there was a wildness in her face. She hadn't cried yet. She was too upset.

I stood. If I'd ever felt more awkward, I couldn't remember when.

"Is everything all right, Bob? Is this your detective friend?"

"Yes. This is Nate Heller."

She came to me and gave me a skull-like smile. "Thank for you coming. Oh, thank you so much for coming. Can you help us?"

"Yes," I said. It was the only thing I could say.

Relief filled her chest and filtered up through her face; but her eyes remained wild.

"Please go sit with Jane," Bob said, patting her arm. He looked at me as if an explanation were necessary. "Jane and her little sister are so very close. She and JoAnn are only two years apart."

I nodded, and the wife went hurriedly away, as if rushing to make sure Jane were still there.

We sat back down.

"I know you've had dealings with the mob," Keenan said. "The problem is . . . so have I. Or actually, the problem is, I haven't."

"Pardon?"

He sighed and shook his head. "I only moved here six months ago. I'd been second-in-command in the New York office. In Albany."

"Of the OPA, you mean?"

"Yes," he said, nodding. "I guess I don't have to tell you the pressures a person in my position is under. We're in charge of everything from building and industrial materials to meat to gasoline to . . . well. Anyway. I didn't play ball with the mobsters out there. There were threats against me, against my family, but I didn't take their money. I asked for a transfer. I was sent here."

Chicago? That was a hell of a place to hide from mobsters.

He read the thought in my face.

"I know," he said, raising an eyebrow, "but I wasn't given a choice in the matter. Oddly, none of that type of people have contacted me here. But then, things are winding down . . . rationing's all but a thing of the past." He laughed mirthlessly. "That's the irony. The sad goddamn irony."

"What is?"

He was shaking his head. "The announcement will be made later this week: the OPA is out of business. They're shutting us down. I'm moving over to a Department of Agriculture position."

"I see." I let out another sigh; it was that kind of situation. "So, because the note said not to notify the authorities, and because you've had threats from gangsters before, you called me in."

I had my hands on my knees; he placed his hand over my nearest one, and squeezed. It was an earnest gesture, and embarrassed hell out of me.

"You've got to help us," he said.

"I will. I will. I'll be glad to serve as an intermediary, and I'll be glad to advise you and do whatever you think will be useful."

"Thank God," he said.

"But first we call the cops."

"What . . . ?"

"Are you a gambling man, Bob?"

"Well, yes, I suppose, in a small way, but not with my daughter's *life*, for God's sake!"

"I know what the odds are in a case like this. In a case like this, children are recovered unharmed more frequently when the police and FBI are brought in."

"But the note said . . . "

"How old is JoAnn?"

"She's six."

"That's old enough for her to be able to describe her kidnappers. That's old enough for her to pick them out of a line-up."

"I don't understand what you're saying."

"Bob." And now I reached over and clasped his hand. He looked at me with haunted, watery eyes. "Kidnapping's a federal offense, Bob. It's a capital crime."

He swallowed. "Then they'll probably kill her, won't they? If she isn't dead already."

"Your chances are better with the authorities in on it. We'll work it from both ends: negotiate with the kidnappers, even as the cops are beating the bushes trying to find the bastards. And JoAnn."

"If she's not already dead," he said.

I just looked at him. Then I nodded.

He began to weep.

I patted his back, gently. There there. There there.

3

The first cop to arrive was Detective Kruger from Summerdale District station; he was a stocky man in a rumpled suit with an equally rumpled face. His was the naturally mournful countenance of a hound. He looked a little more mournful than usual as he glanced around the child's bedroom.

Keenan was tagging along, pointing things out. "That window," Keenan said, "I only had it open maybe five inches, last night, to let in the breeze. But now it's wide open."

Kruger nodded, taking it all in.

"And the bed covers—JoAnn would never fold them back neatly like that."

Kruger looked at Keenan with eyes that were sharp in the folds of his face. "You heard nothin' unusual last night?"

Keenan flinched, almost as if embarrassed. "Well . . . my wife did."

"Could I speak to her?"

"Not just yet. Not just yet."

"Bob," I said, prompting him, trying not to intrude on Kruger but wanting to be of help, "what did Norma hear?"

"She heard the neighbor's dog barking—sometime after midnight. She sat up in bed, wide awake, thought she heard JoAnn's voice. Went to JoAnn's door, listened, didn't hear anything . . . and went back to bed."

Kruger nodded somberly.

"Please don't ask her about it," Keenan said. "She's blaming herself."

We all knew that was foolish of her; but we all also knew there was nothing to done about it.

The Scientific Crime Detection Laboratory team arrived, as did the photographer attached to Homicide, and soon the place was swarming with suits and ties. Kruger, who I knew a little, which was why I'd asked for him specifically when I called the Summerdale station, buttonholed me.

"Look, Heller," he said pleasantly, brushing something off the shoulder of my suit coat. "I know you're a good man, but there's people on the force who think you smell."

A long time ago, I had testified against a couple of crooked cops— crooked even by Chicago standards. By my standards, even. But cops, like crooks, weren't supposed to rat each other out; and even fifteen years later that put me on a lot of shit lists.

"I'll try to stay downwind," I said.

"Good idea. When the feds show, they're not going to relish havin' a private eye on the scene, either."

"I'm only here because Bob Keenan wants me."

"I think he needs you here," Kruger said, nodding, "for his peace of mind. Just stay on the sidelines."

I nodded back.

Kruger had turned to move on, when as an afterthought he looked back and said, "Hey, uh—sorry about your pal Drury. That's a goddamn shame."

I'd worked with Bill Drury on the pickpocket detail back in the early '30s; he was that rare Chicago animal: an honest cop. He also had an obsessive hatred for the Outfit which had gotten him in trouble. He was currently on suspension.

"Let that be a lesson to you," I said cheerfully. "That's what happens to cops who do their jobs."

Kruger shrugged and shambled off, to oversee the forensic boys.

The day was a long one. The FBI arrived in all their officious glory; but they were efficient, putting a tape recorder on the phone, in case a ransom call should come in. Reporters got wind of the kidnapping, but outside the boys in blue roped off the area and were keeping them out for now—a crime lab team was making plaster impressions of footprints and probable ladder indentations under the bedroom window.

A radio station crew was allowed to come in so Bob could record pleas to the kidnappers ("She's just a little girl . . . please don't hurt her . . . she was only wearing her pajamas, so wrap a blanket around her, please"). Beyond the fingerprinting and photos, the only real police work I witnessed was a brief interrogation of the maid of the family upstairs; a colored girl named Leona, she reported hearing JoAnn say, "I'm sleepy," around half past midnight. Leona's room was directly above the girl's.

Kruger came over and sat on the couch next to me, around lunch time. "Want to grab a bite somewhere, Heller?"

"Sure."

He drove me to a corner cafe four blocks away and we sat at the counter. "We found a ladder," he said. "In a back yard a few houses to the south of Keenan's."

"Yeah? Does it match the indentations in the ground?"

Kruger nodded.

"Any scratches on the bricks near the window?"

Kruger nodded again. "Matches those, too. Ladder was a little short."

The first floor window was seven and a half feet off the ground; the basement windows of the building were mostly exposed, in typical Chicago fashion.

"Funny thing," Kruger said. "Ladder had a broken rung."

"A broken rung? Jesus. Just like . . . " I cut myself off.

"Like the Lindbergh case," Kruger said. "You worked that, didn't you?"

"Yeah."

"They killed that kid, didn't they?"

"That's the story."

"This one's dead, too, isn't she?"

The waitress came and poured us coffee.

"Probably," I said.

"Keenan thinks maybe the Outfit's behind this," Kruger said.

"I know he does."

"What do you think, Heller?"

I laughed humorlessly. "Not in a million years. This is an amateur, and a stupid one."

"Oh?"

"Who else would risk the hot seat for twenty grand?"

He considered that briefly. "You know, Heller—Keenan's made some unpopular decisions on the OPA board."

"Not unpopular enough to warrant something like this."

"I suppose." He was sugaring his coffee—overdoing it, now that sugar wasn't so scarce. His hound-dog face studied the swirling coffee as his spoon churned it up. "How do you haul a kid out of her room in the middle of the night without causing a stir?"

"I can think of two ways."

"Yeah?"

"It was somebody who knew her, and she went willingly, trustingly."

"Yeah."

"Or," I said, "they killed her in bed, and carried her out like a sack of sugar."

Kruger swallowed thickly; then he raised his coffee and sipped. "Yeah," he said.

4

I left Kruger at the counter where he was working on a big slice of apple pie, and used a pay phone to call home.

"Nate," Peg said, before I'd had a chance to say anything, "don't you know that fellow Keenan? Robert Keenan?"

"Yes," I said.

"I just heard him on the radio," she said. Her voice sounded both urgent and upset. "His daughter . . . "

"I know," I said. "Bob Keenan is who called me this morning. He called me before he called the police."

There was a pause. Then: "Are you working on the case?"

"Yes. Sort of. The cops and the FBI, it's their baby." Poor choice of words. I moved ahead quickly: "But Bob wants me around. In case an intermediary is needed or something."

"Nate, you've got to help him. You've got to help him get his little girl back."

This morning was forgotten. No talk of divorce now. Just a pregnant mother frightened by the radio, wanting some reassurance from her man. Wanting him to tell her that this glorious post-war world really was a wonderful, safe place to bring a child into.

"I'll try, Peg. I'll try. Don't wait supper for me."

That afternoon, a pair of plainclothes men gave Kruger a sobering report. They stayed out of Keenan's ear-shot, but Kruger didn't seem to mind my eavesdropping.

They—and several dozen more plainclothes dicks—had been combing the neighborhood, talking to neighbors and specifically to the janitors of the many apartment buildings in the area. One of these janitors had found something disturbing in his basement laundry room.

"Blood smears in a laundry tub," a thin young detective told Kruger.

"And a storage locker that had been broken into," his older, but just as skinny partner said. "Some shopping bags scattered around—and some rags that were stained, too. Reddish-brown stains."

Kruger stared at the floor. "Let's get a forensic team over there."

The detectives nodded, and went off to do that.

Mrs. Keenan and ten-year-old Jane were upstairs, at the neighbors, through all of this; but Bob stayed right there, at the phone, waiting for it to ring. It didn't.

I stayed pretty close to him, though I circulated from time to time, picking up on what the detectives were saying. The mood was grim. I drank a lot of coffee, till I started feeling jumpy, then backed off.

Late afternoon, Kruger caught my eye and I went over to him.

"That basement with the laundry tubs," he said quietly. "In one of the drains, there were traces of blood, chips of bone, fragments of flesh, little clumps of hair."

"Oh God."

"I'm advising Chief of Detectives Storm to send teams out looking."

"Looking for what?"

"What do you think?"

"God."

"Heller, I want to get started right now. I can use you. Give Keenan some excuse."

I went over to Bob, who sat on the edge of a straightback chair by the phone stand. His glazed eyes were fixed on the phone.

"I'm going to run home for supper," I told him. "Little woman's in the family way, you know, and I got to check in with her or get in dutch. Can you hold down the fort?"

"Sure, Nate. Sure. You'll come back, though?"

I patted his shoulder. "I'll come right back."

Kruger and I paired up; half a dozen other teams, made up of plainclothes and uniformed men already at the scene, went out into the field as well. More were on the way. We were to look under every porch, behind every bush, in every basement, in every coal bin, trash can, any possible hiding place where a little body—or what was left of one—might be stowed.

"We'll check the sewers, too," Kruger said, as we walked down the sidewalk. It was dusk now; the streetlamps had just come on. Coolness off the lake helped you forget it was July. The city seemed washed in gray-blue, but night hadn't stolen away the clarity of day.

I kept lifting manhole covers and Kruger would cast the beam of his flashlight down inside, but we saw nothing but muck.

"Let's not forget the catch basins," I said.

"Good point."

We began checking those as well, and in the passageway between two brick apartment buildings directly across from the similar building that housed those bloody laundry tubs, the circular iron catch basin lid —like a manhole cover, but smaller—looked loose.

"Somebody opened that recently," Kruger said. His voice was quiet but the words were ominous in the stillness of the darkening night.

"We need something to pry it up a little," I said, kneeling. "Can't get my fingers under it."

"Here," Kruger said. He plucked the badge off the breast pocket of his jacket and, bending down, used the point of the star to pry the lid up to where I could wedge my fingers under it.

I slid the heavy iron cover away, and Kruger tossed the beam of the flashlight into the hole.

A face looked up at us.

A child's face, framed in blonde, muck-darkened hair.

"It looks like a doll," Kruger said. He sounded out of breath.

"That's no doll," I said, and backed away, knowing I'd done as my wife had requested: I'd found Bob Keenan's little girl.

Part of her, anyway.

We fished the little head out of the sewer; how exactly, I'd rather not go into. It involved the handle of a broom we borrowed from the janitor of one of the adjacent buildings.

Afterward, I leaned against the bricks in the alley-like passageway, my back turned away from what we'd found. Kruger tapped me on the shoulder.

"You all right, Heller?"

Uniformed men were guarding the head, which rested on some newspapers we'd spread out on the cement near the catch basin; they were staring down at it like it was some bizarre artifact of a primitive culture.

"About lost my lunch," I said.

"You're white as an Irishman's ass."

"I'm okay."

Kruger lighted up a cigarette; its amber eye glowed.

"Got another of those?" I asked.

"Sure." He got out a deck of Lucky Strikes. Shook one out for me. I took it hungrily and he thumbed a flame on his Zippo and lit me up. "Never saw you smoke before, Heller."

"Hardly ever do. I used to, overseas. Everybody did, over there."

"I bet. You were on Guadalcanal, I hear."

"Yeah."

"Pretty rough?"

"I thought so till tonight."

He nodded. "I made a call. Keenan's assistant, guy that runs the ration board, he's on his way. To make the ID. Can't put the father through that shit."

"You're thinking, Kruger," I said, sucking on the cigarette. "You're all right."

He grunted noncommittally and went over to greet various cops, uniform and plainclothes, who were arriving; I stayed off to one side, back to the brick wall, smoking my cigarette.

The janitor we'd borrowed the broom from sought me out. He was a thick-necked, white-haired guy in his early fifties; he wore coveralls over a flannel shirt rolled up at the sleeves.

"So sad," he said. His face was as German as his accent.

"What's on your mind, pop?"

"I saw something."

"Oh?"

"Maybe is not important."

I called Lieutenant Kruger over, to let him decide.

"About five this morning," the bull-necked janitor said, "I put out some trash. I see man in brown raincoat walking. His head, it was down, inside his collar, like it was cold outside, only it was not cold and not raining, either. He carry shopping bag."

Kruger and I exchanged sharp glances.

"Where did you see this man walking, exactly?" Kruger asked the janitor.

The stocky Kraut led us into the street; he pointed diagonally— right at the brick mansion where the Keenans lived. "He cut across that lawn, and walk west."

"What's your name, pop?" I asked.

"Otto. Otto Bergstrum."

Kruger gave Otto the janitor over to a pair of plainclothes dicks and they escorted him off to Summerdale District station to take a formal statement.

"Could be a break," Kruger said.

"Could be," I said.

Keenan's OPA co-worker, Walter Munsen, a heavy-set fellow in his late forties, was allowed through the wall of blue uniforms to look at the chubby-cheeked head on the spread-out papers. It looked up at him, its sweet face nicked with cuts, its neck a ragged thing. He said, "Sweet Jesus. That's her. That's little JoAnn."

That was good enough for Kruger.

We walked back to the Keenan place. A starless, moonless night had settled on the city, as if God wanted to blot out what man had done. It didn't work. The flashing red lights of squad cars, and the beams of cars belonging to the morbidly curious, fought the darkness. Reporters and neighbors infested the sidewalks in front of the Keenan place. Word of our grim discovery had spread—but not to Keenan himself.

At the front door, Kruger said, "I'd like you to break it to him, Heller."

"Me? Why the hell me?"

"You're his friend. You're who he called. He'll take it better from you."

"Bullshit. There's no 'better' *in* this."

But I did the deed.

We stood in one corner of the living room. Kruger was at my side, but I did the talking. Keenan's wife was still upstairs at the neighbors. I put a hand on his shoulder and said, "It's not good, Bob."

He already knew from my face. Still, he had to say: "Is she dead?" Then he answered his own question: "You've found her, and she's dead."

I nodded.

"Dear lord. Dear lord." He dropped to one knee, as if praying; but he wasn't.

I braced his shoulder. He seemed to want to get back on his feet, so I helped him do that.

He stood there with his head hung and said, "Let me tell JoAnn's mother myself."

"Bob—there's more."

"More? How can there be more?"

"I said it was bad. After she was killed, whoever did it disposed of her body by . . . " God! What words were there to say this? How do you cushion a goddamn fucking blow like this?

"Nate? What, Nate?"

"She was dismembered, Bob."

"Dismembered . . . ?"

Better me than some reporter. "I found her head in a sewer catch basin about a block from here."

He just looked at me, eyes white all around; shaking his head, trying to make sense of the words.

Then he turned and faced the wall; hands in his pockets.

"Don't tell Norma," he said, finally.

"We have to tell her," Kruger said, as kindly as he could. "She's going to hear soon enough."

He turned and looked at me; his face was streaked with tears. "I mean . . . don't tell her about . . . the . . . dismembering part."

"Somebody's got to tell her," Kruger insisted.

"Call their parish priest," I told Kruger, and he bobbed his dour hound-dog head.

The priest—Father O'Shea of St. Gertrude's church—arrived just as Mrs. Keenan was being ushered back into her apartment. Keenan took his wife by the arm and walked her to the sofa; she was looking at her silent husband's tragic countenance with alarm.

The priest, a little white-haired fellow with Bible and rosary in hand, said, "How strong is your faith, my child?"

Keenan was sitting next to her; he squeezed her hand, and she looked up with clear eyes, but her lips were trembling. "My faith is strong, father."

The priest paused, trying to find the words. I knew the feeling.

"Is she all right, father?" Norma Keenan asked. The last vestiges of hope clung to the question.

The priest shook his head no.

"Is . . . is she hurt?"

The priest shook his head no.

Norma Keenan knew what that meant. She stared at nothing for several long moments. Then she looked up again, but the eyes were cloudy now. "Did they . . . " She began again. "Was she . . . disfigured?"

The priest swallowed.

I said, "No she wasn't, Mrs. Keenan."

Somebody had to have the decency to lie to the woman.

"Thank God," Norma Keenan said. "Thank God."

She began to sob, and her husband hugged her desperately.

6

Just before ten that night, a plainclothes team found JoAnn's left leg in another catch basin. Less than half an hour later, the same team checked a manhole nearby and found her right leg in a shopping bag.

Not long after, the torso turned up—in a sewer gutter, bundled in a fifty-pound cloth sugar bag.

Word of these discoveries rocketed back to the Keenan apartment, which had begun to fill with mucky-mucks—the Police Commissioner, the Chief of Detectives and his Deputy Chief, the head of the homicide detail, the Coroner and, briefly, the Mayor. The State's Attorney and his right-hand investigator Captain Daniel "Tubbo" Gilbert came and stayed.

The big shots showing didn't surprise me, with a headline-bound crime like this. But the arrival of Tubbo Gilbert, who was Outfit all the way, was unsettling—considering Bob Keenan's early concerns about mob involvement.

"Heller," well-dressed Tubbo said amiably, "what rock did you crawl out from under?"

Tubbo looked exactly like his name sounded.

"Excuse me," I said, and brushed past him.

It was time for me to fade.

I went to Bob to say my goodbyes. He was seated on the couch, talking to several FBI men; his wife was upstairs, at the neighbors again, under sedation.

"Nate," Keenan said, standing, patting the air with one hand, his bloodshot eyes beseeching me, "before you go . . . I need a word. Please."

"Sure."

We ducked into the bathroom. He shut the door. My eyes caught a child's yellow rubber duck on the edge of the claw-footed tub.

"I want you to stay on the job," Keenan said.

"Bob, every cop in town is going to be on this case. The last thing you need, or they want, is a private detective in the way."

"Did you see who was out there?"

"A lot of people. Some very good people, mostly."

"That fellow Tubbo Gilbert. I know about him. I was warned about him. They call him 'the Richest Cop in Chicago,' don't they?"

"That's true." And that was saying something, in Chicago.

Keenan's eyes narrowed. "He's in with the gangsters."

"He's in with a lot of people, Bob, but . . . "

"I'll write you a check . . . " And he withdrew a checkbook from his pants pocket and knelt at the toilet and began filling a check out, frantically, using the lid as a writing table.

This was as embarrassing as it was sad. "Bob . . . please don't do this . . . "

He stood and handed me a check for one thousand dollars. The ink glistened wetly.

"It's a retainer," he said. "All I want from you is to keep an eye on the case. Keep these Chicago cops honest."

That was a contradiction of terms, but I let it pass.

"Okay," I said, and folded the check up and slipped it in my pocket, smearing the ink probably. I didn't think I'd be keeping it, but the best thing to do right now was just take it.

He pumped my hand and his smile was an awful thing. "Thank you, Nate. God bless you, Nate. Thank you for everything, Nate."

We exited the bathroom and everybody eyed us strangely, as if wondering if we were perverts. Many of these cops didn't like me much, and were glad to see me go.

Outside, several reporters recognized me and called out. I ignored them as I moved toward my parked Plymouth; I hoped I wasn't blocked in. Hal Davis of the *News*, a small man with a big head, bright-eyed and boyish despite his fifty-some years, tagged along.

"You want to make an easy C-note?" Davis said.

"Why I'm fine, Hal. How are you?"

"I hear you were the one that fished the kid's noggin outta the shit soup."

"That's touching, Hal. Sometimes I wonder why you haven't won a Pulitzer yet, with your way with words."

"I want the exclusive interview."

I walked faster. "Fuck you."

"Two C's."

I stopped. "Five."

"Christ! Success has gone to your head, Heller."

"I might do better elsewhere. What's the hell's that all about?"

In the alley behind the Keenan house, some cops were holding reporters back while a crime-scene photographer faced a wooden fence, flashbulbs popping, making little explosions in the night.

"Damned if I know," Davis said, and was right behind me as I moved quickly closer.

The cops kept us back, but we could see it, all right. Written on the fence, in crude red lettering, were the words: "Stop me before I kill more."

"Jesus Christ," Davis said, all banjo-eyed. "Is *that* who did this? The goddamn *lipstick* killer?"

"The lipstick killer," I repeated numbly.

Was that who did this?

7

The Lipstick Killer, as the press had termed him, had hit the headlines for the first time last January.

Mrs. Caroline Williams, an attractive forty-year-old widow with a somewhat shady past, was found nude and dead in bed in her modest North Side apartment. A red skirt and a nylon stocking were tied tightly around the throat of the voluptuous brunette corpse. There had been a struggle, apparently—the room was topsy-turvy. Mrs. Williams had been beaten, her face bruised, battered.

She'd bled to death from a slashed throat, and the bed was soaked red; but she was oddly clean. Underneath the tightly tied red dress and nylon, the coroner found an adhesive bandage over the neck wound.

The tub in the bathroom was filled with bloody water and the victim's clothing, as if wash were soaking.

A suspect—an armed robber who was the widow's latest gentlemen friend—was promptly cleared. Caroline Williams had been married three times, leaving two divorced husbands and one dead one. Her ex-husbands had unshakable alibis, particularly the latter.

The case faded from the papers, and dead-ended for the cops.

Then just a little over a month ago, a similar crime—apparently, even obviously, committed by the same hand—had rattled the city's cage. Mrs. Williams, who'd gotten around after all, had seemed the victim of a crime of passion. But when Margaret Johnson met a disturbingly similar fate, Chicago knew it had a madman at large.

Margaret Johnson—her friends called her Peggy (my wife's nickname)—was twenty-nine years old and a beauty. A well-liked, church-going, small-town girl, she'd just completed three years of war service with the Waves to go to work in the office of a business-machine company in the Loop. She was found nude and dead in her small flat in a North Side residential hotel.

When a hotel maid found her, Miss Johnson was slumped, kneeling, at the bathtub, head over the tub. Her hair was wrapped turban-like in a towel, her pajama top tied loosely around her neck, through which a bread knife had been driven with enough force to go in one side and poke out the other.

She'd also been shot—once in the head, again in the arm. Her palms were cut, presumably from trying to wrest the knife from the killer's hand.

The blood had been washed from the ex-Wave's body. Damp, bloody towels were scattered about the bathroom floor. The outer room of the small apartment was a shambles, blood-stains everywhere. Most significantly, fairly high up on the wall, in letters three to six inches tall, printed in red with the victim's lipstick, were the words:

> For heavens
> Sake catch me
> Before I Kill More
> I cannot control myself.

The cops and the papers called the Lipstick Killer (the nickname was immediate) a "sex maniac," though neither woman had been raped. The certainty of the police in that characterization made me suspicious that something meaningful had been withheld.

I had asked Lieutenant Bill Drury, who before his suspension had worked the case out of Town Hall station, and he said semen had been found on the floor in both apartments, near the windows that had apparently given the killer entry in either flat.

What we had here was a guy who needed one hell of a visual aid to jack off.

What these two slain women had in common with the poor butchered little JoAnn Keenan, I wasn't sure, other than violent death at the hands of a madman with something sharp; the body parts of the child were largely drained of blood. That was about it.

But the lipstick message on that alley fence—even down to the child-like lettering—would serve to fuel the fires of this investigation even further. The papers had already been calling the Lipstick Killer "Chicago's Jack the Ripper." With the slaying of the kidnapped girl, the city would undoubtedly go off the deep end.

"The papers have been riding the cops for months," I told my Peg that night, as we cuddled in bed; she was trembling in the hollow of my arm. "Calling them Keystone Kops, ridiculing the ineffectiveness of their crime lab work. And their failure to nab the Lipstick Killer has been a club the papers've beat 'em with."

"You sound like you think that's unfair," Peg said.

"I do, actually. A lunatic can be a lot harder to catch than a career criminal. And this guy's MO is all over the map."

"MO?"

"The way he does his crimes, the kind of crimes he does. Even the two women he killed, there are significant differences. The second was shot, and that, despite the knife through the throat, was the cause of death. Is it okay if I talk about this?"

She nodded. She was a tough cookie.

"Anyway," I went on, "the guy hasn't left a single workable fingerprint."

"Cleans up after himself," she said.

"Half fetish," I said, "half cautious."

"Completely nuts."

"Completely nuts," I agreed. I smiled at her. It was dark in the bedroom, but I could see her sweet face, staring into nothing.

Quietly, she said, "You told your friend Bob Keenan that you'd stay on the job."

"Yeah. I was just pacifying him."

"You *should* stay on it."

"I don't know if I can. The cops, hell the feds, they're not exactly going to line up for my help."

"Since when does that kind of thing stop you? Keep on it. You've got to find this fiend." She took my hand and placed it on her full tummy. "Got to."

"Sure, Peg. Sure."

I gave her tummy the same sort of "there there" pat I'd given Bob Keenan's shoulder. And I felt a strange, sick gratefulness to the Lipstick Killer, suddenly: the day had begun with my wife asking for a divorce.

It had ended with me holding her, comforting her.

In this glorious post-war world, I'd take what I could get.

8

Two days later, I was treating my friend Bill Drury to lunch in the bustling Loop landmark of a restaurant, the Berghoff.

Waiters in tuxes, steaming platters of food lifted high, threaded around tables like runners on some absurd obstacle course. The patrons—mostly businessmen, though a few lady shoppers and matinee-goers were mixed in—created a din of conversation and clinking tableware that made every conversation in this wide-open space a private one.

Bill liked to eat, and had accepted my invitation eagerly, even though it had meant driving in from his home on the North Side. Even out of work, he was nattily dressed—dark blue vested suit with wide orange tie with a jeweled stickpin. His jaw jutted, his eyes were dark and sharp, his shoulders broad, his carriage intimidating. Only a pouchiness under his eyes and a touch of gray in his dark thinning hair revealed the stress of recent months.

"I'm goddamn glad you beat the indictment," I said.

He shrugged, buttered up a slice of rye; our Wiener Schnitzel was on the way. "There's still this Grand Jury thing to deal with."

"You'll beat it," I said, but I wasn't so sure. Bill had, in his zeal to nail certain Outfit guys, paid at least one witness to testify. I'd been there when the deal was struck.

"In the meantime," he said cheerfully, "I sit twiddling my thumbs at the old homestead, making the little woman nervous with my unemployed presence."

"You want to do a little work for A-1?"

He shook his head, frowned regretfully. "I'm still a cop, Nate, suspended or not."

"It'd be just between us girls. You still got friends at Town Hall station, don't you?"

"Of course."

A waiter old enough to be our father, and looking stern enough to want to spank us, delivered our steaming platters of veal and German fried potatoes and red cabbage.

"I'm working the Keenan case," I said, sipping my beer.

"Still? I figured you'd have dropped out by now." He snorted a laugh. "My brother says you picked up a pretty penny for that interview."

His brother John worked for the *News*.

"Davis met my price," I shrugged. "Look, Bob Keenan seems to want me aboard. Makes him feel better. Anyway, I just intend to work the fringes."

He was giving me his detective look. "That ten grand reward the *Trib* posted wouldn't have anything to do with your decision to stick, would it?"

I smiled and cut my veal. "Maybe. You interested?"

"What can *I* do?"

"First of all, you can clue me in if any of your cop buddies over at Town Hall see any political strings being pulled, or any Outfit strings, either."

He nodded and shrugged, as he chewed; that meant yes.

"Second, you worked the Lipstick killings."

"But I got yanked off, in the middle of the second."

"So play some catch-up ball. Go talk to your buddies. Sort through the files. See if something's slipped through the cracks."

His expression was skeptical. "Every cop in town is on this thing, like ugly on a monkey. What makes you think either one of us can find something *they'd* miss?"

"Bill," I said pleasantly, eating my red cabbage, "we're better detectives than they are."

"True," he said. He cut some more veal. "Anyway, I think they're going down the wrong road."

"Yeah?"

He shrugged a little. "They're focusing on sex offenders; violent criminals. But look at the MO. What do you make of it? Who would *you* look for, Nate?"

I'd thought about that a lot. I had an answer ready: "A second-story man. A cat burglar who wasn't stealing for the dough he could find, or the goods he could fence, not primarily. But for the kicks."

Drury looked at me with shrewd, narrowed eyes. "For the kicks. Exactly."

"Maybe a kid. A JD, or a JD who's getting just a little older, into his twenties maybe."

"Why do you say that?"

"Thrill-seeking is a young at heart kind of thing, Bill. And getting in the Johnson woman's apartment took crawling onto a narrow ledge from a fire-escape. Took some pretty tricky, almost acrobatic skills. And some recklessness."

He held up his knife. "Plus, it takes strength to jam a bread knife through a woman's neck."

"I'll have to take your word for that. But it does add up to somebody on the young side."

He pointed the knife at me. "I was developing a list of just that kind of suspect . . . only I got pulled off before I could follow up."

I'd hoped for something like this.

"Where's that list now?"

"In my field notes," Drury said. "But let me stop by Town Hall, and nose around a little. Before I give you anything. You want me to check around at Summerdale station, too? I got pals there."

"No," I said. "I already got Kruger, there. He's going to keep me in the know."

"Kruger's okay," Drury said, nodding. "But why's he cooperating with you, Nate?"

The fried potatoes were crisp and salty and fine, but I wished I'd asked for gravy. "That reward the *Trib*'s promising. Cops aren't eligible to cash in."

"Ah," Drury said, and drank some dark beer. "Which applies to me, as well."

"Sure. But that's no problem."

"I'm an honest cop, Nate."

"As honest as they come in this town. But you're human. We'll work something out, Bill, you and me."

"We'll start," Bill said, pushing his plate aside, grinning like a goof, "with dessert."

9

That night I stopped in at the funeral home on East Erie. Peg wasn't up to it—felt funny about it, since she'd never met the Keenans; so I went alone. A cop was posted to keep curiosity seekers out, but few made the attempt—the war might have been over, but the memory of personal sorrows was fresh.

The little girl lay dressed in white satin with pink flowers at her breast; you couldn't see the nicks on her face—she was even smiling, faintly. She looked sweetly asleep. She was arranged so that you couldn't tell the arms were still missing.

Norma Keenan had been told, of course, what exactly had happened to her little girl. My compassionate lie had only lessened her sorrow for that first night. Unbelievably, it had gotten worse: the coroner had announced, this afternoon, that there had been "attempted rape."

The parents wore severe black and, while family and friends stood chatting *sotto voce*, were seated to one side. Neither was crying. It wasn't that they were bearing up well: it was shock.

"Thanks for coming, Nate," Bob said, rising, and squeezed my hand. "Will you come to the Mass tomorrow?"

"Sure," I said. It had been a long time since I'd been to Mass; my mother had been Catholic, but she died when I was young.

At St. Gertrude's the next morning, it turned out not to be a Requiem Mass, but the Mass of the Angels, as sung by the one hundred tender voices of the children's choir. "A song of welcome," the priest said, "admitting another to sing before the throne of God."

JoAnn had belonged to this choir; last Christmas, she'd played an angel in the Sacred Heart school pageant.

Now she was an armless corpse in a casket at the altar rail; even the beauty of the children's voices and faces, even the long, tapering white candles that cast a flickery golden glow on the little white coffin, couldn't erase that from my mind. When the priest reminded those in attendance that "there is no room for vengeance in our hearts," I bit my tongue. *Speak for yourself, padre.*

People wept openly, men and women alike, many hugging their own children. Some thirteen hundred had turned out for the Mass; a detail of policemen protected the Keenans as they exited the church. The crowd, however, was well-behaved.

And only a handful of us were at the cemetery. The afternoon was overcast, unseasonably chilly, and the wind coursed through All Saint's like a guilty conscience. After a last blessing of holy water from the priest, the little white casket was lowered into a tiny grave protected by a solitary maple. Flowers banking the grave fluttered and danced in the breeze.

I didn't allow myself to cry, not at first. I told myself Keenan was an acquaintance, not a friend; I reminded myself that I had never met the little girl—not before I fished her head out of a goddamn sewer, anyway. I held back the tears, and was a man.

It wasn't till I got home that night, and saw my pregnant wife, that it hit me; knocked the slats right out from under me.

Then I found myself sitting on the couch, crying like a baby, and this time she was comforting me.

It didn't last long, but when it stopped, I came to a strange and disturbing realization: everything I'd been through in this life, from close calls as a cop to fighting Japs in the Pacific, hadn't prepared me for fear like this. For the terror of being a parent. Of knowing something on the planet was so precious to you the very thought of losing it invited madness.

"You're going to help your friend," Peg said. "You're going to get whoever did this."

"I'm going to try, baby," I said, rubbing the wetness away with the knuckles of one hand. "Hell, the combined rewards are up to thirty-six grand."

10

The next day, however, I did little on the Keenan case. I did check in with both Kruger and Drury, neither of whom had much for me—nothing that the papers hadn't already told me.

Two janitors had been questioned, and considered suspects, briefly. One of them was the old Kraut we'd borrowed the broomstick from—Otto Bergstrum. The other was an Army vet in his early twenties named James Watson, who was the handyman for the nursery from which the kidnap ladder had been stolen. Watson was a prime suspect because, as a juvenile offender, he'd been arrested for molesting an eight-year-old girl.

That long-ago charge had been knocked down to disorderly conduct, however, and meanwhile, back in the present, both

Bergstrum and Watson had alibis. Also, they both passed lie-detector tests.

"It doesn't look like there's any significance," Kruger told me on the phone, "to that locker the killer broke into."

"In the so-called 'murder cellar,' you mean?"

"Yeah. Kidnapper stole rags and shopping bags out of it. The guy's clean, whose locker that is."

"Any good prints turn up?"

"No. Not in the murder cellar, or the girl's room. We had two on the window that turned out to be the cleaning lady. We do have a crummy partial off the kidnap note. And we have some picture-frame wire, a loop of it, we found in an alley near the Keenan house; might've been used to strangle the girl. The coroner says she was dead before she was cut up."

"Thank God for that much."

"We have a couple of odd auto sightings, near the Keenan house, in the night and early morning. We're looking into that."

"A car makes sense," I said. "Otherwise, you'd think somebody would've spotted this maniac hand-carrying the body from the Keenans over to that basement."

"I agree. But it was the middle of the night. Time of death, after all, was between one-thirty and two AM."

Kruger said he'd keep me posted, and that had been that, for me and the Keenan case, on that particular day.

With one rather major exception.

I was about to get into my Plymouth, in a parking garage near the Rookery, when a dark blue 1946 Mercury slid up and blocked me in.

Before I had the chance to complain, the driver looked out at me and grinned. "Let's take a spin, Heller."

He was a thin-faced, long-chinned, beak-nosed, gray-complected guy about forty; he wasn't big, but his presence was commanding. His name was Sam Flood, and he was a fast-rising Outfit guy, currently Tony Accardo's chauffeur/bodyguard. He was also called "Mooney," which was West Side street slang for nuts.

"A 'spin,' Sam—or a 'ride'?"

Sam laughed. "Come on, Heller. I got a proposition for you. Since when do you turn your nose up at dough?"

I wasn't armed, but it was cinch Flood was. Flood was a West Side boy, like me, only I grew up around Maxwell Street while he was from the Near West Side's notorious "Patch," and a veteran of the infamous street gang, the 42's.

"Let's talk right here, Sam," I said. "Nobody's around."

He thought about that; his dark eyes glittered. He pretended to like me, but I knew he didn't. He hated all cops, including ex-cops. And my status with the Outfit largely had to do with my one-time friendship with the late Frank Nitti, whom Sam had no particular respect for. Sam was, after all, a protégé of Paul Ricca, who had forced Nitti out.

"Okay," Sam said. He spoke softly, and almost haltingly. "I'm gonna park it right over there in that space. You come sit and talk. Nothing bad's gonna happen to you in my own fuckin' car."

So we sat and talked.

Sam, wearing a dark well-tailored suit and a Kelly-green snapbrim, half-turned to look at me. "You know who speaks well of you?"

"Who?"

"Louie Campagna." He thumbed his chest. "I kept an eye on his missus for him while he was in stir on the movie-union rap."

"Louie's all right," I said politely. Campagna had been Nitti's right arm; for some reason, Sam wanted to reassure me that we were pals. Or at least, had mutual pals. Back in '44, I'd encountered Sam for the first time when Outfit treasurer Jake Guzik got kidnapped and I was pulled in as a neutral go-between. From that experience I had learned Sam "Mooney" Flood was one ruthless fucker, and as manipulative as a carnival barker.

"You're on this Keenan case," he said.

That would've tensed me right there, only I was already wound tight.

"Yeah," I said casually. "Not in a big way. The father's a friend, and he wants somebody to keep the cops honest."

That made him laugh. Whether it was the idea of *me* keeping somebody honest, or anybody keeping the cops honest, he didn't say.

I decided to test the waters. "You know why Keenan called me in, don't you?"

"No," Sam said. It seemed a genuine enough response.

"He was afraid the kidnapping might have been the mob getting back at him for not playing ball back east. You know, in his OPA job."

Sam nodded, but then shook his head, no. "That's not likely, Heller. The eastern mobs don't make a play on our turf without checking first."

I nodded; that made sense.

"But just so you know—if you don't already—up to very recent, I was in the gas and food stamp business."

I had known that, which was why seeing the little hood show up on my figurative doorstep was so chilling; not that meeting with Sam Flood would warm me up under any circumstances.

"But that's over," Sam said. "In fact, it's been over for a couple months. That racket's gone the way of speakeasies. And Heller—when we was in that business, I never, and to my knowledge, no Outfit guy never made no approach to that Keenan guy."

"He never said you did."

The gaunt face relaxed. "Good. Now—let me explain my interest in this case."

"Please do."

"It's looking like that fucking Lipstick Killer did this awful crime on this little child."

"Looks like. But some people think a crank might've written that lipstick message in the alley."

His eyes tightened. "I hear the family received a lipstick letter, too, with the same message: 'Stop me before I kill more' or whatever."

"That's true."

He sighed. Then he looked at me sharply. "Does attorney-client privilege apply to you and me, if I give you a retainer?"

"Yeah. I'd have to send you a contract with an attorney I work with, to keep it legal. Or we could do it through your attorney. But I don't know that I want you as a client, Sam. No offense."

He raised a finger. "I promise you that working for me will in no way compromise you or put you in conflict of interest with your other client, the Keenan father. If I'm lying, then the deal's off."

I said nothing.

He thrust a fat, sealed envelope into my lap. "That's a grand in fifties."

"Sam, I . . . "

"I'm your client now, Heller. Got that?"

"Well . . . "

"Got it?"

I swallowed and nodded. I slipped the envelope in my inside suit coat pocket.

"The Lipstick Killer," Sam said, getting us back on the track. "The first victim was a Mrs. Caroline Williams."

I nodded.

He thrust his finger in my face; I looked at it, feeling my eyes cross. It was like looking into a gun barrel. "No one, Heller, no one must know about this." The finger withdrew and the ferret-like gangster sighed and looked out the windshield at the cement wall beyond. "I have a family. Little girls. Got to the protect them. Are you a father, Heller?"

"My wife's expecting."

Sam grinned. "That's great! That's wonderful." Then the grin disappeared. "Look, I'd do anything to protect my Angeline. Some guys, they flaunt their other women. Me, far as my family knows, I never strayed. Never. But . . . you're a man—you understand the needs of a man."

I was starting to get the picture; or at least part of it.

"The thing is, I was seeing this woman, this Caroline Williams. For the most part, it was pretty discreet."

It must have been, if Bill Drury hadn't found out about it; he'd been on that case, after all, and his hate-on for the Outfit was legendary.

As if reading my mind, Sam said, "Not a word to your pal Drury about this! Christ. That guy's nuts."

Mooney should know.

"Anyway, there was this photo of us together. Her and me, together. I want it back."

"Not for sentimental reasons, either."

"No," he admitted frankly. "It crushed me that my friend Mrs. Williams had the bad luck to be this maniac's victim. But from what I hear, this guy was not just a sex killer. He was some kind of weirdie second-story man."

"I think so," I said. "I think he was a burglar with a hobby."

"The police reports indicated that stuff was missing. Under-garments, various personal effects. Anyway, even with Drury on the case, I was able to find out that the picture album she had the photo in wasn't among her effects."

"Maybe her family got it."

"I checked that out myself—discreetly."

"Then you think . . . the killer took the photo album?"

Sam nodded. "Yeah. She had photos of herself in bathing suits and shit. If he took her underwear with him, he could've taken that, too."

"So what do you want from me?"

He looked at me hard; he clutched my arm. "All I want is that photo album. Not even that—just that one photo. It was taken in a restaurant, by one of them photo girls who come around."

"How I am supposed to find it?"

"You may find this guy before the cops do. Or, you're tight enough with the cops on the case to maybe get to it before they do. The photo album, I mean. It would embarrass me to have that come out. It would open up an ugly can of worms, and it wouldn't have nothing to do with nothing, where these crackpot killings are concerned. It would hurt me and my family and at the same time only muddy up the waters, where the case against the maniac is concerned."

I thought about that. I had to agree.

"So all you want," I said, "is that photo."

"And your discretion."

"You'd be protected," I said. "It would be through an attorney, after all. You'd be his client and he would be my client. I couldn't say a word if I wanted to."

"You'll take the job?"

"I already took your money. But what if I don't get results?"

"You keep the retainer. You find and return that picture, you get another four grand."

"What I really want," I said, "is that little girl's murderer. I want to kill that son of a bitch."

"Have all the fun you want," Sam said. "But get me my picture back."

11

Lou Sapperstein, who had once been my boss on the pickpocket detail, was the first man I added when the A-1 expanded. Pushing sixty, Lou had the hard muscular build of a linebacker and the tortoise shell glasses and bald pate of a scholar; in fact, he was a little of both.

He leaned a palm on my desk in my office. As usual, he was in rolled-up shirtsleeves, his tie loose around his collar. "I spent all morning in the *Trib* morgue—went back a full year."

I had asked Lou to check on any breaking-and-entering cases involving assault on women. It had occurred to me that if, as Drury and I theorized, the Lipstick Killer was a cat burglar whose thrill-seeking had escalated to murder, there may have been an intermediate stage, between bloodless break-ins and homicidal ones.

"There are several possibilities," Lou said, "but one jumped right out at me. . . . "

He handed me a sheet torn from a spiral pad.

"Katherine Reynolds," I read aloud. Then I read the rest to myself, and said, "Some interesting wrinkles here."

Lou nodded. "Some real similarities. And it happened right smack in between killings number one and two. You think the cops have picked up on it?"

"I doubt it," I said. "This happened on the South Side. The two women who were killed were both on the North Side."

"The little girl, too."

To Chicago cops, such geographic boundaries were inviolate—a North Side case was a North Side case and a crime that happened on the South Side might as well have happened on the moon. Unfortunately, crooks didn't always think that way.

So, late that afternoon, I found myself knocking at the door of the top-floor flat of an eight-story apartment building on the South Side, near the University of Chicago. The building had once been a nurse's dormitory—Billings Hospital was nearby—and most of the residents here still were women in the mercy business.

Like Katherine Reynolds, who was wearing crisp nurse's whites, cap included, when she answered the door.

"Thanks for seeing me on such short notice, Miss Reynolds," I said, as she showed me in.

I'd caught her at the hospital, by phone, and she'd agreed to meet me here at home; she was just getting off.

"Hope I'm not interfering with your supper," I added, hat in hand.

"Not at all, Mr. Heller," she said, unpinning her nurse's cap. "Haven't even started it yet."

She was maybe thirty, a striking brunette, with her hair chopped off in a boyish cut with page-boy bangs; her eyes were large and brown and luminous, her nose pug, her teeth white and slightly, cutely bucked. Her lips were full and scarlet with lipstick. She was slender but nicely curved and just about perfect, except for a slight medicinal smell.

We sat in the living room of the surprisingly large apartment; the furnishings were not new, but they were nice. On the end table next to the couch, where we sat, was a hand-tinted color photographic portrait of a Marine in dress blues, a grinning lantern-jawed young man who looked handsome and dim.

She crossed her legs and the nylons swished. I was a married man, a professional investigator here on business, and her comeliness had no effect on me whatsoever. I put my hat over my hard-on.

"Nice place you got here," I said. "Whole floor, isn't it?"

"Yes," she said. She smiled meaninglessly. "My sister and another girl, both nurses, share it with me. I think this was the head nurse's quarters, back when it was a dorm. All the other flats are rather tiny."

"How long ago was the incident?"

This was one of many questions I'd be asking her that I already knew the answer to.

"You mean the assault?" she said crisply, lighting a cigarette up. She exhaled smoke; her lips made a perfect, glistening red O. "About four months ago. The son of a bitch came in through the skylight." She gestured to it. "It must have been around seven AM. Sis and Dottie were already at work, so I was alone here. I was still asleep . . . actually, just waking up."

"Or did something wake you up?"

"That may have been it. I half-opened my eyes, saw a shadowy figure and then something crashed into my head." She touched her brown boyish hair. "Fractured my skull. I usually wear my hair longer, you know, but they cut a lot of it off."

"Looks good short. Do you know what you were hit with?"

"Your classic blunt instrument. I'd guess, a lead pipe. I took a good knock."

"You were unconscious."

"Oh yes. When I woke up, on the floor by the bed, maybe forty minutes later, blood was streaming down my face, and into my eyes. Some of it was sticky, already drying. My apartment was all a kilter. Virtually ransacked. My hands were tied with a lamp cord, rather loosely. I worked myself free, easily. I looked around and some things were missing." She made an embarrassed face, gestured with a cigarette in hand. "Underwear. Panties. Bras. But also a hundred and fifty bucks were gone from my purse."

"Did you call the police at that point?"

"No. That's when I heard the knock at the door. I staggered over there and it was a kid—well, he could've been twenty, but I'd guess eighteen. He had dark hair, long and greased back. Kind of a good-looking kid. Like a young Cornell Wilde. Looked a little bit like a juvenile delinquent, or anyway, like a kid trying to look like one and not quite pulling it off."

"What do you mean?"

"Well, he wore a black leather jacket, and a T-shirt and dungarees . . . but they looked kind of new. Too clean. More like a costume than clothing."

"What did he want?"

"He said he was a delivery boy—groceries, and he was looking for the right apartment to make his delivery."

"He was lost."

"Yes, but we didn't spend much time discussing that. He took one look at my bloody face and said he would get some help right away."

"And did he?"

She nodded; exhaled smoke again. "He found the building manager, told him the lady in the penthouse flat was injured, and needed medical attention. And left."

"And the cops thought he might have been the one who did it? Brought back by a guilty conscience?"

"Yes. But I'm not sure I buy that."

I nodded. But to me it tied in: the murderer who washed and bandaged his victims' wounds displayed a similar misguided *stop-me-catch-me* remorse. Even little JoAnn's body parts had been cleansed— before they were disposed of in sewers.

"The whole thing made me feel like a jerk," she said.

That surprised me. "Why?"

She lifted her shoulders; it did nice things to her cupcake breasts. Yes, I know. I'm a heel. "Well, if only I'd reacted quicker, I might have been able to protect myself. I mean, I've had all sorts of self-defense training."

"Oh?"

She flicked ashes into a glass tray on the couch arm. "I'm an army nurse—on terminal leave. I served overseas. European theater."

"Ah."

She gave me a sly smile. "You were in the Pacific, weren't you?"

"Well, uh, yes."

"I read about you in the papers. I recognized your name right away. You're kind of well-known around town."

"Don't believe everything you read in the papers, Miss Reynolds."

"You won the Silver Star, didn't you?"

I was getting embarrassed. I nodded.

"So did Jack."

"Jack?"

"My husband. He was a marine, too. You were on Guadalcanal?"

"Yes."

"So was Jack." She smiled. Then the smile faded and she sucked smoke in again. "Only he didn't come back."

"Lot of good men didn't. I'm sorry."

She made a dismissive gesture with a red-nailed hand. "Mr. Heller, why are you looking into this?"

"I think it may relate to another case; that's all."

"The Lipstick Killer?"

I hesitated, then nodded. "But I'd appreciate it if you didn't say anything about it to anybody just yet."

"Why haven't the cops done anything about this?"

"You mean, the Lipstick Killer, or what happened to you . . . ?"

"Both! And, why have *you* made this connection, when they haven't?"

I shrugged. "Maybe I'm more thorough. Or maybe I'm just grasping at straws."

"Well, it occurred to *me* there might be a connection. You'd think it would've occurred to the police, too!"

"You'd think."

"You know, there's something . . . never mind."

"What?"

She shook her head, tensed her lips. "There was something . . . creepy . . . that I never told anybody about." She looked at me with eyes impossibly large, so dark brown the irises were lost. "But I feel like I can talk to you."

She touched my hand. Hers was warm. Mine felt cold.

"On the floor . . . in the bathroom . . . I found something. Something I just . . . cleaned up. Didn't tell anybody about. It embarrassed me."

"You're a nurse. . . . "

"I know. But I was embarrassed just the same. It was . . . come."

"What?"

"There was come on the floor. You know—ejaculate. Semen."

12

When I got home, I called Drury and told him about Katherine Reynolds.

"I think you may be on to something," Drury said. "You should tell Lieutenant Kruger about this."

"I'll call him tomorrow. But I wanted to give you the delivery boy's description first—see if it rang any bells."

Drury made a clicking sound. "Lot of kids in those black leather jackets these days. Don't know what the world's coming to. Lot of kids trying to act like they're in street gangs, even when they're not."

"Could he be a University of Chicago student?"

"Pulling crimes on the North Side?"

Even a cop as good as Drury wore the geographical blinders.

"Yeah," I said. "There's this incredible new mode of transportation they call the El. It's just possible our boy knows about it."

Drury ignored the sarcasm. "Lot of greasy-haired would-be underage hoods around, Nate. Doesn't really narrow the field much."

"That look like a young Cornell Wilde?"

"That want to," Drury said, "yes."

We sighed, and hung up.

Eavesdropping, Peg was half in the kitchen, half in the hall. She wore a white apron over the swell of her tummy. She'd made meat loaf. The smell of it beckoned. Despite herself, Peg was a hell of a cook.

"Good looking?" she asked.

"What?"

"This nurse you went and talked to," she said.

"Oh. I didn't notice."

She smirked; went back into the kitchen. I followed. I waited at the table while she stirred gravy.

"Blonde?" she asked, her back to me.

"No. Brunette, I think."

She looked over her shoulder at me. "You think?"

"Brunette."

"Nice and slender, I'll bet. With a nice shape. Not fat and sloppy. Not a cow. Not an elephant."

"Peg . . ."

She turned; her wooden spoon dripped brown gravy onto the linoleum. "I'm going crazy out here, Nate. I'm ugly, and I'm bored."

"You're not ugly. You're beautiful."

"Fuck you, Heller! I'm an ugly cow, and I'm *bored* out here in the sticks. Jesus, couldn't we live someplace where there's somebody for me to talk to?"

"We have neighbors."

"Squirrels, woodchucks and that dip down the street who mows his lawn on the even days and washes his car on the odd. It's all vacant lots and nurseries and prairie out here. Why couldn't we live closer to the city? I feel like I'm living in a goddamn pasture. Which is where a cow like me belongs, I suppose."

I stood. I went to her and held her. She was angry, but she let me.

She didn't look at me as she bit off the words. "You go off to the Loop and you can be a businessman and you can be a detective and you have your co-workers and your friends and contacts and interview beautiful nurses and you make the papers and you're living a real life. Not stuck out here in a box with a lawn. Listening to 'Ma Perkins.' Peeling potatoes. Ironing shirts."

"Baby . . . "

She thumped her chest with a forefinger. "I used to have a life. I was a professional woman. I was an executive secretary."

"I know, I know."

"Nate—Nate, I'm afraid."

"Afraid?"

"Afraid I'm not cut out to be a housewife. Afraid I'm not cut out to be a mother."

I smiled at her gently; touched her face the same way. Touched her tummy. "You're already a mother, by definition. Give it a chance. The kid will change things. The neighborhood will grow."

"I hate it here."

"Give it a year. You don't like it, we'll move. Closer to town."

She smiled tightly, bravely. Nodded. Turned back to the stove.

The meal was good. We had apple pie, which may have been sarcasm on Peg's part, but if so it was delicious sarcasm. We chatted about business; about family. After the tension, things got relaxed.

We were cuddled on the couch listening to big band music on the radio when the phone rang. It was Drury again.

"Listen," he said, "sorry to bother you, but I've been thinking, and something did jog loose, finally."

"Swell! What?"

"There was this kid I busted a few years back. He was nice-looking, dark-haired, but kind of on the hoody side, though he had a good family. His dad was a security guard with a steel mill. Anyway, the boy was a good student, a bright kid—only for kicks, he stole. Furs, clothes, jewelry, old coins, guns."

"You were working out of Town Hall station at the time?"

"Yeah. All his robberies were on the North Side. He was just thirteen."

"How old is he now?"

"Seventeen."

"Then this was a while ago."

"Yeah, but I busted him again, on some ten burglaries, two years ago. He's agile, Nate—something of human fly, navigating ledges, fire escapes . . . going in windows."

"I see."

"Anyway, he did some time at Gibault." That was a correctional institution for boys at Terre Haute. "But supposedly he came out reformed. He's a really good student—so good, at seventeen, he's a sophomore in college."

"At the University of Chicago?" I said.

"Yeah," Drury said. "And guess what his part-time job is?"

"Delivery boy," I said.

"What a detective you are," Drury said.

13

Jerome Lapps, precocious seventeen-year-old sophomore science student, resided at a dormitory on the University of Chicago campus.

On the phone Drury had asked, "You know where his folks live?"

"What, you take me for a psychic?"

"You could've tripped over this kid, Nate. The Lapps family lives in Lincolnwood."

He gave me the address; not so far from Peg and me.

Sobering as that was, what was more interesting was that the kid lived at school, not home; even during summer session. Specifically, he was in Gates Hall on the Midway campus.

The Midway, a mile-long block-wide parkway between 59th and 60th, connected Washington and Jackson parks, and served to separate Hyde Park and the University eggheads from the real South Side. Just beyond the Midway were the Gothic limestone buildings and lushly landscaped acres of the university. At night the campus looked like another world. Of course, it looked like another world in the daylight, too.

But this was night, and the campus seemed largely deserted. That was partly summer, partly not. I left the Plymouth in a quadrangle parking lot and found my way to the third floor of Gates Hall, where I went to Lapps's room and knocked on the door. No answer. I knocked again. No answer. The door was locked.

A student well into his twenties—probably a vet on the GI Bill— told me where to find the grad student who was the resident assistant in charge of that floor.

The resident assistant leaned against the door jamb of his room with a bottle of beer in his hand and his shirt half-tucked in. His hair was red, his eyes hooded, his mouth smirky. He was perhaps twenty years old.

"What can I do for you, bud?" the kid asked.

"I'm Jerry Lapps's uncle. Supposed to meet him at his room, but he's not in."

"Yeah?"

"You got a key? I'd like to wait inside."

He shrugged. "Against the rules."

"I'm his uncle Abraham," I said. And I showed him a ten-dollar bill. "I'm sure it'll be okay."

The redheaded kid brightened; his eyes looked almost awake. He snatched the ten-spot and said, "Ah. Honest Abe. Jerry mentioned you."

He let me into Lapps's room and went away.

Judging by the pair of beds, one against either wall, Jerome Lapps had a roommate. But the large single room accommodated two occupants nicely. One side was rather spartan and neat as a boot— camp barracks, while across the room an unmade bed was next to a plaster wall decorated with pictures of baseball players and heart-throb movie actors. Each side of the room had its own writing desk, and again, one was cluttered, while the other was neat.

It didn't take long to confirm my suspicion that the messy side of the room belonged to the seventeen-year-old. Inside the calculus text on the sloppy desk, the name Jerome C. Lapps was written on the flyleaf in a cramped hand. The handwriting on a notepad, filled with doodles, looked the same; written several times, occasionally underlined, were the words: "Rogers Park."

Under Jerome C. Lapps's bed were three suitcases.

In one suitcase were half of the panties and bras in the city of Chicago.

The other suitcase brimmed with jewelry, watches, two revolvers, one automatic, and a smaller zippered pouch of some kind, like an oversize shaving kit. I unzipped it and recoiled.

It was a medical kit, including hypos, knives and a surgical saw.

I put everything back and stood there and swallowed and tried to get the image of JoAnn Keenan's doll-like head out of my mind. The best way to do that was to get back to work, which I did, proceeding to the small closet on Jerome's side of the room. On the upper shelf I found a briefcase.

I opened it on the neater bed across the way. Inside were several thousand bucks in war bonds and postal savings certificates. He'd apparently put any cash he'd stolen into these, and any money from fenced goods, although considering that well-stuffed suitcase of jewelry and such, I couldn't imagine he'd bothered to fence much if any of what he'd taken.

As typically teen-ager sloppy as his side of the dorm room was, Jerry had neatly compartmentalized his booty: ladies underwear in one bag; jewelry and watches in another; and paper goods in the briefcase. Included in the latter were clipped photos of big-shot Nazis. Hitler, Goering and Goebbels.

Jerry had some funny fucking heroes.

Finally, in the briefcase, was a photo album. Thumbing through it, I saw photos of an attractive woman, frequently in a bathing suit and other brief, summer apparel. There was also a large photo of the same woman with a ferret-faced male friend in a nightclub setting; you could see a table of men sitting behind them as well, clearly, up a tier. A sweet and tender memento of Caroline Williams and Sam Flood's love affair.

I removed the photo, folded it without creasing it, and slipped it into my inside suit coat pocket. I put the photo album back, closed up the briefcase and was returning it to the upper shelf of the closet when the dorm-room door opened.

"What the hell are you doing?" a male voice demanded.

I was turning around and slipping my hand under my jacket to get at my gun, at the same time, but the guy reacted fast. His hand must have hit the light switch, because the room went black and I could hear him coming at me, and then he was charging into me.

I was knocked back into the corner, by the many-paned windows, through which some light was filtering, and I saw a thin face, its teeth clenched, as the figure pressed into me and a single fist was smashing into my stomach, powerfully.

The damn guy was almost sitting on me, and I used all my strength to lift up and lift him off, heaving him bodily onto the floor. He was scrambling to his feet when I stuck the nine millimeter in his face and said, "Don't."

Somebody hit the lights.

It was the red-headed dorm assistant. Even drunk, he didn't like the looks of this.

Neither did I: the guy in front of me was not Jerome Lapps, but a slender, tow-headed fellow in his mid-twenties. The empty sleeve of his left arm was tucked into a sport coat pocket.

I was a hell of a tough character: I'd just bested a cripple. Of course, I had to pull a gun to do it.

"What the hell . . . " the red-headed kid began. His eyes were wide at the sight of the gun in my hand. The one-armed guy in front of me seemed less impressed.

"Police officer," I said to the redhead. "Go away."

He swallowed, nodded, and went.

"You're Jerome's roommate?" I asked the one-armed fellow.

"Yeah. Name's Robinson. Who are you? You really a cop?"

"I run a private agency," I said. "What branch were you in?"

"Army."

I nodded. "Marines," I said. I put the gun away. "You got a smoke?"

He nodded; with the one hand he had left, he got some Chesterfields out of his sport coat pocket. Shook one out for me, then another for himself. He put the Chesterfields back and got out a silver Zippo. He lit us both up. He was goddamn good with that hand.

"Thank God them bastards left me with my right," he grinned sheepishly.

He sat on his bed. I sat across from him on Lapps's.

We smoked for a while. I thought about a punk kid cutting out pinups of Hitler while sharing a room with a guy who lost an arm over there. I was so happy I'd fought for the little fucker's freedoms.

"You're looking for Jerry, aren't you?" he asked. His eyes were light blue and sadder than a Joan Crawford picture.

"Yeah."

He shook his head. "Figured that kid would get himself into trouble."

"You roomed with him long?"

"Just for summer session. He's not a bad kid. Easy to get along with. Quiet."

"You know what he's got under his bed?"

"No."

"Suitcases full of stolen shit. If you need a new wristwatch, you picked the right roomie."

"I didn't know he was doing anything like that."

"Then what made you think he was going to get himself in trouble?"

"That black leather jacket of his."

"Huh?"

He shrugged. "When he'd get dressed up like a juvie. That black leather jacket. Dungarees. White T-shirt. Smoking cigarettes." He sucked on his own cigarette, shook his head. "He'd put that black leather jacket on, not every night, more like every once in a while. I'd ask him where he was going. You know what he'd say?"

"No."

"On the prowl."

I thought about that.

"Is his black-leather jacket hanging in that closet you were lookin' in?"

"No," I said.

"Then guess where he is right now."

"On the prowl," I said.

He nodded.

14

Now I was on the prowl.

I went up Lakeshore, turned onto Sheridan and followed it up to the Loyola El stop. The notepad on Lapps's desk had sent me here, to Rogers Park, the northernmost neighborhood in Chicago; beyond was Evanston. Here, in a three-block wide and fourteen-block long band between the lake and the El tracks was the middle-class residential area that would suit the kid's MO.

Lapps seemed partial to a certain type of building; according to Drury, many of the boy's burglaries were pulled off in tall, narrow apartment buildings consisting of small studio apartments. Same was true of where the two women who'd been killed had lived, and Katherine Reynolds, too.

First I would look for the dark-haired, black-leather-jacketed Lapps around the El stops—he had no car—and then I would cruise the side streets off Sheridan, looking in particular for that one type of building.

Windows rolled down, half-leaned out, I crawled slowly along, cutting the Plymouth's headlights as I cruised the residential neighborhoods; that way I didn't announce myself, and I seemed to be able to eyeball the sidewalks and buildings better that way. Now and then another car blinked its brights at me, but I ignored them and cruised on through the unseasonably cool July night.

About two blocks down from the Morse Avenue business district, on a street of modest apartment buildings, I spotted two guys running back the direction I'd come. The one in the lead was a heavy-set guy in his T-shirt; close on his heels was a fellow in a plaid shirt. At first I thought one was chasing the other, but then it was clear they were together, and very upset.

The heavy-set guy was slowing down and gesturing with open hands. "Where d'he go? Where d'he go?"

The other guy caught up to him and they both slowed down; in the meantime, I pulled over and trotted over to them.

"The cops, already!" the heavy-set guy said joyously. He was a bald guy in his forties; five o'clock shadow smudged his face.

I didn't correct their assumption that was a cop. I merely asked, "What gives, gents?"

The guy in the plaid shirt, thin, in his thirties, glasses, curly hair, pointed at nothing in particular and said, in a rush, "We had a prowler in the building. He was in my neighbor's flat!"

"I'm the janitor," the fat guy said, breathing hard, hands on his sides, winded. "I caught up to the guy in the lobby, but he pulled a gun on me." He shook his head. "Hell, I got a wife in the hospital, and three kids, that all need me unventilated. I let 'im pass."

"But Bud went and got reinforcements," the thin guy said, taking over, pointing to himself, "and my wife called the cops. And we took chase."

That last phrase almost made me smile, but I said, "Was it a dark-haired kid in a black-leather jacket?"

They both blinked and nodded, properly amazed.

"He's going to hop the El," I said. I pointed to the thin guy. "You take the Morse El stop, I'll . . . "

A scream interrupted me.

We turned toward the scream and it became a voice, a woman's voice, yelling, "He's up *there!*"

We saw her then, glimpsed between two rather squat apartment houses: a stout, older woman, lifting her skirts almost daintily as she barreled down the alley. I ran back there; the two guys were trailing well behind, and not eagerly. A lame horse could have gained the same lead.

The fleeing woman saw me, and we passed each other, her going in one direction, me in the other. She looked back and pointed, without missing a step, saying, "Up on the second-floor porch!" Then she continued on with her escape.

It would have been a comic moment, if the alley hadn't been so dark and I hadn't been both running and scrambling for my nine millimeter.

I slowed to face the back yard of a two-story brick building and its exposed wooden back stairways and porches. Despite what the fleeing woman had said, the second floor porch seemed empty, though it was hard to tell: it was dark back here, the El tracks looming behind me, casting their shadow. Maybe she meant the next building down. . . .

As I was contemplating that, a figure rose on the second-floor porch and pointed a small revolver at me and I could see the hand moving, he was pulling the trigger, but his gun wasn't firing, wasn't working.

Mine was. I squeezed off three quick rounds and the lattice-work wood near him got chewed up, splinters flying. I didn't know if I'd hit him or not, and didn't wait to see; I moved for those steps, and bolted up one flight, and was the bottom of the second when the figure loomed up above me, at the top of the stairs, and I saw him, his pale handsome face under long black greasy hair, his black leather jacket, his dungarees, and he threw the revolver at me like a baseball, and I ducked to one side, and swung my nine millimeter up just as he leaped.

He knocked me back before I could fire, back through the railing of the first-floor porch, snapping it into pieces like so many matchsticks, and we landed in a tangle on the grass, my gun getting lost on the trip. Then he was on top of me, like he was fucking me, and he was a big kid, powerful, pushing me down, pinning me like a wrestler, his teeth clenched, his eyes wide and maniacal.

I heaved with all my strength and weight and pitched him off to one side, but he didn't lose his grip on me, and we rolled, and I was on top now, only he hadn't given up, he hadn't let go, he had me more than I had him and that crazed, glazed look on his face scared the shit out of me. I couldn't punch him, even though I seemed to have the advantage, couldn't get my arms free, and he rocked up, as if he wanted to take a bite out of my face.

I was holding him down, but it was a stand-off at best.

Then I sensed somebody coming up—that janitor and his skinny pal, maybe.

But the voice I heard didn't belong to either of them: "Is that the prowler?"

Still gripping my powerful captive by his arms, I glanced up and saw hovering over us a burly guy in swimming trunks holding a clay flower pot in his hands.

"That's him," I said, struggling.

"That's all I wanted to know," the burly guy said, and smashed the flower pot over the kid's head.

15

On the third smack, the flower pot—which was empty—shattered into fragments and the kid's eyes rolled back and went round and white and blank like Orphan Annie's, and then he shut them. Blood was streaming down the kid's pale face. He was ruggedly handsome, even if Cornell Wilde was stretching it.

I got off him and gulped for my breath and the guy in his bathing trunks said, "Neighbors said a cop was after a prowler."

I stuck my hand out. "Thanks, buddy. I didn't figure the cavalry would show up in swim trunks, but I'll take what I can get."

His grasp was firm. He was an affable-looking, open-faced, hairy-chested fellow of maybe thirty-five. We stood over the unconscious kid like hunters who just bagged a moose.

"You a cop?"

"Private," I said. "My name's Nate Heller."

He grinned. "I thought you looked familiar. You're Bill Drury's pal, aren't you? I'm Chet Dickinson—I work traffic in the Loop."

"You're a cop? What's that, summer uniform?"

He snorted a laugh. "I live around here. My family and me was just walking back from a long day at the beach, when we run into this commotion. I sent Grace and the kids on home and figured I better check it out. Think we ought to get this little bastard to a hospital?"

I nodded. "Edgewater's close. Should we call for an ambulance? I got a car."

"You mind? The son of a bitch could have a concussion." He laughed again. "I saw you two strugglin', and I grabbed that flower pot off a window sill. Did the trick."

"Sure did."

"Fact, I mighta over-did it."

"Not from my point of view."

After Dickinson had found and collected the kid's revolver and contributed his beach towel to wrap the kid's head in, we drunk-walked Lapps to my car.

The burly bare-chested cop helped me settle the boy in the rider's seat. "I'll run over home, and call in, and get my buggy, and meet you over at Edgewater."

"Thanks. You know, I used to work traffic in the Loop."

"No kiddin'. Small world."

I had cuffs in the glove box; I cuffed the unconscious kid's hands behind him, in case he was faking it. I looked at the pleasant-faced cop. "Look—if anything comes of this, you got a piece of the reward action. It'll be just between us."

"Reward action?"

I put a hand on his hairy shoulder. "Chet—we just caught the goddamn Lipstick Killer."

His jaw dropped and I got in and pulled away, while he ran off, looking in those trunks of his like somebody in a half-assed track meet.

Then I pulled over around a corner and searched the kid. I figured there was no rush getting him to the hospital. If he died, he died. He had two five-hundred-buck postal savings certificates in a pocket of his leather jacket. In his billfold, which had a University of Chicago student ID card in the name Jerome C. Lapps, was a folded-up letter, typed. It was dated last month. It said:

Jerry—

I haven't heard from you in a long time. Tough luck about the jail term. You'll know better next time.

I think they're catching up to me, so I got to entrust some of my belongings to you. I'll pick these suitcases up later. If you get short of cash, you can dip into the postal certificates.

I appreciate you taking these things off my hands when I was being followed. Could have dumped it, but I couldn't see losing all that jewelry. I'll give you a phone call before I come for the stuff.

George

I was no handwriting expert, but the handwritten signature sure looked like Lapps's own cramped handwriting from the inside cover of his calculus book.

The letter stuck me immediately as a lame attempt on the kid's part to blame the stolen goods stashed in his dorm room on some imaginary accomplice. Carrying it around with him, yet—an alibi in his billfold.

He was stirring.

He looked at me. Blinked. His lashes were long. "Who are you, mister? Where am I?"

I threw a sideways forearm into his stomach and doubled him over. He let the air out with a groan of pain that filled the car and made me smile.

"I'm somebody you tried to shoot, is who I am," I said. "And where you are is up shit creek without a paddle."

He shook his head, licked his lips. "I don't remember trying to shoot anybody. I'd never do a thing like that."

"Oh? You pointed a revolver at me, and when it wouldn't shoot, you hurled it at me. Then you jumped me. This just happened, Jerry."

A comma of greasy black hair fell to his forehead. "You . . . you know my name? Oh. Sure." He noticed his open billfold on the seat next to us.

"I knew you before I saw your ID, Jerry. I been on your trail all day."

"I thought you cops worked in pairs."

"I don't work for the city. Right now, I'm working for the Robert Keenan family."

He recognized the name—anybody in Chicago would have—but his reaction was one of confusion, not alarm, or guilt, or anything else I might have expected.

"What does that have to do with me, mister?"

"You kidnapped their little girl, Jerry—you strangled her and then you tried to fuck her and then you cut her in pieces and threw the pieces in the sewer."

"What . . . what are you . . . "

I sidearmed him in the stomach again. I wanted to shove his head against the dash, but after those blows to the skull with that flower pot, it might kill him. I wasn't particularly interested in having him die in my car. Get blood all over my new Plymouth. Peg would have a fit.

"You're the Lipstick Killer, Jerry. And I caught you going up the back stairs, like the cheap little sneak thief you are."

He looked down at his lap, guiltily. "I didn't kill those women."

"Really. Who did?"

"George."

The letter. The alibi.

"George," I said.

"Yeah," he said. "George did it."

"George did it."

"Sometimes I went along. Sometimes I helped him prepare. But I never did it. George did."

"Is that how you're going to play it?"

"George did it, mister. George hurt those women."

"Did George jack off the floor, or did you, Jerry?"

Now he started to cry.

"I did that," he admitted. "But George did the killings."

"JoAnn Keenan too?"

Lapps shook his head; his face glistened with tears. "He must have. He must have."

16

Cops in uniform, and plainclothes too, were waiting at the hospital when I deposited Lapps at the emergency room. I didn't talk to the kid after that, though I stuck around, at the request of a detective from Rogers Park.

The word spread fast. Dickinson, when he called it in, had spilled the Lipstick Killer connection. The brass started streaming in, and Chief of Detectives Storm took me off to one side and complimented me on my fine work. We decided that my visit to Lapps's dorm room would be off the record for now; in the meantime, South Side detectives were already on the scene making the same discoveries I had, only with the proper warrants.

I got a kick out of being treated like somebody special by the

Chicago police department. Storm and even Tubbo Gilbert were all smiles and arms around my shoulder, when the press showed, which they quickly did. For years I'd been an "ex—cop" who left the force under a cloud in the Cermak administration; now, I was a "distinguished former member of the Detective Bureau who at one time was the youngest plainclothes officer on the force."

It soon became a problem, having the emergency area clogged with police personnel, politicians and reporters. Lapps was moved upstairs, and everybody else moved to the lobby.

Dickinson, when he'd gone home, had taken time to get out of his trunks and into uniform, which was smart; the flashbulbs were popping around the husky, amiable patrolman. We posed for a few together, and he whispered to me, "We done good."

"You and your flower pot."

"You're a hell of cop, Heller. I don't care what anybody says."

That was heartwarming.

My persistent pal Davis of the *News* was among the first of the many reporters to arrive and he buttonholed me with an offer of a grand for an exclusive. Much as I hated to, I had to turn him down.

From his expression you'd think I'd pole-axed him. "Heller turning down a pay-off? Why?"

"This is too big to give to one paper. I got to let the whole world love me this time around." Most of the reward money—which was up to forty grand, now—had been posted by the various newspapers (though the city council had anted up, too) and I didn't want to alienate anybody.

"It's gonna be months before you see any of that dough," Davis whined. "It's all contingent upon a conviction, you know."

"I know. I can wait. I'm a patient man. Besides, I got a feeling the A-1 isn't going to be hurting for business after this."

Davis smirked. "Feelin' pretty cocky aren't you? Pretty smug."

"That's right," I said, and brushed by him. I went to the pay phones and called home. It was almost ten, but Peg usually stayed up at least that late.

"Nate! Where have you been . . . it's almost . . . "

"I know. I got him."

"What?"

"I got him."

There was a long pause.

"I love you," she said.

That beat reward money all to hell.

"I love you, too," I said. "Both of you."

I was slipping out of the booth when Lieutenant Kruger shambled over. His mournful-hound puss was twisted up in a grin. He extended his hand and we shook vigorously.

He took my arm, spoke in my ear. "Did you take a look at the letter in Lapps's billfold?"

I nodded. "It's his spare-tire of an alibi. He told me 'George' did the killings. Is he sticking to that story?"

Kruger nodded. "Only I don't think there is a George."

"Next you'll be spoiling Santa Claus and the Easter Bunny for me."

"I don't think that's what he's up to."

"Oh? What is he up to, lieutenant?"

"I think it's a Jekyll and Hyde routine."

"Oh. *He's* George, only he doesn't know it. Split personality. There's a post-war scam for you."

Kruger nodded. "Insanity plea."

"The papers will love that shit."

"They love the damnedest things." He grinned again. "Tonight they even love you."

Chief of Detectives Storm came and found me, shortly after that, and said, "There's somebody who wants to talk to you."

He led me back behind the reception counter to a phone, and he smiled quietly as he handed me the receiver. He might have been presenting an award of valor.

"Nate?" the voice said.

"Bob?"

"Nate. God bless you, Nate. You found the monster. You found him."

"It's early yet, Bob. The real investigation has just started. . . . "

"I knew I did the right thing calling you. I knew it."

I could tell he was crying.

"Bob. You give Norma my love."

"Thank you, Nate. Thank you."

I didn't know what to say. So I just said, "Thanks, Bob. Good night."

I gave a few more press interviews, made an appointment with Storm to come to First District station the next morning and give a formal statement, shook Kruger's hand again, and wandered out into the parking lot. Things were winding down. I slipped behind the wheel of Plymouth and was about to start the engine when I saw the face in my rear-view mirror.

"Hello, Heller," the man said.

His face was all sharp angles and holes: cheek-bones, pock-marks, sunken dead eyes, pointed jaw, dimpled chin. His suit was black and well-tailored—like an undertaker with style. His arms were folded, casually, and he was wearing kid gloves. In the summer.

He was one of Sam Flood's old cronies, a renowned thief from the 42 gang in the Patch. Good with a knife. His last name was Morello.

"We need to talk," he said. "Drive a while."

His first name was George.

17

"Sam couldn't come himself," George said. "Sends his regards, and apologies."

We were on Sheridan, heading toward Evanston.

"I was going to call Sam when I got home," I said, watching him in the rearview mirror. His eyes were gray under bushy black brows; spooky fucking eyes.

"Then you did make it to the kid's pad, before the cops." George sighed; smiled. A smile on that slash of a craggy face was not a festive thing.

"Yeah."

"And you got what Sam wants?"

"I do."

"The photo?"

"Yes."

"That's swell. You're all right, Heller. You're all right. Pull over into the graveyard, will you?"

Calvary Cemetery was the sort of gothic graveyard where Bela Lugosi and Frankenstein's monster might go for a stroll. I pulled in under the huge limestone archway and, when George directed, pulled off the main path onto a side one, and slowed to a stop. I shut the engine off. The massive granite wall of the cemetery muffled the roar of traffic on Sheridan; the world of the living seemed suddenly very distant.

"What's this about, George?" At Statesville, they say, where he was doing a stretch for grand-theft auto, George was the prison shiv artist;

an iceman whose price was five cartons of smokes, for which an individual that was annoying you became deceased.

Tonight George's voice was pleasant; soothing. A Sicilian disc jockey. "Sam just wants his photo, that's all."

"What's the rush?"

"Heller—what's it to you?"

"I'd rather turn it over to Sam personally."

He unfolded his arms and revealed a silenced Luger in his gloved right hand. "Sam says you should give it to me."

"It's in the trunk of the car."

"The trunk?"

"I had the photo in my coat pocket, but when I realized cops were going to be crawling all over, I slipped it in an envelope in my trunk, with some other papers."

That was the truth. I did that at the hospital, before I took Lapps inside.

"Show me," George said.

We got out of the car. George made me put my hands up and, gun in his right hand, he calmly patted me down with his left. He found the nine millimeter under my arm, slipped it out and tossed it gently through the open window of the Plymouth onto the driver's seat.

Calvary was a rich person's cemetery, with mausoleums and life-size statues of dear departed children and other weirdness, all casting their shadows in the moonlight. George kept the gun in hand, but he wasn't obnoxious about it. I stepped around back of the Plymouth, unlocked the trunk and reached in. George took a step forward. I doubled him over with the tire iron, then whacked the gun out of his hand, and swung the iron sideways against his cheek as he began to rise up.

I picked up his Luger and put a knee on his chest and the nose of the silenced gun against his bloody cheekbone. I would have to kill him. There was little doubt of that. His gray eyes were narrowed and full of hate and chillingly absent of fear.

"Was killing me Sam's idea, or yours?"

"Who said anything about killing you?"

I forced the bulky silenced nose of the gun into his mouth. Time for the Chicago lie-detector test.

Fear came into his eyes, finally.

I removed the gun, slowly, not taking any teeth, and said, "Your idea or Sam's?"

"Mine."

"Why, George?"

"Fuck you, Heller."

I put the gun in his mouth again.

After I removed it, less gently this time, cutting the roof of his mouth, he said through bloody spittle, "You're a loose end. Nobody likes loose ends."

"What's it to you, George?"

He said nothing; he was shaking. Most of it was anger. Some of it was fear. An animal smell was coming up off him.

"I said, what's it to you, George? What was your role in it?"

His eyes got very wide; something akin to panic was in them.

And then I knew.

Don't ask me how, exactly, but I did.

"You killed her," I said. It was part question, part statement. "*You* killed Sam's girl friend. For Sam?"

He thought about the question; I started to push the gun back in his mouth and he began to nod, lips kissing the barrel. "It was an accident. Sam threw her over, and she was posing a problem."

I didn't ask whether that problem was blackmail or going to the press or cops or what. It didn't much matter.

"So he had you hit her?"

"It was a fuck-up. I was just suppose to put the fear of God in her and get that fucking picture."

I pressed the gun into his cheek; the one that wasn't bloody. "That kid—Lapps . . . he was your accomplice?"

"No! I didn't know who the hell he was. If we knew who he was, we coulda got that photo long time ago. Why the fuck you think *you* were hired?"

That made sense; but not much else did. "So what was the deal, George?"

His eyes tightened; his expression said: *You know how it is.* "I was slapping her around, trying to get her to tell me where that picture was. I'd already tossed the place, but just sorta half-ass. She was arrogant. Spitting at me. All of a sudden her throat got cut."

Accidents will happen. "How did that kid get the photo album, then?"

"I heard something at the window; I looked up and saw this dark shape there, out on the fire escape . . . thought it was a cop or something."

The black-leather jacket.

"I thought *fuck it* and cut out," he said. "The kid must've come in, stole some shit, found that photo album someplace I missed, and left with it and bunch of other stuff."

But before that, he washed the victim's wounds and applied a few bandages.

"What about the second girl?" I demanded. "Margaret Johnson? And the Keenan child?"

"I had nothing to do with them crimes. You think I'm a fuckin' psycho?"

I thought that one best left unanswered.

"George," I said calmly, easing the gun away from his face, "you got any suggestions on how we can resolve our differences, here? Can you think of some way both of us can walk out of this graveyard tonight?"

He licked his lips. Smiled a ghastly, blood-flecked smile. "Let bygones be bygones. You don't tell anybody what you know—Sam included—and I just forget about you working me over. That's fair. That's workable."

I didn't see where he got the knife; I hadn't seen a hand slip into a pocket at all. He slashed through my sleeve, but didn't cut me. When I shot him in the head, his skull exploded, but almost none of him got on me. Just my gun hand. A limestone angel, however, got wreathed in blood and brains.

I lifted up off him and stood there panting for a while. The sounds of muted traffic reminded me there was a world to go back to. I checked his pockets, found some Camels and lit one up; kept the pack. Then I wiped my prints off his gun, laid it near him, retrieved my tire iron, put it back in the trunk, which I closed up, and left him there with his peers.

18

The phone call came late morning, which was a good thing: I didn't even make it into the office till after ten.

"You were a busy fella yesterday, Heller," Sam Flood's voice said cordially.

"I get around, Sam."

"Papers are full of you. Real hero. There's other news, though, that hasn't made the papers yet."

"By the afternoon edition, it'll be there."

We each knew what the other was talking about: soon Giorgio (George) Morello would be just another of the hundreds of Chicago's unsolved gangland killings.

"Lost a friend of mine last night," Sam said.

"My condolences. But I don't think he was such a good friend. He loused up that job with the girl, and he tried to sell me a cemetery plot last night."

The possibility of a phone tap kept the conversation elliptical; but we were right on track with each other.

"In other words," Sam said, "you only did what you had to do."

"That's right."

"What about that item you were gonna try to obtain for me?"

"It's in the hands of the U.S. Postal Service right now. Sealed tight —marked personal. I sent it to you at your liquor store on the West Side."

"That was prompt. You just got hold of the thing last night, right?"

"Right. No time to make copies. I didn't *want* a copy, Sam. Your business is your business. Anything I can do to make your happy home stay that way is fine with me. I got a wife, too. I understand these things."

There was a long, long pause.

Then: "I'll put your check in the mail, Heller. Pleasure doin' business with you."

"Always glad to hear from a satisfied customer."

There was a briefer pause.

"You wouldn't want to go on a yearly retainer, would you, Heller?"

"No thanks, Sam. I do appreciate it. Like to stay on your good side."

"That's wise, Heller. Sorry you had that trouble last night. Wasn't my doing."

"I know, Sam."

"You done good work. You done me a favor, really. If I can pay you back, you know the number."

"Thanks, Sam. That check you mentioned is plenty, though."

"Hey, and nice going on that other thing. That sex-maniac guy. Showed the cops up. Congratulations, war hero."

The phone clicked dead.

I swallowed and sat there at my desk, trembling.

While I had no desire to work for Sam Flood ever again, I did truly want to stay on his good side. And I had made no mention of what I knew was a key factor in his wanting that photo back.

It had little, if anything, to do with keeping his wife from seeing him pictured with his former girl friend: it was the table of Sam's friends, glimpsed behind Sam and the girl in the photo. Top mobsters from Chicago, New York, Cleveland and Detroit. Some of kind of informal underworld summit meeting had been inadvertently captured by a nightclub photographer. Proof of a nationwide alliance of organized crime families, perhaps in a major meeting to discuss post-war plans.

If Sam suspected that I knew the true significance of that photo, I might not live to see my kid come into the world.

And I really wanted to.

19

A little over a week later, I was having lunch at Binyon's with Ken Levine, the attorney who had brought Bob Keenan and me together. The restaurant was a businessman's bastion, wooden booths, spartan decor; my old office was around the corner, but for years I'd been only an occasional customer here. Now that business was good, and my suits were Brooks Brothers not Maxwell Street, I could afford to hobnob on a more regular basis with the brokers, lawyers and other well-to-do thieves.

"You couldn't ask for better publicity," Ken said. He was a small handsome man with sharp dark eyes that didn't miss anything and a hairline that was a memory.

"I'm taking on two more operatives," I said, sipping my rum cocktail.

"That's great. Glad it's working out so well for you." He made a clicking sound in his cheek. "Of course, the Bar Association may have something to say about the way that Lapps kid has been mistreated by Chicago's finest."

"I could bust out crying at the thought," I said.

"Yeah, well they've questioned him under sodium pentathol, hooked his nuts up to electrodes, done all sorts of zany stuff. And then they leak these vague, inadmissible 'confessions' to the papers. These wild stories of 'George' doing the crimes."

Nobody had connected George Morello to the case. Except me, of course, and I wasn't talking.

"The kid faked a coma for days," I said, "and then claimed amnesia. They had to do something."

Ken smiled wryly. "Nate, they brought in a priest and read last rites over him, to try to trick him into a 'death-bed' confession. They didn't feed him any solid food for four days. They held him six days without charging him or letting him talk to a lawyer. They probably beat the shit out of him, too."

I shrugged, sipped my cocktail. It was my second.

"Only it may backfire on 'em," Ken said. "All this dual personality stuff has the makings of an insanity plea. He's got some weird sexual deviation—his burglaries were sexually based, you know."

"How do you mean?"

"He got some kind of thrill out of entering the window of a strange apartment. He'd have a sexual emission shortly after entering. Must've been symbolic in his mind—entering through the window for him was like . . . you know." He shrugged. "Apparently the kid's never had normal sex."

"Thank you, Dr. Freud."

Ken grinned. "Hey, I could get that little bastard off."

I was glad it wasn't Ken's case.

"Whatever his sex quirk," I said, "they tied him to the assault on that nurse, Katherine Reynolds. They matched his prints to one left in her apartment. And to a partial print on the Keenan kidnap note."

"The key word is partial," Ken said, raising a finger. "They got six points of similarity on the note. Eleven are required for a positive ID."

"They've got an *eye witness* ID."

Ken laughed; there was genuine mirth in it. Lawyers can find the humor in both abstract thinking and human suffering. "Their eye witness is that old German janitor who was their best suspect till you nabbed Lapps. The old boy looked at four overweight, middle-aged cops and one seventeen-year-old in a line-up and somehow managed to pick out the seventeen-year-old. Before that, his description of the guy he saw was limited to 'a man in a brown raincoat with a shopping bag.' Did you know that that janitor used to be a butcher?"

"There was something in the papers about it. That doesn't mean he cuts up little girls."

"No. But if he lost his job during the war, 'cause of OPA restrictions, he could bear Bob Keenan a grudge."

"Bob wasn't with the OPA long enough for that to be possible. He was with the New York office. Jesus, Ken, what's your point, here?"

Like most attorneys, Ken was argumentative for the sheer hell of it; but he saw this was getting under my skin and backed off. "Just making conversation, Nate. That kid's guilty. The prosecutors are just goddamn lucky they got a mean little JD who carried Nietzsche around and collected Nazi memorabilia. 'Cause without public opinion, they couldn't win this one."

Ken headed back to court and I sat working at my cocktail, wondering if I could get away with a third.

I shared some of Ken's misgivings about the way the Lapps case was being handled. A handwriting expert had linked the lipstick message on the late Margaret Johnson's wall with that of the Keenan kidnap note; then matched those to recreations of both Lapps was made to give.

This handwriting expert's claim to fame was the Lindbergh case—having been there, I knew the Lindbergh handwriting evidence was a crock—and both the lipstick message and kidnap notes were printed, which made handwriting comparison close to worthless.

Of course, Lapps had misspelled some of the same words as in the note: "waite" and "safty." Only I'd learned in passing from Lieutenant Kruger that Lapps had been told to copy the notes, mistakes and all.

A fellow named Bruno Hauptmann had dutifully done the same in his handwriting samples, some years before. The line-up trick Ken had mentioned had been used to hand Hauptmann on a platter to a weak, elderly eye-witness, too. And the press had played their role in Bruno's railroading—one over-eager reporter had written an incriminating phone number inside Hauptmann's apartment, to buy a headline that day, and that little piece of creative writing on wainscoting became an unrefuted key prosecution exhibit.

But so what? Bruno was (a) innocent and (b) long-dead. This kid was alive, well and psycho—and as guilty as the Nazi creeps he idolized. Besides which, what Ken had said about the kid's sexual deviation had made something suddenly clear to me.

I knew Lapps was into burglary for kicks, but I figured it was the violence against women that got him going. This business about strange buildings—and he'd had a certain of type of building, hadn't he, like some guys liked blondes or other guys were leg men—made a screwy sort of sense.

Lapps must have been out on the fire escape, peeking into Caroline Williams's apartment, casing it for a possible break-in, when he saw

George slapping the girl around in the bedroom. He must have heard the Williams woman calling George by name—that planted the "George did it" seed—and got a new thrill when he witnessed George cut the woman's throat.

Then George had seen the dark, cop-like figure out the window, got spooked and lammed; and Lapps entered the apartment, spilled his seed, did his sick, guilty number washing and bandaging the corpse, and took various mementos, including undies and the photo album.

This new thrill had inspired Lapps to greater heights of madness, and the second girl—Margaret Johnson—had been all his. All his own twisted handiwork . . . though perhaps in his mind George had done that, as well.

But Lapps, like so many men after even a normal sexual release, felt a sadness and even guilt and had left that lipstick plea on the wall.

That pretty nurse, Katherine Reynolds, had been lucky. Lapps hadn't been able to kill again; he'd stopped at assault—maybe he'd had his sexual release already, and his remorse kicked in before he could kill her. He'd even come back to help her.

What was bothering me, though, was the Keenan child. Nothing about Lapps's MO fit this crime. The building wasn't his "type." Kidnapping wasn't his crime, let alone dismembering a child. Had Lapps's thrill-seeking escalated into sheer depravity?

Even so, one thing was so wrong I couldn't invent any justification for it. Ken had said it: the kid had probably never had normal sex. The kid's idea of a fun date was going through a strange window and coming on the floor.

But rape had been attempted on the little girl. The coroner said so. Rape.

"Want some company, Heller?"

Hal Davis, with his oversize head and sideways smile, had already slid in across from me in the booth.

"Sure. What's new in the world of yellow journalism?"

"Slow day. Jeez, Heller, you look like shit."

"Thanks, Hal."

"You should be on top of the world. You're a local hero. A celebrity."

"Shut up, Hal."

Davis had brought a scotch along with him. "Ain't this case a pip. Too bad they can't fry this kid, but in this enlightened day and age, he'll probably get a padded cell and three squares for the rest of his miserable life."

"I don't think they'll fry a seventeen-year-old, even in a case like this."

"What a case it's been. For you, especially."

"You got your share of mileage out of it, too, Hal."

He laughed; lit up a cigarette. Shook his head. "Funny."

"What is?"

"Who'd a thunk it?"

"Thunk what?"

He leaned over conspiratorially. His breath was evidence that this was not his first scotch of the afternoon. "That the Keenan kidnapper really would turn out to be the Lipstick Killer. For real."

"Why not? He left his signature on Keenan's back fence. 'Stop me before I kill more . . .'"

"That's the funny part." He snorted smugly. "Who do you think wrote that on the fence?"

I blinked. "What do you mean?"

Davis leaned across with a one-sided smirk that split his boyish face. "Don't be a jerk. Don't be so gullible. *I* wrote that there. It made for a hell of a byline."

I grabbed him by his lapels and dragged him across the table. His scotch spilled and my drink went over and his cigarette went flying and his eyes were wide, as were those of the businessmen finishing up their two- and three-martini lunches.

"You *what*?" I asked him through my teeth.

"Nate! You're hurting me! Let go! You're makin' a scene. . . ."

I shoved him back against the booth. I got out. I was shaking. "You did do it, didn't you, you little cocksucker."

He was frightened, but he tried not to show it; he made a face, shrugged. "What's the big fucking deal?"

I grabbed him by the tie and he watched my fist while I decided whether to smash in his face.

Then the fist dissolved into fingers, but I retained my grip on his tie.

"Let's go talk to the cops," I said.

"I was just bullshitting," he said, lamely. "I didn't do it. Really. It was just the booze talking."

I put a hand around his throat and started to squeeze. His eyes popped. I was sneering at him when I said, "Stop me, Hal—before I kill more."

Then I shoved him against the wall, rattling some framed pictures, and got the hell out of there.

20

The cellar was lit by a single hanging bulb. There were laundry tubs and storage lockers, just like the basement where JoAnn Keenan was dismembered.

But this was not that basement. This was a slightly smaller one in a building near the "murder cellar," a tidy one with tools and cleaning implements neatly lining the walls, like well-behaved prisoners.

This was janitor Otto Bergstrum's domain.

"Why you want meet with me?" the thick-necked, white-haired Bergstrum asked.

Outside, it was rainy and dark. Close to midnight. I was in a drenched trenchcoat, getting Bergstrum's tidy cellar damp. I left my hat on and it was dripping, too.

"I told you on the phone," I said. "Business. A matter of money."

As before, the husky old fellow was in coveralls, his biceps tight against the rolled-up sleeves of his flannel shirt; his legs were planted well apart and firmly. His hands were fists and the fists were heavily veined.

"You come about reward money," he said. His eyes were blue and unblinking and cold under unruly salt-and-pepper eyebrows. "You try talk me out of claim my share."

"That's not it exactly. You see, there's going to be several people put in claims."

"Cops not eligible."

"Just city cops. I'm eligible."

"But they not."

"Right. But I have to kick back a few bucks to a couple of 'em, out of what I haul to shore."

"So, what? You think I should help you pay them?"

"No. I think you should kick your share back to me."

His eyes flared; he took a step forward. We were still a number of paces apart, though. Christ, his arms and shoulders were massive.

"Why should I do this?"

"Because I think you kidnapped the Keenan girl," I said.

He took a step back. His mouth dropped open. His eyes widened.

"I'm in clear," he said.

That was less than a denial, wasn't it?

"Otto," I said, "I checked up on you, this afternoon. Discreetly. You're a veteran, like me—only you served in the first war. On the other side."

He jutted his jaw. "I am proud to be German."

"But you were an American immigrant at the time. You'd been in this country since you were a kid. But still you went back home, to fight for the fatherland . . . then after they lost their asses, you had the nerve to come back."

"I was not alone in doing such."

He wasn't, either: on the North Side, there was a whole organization of these German World War I vets who got together. They even had dinners with American vets.

"The Butcher's Union knew about you," I said, "but you were never a member."

"Communists," he said.

"You worked as a butcher in a shop on the West Side, for years—till meat shortages during the war . . . this *last* war . . . got you laid off. You were non-union, couldn't find another butcher job . . . with your background, anything defense-related was out. You wound up here. A janitor. It's your sister's building, isn't it?"

"You go to hell, mister."

"You know what I think, Otto? I think you blamed the New Deal for your bad deal. I think you got real mad at the government. I think you in particular blamed the OPA."

"Socialists," he said.

"Bob Keenan wasn't even in Chicago when you got laid off, you stupid old fart. But he was in the OPA now, and he was in the neighborhood. He had money, and he had a pretty little daughter. He was as good a place as any for Otto Bergstrum to get even."

"There is no proof of any of this. It is all air. Wind. You are the fart."

"What, did you get drunk, was it spur of the moment, or did you plan it? The kidnapping I can see. What I don't understand is killing the little girl. Did she start to make noise in bed, and you strangled her? Were you just too strong, and maybe drunk, and it was an accident of sorts?"

Now his face was an expressionless mask. His hands weren't fists anymore. His eyes were hooded; his head was slack.

"What I really don't get, Otto, is the rape. Trying to rape a little girl. Was she already dead? You sick fucker."

He raised his head. "You have filthy mouth. Maybe I wash it out with lye."

"I'm going to give you a choice, old man. You can come with me, and come clean at Summerdale station. Or I can kill you right here."

"You have gun in your coat pocket?"

"I have gun in my coat pocket, yeah."

"Ah. But my friend has knife."

I hadn't heard him. I have no idea where he came from; coal bin, maybe. He was as quiet as nobody there. He was just suddenly behind me and he did have a knife, a long, sharp butcher knife that caught the single bulb's glow and reflected it, like the glint of a madman's eyes. Like the glint of this madman's eyes, as I stepped quickly to one side, the knife slashing down, cutting through the arm of my raincoat, cutting cloth and ripping a wound along my shoulder. My hand involuntarily released the gun, and even though both it and my hand were in the same coat pocket, I was fumbling for it, the gun caught in the cloth, my fingers searching for the grip. . . .

I recognized this rail-thin, shorthaired, sunken-cheeked young man as James Watson—but only from the papers. I'd never met him. He was the handyman at the nursery from which the kidnap ladder had been "stolen"; an Army vet and an accused child molester and, with Otto, a suspect in this case till I hauled Jerome Lapps onstage.

He was wearing a rain slicker, yellow, and one of those floppy yellow wide-brimmed rain hats; but he didn't look like he'd been outside. Maybe his raincoat was to keep the blood off.

He had the knife raised in such a corny fashion; raised in one fist, level with his head, and walking mummy-slow. His dark blue eyes were wide and his grin glazed and he looked silly, like a scarecrow with a knife, a caricature of a fiend. I could have laughed at how hokey this asshole looked, only Otto had grabbed me from behind as Watson advanced.

With my arms pulled back, one of them bleeding and burning from the slash of a knife that was even now red with my blood, I struggled but with little success. The old German janitor had me locked in his thick hands.

Watson stabbed savagely with the knife and I moved to the left and the blade, about half of it, went into Otto's neck and blood spurted.

Otto went down, clutching his throat, his life oozing through his fingers, and I was free of him, and while Watson still had the knife in his hand—he'd withdrawn the blade almost as quickly as he'd accidentally sunk it into his cohort's throat—the handyman was stunned by the turn of events, his mouth hanging open, as if awaiting a dentist's drill. I grabbed his wrist with my two hands and swung his hand and his knife in a sudden arc down into his stomach.

The sound was like sticking your foot in thick mud.

He stood there, doing the oddest little dance, for several seconds, his hand gripped around the handle of the butcher knife, which I had driven in almost to the hilt. He looked down at himself with a look of infinite stupidity and danced some more.

I pushed his stupid face with the heel of my hand and he went ass-over-tea-kettle. He lay on his back twitching. He'd released the knife handle. I yanked the knife out of his stomach; there was a little hole in the rain slicker where the knife went in.

And the sound was like pulling your foot out of thick mud.

"You're the one who tried to rape that little girl, aren't you, Jim?"

He was blinking and twitching; a thin geyser of blood was coming from the hole in the yellow rain slicker.

"Poor old Otto just wanted to get even. Pull a little kidnap, make a little money off those socialist sons of bitches who cost him his job. But he picked a bad assistant in you, Jim. Had to play butcher on that dead little girl, trying to clean up after you."

There was still life in Watson's eyes. Otto was over near the laundry tubs, gurgling. Alive, barely.

I had the knife in one hand, and my blood was soaking my shirt under the raincoat, though I felt little if any pain. I gave some serious thought to whaling away on Watson with the butcher knife; just carving the fucker up. But I couldn't quite cross the line.

I had George Morello's pack of Camels in my suit coat pocket. I dug them out and smoked while I watched both men die.

Better part of two cigarettes, it took.

Then I wiped off anything I'd touched, dropped the butcher knife near Watson, and left that charnel house behind; went out into a dark, warm summer night and a warm, cleansing summer rain, which put out the second cigarette.

It was down to the butt, anyway. I tossed it in a sewer.

The deaths of Otto Bergstrum and James Watson made a bizarre sidebar in the ongoing saga of the Lipstick Killer, but neither the cops nor the press allowed the "fatal falling out between friends" to influence the accepted scenario.

It turned out there was even something of a motive: Watson had loaned Otto five hundred dollars to pay off a gambling debt; Otto played the horses, it seemed. Speculation was that Watson, knowing Otto was due reward money from the Keenan case, had demanded payment. Both men were known to have bad tempers. Both had killed in the war—well, each in his individual war.

The cops never figured out how the two men had managed to kill each other with the one knife, not that anybody seemed to care. It was fine with me. Nobody had seen me in the vicinity that rainy night, or at least nobody who bothered to report it.

Lapps was indicted on multiple burglary, assault, and murder charges. His lawyers entered into what years later an investigative journalist would term "a strange, unprecedented cooperative relationship" with the State's Attorney's office.

In order to save their client from the electric chair, the defense lawyers—despite the prosecution's admission of the "small likelihood of a successful murder prosecution of Jerome Lapps"—advised the boy to cop a plea.

If Lapps were to confess to the murders of Caroline Williams, Margaret Johnson and JoAnn Keenan, the State's Attorney would seek concurrent life sentences. That meant parole in twenty years.

Lapps—reluctantly, I'm told—accepted the plea bargain, but when the boy was taken into a judge's presence to make a formal admission of guilt, he said instead, "I don't remember killing anybody."

The recantation cost him. Even though Lapps eventually gave everybody the confession they wanted, the deal was off: all he got out of it was avoiding the chair. His three life terms were concurrent with a recommendation of no parole. Ever.

He tried to hang himself in his cell, but it didn't take.

I took a ride on the Rock Island Rocket to Joliet to visit Lapps, about a year after he was sent up.

The visiting room at Stateville was a long narrow room cut in half by a long wide table with a glass divider. I'd already taken my seat with the other visitors when guards paraded in a handful of prisoners.

Lapps, like the others, wore blue denims and a blue-and-white striped shirt, which looked like a normal dress shirt, unless the wearer turned to reveal a stenciled number across the back. The husky, good-looking kid had changed little in appearance; maybe he was a little heavier. His dark, wavy hair, though no shorter, was cut differently—it was neater looking, a student's hair, not a JD's.

He sat and smiled shyly. "I remember you."

"You should. You tried to shoot me."

"That's what I understand. I'm sorry."

"You don't remember?"

"No."

"The gun you used was one you'd stolen. The owner identified it along with other stuff of his you took."

He shrugged; this was all news to him.

I continued: "The owner said the gun had been his father's and had been stuck in a drawer for seventeen years. Hadn't been fired for a long time."

His brow knit. "That's why the gun didn't go off, when I shot at you?"

"Yes. But a ballistics expert said the third shot *would* have gone off. You'd reactivated the trigger."

"I'm glad it didn't."

"Me too."

We looked at each other. My gaze was hard, unforgiving; his was evasive, shy.

"Why are you here, Mr. Heller?"

"I wanted to ask you a question. Why did you confess to all three murders?"

He shrugged again. "I had to. Otherwise, I'd be dead, my lawyers say. I just made things up. Told them what they wanted to hear. Repeated things back to them. Used what I read in the papers." One more shrug. Then his dark eyes tightened. "Why? You asked me like . . . like you knew I didn't do them."

"You did one of them, Jerry. You killed Margaret Williams and you wrote that lipstick message on her wall."

Something flickered in his eyes. "I don't remember."

"Maybe not. But you also assaulted Katherine Reynolds, and you tried to shoot me. As far as I'm concerned, that's why you're here."

"You don't think I killed that little girl?"

"I know you didn't."

An eagerness sprang into his passive face. "Have you talked to my lawyers?"

I shook my head no.

"Would you talk to my . . . "

"No. I'm not going to help you, Jerry."

"Why . . . why are you telling this, then . . . ?"

My voice was barely above a whisper; this was just between us guys. "In case you're not faking. In case you really don't remember what you did. I think you got a right to know what you're doing time for. What you're really doing time for. And you did kill the second girl. And you almost killed the nurse. And you damn near killed me. That's why you're here, Jerry. That's why I'm leaving you here to rot, and don't bother repeating what I'm telling you, because I can out-lie every con in Stateville. I used to be a Chicago cop."

He was reeling. "Who . . . who killed the first girl? Who killed that Caroline Williams lady?"

"Jerry," I said, rising to go, "George did it."

22

Lapps, as of this writing, is still inside. That's why, after all these years, as I edge toward senility in my Coral Springs condo, in the company of my second wife, I have put all this down on paper. The Parole for Lapps Committee requested a formal deposition, but I preferred that this take the same form, more or less, as other memoirs I've scribbled in my dotage.

Jerry Lapps is an old man now—not as old as me, but old. A gray-haired, paunchy old boy. Not the greasy-haired JD who I was glad to see go to hell and Stateville. He's been in custody longer than any other inmate in the Illinois prison system. Long before courses were offered to prisoners, he was the first Illinois inmate to earn a college degree. He then helped and advised other convicts with organizing similar self-help correspondence-course programs. He taught himself electronics and became a pretty fair watercolor artist. Right now he's in Vienna prison, a minimum-security facility with no fences and no barred windows. He's the assistant to the prison chaplain.

Over the years, the press and public servants and surviving relatives of the murder victims—including JoAnn's sister Jane—have fought Lapps' parole. He is portrayed as the first of a particular breed of American urban monster—precursor to Richard Speck, John Wayne Gacy and Ted Bundy.

Bob Keenan died last year. His wife Norma died three years ago.

Sam Flood—a.k.a. Sam Giancana—was hit in his home back in '75, right before he was supposed to testify before a Senate committee about Outfit/CIA connections.

Of the major players, Lapps is the only one left alive. Lapps and me.

What the hell. I've had my fill of revenge.

Let the bastard loose.

If he's faking rehabilitation like he once faked amnesia, if he hurts anybody else, shit—I'll haul the nine millimeter out of mothballs and hobble after him myself.

23

My son was born just before midnight, on September 27, 1947.

We named him Nathan Samuel Heller, Jr.

His mother—exhausted after twelve hours of labor, face slick with sweat, hair matted down—never looked more beautiful to me. And I never saw her look happier.

"He's so small," she said. "Why did he take so long making his entrance?"

"He's small but he's stubborn. Like his mother."

"He's got your nose. He's got your mouth. He's gorgeous. You want to hold him, Nate?"

"Sure."

I took the little bundle, and looked at the sweet small face and experienced, for the first and only time before or since, love at first sight.

"I'm Daddy," I told the groggy little fellow. He made saliva bubbles. I touched his tiny nose. Examined his tiny hand—the miniature palm, the perfect little fingers. How could something so miraculous happen in such an awful world?

I gave him back to his mother and she put him to her breast and he began to suckle. A few minutes on the planet, and he was getting tit already. Life wasn't going get to much better.

I sat there and watched them and waves of joy and sadness

alternated over me. It was mostly joy, but I couldn't keep from thinking that a hopeful mother had once held a tiny child named JoAnn in her arms, minutes after delivery; that another mother had held little Jerry Lapps in her gentle grasp. And Caroline Williams and Margaret Johnson were once babes in their mother's arms. One presumes even Otto Bergstrum and James Watson and, Christ, George Morello were sweet infants in their sweet mother's arms, once upon a time.

I promised myself that my son would have it better than me. He wouldn't have to have it so goddamn rough; the Depression was ancient history, and the war to end all wars was over. He'd want for nothing. Food, clothing, shelter, education, they were his birthright.

That's what we'd fought for, all of us. To give our kids what we never had. To give them a better, safer place to live in. Life, liberty and the pursuit of happiness.

For that one night, settled into a hard hospital chair, in the glow of my brand-new little family, I allowed myself to believe that that hope was not a vain one. That anything was possible in this glorious post-war world.

AUTHOR'S NOTE

My friend and research associate George Hagenauer did hours of newspaper research on the William Heirens case (the real-life basis for this novella), and took me on a walking tour of the various crime scenes. Bill Drury, Sam Giancana, and a few others appear under their true names, but most characters here are fictional with real-life counterparts. Sources include *The Don* (1977), William Brashler; *Murders Sane and Mad* (1965), Miriam Allen deFord; *Murder Man* (1984), Thomas Downs; *"Before I Kill More . . . "* (1955), Lucy Freeman; *Mafia Princess* (1984), Antoinette Giancana and Thomas C. Renner; and *Wartime Racketeers* (1945), Harry Lever and Joseph Young. Also, the article "Kill-Crazed Animal?" by Robert McClory (*The Chicago Reader*, August 25 1989).

A Little Missionary Work

by Sue Grafton

S OMETIMES YOU have to take on a job that constitutes pure missionary
work. You accept an assignment not for pay, or for any hope of
tangible reward, but simply to help another human being in distress.
My name is Kinsey Millhone. I'm a licensed private eye . . . in business
for myself . . . so I can't really afford professional charity, but now and
then somebody gets into trouble and I just can't turn my back.

I was standing in line one Friday at the bank, waiting to make a
deposit. It was almost lunchtime and there were eleven people in front
of me, so I had some time to kill. As usual, in the teller's line, I was
thinking about Harry Hovey, my bank-robber friend, who'd once been
arrested for holding up this very branch. I'd met him when I was
investigating a bad-check case. He was introduced to me by another
crook as an unofficial "expert" and ended up giving me a crash course
in the methods and practices of passing bad paper. Poor Harry. I
couldn't remember how many times he'd been in the can. He was
skilled enough for a life of crime, but given to self-sabotage. Harry was
always trying to go straight, always trying to clean up his act, but
honest employment never seemed to have much appeal. He'd get out of
prison, find a job, and be doing pretty well for himself. Then something
would come along and he'd succumb to temptation—forge a check, rob
a bank, God only knows what. Harry was hooked on crime the way
some people are addicted to cocaine, alcohol, chocolate, and unrequited
love. He was currently doing time in the federal correctional institution
in Lompoc, California, with all the other racketeers, bank robbers,
counterfeiters, and former White House staff bad boys. . . .

I had reached the teller's window and was finishing my transaction when Lucy Alisal, the assistant bank manager, approached. "Miss Millhone? I wonder if you could step this way. Mr. Chamberlain would like a word with you."

"Who?"

"The branch vice president," she said. "It shouldn't take long."

"Oh. Sure."

I followed the woman toward Mr. Chamberlain's glass-walled enclosure, wondering the whole time what I'd done to deserve this. Well, okay. Let's be honest. I'd been thinking about switching my account to First Interstate for the free checking privileges, but I didn't see how he could have found out about that. As for my balances, I'd only been overdrawn by the teensiest amount and what's a line of credit for?

I was introduced to Jack Chamberlain, who turned out to be someone I recognized from the gym, a tall, lanky fellow in his early forties, whose workouts overlapped mine three mornings a week. We'd exchange occasional small talk if we happened to be doing reps on adjacent machines. It was odd to see him here in a conservative business suit after months of sweat-darkened shorts and T-shirts. His hair was cropped close, the color a wiry mixture of copper and silver. He wore steel-rimmed glasses and his teeth were endearingly crooked in front. Somehow, he looked more like a high-school basketball coach than a banking exec. A trophy sitting on his desk attested to his athletic achievements, but the engraving was small and I couldn't quite make out the print from where I sat. He caught my look and a smile creased his face. "Varsity basketball. We were state champs," he said as he shook my hand formally and invited me to take a seat.

He sat down himself and picked up a fountain pen, which he capped and recapped as he talked. "I appreciate your time. I know you do your banking on Fridays and I took the liberty," he said. "Someone told me at the gym that you're a private investigator."

"That's right. Are you in the market for one?"

"This is for an old friend of mine. My former high-school sweetheart, if you want the truth. I probably could have called you at your office, but the circumstances are unusual and this seemed more discreet. Are you free tonight by any chance?"

"Tonight? That depends," I said. "What's going on?"

"I'd rather have her explain it. This is probably going to seem paranoid, but she insists on secrecy, which is why she didn't want to make contact herself. She has reason to believe her phone is tapped. I hope you can bear with us. Believe me, I don't ordinarily do business this way."

"Glad to hear that," I said. "Can you be a bit more specific? So far, I haven't really heard what I'm being asked to do."

Jack set the pen aside. "She'll explain the situation as soon as it seems wise. She and her husband are having a big party tonight and she asked me to bring you. They don't want you appearing in any professional capacity. Time is of the essence, or we might go about this some other way. You'll understand when you meet her."

I studied him briefly, trying to figure out what was going on. If this was a dating ploy, it was the weirdest one I'd ever heard. "Are you married?"

He smiled slightly. "Divorced. I understand you are, too. I assure you, this is not a hustle."

"What kind of party?"

"Oh yes. Glad you reminded me." He removed an envelope from his top drawer and pushed it across the desk. "Cocktails. Five to seven. Black tie, I'm afraid. This check should cover your expenses in the way of formal dress. If you try the rental shop around the corner, Roberta Linderman will see that you're outfitted properly. She knows these people well."

"What people? You haven't even told me their names."

"Karen Waterston and Kevin McCall. They have a little weekend retreat up here."

"Ah," I said, nodding. This was beginning to make more sense. Karen Waterson and Kevin McCall were actors who'd just experienced a resurgence in their careers, starring in a new television series called *Shamus, PI*, an hour-long spoof of every detective series that's ever aired. I don't watch much TV, but I'd heard about the show, and after seeing it once, I'd found myself hooked. The stories were fresh, the writing was superb, and the format was perfect for their considerable acting talents. Possibly because they were married in "real" life, the two brought a wicked chemistry to the screen. As with many new shows, the ratings hadn't yet caught up with the rave reviews, but things looked promising. Whatever their problem, I could understand the desire to keep their difficulties hidden from public scrutiny.

Jack was saying, "You're in no way obligated, but I hope you'll say yes. She really needs your help."

"Well. I guess I've had stranger requests in my day. I better give you my address."

He held up the signature card I'd completed when I opened my account. "I have that."

I soon learned what "cocktails five to seven" means to the very rich. Everybody showed up at seven and stayed until they were dead drunk. Jack Chamberlain, in a tux, picked me up at my apartment at 6:45. I was decked out in a slinky beaded black dress with long sleeves, a high collar, and no back; not my usual apparel of choice. When Jack helped me into the front seat of his Mercedes, I shrieked at the shock of cold leather against my bare skin.

Once at the party, I regained my composure and managed to conduct myself (for the most part) without embarrassment or disgrace. The "little weekend retreat" turned out to be a sprawling six-bedroom estate, decorated with a confident blend of the avant-garde and the minimalist; unadorned white walls, wide, bare, gleaming expanses of polished hardwood floor. The few pieces of furniture were draped with white canvas, like those in a palatial summer residence being closed up for the season. Aside from a dazzling crystal chandelier, all the dining room contained was a plant, a mirror, and a bentwood chair covered with an antique paisley shawl. . chic. They'd probably paid thousands for some interior designer to come in and haul all the knickknacks away.

As the party picked up momentum the noise level rose, people spilling out onto all the terraces. Six young men, in black pants and pleated white shirts, circulated with silver platters of tasty hot and cold morsels. The champagne was exquisite, the supply apparently endless, so that I was fairly giddy by the time Jack took me by the arm and eased me out of the living room. "Karen wants to see you upstairs," he murmured.

"Great," I said. I'd hardly laid eyes on her except as a glittering wraith along the party's perimeters. I hadn't seen Kevin at all, but I'd overheard someone say he was off scouting locations for the show coming up. Jack and I drifted up the spiral stairs together, me hoping that in my half-inebriated state, I wouldn't pitch over the railing and land with a splat. As I reached the landing I looked down and was startled to see my friend Vera in the foyer below. She caught sight of me and did a double take, apparently surprised to see me in such elegant surroundings, especially dressed to the teeth. We exchanged a quick wave.

The nearly darkened master suite was carpeted to a hush, but again, it was nearly empty. The room was probably fifty feet by thirty, furnished dead center with a king-size bed, a wicker hamper, two fichus trees, and a silver lamp with a twenty-five-watt bulb on a long, curving neck.

As Jack ushered me into the master bathroom where the meeting was to take place, he flicked me an apologetic look. "I hope this doesn't seem too odd."

"Not at all," I said, politely . . . like a lot of my business meetings take place in the WC.

Candles flickered from every surface. Sound was dampened by thick white carpeting and a profusion of plants. Karen Waterston sat on the middle riser of three wide, beige, marble steps leading up to the Jacuzzi. Beside her, chocolate-brown bath towels were rolled and stacked like a cord of firewood. She was wearing a halter-style dress of white chiffon, which emphasized the dark even tan of her slender shoulders and arms. Her hair was silver blond, coiled around her head in a twist of satin ropes. She was probably forty-two, but her face had been cosmetically backdated to the age of twenty-five, a process that would require ever more surgical ingenuity as the years went by. Jack introduced us and we shook hands. Hers were ice cold, and I could have sworn she wasn't happy to have me there.

Jack pulled out a wicker stool and sat down with his back to Karen's makeup table, his eyes never leaving her face. My guess was that being an ex-high-school sweetheart of hers was as much a part of his identity as being a former basketball champ. I leaned a hip against the marble counter. There was a silver-framed photograph of Kevin McCall propped up beside me, the mirror reflecting endless reproductions of his perfect profile. To all appearances, he'd been allowed to retain the face he was born with, but the uniform darkness of his hair, with its picturesque dusting of silver at the temples, suggested that nature was being tampered with, at least superficially. Still, it was hard to imagine that either he or Karen had a problem more pressing than an occasional loose dental cap.

"I appreciate your coming, Miss Millhone. It means a lot to us under the circumstances." Her voice was throaty and low, with the merest hint of tremolo. Even by candlelight, I could see the tension in her face. "I wasn't in favor of bringing anyone else into this, but Jack insisted. Has he explained the situation?"

She glanced from me to Jack, who said, "I told her you preferred to do that yourself."

She seemed to hug herself for warmth and her mouth suddenly looked pinched. Tears welled in her eyes and she placed two fingers on the bridge of her nose as if to quell their flow. "You'll have to forgive me. . . ."

I didn't think she'd be able to continue, but she managed to collect herself

"Kevin's been kidnapped. . . ." Her voice cracked with emotion and she lifted her dark eyes to mine. I'd never seen such a depth of pain and suffering.

At first, I didn't even know what to say to her. "When was this?"

"Last night. We're very private people. We've never let anyone get remotely close to us—" She broke off again.

"Take your time," I said.

Jack moved over to the stair and sat down beside her, putting an arm protectively around her shoulders. The smile she offered him was wan and she couldn't sustain it.

He handed her his handkerchief and I waited while she blew her nose and dabbed at her eyes. "Sorry. I'm just so frightened. This is horrible."

"I hope you've called the police," I said.

"She doesn't want to take the risk," Jack said.

Karen shook her head. "They said they'd kill him if I called in the police."

"Who said?"

"The bastards who snatched him. I was given this note. Here. You can see for yourself. It's too much like the Bender case to take any chances." She extracted a piece of paper from the folds of her long dress and held it out to me.

I took the note by one corner so I wouldn't smudge any prints, probably a useless precaution. If this was truly like the Bender case, there wouldn't be any prints to smudge. The paper was plain, the printing in ballpoint pen and done with a ruler.

Five hundred thou in small bills buys your husband back. Go to the cops or the feds and he's dead meat for sure. We'll call soon with instructions. Keep your mouth shut or you'll regret it. That's a promise, baby cakes.

She was right. Both the format and the use of language bore an uncanny similarity to the note delivered to a woman named Corey Bender, whose husband had been a kidnapped about a year ago. Dan Bender was the CEO of a local manufacturing company, a man who'd made millions with a line of auto parts called Fender-Benders. In that situation, the kidnappers had asked for five hundred thousand dollars in tens and twenties. Mrs. Bender had contacted both the police and the FBI, who had stage-managed the whole transaction, arranging for a suitcase full of blank paper to be dropped according to the kidnappers' elaborate telephone instructions. The drop site had been staked out, everyone assuring Mrs. Bender that nothing could possibly go wrong. The drop went as planned except the suitcase was never picked up and Dan Bender was never seen alive again. His body . . . or what was left of it . . . washed up on the Santa Teresa beach two months later.

"Tell me what happened," I said

She got up and began to pace, describing in halting detail the circumstances of Kevin McCall's abduction. The couple had been working on a four-day shooting schedule at the studio down in Hollywood. They'd been picked up from the set by limousine at 7:00 PM on Thursday and had been driven straight to Santa Teresa, arriving for the long weekend at nine that night. The housekeeper usually fixed supper for them and left it in the oven, departing shortly before they were due home. At the end of a week of shooting, the couple preferred all the solitude they could get.

Nothing seemed amiss when they arrived at the house. Both interior and exterior lights were on as usual. Karen emerged from the limo with Kevin right behind her. She chatted briefly with the driver and then waved good-bye while Kevin unlocked the front door and disarmed the alarm system. The limo driver had already turned out of the gate when two men in ski masks stepped out of the shadows armed with automatics. Neither Karen nor Kevin had much opportunity to react. A second limousine pulled into the driveway and Kevin was hustled into the backseat at gunpoint. Not a word was said. The note was thrust into Karen's hand as the gunmen left. She raced after the limo as it sped away, but no license plates were visible. She had no real hope of catching up and no clear idea what she meant to do anyway. In a panic, she returned to the house and locked herself in. Once the shock wore off, she called Jack Chamberlain, their local banker, a former high-school classmate—the only person in Santa Teresa she felt she could trust. Her first thought was to cancel tonight's party altogether, but Jack suggested she proceed.

"I thought it would look more natural," he filled in. "Especially if she's being watched."

"They did call with instructions?" I asked.

Again she nodded, her face pale. "They want the money by midnight tomorrow or that's the last I'll see of him."

"Can you *raise* five hundred thousand on such short notice?"

"Not without help," she said, and turned a pleading look to Jack.

He was already shaking his head and I gathered this was a subject they'd already discussed at length. "The bank doesn't keep large reservoirs of cash on hand," he said to me. "There's no way I'd have access to a sum like that, particularly on a weekend. The best I can do is bleed the cash from all the branch ATMs."

"Surely you can do better than that," she said. "You're a bank vice president."

He turned to her, with a faintly defensive air, trying to persuade her the failing wasn't his. "I might be able to put together the full amount by Monday, but even then, you'd have to fill out an application and go through the loan committee."

She said, "Oh, for God's sake, Jack. Don't give me that bureaucratic bullshit when Kevin's life is at stake! There has to be a way."

"Karen, be reasonable. . . ."

"Forget it. This is hopeless. I'm sorry I ever brought you into this."

I watched them bicker for a moment and then broke in. "All right, wait a minute. Hold on. Let's back off the money question, for the time being."

"Back *off*?" she said.

"Look. Let's assume there's a way to get the ransom money. Now what?"

Her brow was furrowed and she seemed to have trouble concentrating on the question at hand. "I'm sorry. What?"

"Fill me in on the rest of it. I need to know what happened last night after you got in touch with Jack."

"Oh. I see, yes. He came over to the house and we sat here for hours, waiting for the phone to ring. The kidnappers . . . one of them . . . finally called at two AM."

"You didn't recognize the voice?"

"Not at all."

"Did the guy seem to know Jack was with you?"

"He didn't mention it, but he swore they were watching the house and he said the phone was tapped."

"I wouldn't bet on it, but it's probably smart to proceed as though it's true. It's possible they didn't have the house staked out last night, but they may have put a man on it since. Hard to know. Did they tell you how to deliver the cash once you got it?"

"That part was simple. I'm to pack the money in a big canvas duffel. At eleven-thirty tomorrow night, they want me to leave the house on my bicycle with the duffel in the basket."

"On a bike? That's a new one."

"Kev and I often bike together on weekends, which they seemed aware of. As a matter of fact, they seemed to know quite a lot. It was very creepy."

Jack spoke up. "They must have cased the place to begin with. They knew the whole routine from what she's told me."

"Stands to reason," I remarked. And then to her, "Go on."

"They told me to wear my yellow jumpsuit—I guess so they can identify me—and that's all there was."

"They didn't tell you which way to ride?"

"I asked about that and they told me I could head in any direction I wanted. They said they'd follow at a distance and intercept when it suited them. Obviously, they want to make sure I'm unaccompanied."

"Then what?"

"When they blink the car lights, I'm to toss the canvas duffel to the side of the road and ride on. They'll release Kevin as soon as the money's been picked up and counted."

"Shoot. It rules out any fudging if they count the money first. Did they let you talk to Kevin?"

"Briefly. He sounded fine. Worried about me . . ."

"And you're sure it was him."

"Positive. I'm so scared. . . ."

The whole time we'd been talking, my mind was racing ahead. She had to call the cops. There was no doubt in my mind she was a fool to tackle this without the experts, but she was dead set against it. I said, "Karen, you can't handle something like this without the cops. You'd be crazy to try to manage on your own."

She was adamant.

Jack and I took turns arguing the point and I could see his frustration surface. "For God's sake, you've got to listen to us. You're way out of your element. If these guys are the same ones who kidnapped Dan Bender, you're putting Kevin's life at risk. They're absolutely ruthless."

"Jack, I'm not the one putting Kevin's life at risk. *You* are. That's exactly what you're doing when you propose calling the police."

"How are you going to get the money?" he said, exasperated.

"Goddammit, how do I know? You're the banker. You tell me."

"Karen, I'm telling you. There's no way to do this. You're making a big mistake."

"Corey Bender was the one who made a mistake," she snapped.

We were getting nowhere. Time was short and the pressures were mounting every minute. If Jack and I didn't come up with some plan, Kevin McCall was going to end up dead. If the cash could be assembled, the obvious move was to have me take Karen's place during the actual delivery, which would at least eliminate the possibility of her being picked up as well. Oddly enough, I thought I had an inkling how to get the bucks, though it might well take me the better part of the next day.

"All right," I said, breaking in for the umpteenth time. "We can argue this all night and it's not going to get us anyplace. Suppose I find a way to get the money, will you at least consent to my taking your place for the drop?"

She studied me for a moment. "That's awfully risky, isn't it? What if they realize the substitution?"

"How could they? They'll be following in a car. In the dark and at a distance, I can easily pass for you. A wig and a jumpsuit and who'd know the difference?"

She hesitated. "I do have a wig, but why not just do what they say? I don't like the idea of disobeying their instructions."

"Because these guys are way too dangerous for you to deal with yourself. Suppose you deliver the money as specified. What's to prevent their picking you up and making Kevin pay additional ransom for your return?"

I could see her debate the point. Her uneasiness was obvious, but she finally agreed. "I don't understand what you intend to do about the ransom. If Jack can't manage to get the money, how can you?"

"I know a guy who has access to a large sum of cash. I can't promise anything, but I can always ask."

Karen's gaze came to rest on my face with puzzlement.

"Look," I said in response to her unspoken question. "I'll explain if I get it. And if not, you have to promise me you'll call the police."

Jack prodded. "It's your only chance."

She was silent for a moment and then spoke slowly. "All right. Maybe so. We'll do it your way. What other choice do I have?"

Before we left, we made arrangements for her to leave a wig, the yellow jumpsuit, and the bicycle on the service porch the next night. I'd return to the house on foot sometime after dark, leaving my car parked a few discreet blocks away. At 11:30, as instructed, I'd peddle down the drive with the canvas duffel and ride around until the kidnappers caught up with me. While I was gone Jack could swing by and pick Karen up in his car. I wanted her off the premises in the event anything went wrong. If I were snatched and the kidnappers realized they had the wrong person, at least they couldn't storm back to the house and get her. We went over the details until we were all in accord. In the end, she seemed satisfied with the plan and so did Jack. I was the only one with any lingering doubts. I thought she was a fool, but I kept that to myself.

I hit the road the next morning early and headed north on 101. Visiting hours at the federal correctional institution at Lompoc run from eight to four on Saturdays. The drive took about an hour with a brief stop at a supermarket in Buellton, where I picked up an assortment of picnic supplies. By ten, I was seated at one of the four sheltered picnic tables with my friend, Harry Hovey. If Harry was surprised to see me, he didn't complain. "It's not like my social calendar's all that full," he said. "To what do I owe the pleasure?"

"Let's eat first," I said. "Then I got something I need to talk to you about."

I'd brought cold chicken and potato salad, assorted cheeses, fruit, and cookies—anything I could grab that didn't look like institutional fare. Personally, I wasn't hungry, but it was gratifying to watch Harry chow down with such enthusiasm. He was not looking well. He was a man in his fifties, maybe five five, heavyset, with thinning gray hair and glasses cloudy with fingerprints. He didn't take good care of himself under the best of circumstances, and the stress of prison living had aged him ten years. His color was bad. He was smoking way too much. He'd lost weight in a manner that looked neither healthful nor flattering.

"How're you doing?" I asked. "You look tired."

"I'm okay, I guess. I been better in my day, but what the hell," he said. He'd paused in the middle of his meal for a cigarette. He seemed distracted, his attention flicking from the other tables to the playground equipment, where a noisy batch of kids were twirling round and round on the swings. It was November and the sun was shining, but the air was chilly and the grass was dead.

"How much time you have to serve yet?"

"Sixteen months," he said. "You ever been in the can?"

I shook my head.

He pointed at me with his cigarette. "Word of advice. Never admit nothin'. Always claim you're innocent. I learned that from the politicians. You ever watch those guys? They get caught takin' bribes and they assume this injured air. Like it's all a mistake, but the truth will out. They're confident they'll be vindicated and bullshit like that. They welcome the investigation so their names can be cleared. They always say that, you know? Whole time I'm in prison, I been saying that myself. I was framed. It's all a setup. I don't know nothing about the money. I was just doing a favor for an old friend, a bigwig. A Very Big Wig. Like I'm implying the governor or the chief of police."

"Has it done you any good?"

"Well, not yet, but who knows? My lawyer's still trying to find a basis for appeal. If I get outta this one, I'm going into therapy, get my head straight, I swear to God. Speaking of which, I may get 'born again,' you know? It looks good. Lends a little credibility, which is something all the money in the world can't buy."

I took a deep breath. "Actually, it's the money I need to talk to you about." I took a few minutes to fill him in on the kidnapping without mentioning any names. Some of Karen Waterston's paranoia had filtered into my psyche and I thought the less I said about the "victim," the better off he'd be. "I know you've got a big cache of money somewhere. I'm hoping you'll contribute some of it to pay the ransom demands."

His look was blank with disbelief. "Ransom?"

"Harry, don't put me through this. You know what ransom is."

"Yeah, it's money you give to guys you never see again. Why not throw it out the window? Why not blow it at the track?"

"Are you finished yet?"

He smiled and a dimple formed. "How much you talking about?"

"Five hundred thousand."

His eyebrows went up. "What makes you think I got money like that?"

"Harry," I said patiently, "an informant told the cops you had over a million bucks. That's how you got caught"

Harry slapped the table. "Bobby Urquhart. That fuck. I should have known it was him. I run into the guy in a bar settin' at this table full of bums. He buys a round of tequila shooters. Next thing I know, everybody else is gone. I'm drunk as a skunk and flappin' my mouth." He dropped his cigarette butt on the concrete and crushed it underfoot. "Word of warning. Never confide in a guy wearing Brut. I must have been nuts to give that little faggot the time of day. The money's gone. I blew it. I got nothin' left."

"I don't believe you. That's bullshit. You didn't have time to blow that much. When you were busted, all you had were a few lousy bucks. Where's the rest of it?"

"Uh-uh. No way."

"Come on, Harry. It isn't going to do you any good in here. Why not help these people out? They got tons of money. They can pay you back."

"They got money, how come they don't pay the shit themselves?"

"Because it's Saturday and the banks are closed. The branch VP couldn't even come up with the cash that fast. A man's life is at stake."

"Hey, so's mine and so what? You ever try life in the pen? I worked hard for that money, so why should I do for some guy I never seen before?"

"Once in a while you just gotta help people out."

"Maybe you do. I don't"

"Harry, please. Be a prince. . . ."

I could see him begin to waiver. Who can resist a good deed now and then?

He put his hand on his chest. "This is giving me angina pains." He wagged his head back and forth. "Jesus. What if the cops get wind of it? How's it gonna look?"

"The cops are never going to know. Believe me, this woman's never going to breathe a word of it. If she trusted the cops, she'd have called them in the first place."

"Who are these people? At least tell me that. I'm not giving up half a million bucks without some ID."

I thought about it swiftly. I was reluctant to trade on their celebrity status. On the other hand, she was desperate and there wasn't time to spare. "Swear you won't tell."

"Who'm I gonna tell? I'm a con. Nobody believes me anyway," he said.

"Kevin McCall and Karen Waterston."

He seemed startled at first. "You're kidding me. No shit? You're talking, *Shamus, PI*? Them two?"

"That's right."

"Whyn't you say so? That's my favorite show. All the guys watch that. What a gas. Karen Waterston is a fox."

"Then you'll help?"

"For that chick, of course," he said. He gave me a stern look. "Get me her autograph or the deal's off."

"Trust me. You'll have it. You're a doll. I owe you one."

We took a walk around the yard while he told me where the money was. Harry had nearly two million in cash hidden in a canvas duffel of his own, concealed in the false back of a big upholstered sofa, which was locked up, with a lot of other furniture, in a commercial self-storage facility.

I headed back to Santa Teresa with the key in my hand. Unearthing the money took the balance of the afternoon. The couch was at the bottom of an eight-by-eight-foot storage locker crammed with goods. Tables, chairs, cardboard boxes, a desk, a hundred or more items, which I removed one by one, stacking them behind me in the narrow aisle between bins. The facility was hot and airless and I could hardly ask for help. By the time I laid my hands on the canvas tote hidden in the couch, there was hardly room in the passageway to turn around. By six o'clock, feeling harried, I had taken all but half a million out of Harry's tote. The rest of the stash, I stuffed back into the couch, piling furniture and boxes helter-skelter on top of it. I'd have to return at some point . . . when the whole ordeal was over . . . and pack the bin properly.

The drop played out according to the numbers, without the slightest hitch. At ten that night, I eased through a gap in the hedge on the north side of the Waterston-McCall property and made my way to the house with Harry's canvas bag in tow. I slipped into the darkened service entry where Karen was waiting. Once the door shut behind me, I shoved Harry's canvas tote into the larger duffel she provided. We chatted nervously while I changed into the wig and yellow jumpsuit. It was just then 10:30 and the remaining wait was long and tense. By 11:30, both of us were strung out on pure adrenaline and I was glad to be on the move.

Before I took off on the bicycle, Karen gave me a quick hug. "You're wonderful. I can't believe you did this."

"I'm not as wonderful as all that," I said uncomfortably. "We need to talk the minute Kevin's home safe. Be sure to call me."

"Of course. Absolutely. We'll call you first thing."

I pedaled down the drive and took a right on West Glen. The cash-heavy duffel threw the bike out of balance, but I corrected and rode on. It was chilly at that hour and traffic was almost nonexistent. For two miles, almost randomly, I bicycled through the dark, cursing my own foolishness for thinking I could pull this off. Eventually, I became aware that a sedan had fallen in behind me. In the glare of the headlights, I couldn't tell the make or the model; only that the vehicle was dark blue and the front license plate was missing. The sedan followed me for what felt like an hour, while I pedaled on, feeling anxious, winded, and frightened beyond belief. Finally, the headlights blinked twice. Front wheel wobbling, I hauled the duffel from the basket and tossed it out onto the shoulder of the road. It landed with a thump near a cluster of bushes and I pedaled away. I glanced back only once as the vehicle behind me slowed to a stop.

I returned to the big house, left the bicycle on the service porch, and made my way back across the blackness of the rear lawn to my car. My heart was still thudding as I pulled away. Home again, in my apartment, I changed into a nightie and robe and huddled on the couch with a cup of brandy-laced hot tea. I knew I should try to sleep, but I was too wired to bother. I glanced at my watch. It was nearly 2:00 AM. I figured I probably wouldn't get word from Karen for another hour best. It takes time to count half a million dollars in small bills. I flipped on the TV and watched a mind-numbing rerun of an old black-and-white film.

I waited through the night, but the phone didn't ring. Around five, I must have dozed, because the next thing I knew, it was 8:35. What was going on? The kidnappers had had ample time to effect Kevin's release. If he's getting out alive, I thought. I stared at the phone, afraid to call Karen in case the line was still tapped. I pulled out the phone book, looked up Jack Chamberlain, and tried his home number. The phone rang five times and his machine picked up. I left a cryptic message and then tried Karen at the house. No answer there. I was stumped. Mixed with my uneasiness was a touch of irritation. Even if they'd heard nothing, they could have let me know.

Without much hope of success, I called the bank and asked for Jack. Surprisingly, Lucy Alisal put me through.

"Jack Chamberlain," he said.

"Jack? This is Kinsey. Have you heard from Karen Waterston?"

"Of course. Haven't you?"

"Not a word," I said. "Is Kevin okay?"

"He's fine. Everything's terrific."

"Would you kindly tell me what's going on?"

"Well, sure. I can tell you as much as I know. I drove her back over to the house about two this morning and we waited it out. Kevin got home at six. He's shaken up, as you might imagine, but otherwise he's in good shape. I talked to both of them again a little while ago. She said she was going to call you as soon as we hung up. She didn't get in touch?"

"Jack, that's what I just said. I've been sitting here for hours without a word from anyone. I tried the house and got no answer."

"Hey, relax. Don't worry. I can see where you'd be ticked, but everything's fine. I know they were going back to Los Angeles. She might have just forgotten."

I could hear a little warning. Something was off here. "What about the kidnappers? Does Kevin have any way to identify them?"

"That's what I asked. He says, not a chance. He was tied up and blindfolded while they had him in the car. He says they drove into a garage and kept him there until the ransom money was picked up and brought back. Next thing he knew, someone got in the car, backed out of the garage, drove him around for a while, and finally set him out in his own driveway. He's going to see a doctor once they get to Los Angeles, but they never really laid a hand on him."

"I can't believe they didn't call to let me know he was safe. I need to talk to her." I knew I was being repetitive, but I was really bugged. I'd promised Harry her autograph, among other things, and while he'd pretended to make a joke of it, I knew he was serious.

"Maybe they thought I'd be doing that. I know they were both very grateful for your help. Maybe she's planning to drop you a note."

"Well. I guess I'll just wait until I hear from them," I said, and hung up.

I showered and got dressed, sucked down some coffee, and drove over to my office in downtown Santa Teresa. My irritation was beginning to wear off and exhaustion was trickling into my body in its wake. I went through my mail, paid a bill, tidied up my desk. I found myself laying my little head down, catching a quick nap while I drooled on my Month-at-a-Glance. There was a knock on the door and I woke with a start.

Vera Lipton, the claims manager for the insurance company next door, was standing on my threshold. "You must have had a better time than I did Friday night. You hung over or still drunk?" she said.

"Neither. I got a lousy night's sleep."

She lifted her right brow. "Sounds like fun. You and that guy from the bank?"

"Not exactly."

"So what'd you think of the glitzy twosome . . . Karen and Kev."

"I don't even want to talk about them," I said. I then proceeded to pour out the whole harrowing tale, including a big dose of outrage at the way I'd been treated.

Vera started smirking about halfway through. By the end of my recital, she was shaking her head.

"What's the matter?" I asked.

"Well, that's the biggest bunch of horsepuckey I ever heard. You've been taken, Kinsey. Most royally had."

"*I* have?"

"They're flat broke. They don't have a dime."

"They do, too!"

She shook her head emphatically. "Dead broke. They're busted."

"They couldn't be," I said.

"Yes, they are," she said. "I bet you dollars to donuts they put the whole scam together to pick up some cash."

"How could they be broke with a house like that? They have a hot new series on the air!"

"The show was canceled. It hasn't hit the papers yet, but the network decided to yank 'em after six episodes. They sank everything they had into the house up here when they first heard they'd been picked up."

I squinted at her. "How do you know all this stuff?"

"Neil and I have been looking for a house for months. Our real-estate agent's the one who sold 'em that place."

"They don't have any money?" I asked.

"Not a dime," she said. "Why do you think the house is so empty? They had to sell the furniture to make the mortgage payment this month."

"But what about the party? That must have cost a mint!"

"I'm sure it did. Their attorney advised them to max out their credit cards and then file for bankruptcy."

"Are you sure?"

"Sure I'm sure."

I looked at Vera blankly, doing an instant replay of events. I knew she was right because it suddenly made perfect sense. Karen Waterston and Kevin McCall had run a scam, that's all it was. No wonder the drop had gone without a hitch. I wasn't being followed by kidnappers . . . it was him. Those two had just successfully pocketed half a million bucks. And what was I going to do? At this point, even if I called the cops, all they had to do was maintain the kidnapping fiction and swear the bad guys were for real. They'd be very convincing. That's what acting is all about. The "kidnappers," meanwhile, would have disappeared without a trace, and they'd make out like bandits, quite literally.

Vera watched me process the revelation. "You don't seem all that upset. I thought you'd be apoplectic, jumping up and down. Don't you feel like an ass?"

"I don't know yet. Maybe not."

She moved toward the door. "I gotta get back to work. Let me know when it hits. It's always entertaining to watch you blow your stack."

I sat down at my desk and thought about the situation and then put a call through to Harry Hovey at the prison.

"This is rare," Harry said when he'd heard me out. "I think we got a winner with this one. Holy shit."

"I thought you'd see the possibilities," I said.

"Holy shit!" he said again.

The rest of what I now refer to as my missionary work, I can only guess at until I see Harry again. According to the newspapers, Kevin McCall and Karen Waterston were arrested two days after they returned to Los Angeles. Allegedly (as they say), the two entered a bank and tried to open an account with nine thousand dollars in counterfeit ten and twenties. Amazingly, Harry Hovey saw God and had a crisis of conscience shortly before this in his prison cell up in Lompoc. Recanting his claims of innocence, he felt compelled to confess . . . he'd been working for the two celebrities for years, he said. In return for immunity, he told the feds where to find the counterfeit plates, hidden in the bottom of a canvas tote, which turned up in their possession just as he said it would.

The Shamus Winners
Volume I (1982-1995)

1982

The Eye (Lifetime Achievement Award): **Ross Macdonald**

Best P.I. Hardcover Novel: *Hoodwink* **by Bill Pronzini**. Other nominees: *A Stab in the Dark* by Lawrence Block. *30 for a Harry* by Richard Hoyt. *Hard Trade* by Arthur Lyons. *Early Autumn* by Robert B. Parker.

Best Original P.I. Paperback: *California Thriller* **by Max Byrd.** Other nominees: *Carpenter, Detective* by Hamilton T. Caine. *Brown's Requiem* by James Ellroy. *The Old Dick* by L.A. Morse. *Murder in the Wind* by George Ogan.

1983

The Eye (Lifetime Achievement Award): **Mickey Spillane**

Best P.I. Hardcover Novel: *Eight Million Ways to Die* **by Lawrence Block.** Other nominees: *A Is for Alibi* by Sue Grafton. *Gravedigger* by Joseph Hansen. *A Piece of the Silence* by Jack Livingston. *Ceremony* by Robert B. Parker.

Best Original P.I. Paperback: *The Cana Diversion* **by William Campbell Gault.** Other nominees: *Nevsky's Return* by Dimitri Gat. *Pieces of Death* by Jack Lynch. *Smoked Out* by Warren Murphy.

Best P.I. Short Story: **"What You Don't Know Can Hurt You" by John Lutz.**

1984

The Eye (Lifetime Achievement Award): **William Campbell Gault**

Best P.I. Hardcover Novel: *True Detective* **by Max Allan Collins.** Other nominees: *Dancing Bear* by James Crumley. *The Glass Highway* by Loren D. Estleman. *The Dark Fantastic* by Stanley Ellin. *The Widening Gyre* by Robert B. Parker.

Best Original P.I. Paperback: *Dead in Centerfield* **by Paul Engelman.** Other nominees: *Finders Weepers* by Max Byrd. *Death and the Single Girl* by Elliot Lewis. *Trace* by Warren Murphy Devlin. *The Steinway Collection* by Robert J. Randisi.

Best Short Story: **"Cat's-Paw" by Bill Pronzini.** Other nominees: "The Oldest Killer" by Michael Collins. "Greektown" by Loren D. Estleman. "The Long Slow Dive" by T. Robin Kanter. "Only One Way To Land" by John Lutz.

1985

The Eye (Lifetime Achievement Award): **Howard Browne**

Best P.I. Hardcover Novel: *Sugartown* **by Loren D. Estleman.** Other nominees: *True Crime* by Max Allan Collins. *Die Again, Macready* by Jack Livingston. *Nightlines* by John Lutz. *Full Contact* by Robert J. Randisi.

Best Original P.I. Paperback: *Ceiling of Hell* **by Warren Murphy.** Other nominees: *Squeeze Play* by Paul Benjamin. *San Quentin* by Jack Lynch. *Trace and 47 Miles of Rope* by Warren Murphy. *The Man Who Risked His Partner* by Reed Stephens.

Best First P.I. Novel: *A Creative Kind of Killer* **by Jack Early.** Other nominees: *Blunt Darts* by Jeremiah Healy. *The Nebraska Quotient* by William J. Reynolds.

Best P.I. Short Story: **"By the Dawn's Early Light" by Lawrence Block.** Other nominees: "Easy Money" by John C. Boland. "Iris" by Stephen Greenleaf. "The Rat Line" by Rob Kantner. "The Big Winners" by Ernest Savage.

1986

The Eye (Lifetime Achievement Award): **Richard S. Prather**

Best P.I. Hardcover Novel: *B is for Burglar* **by Sue Grafton**. Other nominees: *The Naked Liar* by Harold Adams. *Hardball* by Doug Hornig. *A Catskill Eagle* by Robert B. Parker. *Bones* by Bill Pronzini.

Best Original P.I. Paperback: *Poverty Bay* by Earl Emerson. Other nominees: *The Rainy City* by Earl Emerson. *The Kill* by Douglas Heyes. *Trace: Pigs Get Fat* by Warren Murphy. *Blue Heron* by Philip Ross.

Best First P.I. Novel: *Hardcover* by Wayne Warga. Other nominees: *New, Improved Murder* by Ed Gorman. *Sleeping Dog* by Dick Lochte. *Embrace the Wolf* by Benjamin Schutz. *Flood* by Andrew Vachss.

Best P.I. Short Story: **"Eight Mile and Dequindre" by Loren D. Estleman**. Other nominees: "Lucky Penny" by Linda Barnes. "Shooting Match" by Wayne Dundee. "Perfect Pitch" by Rob Kantner. "The Snaphaunce" by Robert J. Randisi.

St. Martin's Press/PWA Best First P.I. Novel Contest: *An Infinite Number of Monkeys* by **Les Roberts.**

1987

The Eye (Lifetime Achievement Award): **Bill Pronzini**

Best P.I. Hardcover Novel: *The Staked Goat* by **Jeremiah Healy**. Other nominees: *When the Sacred Ginmill Closes* by Lawrence Block. *In La-La Land We Trust* by Robert Campbell. *The Million Dollar Wound* by Max Allan Collins. *C is for Corpse* by Sue Grafton.

Best Original P.I. Paperback: *The Back Door Man* by **Rob Kantner**. Other nominees: *Melting Point* by Kenn Davis. *Nervous Laughter* by Earl Emerson. *Dark Fields* by T.J. MacGregor. *Trace: Too Old a Cat* by Warren Murphy.

Best First P.I. Novel: *Jersey Tomatoes* by J.W. Rider. Other nominees: *No One Rides for Free* by Larry Beinhart. *Tourist Season* by Carl Hiassen.

Best P.I. Short Story: **"Fly Away Home" by Rob Kantner**. Other nominees: "Quint and the Braceros" by Paul Bishop. "Body Count" by Wayne D. Dundee. "I'm in the Book" by Loren D. Estleman. "Between the Sheets" by Sue Grafton.

St. Martin's Press/PWA Best First P.I. Novel Contest: *Fear of the Dark* by **Gar Anthony Haywood.**

1988

The Eye (Lifetime Achievement Awards): **Dennis Lynds; Wade Miller (Robert Wade and Bob Miller)**

Best P.I. Hardcover Novel: *A Tax in Blood* by **Benjamin Schutz**. Other nominees: *Lady Yesterday* by Loren D. Estleman. *Ride the Lightning* by John Lutz. *A Trouble of Fools* by Linda Barnes. *The Autumn Dead* by Ed Gorman.

Best Original P.I. Paperback: *Wild Night* by **L.J. Washburn**. Other nominees: *The Monkey's Raincoat* by Robert Crais. *Snake Eyes* by Gaylord Dold. *Recount* by David Everson. *Madelaine* by Joseph Louis.

Best First P.I. Novel: *Death on the Rocks* by **Michael Allegretto**. Other nominees: *The House of Blue Lights* by Robert Bowman. *Shawnee Alley Fire* by John Douglas. *Detective* by Parnell Hall. *An Infinite Number of Monkeys* by Les Roberts.

Best P.I. Short Story: **"Turn Away" by Ed Gorman**. Other nominees: "Bodyguards Shoot Second" by Loren Estleman. "The Kerman Kill" by William Campbell Gault. "Merely Players" by Joseph Hansen. "My Brother's Life" by Rob Kantner.

St. Martin's Press/PWA Best First P.I. Novel Contest: *Katwalk* by **Karen Kijewski.**

1989

The Eye (Lifetime Achievement Award): No Award Given

Best P.I. Hardcover Novel: *Kiss* by **John Lutz**. Other nominees: *Neon Mirage* by Max Allan Collins. *Deviant Behavior* by Earl Emerson. *Swan Dive* by Jeremiah Healy. *Blood Shot* by Sara Paretsky.

Best Original P.I. Paperback: *Dirty Work* by **Rob Kantner**. Other nominees: *The Last Private Eye* by John Birkett. *Bonepile* by Gaylord Dold. *Rebound* by David Everson. *The Crystal Blue Persuasion* by W. R. Philbrick.

Best First P.I. Novel: *Fear of the Dark* by **Gar Anthony Haywood**. Other nominees: *Lost Daughter* by Michael Cormany. *Burning Season* by Wayne D. Dundee. *Wall of Glass* by Walter Satterthwait. *Slow Dance in Autumn* by Philip Lee Williams.
Best P.I. Short Story: **"The Crooked Way" by Loren D. Estleman**. Other nominees: "The Man Who Knew Dick Bong" by Robert Crais. "The Reason Why" by Ed Gorman. "In the Line of Duty" by Jeremiah Healy. "Incident in a Neighborhood Tavern" by Bill Pronzini.
St. Martin's Press/PWA Best First P.I. Novel Contest: *Kindred Crime* by **Janet Dawson**.

1990
The Eye (Lifetime Achievement Award): No Award Given
Best P.I. Hardcover Novel: *Extenuating Circumstances* by **Jonathan Valin**. Other nominees: *Out on The Cutting Edge* by Lawrence Block. *The Skintight Shroud* by Wayne Dundee. *The Shape of Dread* by Marcia Muller. *The Killing Man* by Mickey Spillane.
Best Original P.I. Paperback: *Hell's Only Half Full* by **Rob Kantner**. Other nominees: *Muscle and Blood* by Gaylord Dold. *Behind The Fac* by Richard Hilary. *Tough Enough* by W. R. Philbrick. *A Collector of Photographs* by Deborah Valentine.
Best First P.I. Novel: *Katwalk* by **Karen Kijewski**. Other nominees: *Medicine Dog* by Geoff Peterson. *Cold Night* by Al Sarrantonio. *Rock Critic Murders* by Jesse Sublett.
Best P.I. Short Story: **"The Killing Man" by Mickey Spillane**. Other nominees: "Deadly Fantasies" by Marcia Muller. "Here Comes Santa Claus" by Bill Pronzini. "The Sure Thing" by Dan A. Sproul. "Sloat's Last Case" by Robert Twohy.
St. Martin's Press/PWA Best First P.I. Novel Contest: *The Loud Adios* by **Ken Kuhlken**.

1991
The Eye (Lifetime Achievement Award): **Roy Huggins**
Best P.I. Hardcover Novel: *G is for Gumshoe* by **Sue Grafton**. Other nominees: *Dead Irish* by John Lescroart. *The Desert Look* by Bernard Schopen. *Polo's Wild Card* by Jerry Kennealy. *Poor Butterfly* by Stuart Kaminsky. *A Ticket to the Boneyard* by Lawrence Block.
Best Original P.I. Paperback: *Rafferty: Fatal Sisters* by **W. Glenn Duncan**. Other nominees: *Made in Detroit* by Rob Kantner. *Bimbo Heaven* by Marvin Albert. *The Blue Room* by Monroe Thompson. *The Queen's Mare* by John Birkett.
Best First P.I. Novel: *Devil in a Blue Dress* by **Walter Mosely**. Other nominees: *Body Scissors* by Jerome Doolittle. *Kindred Crimes* by Janet Dawson. *The Stone Veil* by Ronald Tierney.
Best P.I. Short Story: **"Final Resting Place" by Marcia Muller**. Other nominees: "Bypass to Murder" by Dick Stodghill. "Battered Spouse" by Jeremiah Healy. "Cigarette Stop" by Loren D. Estleman. "Naughty, Naughty" by Wayne D. Dundee. "A Poison That Leaves No Trace" by Sue Grafton.
St. Martin's Press/PWA Best First P.I. Novel Contest: *A Sudden Death at the Norfolk Cafe* by **Winona Sullivan**.

1992
The Eye (Lifetime Achievement Award): **Joseph Hansen**
Best P.I. Hardcover Novel: *Stolen Away* by **Max Allan Collins**. Other nominees: *Dance at the Slaughterhouse* by Lawrence Block. *Where Echoes Live* by Marcia Muller. *A Fistful of Empty* by Benjamin Schutz. *Second Chance* by Jonathan Valin.
Best Original P.I. Paperback: *Cool Blue Tomb* by **Paul Kemprecos**. Other nominees: *Black Light* by Daniel Hearn. *House of Cards* by Kay Hooper. *The Thousand Yard Stare* by Rob Kantner.
Best First P.I. Novel: *Suffer Little Children* by **Thomas Davis**. Other nominees: *The January Corpse* by Neil Albert. *Dead on the Island* by Bill Crider. *Best Performance by a Patsy* by Stan Cutler. *Cool Breeze on the Underground* by Don Winslow.
Best P.I. Short Story: **"Dust Devil" by Nancy Pickard**. Other nominees: "Dying in the Post War World" by Max Allan Collins. "The Man Who Loved Noir" by Loren D. Estleman. "Full Circle" by Sue Grafton.

St. Martin's Press/PWA Best First P.I. Novel Contest: *Storm Warning* **by A.C. Ayres** (published as *Hour of the Manatee*).

1993

The Eye (Lifetime Achievement Award): **Marcia Muller**

Best P.I. Hardcover Novel: *The Man Who was Taller Than God* **by Harold Adams**. Other nominees: *Cassandra in Red* by Michael Collins. *Lullaby Town* by Robert Crais. *Shallow Graves* by Jeremiah Healy. *Special Delivery* by Jerry Kennealy.

Best Original P.I. Paperback: *The Last Tango of Delores Delgado* **by Marele Day**. Other nominees: *Lay It on the Line* by Catherine Damn. *Dirty Money* by Mark Davis. *The Brutal Ballet* by Wayne D. Dundee.

Best First P.I. Novel: *The Woman Who Married a Bear* **by John Straley**. Other nominees: *Return Trip Ticket* by David C. Hall. *Switching the Odds* by Phyllis Knight. *The Long-Legged Fly* by James Sallis.

Best P.I. Short Story: **"Mary, Mary, Shut the Door" by Benjamin Schutz**. Other nominees: "The Messenger" by Jacklyn Butler. "Safe House" by Loren D. Estleman. "A Little Missionary Work" by Sue Grafton. "Rest Stop" by Jeremiah Healy.

St. Martin's Press/PWA Best First P.I. Novel Contest: *The Harry Chronicles* **by Allan Pedrazas**.

1994

The Eye (Lifetime Achievement Award): **Stephen J. Cannell**

Best P.I. Hardcover Novel: *The Devil Knows You're Dead* **by Lawrence Block**. Other nominees: *Foursome* by Jeremiah Healy. *Wolf in the Shadows* by Marcia Muller. *Moth* by James Sallis. *The Lies That Bind* by Judith Van Gieson.

Best Original P.I. Paperback: *Brothers and Sinners* **by Rodman Philbrick**. Other nominees: *The Half-hearted Detective* by Milton Bass. *A Minyan for the Dead* by Richard Fliegel. *Shadow Games* by Edward Gorman. *Torchtown Boogie* by Steven Womack.

Best First P.I. Novel: *Satan's Lambs* **by Lynn Hightower**. Other nominees: *Brotherly Love* by Randye Lordon. *By Evil Means* by Sandra West Prowell.

Best P.I. Short Story: **"The Merciful Angel of Death" by Lawrence Block**. Other nominees: "The Sultans of Soul" by Doug Allyn. "Nobody Wins" by Charles Ardai. "The Bagged Man" by Jeremiah Healy. "The Watt's Lion" by Walter Mosley.

St. Martin's Press/PWA Best First P.I. Novel Contest: *The Heaven Stone* **by David Daniel**.

1995

The Eye (Lifetime Achievement Award): **John Lutz; Robert B. Parker**

Best P.I. Hardcover Novel: *K Is for Killer* **by Sue Grafton**. Other nominees: *A Long Line of Dead Men* by Lawrence Block. *Carnal Hours* by Max Allan Collins. *The Killing of Monday Brown* by Sandra West Prowell. *The Lake Effect* by Les Roberts.

Best First P.I. Novel: *A Drink Before the War* **by Dennis Lehane**. Other nominees: *The Heaven Stone* by David Daniel. *One for the Money* by Janet Evanovich. *The Fall-down Artist* by Thomas Lipinski. *When Death Comes Stealing* by Valerie Wilson Wesley.

Best Original P.I. Paperback: *Served Cold* **by Ed Goldberg**. Other nominees: *Double Plot* by Leo Axler. *Lament for a Dead Cowboy* by Catherine Dain. *Dead Ahead* by Bridget Mckenna. *Deadly Devotion* by Patricia Wallace.

Best P.I. Short Story: **"Necessary Brother" by Brendan DuBois**. Other nominees: "A Matter of Character" by Michael Collins. "Slipstream" by Loren Estleman. "Split Decision" by Clark Howard. "The Romantics" by John Lutz.

St. Martin's Press/PWA Best First P.I. Novel Contest: *Diamond Head* **by Charles Knief**.

Short story collections from www.PerfectCrimeBooks.com

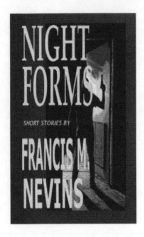

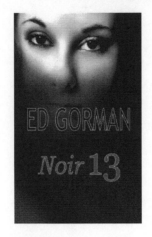

NIGHT FORMS
Francis M. Nevins
378 pages $16.95
ISBN: 978-1-935797-00-5

NOIR 13
Ed Gorman
250 pages $14.95
ISBN: 978-0-9825157-5-4
"Strong collection."
  Publishers Weekly

THE HOLLYWOOD OP
Terence Faherty
246 pages $14.95
ISBN: 978-1-935797-08-1
"Writes this era like he was there." Crime Spree

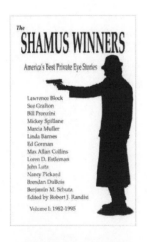

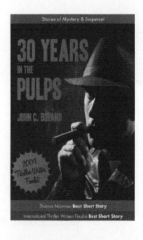

THE SHAMUS WINNERS
Volumes I & II
$14.95 each
Vol I ISBN: 978-0-9825157-4-7
Vol II ISBN: 978-0-9825157-6-1
"Must-have items."
James Reasoner

THE GUILT EDGE
Robert J. Randisi
232 pages $13.95
ISBN: 978-0-9825157-3-0
"One of the best."
  Michael Connelly

30 YEARS IN THE PULPS
John C. Boland
346 pages $14.95
ISBN: 978-0-9825157-2-3
"Style, substance, versatility." EQMM

13179926R00197

Printed in Great Britain
by Amazon.co.uk, Ltd.,
Marston Gate.